The Burdens
of a
Bachelor

Also by
Rebecca Connolly

An Arrangement of Sorts
Married to the Marquess
Secrets of a Spinster
The Dangers of Doing Good

Coming Soon
A Bride Worth Taking

More romance coming soon from
Phase Publishing

by
Emily Daniels
Lucia's Lament

by
Grace Donovan
Saint's Ride

The Burdens
of a
Bachelor

Rebecca Connolly

Phase Publishing, LLC
Seattle

Text copyright © 2017 by Rebecca Connolly
Cover art copyright © 2017 by Rebecca Connolly

Cover art by Tugboat Design
http://www.tugboatdesign.net

Phase Publishing, LLC first paperback edition
April 2017

ISBN 978-1-943048-24-3
Library of Congress Control Number 2017936379
Cataloging-in-Publication Data on file.

Acknowledgements

To all of the men in my family, who love me and support me, but will never know this dedication is here since they don't read romances. I promise not to write any unflattering characters with your names or physical features, and apologize for the lack of explosions and car chases to make this book your sort of thing. But it's better than a homemade book of self-written poems in your stockings, right?

And to Tom Hiddleston. You are perfection, sir, and I defy any person alive to say differently. A true gentleman of the highest class, and I give you my unending support in all things. Perhaps now we can meet…?

Thanks go out to Chris Bailey and the Phase family for getting me here and letting me stay here, to Deborah Bradseth of Tugboat Design for being the illustrator of my imagination and the best darn cover artist ever, and to Whitney Hinckley for making my writing look good with her magic polishing skills.

Thanks to the family for being the best of the best of the best. With honors.

Thanks, as always, to my musketeers. Not even Thin Mints are as good as you guys. Well, okay, maybe Thin Mints, but not the other cookies.

Chapter One
London, 1820

*I*t was far too early in the day for anyone to be wandering the London streets. Such activities spoke of poor regard for health, a lack of social engagements, or a loss of ambition, and was undoubtedly a precursor for certain ruin. It was not a wise notion for any sensible creature of Society.

It was even worse when that person was Colin Gerrard. He couldn't bring himself to care, whatever statement it might make about him, should he be seen.

When one is woken from a nightmare, the screams of his name still ringing in his own ears, there was nothing else to do but wander in the hopes of clearing his head.

Colin had been more than familiar with that particular dream in the past, unfortunately. But it had been at least ten years and he'd thought himself long past it.

If only it had been just a dream.

If only it hadn't been a memory.

He remembered all too well standing there in the middle of the road that rainy day in Seabrook, listening as the love of his life told him she was leaving, and worst of all, she was getting married. His family was not proper, she'd said. She had no choice, she'd said.

This was where his dream had varied from reality. In his dream, she had started to cry, had kissed him with all of the passion her innocence could conjure up, clinging to him. She'd been torn from his embrace and hauled away by her family, who had found Colin beneath their precious station. He was always unable to move, incapable of getting to her, as her screams of his name reverberated all around him.

He growled in irritation. He had no desire to dream of her; not now, not ever.

What a fool that seventeen-year-old had been.

She had not been taken from him.

She had walked away.

Head high, no tears, no dramatics. Just walked out of his life to marry someone else. Someone she wouldn't identify.

Susannah Merritt, as she had been then, had been the love of his youth.

And had taken his heart with her that day.

Oh, he had known his little flirtations since that time, had made himself quite the catch for Society. It had taken a lot of work, for him and for Kit, to undo the damage their family's reputation had suffered over the years. No one even thought of it now, because Colin distracted them too much, and Kit... well, Kit had his own troubles with reputation and rumors, but there was nothing he could do about that.

But it was all for show.

He grunted and shook his head, the limp form of his loosely tied cravat dancing against him. He had not bothered with a waistcoat and jacket, just his greatcoat, as the morning was chilly.

Besides, it was early in the day, too early for many people to be out and about, and if they were, he would only stir their imaginations with his appearance.

Was he up all night doing scandalous things? Had he been in a drunken brawl? Had he been in late meetings with ambassadors and foreign kings? The possibilities were endless and far-fetched, but he had heard them all before. Wherever he went and whatever he did, he attracted attention and tales.

He did that on purpose.

It was all a distraction.

Pretending at disreputable yet charming behaviors was easier than letting anyone see inside of him. Even his friends had no idea of his past. Oh, they knew a good deal, he had been friends with them for years and years. They knew him better than anyone else outside of his brother.

But they were not here.

And life in London was unbearably dull without them.

He wandered the London streets silently, nodding at those who recognized him, smirking at their whispers as he passed. He could not say his life was bleak. In fact, he had quite a good life, when he thought about it, at thirty-two years of age, considering his fortune and good looks were still intact.

But there was one thing he had admitted to himself recently that he never thought he would: he was lonely.

Colin Theodore Sebastian Albert Gerrard was lonely.

Worse than that, as shocking and miserable as that alone was, he was lonely and bored. He had never suffered from such an ailment in his entire life, and, as usual, he was not in the least to blame. His friends had rudely abandoned him without so much as a "fare thee well".

His four best friends had all married now, or in Derek's case, revitalized his marriage-in-name-only to a real one, and were all in various stages of matrimonial bliss. Two had recently partaken yet again in the ill-advised state of fatherhood, one had married and was enjoying attempting to join the others in the aforementioned ill-advised state, and the other… Well, he was still acting a newlywed and Colin was pleased to be rid of that lovesick lunatic. His nausea was only now just beginning to fade.

And so it happened that Colin found himself in this rarest of states, without even his twin for entertainment. Kit was rarely in London anymore, and never home when he was. He could hardly blame him, with all he had to be getting along with.

With absolutely nothing to do and absolutely nobody to do nothing with, he ventured to do something he had not done in nearly ten years, and never of his own free will and volition: he went calling. But so out of practice was he, and so early was the hour, and such was the sad state of London in the early weeks of autumn that, after much deliberation, he only called upon one person the whole of the day. And when that person was Lady Raeburn, the eccentric aunt of his good friend Duncan Bray, the toast of Society's older set, the wealthy widow of at least three men he knew of, and the single most terrifying woman on the planet, one person was quite enough to be getting on with.

Tibby was rather like Colin, when one looked at it objectively. Showy, bold, brazen, but still so respected and admired that nobody thought anything ill of them at all. It was a fine line between being the brunt of Society's mockery and the height of its eccentricity. Both of them had learned to balance it quite precariously, but with such flourish that no one could tell what was truth and what was fiction.

And that was just how they liked it.

He had always gotten along rather well with her, even as a boy. As his family consisted of himself and his brother, and a host of faceless relatives in various places who would not claim them, she had rather become his aunt too.

She certainly scolded him like an aunt would.

And if the look on her face at this moment was anything to go by, he was about to be scolded again.

Tibby looked radiant for being roused from sleep. Or, he strongly suspected, being forced to get out of a bed she had been wide awake in for several hours. She wore an elegant day dress of the old French style, her fiery red hair still in curlers and set beneath a cap that did not suit her temperament, but made him smile.

"Don't you smile at me like that, Colin Gerrard," she snapped, though her lips quirked. "Calling before breakfast is abominably rude, and I am quite determined to toss you out of the house at once."

He pouted. "But Tibby, you have such a lovely house. The renovations are so delightful, it would be a shame to waste them by not admiring them as grandly as I can."

She pursed her lips, her eyes twinkling. "Yes, well, if you had come three months ago when I reoccupied the place, I might have given you a tour. Now it is far too late."

He clasped a hand to his heart as if in agony. "Oh, my heart. Tibby, I am an abominable rogue, but you must know I never attend when I ought. Lateness is my way, and I could hardly disappoint you by being unexpectedly early. People might think I've turned respectable." He shuddered at the thought.

She laughed merrily and grinned at him, holding out her hand with a wink. "You darling idiot. Have you had breakfast?"

He grinned and kissed her offered hand. "No, my lady, I have not."

"You will join me."

"Of course." He offered her his arm, then frowned. "I have no idea where we are going, but I will escort you anyway."

She rolled her eyes and directed him towards her new breakfast room, where they sat together and enjoyed some truly delicious food. She asked after his brother, he asked after Marianne, and they both pointedly ignored the fact that the two were somehow inexplicably connected.

They had asked no questions about it, and neither of the persons in question had ever volunteered any information.

The two of them chatted aimlessly for a while, and then Tibby sat back, pushing her plate aside and letting a servant take it. "Colin."

"Yes, Tibby?"

She smirked at his cheeky response. "You are making small talk with me at an early hour on a Thursday in autumn."

He frowned, unsure where she was heading with her comments. "So I am…"

"You do not make small talk. You do not do early hours. And you hate autumn."

"I do not," he said with a snort.

She gave him a look that wiped away his amusement. "You have not been in London in autumn for the last three years in a row. I have not your gossip sources, but I do know quite a bit. What are you doing?"

"Nothing."

"Colin…"

"No, I mean it," he said, letting earnestness shine through. "I am doing nothing. There is no one to see and nothing to do. I… I feel rather pointless, actually."

Tibby made a clucking sound and put her hand over his. "I think you need to find a wife, Colin."

He withdrew his hand and shook his head. "No, I think not. They can hunt all they like, but there will be no wife for Colin Gerrard, I can promise you that." He rose and gave her a smile, grandly picking up her hand and kissing it. "Thank you for breakfast, Tibby. I shall call on you again soon, at a more reasonable hour."

"Who broke your heart, Colin?" she asked softly, her eyes searching his. "What happened to you?"

He stiffened briefly, and stepped back, trying to find his usual façade. "You know me, Tibby," he commented drily, his tone very off indeed. "I have no heart." He bowed and turned from the room.

"Not true," she called after him. "I know it, and you know it."

He did not reply, and left the house.

The neighborhood was much more populated than it had been when he had arrived, and he wished he'd had the foresight to dress better. Now the comments would be aplenty, and he'd have to create something to talk about because of it. Not that it was uncommon; he was really quite good at making up stories about himself.

After all, he'd convinced the entire world he was a reckless bachelor who thought of nothing serious and had no thought but fun and laughter.

No one knew there was a darker truth.

His eyes glanced over the faces of the people passing him, not really marking any of them, when suddenly his heart leapt into his throat and he whirled around.

She'd been there. Right in front of him. He'd barely glanced at her as she'd walked by, but then recognition set in, and fifteen years was not so long as to change her so.

He would have known her anywhere, at any age. He'd known her since he was eleven, had seen her every summer between then and that fateful day… He knew her, even now.

But looking around, he could see nothing that resembled her. Not a single woman met her size or stature, no shade of hair was hers.

Susannah Merritt.

Or whatever her name was now.

Could she be in London?

"Someday we'll meet in London, and I'll be a fine lady, and you a gentleman. And we'll take the place by storm, Colin. Just you wait."

His panicked breathing began to calm, and he shook his head frantically, desperate to wipe the memory from his mind, from existence. Her sweet little voice, echoing in his ears, sent his heart racing just as madly as seeing her face had.

Or thinking he'd seen it.

She could not have been here.

She'd never come yet.

Frustrated that he still apparently looked for her, he whirled on his heel and made for home quickly. He would need to soak his head for a while. Perhaps he'd had too much to drink last night, or the breakfast at Tibby's was not sitting well with him, or he was taken ill. Perhaps he was ill. That would do it. He would call for the doctor immediately; he undoubtedly had some deadly, incurable illness that was making his past flash before his eyes as if it were the present. He was feeling things and thinking things that he'd spent years burying, and that had to be a curious symptom for anyone to suddenly suffer from.

He hoped he wouldn't die unexpectedly next week. There was much he needed to do, and Kit would not take kindly to having to deal with the funeral arrangements.

Now he was being ridiculous. One step in front of the other; hurry home, and go back to bed. Or perhaps drink. A good drink could drown out anything. He hadn't really done that in years, he'd rather lost his taste for strong drink, but if it could take her away, he'd become a raving drunkard.

So intent was he on the path before him that he hardly noticed the butler as he entered his house. It wasn't until he was halfway up the stairs that it occurred to him that he was being addressed.

He frowned, and turned back. "I'm sorry, Bartlet, what were you saying?"

His butler, a rather stout man with no emotions, looked positively ghost-like and appeared to have developed a tremor.

"Good heavens, Bartlet," he said in a rush, hurrying down. "Are you ill? Is someone dead? Where's Kit?"

Bartlet shook his head, his thinning hair slicked against his skin with perspiration. "No, sir. I am well, no one has died, and Master Christopher is still unaccounted for, but his valet has sent for some things."

Colin sighed just a touch, but looked at the man carefully. "So what ails you, man? Pardon me for saying so, but you really look like death."

Bartlet swallowed hard. "Forgive my lack of composure, sir, but…" He gestured towards the morning room, and Colin turned.

The door was wide open, and a man in a rather common ensemble stood there, looking fatigued and grumpy, watching them.

"Can I help you?" Colin asked, not at all caring for the sudden gleam in the man's eye.

"Are you Mr. Gerrard?" he asked in a rough, foreign accent.

"One of them." He was in no mood for impertinence, which was why he would be impertinent. It was always so worthwhile and stirred up the most enjoyable scuffles.

The man's thick brow lowered. "Which one?"

Colin snorted. "Samuel."

The foreign frown deepened. "Are you Colin or Christopher?"

He sighed and rolled his eyes. "Colin, for pity's sake. What do you want?"

"So you are the second son of Lord Loughton."

Now Colin was taken aback and actually staggered sideways a little. Not many people knew that, except the oldest families and his friends. His father had not lived in England in twenty some odd years, and that was just barely long enough for the family legacy to have been wiped from memory. Nobody remembered they were technically in the aristocracy, though only just, and Loughton had nearly stripped the family of any shred of respectability they might have had.

If he knew that…

Colin swallowed. "I am. What do you want?"

The man heaved a massive sigh that sounded suspiciously like relief. "Then these are under your care now. Farewell." He inclined his head and left.

These? These what?

Colin warily approached the room, noticing his butler remained where he was. He peered cautiously into it, then suddenly jerked with such force that he slammed back against the doorframe, and the sound echoed through the house.

Three small girls in travel-worn clothing stood in the room, the youngest barely older than a toddler, and the other two looking quite terrified. They all stared at him with the same wide, blue eyes.

And all three looked unnervingly like him.

He swallowed his shock, blinked a few times, and when they still stood before him, watching him, he spoke the one concise thought that had entered his mind:

"Damn."

Chapter Two

That had been far too close.

She was still tucked against the side of a brick house, hand clutching at her heart, as if that alone would stop its anguished throbbing.

Colin Gerrard.

In London.

It should not have been too unexpected; he was certainly of an age now where he ought to be in London on occasion, particularly if he were trying to find a wife.

She winced and pushed off of the wall, peering around the corner of the house. It had been at least a quarter of an hour that she had been hiding here. Surely he ought to be long gone by now.

Unless he had been looking for her.

She shook her head with a derisive snort and continued on towards her destination. She was being ridiculous; why in the world would he want to look for her? It had been fifteen years since she had given him the cruelest sort of news imaginable, and if she knew anything about Colin Gerrard, which she was quite certain she did, he would not easily forget that.

No, he would most certainly not look for her. Perhaps he had already forgotten her.

He ought to forget her. She was nothing anymore, not to him, not to anyone.

Lady Susannah Hawkins-Dean was a name few knew, and even fewer would be pleased to. Even she shuddered when she heard it. She wished she could be Susannah Merritt once more, but that name had not meant very much either. It had certainly caused enough damage in its time, though she'd only borne it for fifteen years. She had not had that name for half of her life now.

She did not even know that name anymore.

Now she had to be Susannah Hart, accomplished spinster, governess, or companion, with few references and even fewer connections. Looking for work in such a pitiful state was feeling rather impossible, and while she would have preferred to work at the hospital, they had no need for help right now unless it was as a volunteer.

She would have done so, had she any choice.

But she needed money.

And she needed it now.

Susannah pushed a strand of her dark honey-colored hair out of her face and carefully tucked it back into the knot she wore at the base of her neck. She had to look as respectable as possible. She still had a fairly youthful face that made her age suspect when revealed. But wearing the severe knot seemed to help in that respect. No young woman looking for a husband would ever wear her hair thus.

And she was certainly not looking for a husband.

No, indeed, Susannah had had quite enough of husbands, thank you very much. One was all that it took for her to tire of ever experiencing the married life again. Sir Martin Hawkins-Dean had been thirty-five when he had married her, and his fortune had saved her family from complete destitution and ruin, which is what had finally made her accept the reality of her situation.

It had all been arranged without her consent, but she had to agree to the conditions set forth before the marriage would take place. And one of the conditions set down by her father was that she had to sever all ties with Colin Gerrard.

He had not been suitable for her, and had her brother not seen them kiss, no one would have known that their relationship had been anything other than platonic. His family had once been a respectable one, but after his mother's death, his father had lost all sense of himself and had carried on in the most shocking of ways. Colin and his brother Kit had been forced to visit their aunt Agatha, who lived at Seabrook, for every school holiday, and it was there they had become acquainted.

She remembered that first day on the shore when they had met. She had been ten years old, her brother Rupert had just been teasing her about growing too fast for her dresses and looking like a stork, and she had been crying. Colin had found her, teased her out of her tears, and they had been best friends ever since.

Until she had broken his heart six years later.

She'd also broken her own. He would never know that. He would never have understood.

But she'd had to. Her family had depended upon her saving them.

Fifteen years later, little had changed except her. She was harder, older, more experienced, her body was not the same as it had been, nor was her heart. But here she was, scurrying about London, hiding from anyone who might have known her, looking for the most readily available work that would still allow her to maintain some sort of respectability.

But that was destined to change soon if she did not have some success.

It was beginning to matter less and less what she did for work as long as money was involved. Beggars could not be choosers, and while she was not a beggar as yet, she was getting dangerously close. And her family was incapable of developing any sort of backbone for themselves.

She shook her head in irritation, desperate to wipe that line of thinking away. Her family could not be blamed entirely for their current state of misfortune. While they were guilty of poorly managing money, and a long history of it, the blame must set where it belonged.

With her blessedly late husband and his infernal inability to think of anyone but himself.

She checked the small watch that was attached to her jacket, the one trinket she had been permitted to keep of her belongings, and sighed. She was going to be late for her interview if she did not make haste, and that would not do at all.

But London was a far larger place than she had ever imagined it to be. If she had been wiser, she would have come weeks ago and taken stock of the place, learned its energy and dangers, and sought out work in all the right places. But she was neither wise enough nor free enough to do as she wished. And her current restrictions pressed upon her such a need for discretion that she had to exercise extreme caution in everything.

And in that sense, London itself might have been more terrifying than Colin Gerrard.

Her mind betrayed her to thinking back on his face just then. He was older, certainly, but somehow, impossibly, he was more handsome for it. He had been a very attractive boy, but now? He would have stopped an entire room of people simply by entering it. And they would have thanked him for giving their eyes such pleasure.

He had looked troubled, which was not an expression his face was supposed to know. Her one consolation all these years had been that he would be happy without her, that his life would have been profoundly blessed by not being mired down with her family and her ties. He would have been better for never knowing how deeply she had loved him.

Had? her mind asked in a taunting voice.

She pushed that aside with an irritated snort. She would not admit to anything but holding onto the memory of Colin all these years. What girl in her situation would have done otherwise? She had to cling to something bright in the world of the black oblivion she had known.

She had loved Colin, as much as her little girl heart had known how.

But that had been a lifetime ago.

She had never told him the name of the man she would marry, and that had been her idea. She knew he would not rest without knowing, but also knew that he would never discover it. Sir Martin had not had their marriage publicized for reasons of what he claimed was practicality, but she knew it had been to keep his indiscretions at bay. She had been a matter of convenience for him, as a wife lent respectability to a name and a title, and an estate wanted for a woman's hand.

She had not touched anything of his their entire marriage, nor had she desired to.

But she was free of it now, and London was her escape.

And her prison, it would seem.

She hurried along the rambling street, unable to keep from smiling. They'd always said they would come to London, that they would meet there one day and explore it together. They would be married and have six children and be infamous for their parties. There was never any thought of money or titles or social politeness, they never cared for that. They wanted the adventure, and they wanted to be together.

It was all they ever wanted.

"Someday we'll meet in London, and I'll be a fine lady, and you a gentleman. And we'll take the place by storm, Colin. Just you wait."

She inhaled sharply at the sudden memory of herself, lying on the grass at his aunt's home, her head near his, looking up at the clouds.

He had laughed at her, but gone along with it, rambling on and on about the things they would do, the places they would go, the things they would see.

But from then on, it had always been London for them.

Now they were both in London. She was a lady and he a gentleman. But that was the end of it.

Colin could never know of her life or that she was here, or that she had clung to so much. He might not even remember her.

But even her mind could not let her believe that.

He was Colin. He remembered everything.

A yell jerked her from her thoughts and she jumped back to avoid being hit by a carriage. A hand seized her arm and she whirled with a gasp towards it, heart galloping faster than the carriages.

"Watch yourself," a familiar accented voice said. "Streets are dangerous this side of town, even in the mornings."

Susannah smiled up at the man, whom she only knew as "the Gent," and who had become the first man she had trusted in over a decade. "You would think I'd have learned that by now."

He grinned and she was astonished again by the straightness, and cleanliness, of his teeth. His clothes were dirty and common, perfectly threadbare and unremarkable, and he was unshaven. By all accounts, his teeth ought to have matched. But they did not. It wasn't the first time she wondered if he was not quite what he seemed.

"Or perhaps you just enjoy being saved by me," he said with a bit of a Cockney drawl.

Susannah rolled her eyes, scoffing softly.

The Gent chuckled a little. "You seem to be lost in thought, Miss Hart. Can I escort you somewhere so you won't be in danger from any more runaway coaches?"

She heaved a little sigh. "Yes, thank you. I'm… not myself today."

He offered his arm very properly. "I understand. I'm not myself most days, it's a confusing state."

Susannah was amused in spite of her distress. The Gent had found her wandering London shortly after her arrival and, after assuring her that he only wanted to help, he showed her about London and helped her get her bearings. She had worried about it at first, but he never asked questions, and he never judged.

And it was nice to have someone looking out for her.

"Where to, then?" the Gent asked, his accent ringing out proudly.

"Mrs. Grovner's," she said. "I'm still in need of work."

He looked down at her, one dark brow rising. "Mrs. Grovner's, eh? Governess or companion?"

"Whichever will take me first," she replied simply. She was in no position to be particular. Her situation was dire and growing more and more desperate.

"Come work for me, I could use a woman like you."

She laughed forcibly at his suggestion. "You couldn't afford me, Gent."

"And you can't afford anything right now."

She pretended to consider that. "Then I accept. What is the position? Sending out runaway carriages so you can save the women in their path?"

He patted her gloved hand and chuckled. "There's some spirit, that's better. I was beginning to doubt my charm."

"Well, I wouldn't want that."

"It would ruin me for the whole city."

"That would be a travesty."

"You have no idea."

They shared a smile and his eyes suddenly looked past her and turned colder. "Don't turn to look," he murmured, still wearing the smile, though it was now forced, "but do you know anybody in London enough for them to watch you?"

She swallowed and nearly looked anyway, but put her gaze squarely on the small area of exposed skin at his throat. "No," she answered truthfully.

He made a small noise of noncommittal assent. "A shortcut, I think."

"I should go," she hissed, shaking her head rapidly as the fear and worry rose within her. "I shouldn't have come, I should have known, you should go…"

"If you think I am leaving you for one minute, you are not nearly as intelligent as you look."

His voice suddenly had such authority, and no hint of an accent, that she looked up at him, fear receding at his calm.

He looked beyond again and grunted. "Gone already. But with how you reacted, I think you must need my help more than the occasional carriage rescue and London tour."

"Gent…"

He snorted and set them to moving again. "Susannah, don't even bother."

She swallowed and tried to pull back, but he wouldn't budge. "Gent, thank you for helping me, but really, I will be fine."

He gave her one look that told her he knew that she was lying and she found no defense to counter with. He turned them down a smaller street, far less filled with people than the previous one.

"Miss Hart," he said simply, his accent returning at last, "you officially have a protector now. You might not always see me, but from here on out, you are safe to walk about as you will. I would

16

recommend being accompanied if possible; it is London, after all. But no harm will come to you, I swear it."

She opened her mouth, but found no words. "You don't know where I live."

He smirked. "You are new to the city, Miss Hart, so I doubt you do either. And you are looking for work, meaning you will not stay somewhere long, if you become employed. Where you live is a very fluid concept at the moment."

Actually, her life was a very fluid concept these days. Rough seas, to be sure, considering the poor state of her boat and the size of the waves, the storms swirling about, and her inability to steer. But he was right. She had no home. No friends. No future.

Yet somehow, she had gained a protector.

"Why are you helping me?" she asked in a low voice as they approached Mrs. Grovner's. "You have no idea who I am or what my troubles are."

He heaved a sigh, as if he had been asking himself that same question the entire walk. "I don't know, Miss Hart. Sometimes, I just can't help myself." He turned to her with a tip of his hat and a wink. "You need anything, you just holler. Help will come."

He turned to leave, but she suddenly grabbed his sleeve. He looked down at her hand, then up at her, just as she'd done to him only moments before. She bit her lip and looked at the agency door.

"There's no shame in it," he murmured, as if he knew the mess of her thoughts.

She nodded once, swallowing. "This isn't what I want," she whispered, unsure why she was admitting that.

"And since when does that make a difference in what happens to us?" he asked with a tilt of his head and the hint of a smile. "You think I like walking around London looking like this and saving people like you?"

She raised her chin suspiciously, suddenly feeling the slightest bit lighter. "Yes, I think you do."

He winked again and turned around, heading in the opposite direction, whistling a jaunty tune. "Don't you tell no one. Good luck!"

Susannah shook her head and turned back towards the door. The

Gent was right, she was doing what she had to. And she might as well face it. She exhaled, and pushed the door open.

The interview did not take long at all, as Mrs. Grovner already had her notes and references, and now she bore a list of suggested places she might fit as either a companion or a governess. Mrs. Grovner would set up appointments for her with each of them, and let her know the results when she could, but Susannah could not think on that now. She had prospects, which was more than she'd had before. For the first time in years, she had something to hope for.

It was an entirely new sensation.

She didn't see the Gent, but she did not expect to. He was, no doubt, saving other wandering females with no sense of the city. Who was he, really? He obviously did not belong any more than she did, yet he mingled so well, disappeared so easily. He was a contradiction, walking and living and breathing, and who knew what his real story was. He had taken an interest in her, for whatever reason, and she was grateful for it.

She was not grateful for many things these days.

The building of apartments in which she was staying looked more dank in the daylight than she recalled, but she had been so grateful for the vacancy that it hadn't mattered. The price was something she could afford, the state of the building something she could overlook, and the smell was something she could learn to accept, she supposed. Something better would come along.

It had to.

She knocked at the door and was let in by the mute doorman, whose name she still had yet to learn, but he nodded at her, belched, and went back to dozing on his stool in the corner.

Oh, but she was a long way from Pavel House.

She removed her bonnet, wincing as the cheap straw caught at her hair, and went up the creaking stairs. The apartments were quiet, which she expected, given the hour of the day, though they had been busy enough last night. Again, she would have to adjust. Nothing would be the same, and it was time to adapt to her new state of living and being.

She reached her apartment and fumbled for her key, sighing with a small smile. Progress had been made today, which must be appreciated.

And she had seen Colin Gerrard.

Her smile faded, and she swallowed. That was something she had never intended.

But no matter. It would not happen again.

It could not.

The door opened before she could do so herself and her neighbor answered, her gown far more decent now than it had been when she'd left, though one shoulder was still bare. "Oh, good," she hiccupped, though she was not drunk, "you meant it when you said not long. So many people lie these days, and I really do have to work."

Susannah smiled and entered. "Yes, Sasha, I meant it. And I do appreciate your helping me."

The woman shrugged her one bare shoulder and gave her a smile. "He's easy enough to please. Been teaching me to read, actually. Never learned before."

Susannah's smile grew and she shook her head. "I'm sure he did. How much do I owe you?"

Sasha held up a hand. "Not a bit, Miz Hart. I'll do it anytime, provided I don't have a chap. I like you, and I like him. And neighbors help each other."

A lump rose in her throat. "Thank you."

Sasha wrinkled her nose in a smirk, and left, calling out, "Bye, love!" as she did so.

Susannah sighed and turned around, hands on her hips, facing the small, curly-haired seven-year-old boy sitting in the chair before the empty fireplace, book open in his lap.

"Good morning, Mama," he giggled, opening his arms for a hug.

She went to him, hugged him back, and kissed his brow. "Good morning, Freddie. What are we reading today and where did you get it from?"

Chapter Three

Colin paced anxiously back and forth, rubbing his hands up and down his arms. "They can't be mine," he muttered, turning on his heel. "They can't be. I mean, they honestly cannot be."

"He's said that already," one of the girls whispered to the other. "Do you think he's mad?"

"Shh!" the other scolded harshly.

He stopped suddenly and looked down at his hands. "They can't be mine. They aren't mine."

"We know that," said the one who'd shushed the other.

He ignored her.

"But Kit…" he said, beginning to pace again. "They could be Kit's. He's a bit of an idiot, he might have been that stupid."

"Here we go," the older girl moaned, sitting down on the floor.

The youngest just watched him pace, as she had been doing, as if it was a game she did not comprehend.

"But he's never been that stupid," he reminded himself, sweeping his hands behind his back. "It seems odd for him to do something so drastically stupid and out of character, and three times, at that."

"We're not Kit's," the oldest one announced.

He ignored her again.

"Letter for you, sir," Bartlet intoned gravely from the doorway, determinedly avoiding looking at the girls.

Colin grabbed it from him. "From Kit? I should hope so, I demand an explanation."

"From the foreign gentleman, sir," Bartlet said with a shake of his head. "He said he forgot to give it to you before."

Colin frowned and tore open the blank seal. "Not a surprise, I don't think his mind actually works most of the time."

"Indeed, sir," Bartlet replied, leaving him.

Colin glanced at the girls, all watching him, then back down at the letter as he opened it.

The handwriting told him immediately that he, and Kit, were safe.

"Oh, thank God," he said, heaving a sigh and leaning back against the doorframe.

It was from their father, Lord Loughton, who never communicated with them unless it was imperative, and would rather not be reminded of their existence. As the feeling was entirely mutual, they had seen no reason to alter the arrangement.

Colin frowned suddenly as his mind leapt forward. If the letter was from Loughton, then…

"Oh, no," he murmured slowly, looking down at the letter and actually beginning to read it.

"And there it is," the impertinent one said loudly as she began to applaud.

He again ignored her as he tried to read the words before him:

Married a French woman some years ago. The three girls are from our relationship. Their mother has died and I have no interest in raising them. I give charge of them to the two of you for the duration of their lives. Official documents will be forthcoming, assuming I can find a lawyer here who understands British law. If funds are needed, inform me and it shall be done.

It was signed only with the great flourishing L that they had learned to expect as a signature from him.

There were hardly any answers in that letter at all.

He turned it over to look at the back, just in case there was a post script.

There wasn't.

"Damn," he hissed, scanning it again.

"He swears a lot," the second girl whispered loudly.

He looked at her in disbelief, which earned him a scowl from the oldest.

"You kind of do," she agreed with a half of a wince.

"Twice," he murmured.

"That we could hear."

They stared at each other for a long moment. Then Colin bellowed, "BARTLET!"

The butler appeared as if by magic, making the girls jump more than Colin's yell had. "Sir?

"Wherever Kit is," Colin said, still in a bit of a daze, "send for him. Now. And tell him it's urgent."

"Yes, sir," Bartlet said with a nod. "And... sir, what about... them?" He inclined his head only towards the girls.

Colin looked at them as the youngest yawned without hesitation. "Prepare a room. We'll have to make arrangements for them. They are staying with us. They... are my sisters."

Bartlet gaped, which was entirely unlike Bartlet, but it would be excused, given the circumstances.

The girls, on the other hand, grinned at each other in delight.

"That will be all, Bartlet," Colin muttered, uncomfortable with their unfettered glee.

Bartlet fairly scampered away.

"What?" he barked when their smiles stayed in place.

The oldest shrugged, still grinning. "We thought you would toss us into the streets and we'd be forced to be paupers."

Colin snorted at the notion and moved to sit on a sofa. "Where did you get a ridiculous idea like that?"

"Loughton," she said simply.

He looked at her then, assessing her carefully. "So you call him that too?"

She nodded, her dark curls bouncing. "It was a right sight better than calling him 'father'."

"Very true."

Again, they stared at one another.

And again, the youngest yawned, now curled on his carpet by the fire.

"Is she going to fall asleep on the floor there?" he asked with a touch of concern. He would not claim to understand children, though he had spent a little time with the children of his friends, and some various others around town, but not with enough consideration to notice much of anything.

"Probably," the oldest said with a sigh, shaking her head. "It's her nap time, and we've been travelling for days and days, without much to eat, and sleep has been difficult."

"No need for dramatics," he scolded with a wave of his hand.

She quirked a brow like he'd seen Kit do every day of his life. "Who said I was being dramatic?"

He was beyond surprised at this little tart-tongued new sister of his. Where in the world did she get off speaking to him that way?

He nearly rolled his eyes at his own stupidity.

She was his sister.

Suddenly, he didn't need any further proof.

"Well," he said with a heavy sigh, "I suppose introductions are in order."

The older two girls stood up and curtseyed.

"No, no, no," he interrupted with a shake of his head, waving his hand once more. "No formalities, although I applaud your education in manners. Your mother, I presume?"

The oldest nodded. "She wanted us to be fine English ladies someday."

He grunted softly, trying not to smile at the hint of accent he heard in her voice. Well, at least one of their parents had sense.

"Come sit down," he told them, gesturing to the sofa opposite him.

They did so, sitting rather close together. The youngest was now sound asleep in front of the fire, and actually looked remarkably cozy. He found himself smiling in spite of himself.

He shook his head rapidly and looked back at the others. "You obviously know that I'm Colin."

They nodded as one.

"I am the second son," he continued. "My twin is Christopher, or Kit, and he'll be around whenever he sees fit to come back. He tends to come and go as he pleases, you'll get used to it. But he's a good man, though not as amusing or handsome as I am."

They did not react except to blink.

Hmm. This was going to be interesting.

"Your turn."

"How old are you?" the smaller of the girls asked.

He fought a smile. "Thirty-two. How old are you?"

Her eyes went wide at his age. "*Zut alors,*" she breathed. "I'm only six."

Now he did smile. "Six is a very good age."

The oldest was finally starting to smile at him. "I'm Rose. Rose Marie Elizabeth Gerrard, but you can call me Rosie. I'm nine."

"Nine is also good, if I remember," he said with a nod.

She shrugged. "Eight was better."

"I remember that too."

Now she did smile. She indicated her sister beside her. "This is Louisa, though she goes by Bitty, I have no idea why."

Bitty shrugged herself and smiled at him. "I'm not very big, so the nurse called me Bitty."

"Makes sense," he murmured, wishing he wasn't so amused by them. "And who is the little Sleeping Beauty over there?"

"That's Genevieve," Rosie informed him with a smile of her own, her accent much more pronounced on her sister's name. "We call her Ginny. She's three."

"Three," he murmured, looking over at her again. "I don't remember three at all."

"She's adorable," Rosie said with a sigh that told him she really was, but also tiresome. "She is curious about everything, a bit shy, and doesn't know enough words to properly communicate. You'll learn how she works fairly quickly."

"I'll try to remember that," he answered drily.

Rosie and Bitty stared at him for a long moment, as if waiting for something. Colin, for the life of him, could not think what it was.

Then the loud, unmistakable sound of a stomach rumbling erupted from one of them, and the girls looked at each other in a mixture of horror and amusement.

In spite of the upheaval this would cause him, in spite of the complete lack of humor involved, and in spite of the fact that he'd already had a trying morning, Colin found himself laughing.

The girls looked at him in surprise, but he was beyond containing it.

They soon joined him and it was quite some time before any of them could stop.

"Apparently," he managed when he could breathe, "one of you is hungry."

Bitty clamped her hands over her stomach and nodded. "Sorry."

"Why are you sorry for that?" he asked her, tilting his head. "I am usually hungry, there is no apology needed. And when you meet my friend Duncan, you will learn that some people are just always hungry and always will be."

Bitty grinned at him. "So… can I have something to eat?"

He smiled back, unable to resist. "Of course, you can! We all can. Let's go down to the kitchens and see what they have."

"But what about Ginny?" Rosie asked as they got up.

Colin looked over at his smallest sister, and felt an unexpected swelling of emotion. He looked back at the other two. "I'll get her, and then lead the way. She can sleep if she wants, and eat when she wants. We'll sort out a schedule later."

He went to the fireplace and pulled the little sleeping girl into his arms. She nuzzled against him, then turned her cheek into his neck and sighed sleepily, her mouth gaping the tiniest bit.

There was no accounting for the sudden lump in his throat, and he could not very well clear it, or he might wake her, and then she might cry, and he had no idea what to do if that happened, so he simply swallowed. It took a few times for the lump to clear, but eventually it did and he rose to his feet.

"Come on," he urged the other two softly, gesturing out the door. "I'll show you where to go."

They passed Bartlet again, who now smiled at the girls in a sort of astonishment.

"Bartlet," Colin hissed, signaling him to come to him.

"Yes, sir?" he asked with a sudden calm.

"I will need notes to be delivered to my friends," he murmured softly, forcing a smile.

Bartlet nodded in understanding. "At once?"

"Yes," he hissed. "Have paper sent down to the kitchens, I will write them there while the girls eat. And then I think I should get a nursemaid or a governess or something. Right?"

Bartlet appeared bewildered at being asked for his opinion. "I, uh…."

"Send for Lady Raeburn," Colin sighed with a look heavenward. "I have no one else to turn to."

"Oh, lord," Bartlet muttered, shaking his head.

"Indeed." He looked down at the girls, watching him in confusion. "But do it."

"Yes, sir."

Colin turned and led his sisters down to the kitchens, wondering what in heaven's name his father had gotten him into.

"All right, Colin, what is it?"

Colin turned from the thick wooden table in surprise and looked at his twin, who strode into the kitchen with his usual purposeful strides and looked rather dapper and fresh for apparently not being in London. He made Colin look like a street peddler, and he knew it. He always did that, and it drove Colin mad.

"So you are in London?" he replied with a bit of a sneer, knowing how Kit hated being taunted. "Amazing. Bartlet was mistaken, then. I shall have to let him down gently, he's never been wrong before in his life."

Kit narrowed his eyes, which matched Colin's to a tee, but held no laughter. He scoffed softly. "Of course, I was in London. Where else would I have been? Now what was so damn urgent?"

Colin tsked and shook his head. "Language, Kit. There are children present."

Kit blinked slowly, but gave no other indication of surprise. "There are… what?"

"Children," Colin repeated with a smirk.

"And a lady!" Tibby called out from the other end of the table, where she had been watching with interest.

Kit turned to see her and bowed very politely. "Lady Raeburn, I apologize, I did not see you."

Tibby inclined her regally turbaned head, where her violent red hair was barely visible beneath the shimmering blue swaths of fabric. "Christopher. Always so formal. Tibby, please."

One side of Kit's mouth quirked up in an almost-smile. "Tibby. Forgive me, old habits." He gave a quarter turn and looked at Colin again. "Children, Colin? What children?"

Colin allowed his smirk to spread and pointed at the girls, sitting on the other side of Tibby, eyes fixed on them both. "Those children."

It said a great deal that Kit, after looking where he was indicating, only blinked again, though his eyes were a good deal wider than before. He swallowed twice, and then looked back at him. "What did you do?" he asked in a low, very controlled voice.

Colin snorted and handed him the letter.

Kit took it and his eyes raced across the page. He swallowed again, closed his eyes, and sighed. "Oh, thank God."

"Why does everyone keep saying that?" Bitty asked Rosie in what she undoubtedly thought was a whisper, her own slight accent making an appearance.

Colin snorted again and gave her a smile. "It's just so wonderful to have sisters, Bitty. Kit is delighted, aren't you, Kit?"

Kit gave him a hard look, but swallowed again and smiled politely. "Yes, very delighted. Colin, would you introduce us?"

Colin fought a grin at his twin's obvious distress. He quickly made the introductions and respective age information, waving Bitty down when she rose to curtsey for her turn, winked at Rosie when she gave a rather impertinent tilt of her chin, and shook his head when Ginny waved and yawned at the same time.

Kit looked as though he had swallowed marbles. "Pleasure to meet all three of you." He turned to Colin. "I think we need to talk."

"Probably wise," Colin agreed with a sage nod, as if his brother were a remarkably intelligent fellow.

Kit turned back to Tibby, his eyes barely grazing the girls. "Tibby, would you mind… erm…" He fought for words as he looked at the girls, and really looked.

It was not surprising that he was so taken aback. They really did look remarkably like them.

Tibby hummed a laugh. "I will watch the girls, my dear. I'm having my seamstress come and measure them. Apparently, their clothing is to follow once it is sent for, but they have nothing to wear now."

Colin gaped and looked back at the three of them. "What, nothing?" he cried.

Kit whirled back, his expression aghast. "Colin, you didn't ask them?"

"I was a little distracted by their existence, let alone appearance, so luggage may have slipped my mind," he protested, running a hand through his hair.

Kit harrumphed and shook his head. "Ridiculous. You never, ever consider the specifics, do you? No, you just ride along as if life is a game. Everything is all creative and fun to you."

"Oh, and you should talk?" Colin retorted with a laugh. "You're so proper and polite and then you randomly disappear, and who has to make your excuses? Oh, yes, your creative, fun, and remarkably loyal younger brother."

"Oh, why don't you…"

"Boys!" Tibby suddenly thundered.

They both looked at Tibby in shock, and the girls let out small giggles.

Tibby shook her head and smiled. "Go elsewhere to fight. The girls and I have fashion to get to." She winked at the girls, whose giggles turned into full blown laughs.

Kit held up a warning finger. "Nothing ostentatious, Tibby."

Colin nodded in agreement, knowing how Tibby could be.

Tibby scoffed and tossed her turbaned head. "Please, Christopher. They are children."

"That would not stop you," Colin muttered, drawing another almost-smile from Kit.

Tibby sniffed once. "They should live up to the Gerrard name, don't you think?"

"Which Gerrard?" Rosie muttered from beside her and looking back and forth between her brothers.

Colin did not have to look at his brother to know he was also struggling to fight laughter. Colin clamped down on his lips hard and tried to look serious.

It didn't work.

Tibby smiled at Rosie far too proudly for comfort.

Colin shook his head and gestured to the door. "Come on, Kit. If we leave now, we can claim blissful ignorance."

Kit followed him with a nod. "Not sure how blissful ignorance is where she is concerned. It rather makes me nervous."

Colin smiled and looked over his shoulder at him. "She has actually been surprisingly helpful this morning. She's offered to help us find a governess for them when they are comfortable and make sure they have everything they need."

"That's good," Kit murmured as they entered the study. "I haven't the faintest idea what to do at this point."

"Nor I. Boys I could have handled, we basically raised ourselves, but girls?" Colin shook his head and sat down in one of the leather back chairs.

"Three of them." Kit ran a hand through his dark hair, which was a sure sign of his turmoil, as his hair was perpetually perfect at all times. "I hate Loughton."

Colin smiled without humor. "So do they. You should have heard Rosie going on about him."

Kit smirked. "She is you, you know."

"Yes, I know."

"Are you sure she's not yours?"

Colin gave him a look, and Kit laughed out loud and held up his hands in surrender.

"All right, all right, I'm sorry." He sighed and looked at the still open door. "How bad do you think it is if Loughton sent them to us?"

Colin shook his head. "I don't want to know. I think they need us, Kit, and badly."

"Well, I was not exactly thinking of turning them out," Kit said with a sigh and a wince. "We are going to be terrible at this."

He snorted. "That much is obvious." He gripped the back of his head and sighed as well. "Well, we are all they've got, so we had better figure it out." Colin let his shoulders drop, suddenly feeling the weight of what they were taking on. He leaned his head back against the wall.

"At least there's two of us," Kit murmured, sounding more resigned than hopeful.

Colin laughed and brought his hand up as if saluting with a sword. "We few, we happy few, we band of brothers…"

Kit gave a quirk of his brow and inclined his head in a salute. "Poetic. And original."

"Shut up."

Chapter Four

$\mathcal{S}$usannah fidgeted with the lace at her bodice nervously, then remembered that a lady of her station never did such a thing, and jerked her expensively gloved hands away and folded them in her lap. She ought to have protested when she had been asked to wait on the bench in the hall, but it had been so long since she had felt like anyone who could expect cordiality, she had done nothing but nod.

She felt as though she were wearing a costume, playing a part in some ghastly play with poor writing and even poorer acting. The deep navy dress she wore was a bit faded, but she was in no position to be particular. The entire ensemble she had borrowed from Sasha, who had quite the selection of costumes to choose from. Some were far less respectable than others, but she knew better than to ask any questions. And she did not care enough to. Once, Susannah would have balked at the merest hint of such people, or such tawdry items. Now she was only grateful.

"Pardon me, madam."

The grating voice of the assistant broke her reverie and she turned her head only with a rather imperious look. She had thought such airs long forgotten, yet it was natural with him.

Whether that spoke of his nature or her desperation, she could not tell.

"Yes?" she replied in a crisp tone.

He bowed stiffly. "Mr. Goulding will see you now."

She sniffed, but tempered it with a faint smile. "Thank you."

The younger man looked a bit taken aback, but pleasantly so.

Blast. She did not need any such admiring, not from him or

anyone. "Will you show me the way or must I find it myself?" she finally snapped when he said nothing.

His thick brow furrowed and he gestured the way. Feeling once again in control, she swept past him and enjoyed once again hearing the sharp clicks of her heels against the floor. The shoes were torturing her feet, as they were at least one size too small, but Sasha assured her that they were necessary if she wanted to be believed.

Once, this had all been normal. The click of heels against a polished floor reminded her of that. And made her a trifle sad.

"Turn left," ordered the assistant from behind her.

Her spine stiffened in response, ugly memories rearing their heads at such a tone of command. She swallowed nervously, forced the memories back, and raised her chin higher. She did not need to reply, no one of her station would dare to comment on such behavior to an inferior.

Once she had made the turn, the office was in plain sight, and was a touch too ornate for a simple solicitor. But when one had the right sort of clientele, she supposed anything was possible. Mr. Goulding had never done her wrong before, in spite of everything else, so she would ignore the finery of his office and not ask where or how he had obtained the funds for such things.

Even the large mahogany desk at which the older man sat, his full and wavy head of graying hair bowed low to it as he scribbled, was carved and detailed in such an extraordinary away that she could easily have seen such a piece of furniture residing at Pavel House. But, of course, she had never seen her husband's offices or private rooms, so there was no way to tell if it actually had come from Pavel House. But it had come from somewhere and from someone.

When Mr. Goulding made no motion in acknowledging her and the assistant made no effort to announce her, she cleared her throat a bit obnoxiously, as her late aunt Harriet used to when she wanted something.

Mr. Goulding raised his head and his eyes widened at once. He sprang from his chair and bowed. "Lady Hawkins-Dean! What a pleasant surprise!"

Behind her, the assistant seemed to croak in distress. Ah, so no one had told him her identity. The poor man, he had no idea with whom he had been so rude. Pity she was not more powerful.

"Mr. Goulding," she replied cordially, taking the seat that the assistant had been quick to pull out for her. "I trust it is no trouble to your schedule to see me on such short notice?"

"No, no, not at all, my lady!" he replied with a swift shake of his head. "I have all the time in the world for you. Thank you, Reynolds, that will be all."

The assistant nodded, bowed to Susannah with a soft and sincere "my lady," and vacated the room, shutting the door firmly behind him.

Mr. Goulding hesitated for a long moment, then took his seat. "I did not know that your ladyship would be in London," he said slowly, folding his hands across the desk.

Susannah had to force herself not to look down at her gloves. "I have some friends in the area who have invited us to stay for a little while, and we were close to Town today, so I thought I should come by and see what the situation is at present."

He nodded in understanding, but his eyes showed a glimmer of disbelief.

She tilted her chin a bit and forced her superior voice to shine through. "Did you receive the funds I sent last month?"

"I did," he said with a hint of a sigh, "but it will not be enough to satisfy them. They want more for settlement. They claim it is not enough for what Sir Martin owed them. It was, after all, a great deal and they did not like our suggestion of portioned payments to make up the difference, but they agreed to it. Now they are increasing the amount demands and claim they will require more interest if you cannot meet it."

Susannah touched her brow and fought back a whimper of distress. If only he, or they, knew what she had given up, what she had sacrificed, in order to meet the previous demand. For more to be required… She did not have more to give, and earning it would be harder than ever before.

"I know it seems a great deal," Goulding murmured softly, sounding as if he spoke from a very great distance, "but surely it will not be so difficult for a woman in your position?"

She nearly laughed. A woman in her position? He had no idea what sort of a position she was in. She used a different solicitor for her own affairs and to get the necessary funding to her family, so as to keep Sir Martin as far from her concerns as humanly possible, and thus Mr. Goulding would never know.

No one would.

She forced herself to smile tightly, as if she were merely displeased. "Of course not. I shall do what I can. And the other matter?"

Mr. Goulding now looked very uncomfortable indeed. That did not bode well. He was a good enough man, had always treated her as fairly as Sir Martin allowed him, and since his death, had done all he could to help Susannah to retain as much as was possible, which had been a pitiful amount. He may not have known how bad her situation was, but he knew enough to understand that it was not good by any stretch. Yet he had always maintained a hope about it, sworn to find a way, and his letters to her had been regular and detailed.

He had not looked this poorly since they had discussed the last will and testament of Sir Martin, and all of its evils revealed.

"There is nothing I can do about that," he told her in a rough tone. "I have had the documents examined by a number of lawyers with more power and influence than myself, have searched for every loophole and alternative possible, but there is nothing. However careless and ill-conceived your late husband's financial affairs were, in this matter he was uncharacteristically thorough and complete. There is no possible reversal of his claim of your son's illegitimacy. He denied ever siring an heir, provided what appears to be irrefutable proof of this, and went so far as to have a physician declare him impotent. Thus, your son cannot inherit any portion of Pavel House, nor any of the other properties, even if they were in a financial position for him to do so."

She closed her eyes in horror. Not that Pavel House had any particular sentimental value to her, but it could have been razed and rebuilt into something fine for Freddie. For his future. But now...

"And does my word mean nothing?" she asked a broken, hoarse

tone.

Mr. Goulding sighed and she heard his elbows squeak on the gleaming desk surface. "I am afraid not, my lady. What with the sale of all the estates, and with such proof on his side…"

"They are not inclined to listen to a woman's side of the story," she finished with an irritated sigh.

Mr. Goulding had the good sense to look sympathetic.

Susannah scowled and muttered, "Does it matter that I could produce a list of the names of several women who have borne his real illegitimate children, and thus disprove his claim? For there were several, I could fill pages, he was perfectly capable…"

Mr. Goulding surprised her by snorting loudly. "I know, my lady."

She gave him a curious look.

"Who do you think had to arrange all of that and pay those women for their silence at the time?" He sat back in his chair and watched her. "There were several things I had to do, my lady, in the service of your husband, that I would rather not recall. I cannot undo them now, though I have tried. There were no provisions in the will about any of the women, nor the illegitimate children. All that remains for me to do in his service is see the debts repaid, and then it is done. Believe me, had I means, I would help you in this regard, but I have not."

"I understand." And she did, in some respect. No one would wish to deal with such unsavory men as they had to in this business, and he was right to wish out of it. He knew as she did that there was no running or hiding, no way out but to do exactly as they wished.

Susannah sighed and straightened. "Is there anything else?"

"Sir Martin's cousin is demanding we pay for the repairs to Pavel House."

"What?" she cried, surging forward in her seat. "That is not possible, he bought it from the creditors, it is not my duty!"

"He feels that the responsibility is that of the late owners. I have convinced him to consent to half, and he has no plans to live there in the next five years, so time is on our side." He smiled at her in what was undoubtedly supposed to be a comforting way. "He is not so demanding and unfeeling as the creditors."

No, he probably was not. But he was also a relation of her late husband, which meant she could not trust a single word he said. And it still tightened the noose around her neck.

"We couldn't convince Sir Martin to make the repairs when he was alive," she moaned to herself.

"I know. It is far from an ideal situation, is it not?"

Susannah gave him a potent look of disbelief. "Far from ideal?" she repeated dangerously. "My son has been declared illegitimate, we have no house, every farthing is spoken for, and more funds are demanded than..." She bit her lip and held the rest back. She again forced the barest hint of a wan smile. "I am afraid, my dear Mr. Goulding, that the phrase 'far from ideal' would be a haven compared to what we now face."

The solicitor swallowed and shuffled papers on his desk. "As I said," he began in quick, nervous bursts of words, "I will continue to do what I can. I trust you can continue to send the funds to me so that I might forward them on?"

She nodded, painfully sliding her cool mask of haughty indifference back into place. "You may expect it, yes. I shall send what I can when I can."

"Excellent." He was all business now, a sure sign that he was vastly uncomfortable. "And should I need to contact you? Where will you be staying in Town?"

"We are not staying in Town," she lied easily. "Our friends travel the country and we will be in their party. I cannot say where I will be or when, so contacting me shall be quite difficult. If I can convince my friends to remain in one place for any given amount of time, I shall send you notice of it."

He stared at her for another long moment, but when her expression did not change, he nodded and rose. It was a breach of protocol for him to rise before she did so, but she was hardly in the mood to demand propriety now. She rose as well and inclined her head, before turning towards the door.

"Lady Hawkins-Dean?"

She turned back and raised a brow.

He pressed his lips together in a tight line. "Do be careful. These men to whom you are in debt are not the sort to be trifled with. They will come for you if they are dissatisfied. And they will be neither kind nor courteous about it."

She took a moment to process that, then nodded. "Thank you. Good day, Mr. Goulding."

And with a heavy heart and numb to all else, Susannah strode from the office, giving neither the assistant nor the butler the courtesy of acknowledgement.

It was all far worse than she could ever have imagined it to be.

She had no leads to finding any sort of employment yet, although Mrs. Grovner assured her that patience was needed. Interviews were apparently forthcoming, though none had been set. Every day without possibilities made Susannah nervous. After all, her references were almost entirely falsified, save for the sisters at the hospital near Pavel House, and there was no way for any of her claims to be verified. Anyone who actually wanted to check her references would be grossly disappointed and her secret would be out.

For the time being, she was working as a laundress and seamstress for the lady who owned and ran the boarding house in which she now resided. She had been forced to do without a maid or any servant to do mending the last few years at Pavel House, so she had learned to do it herself, and had grown quite accomplished at it. It had come in handy when she had worked at the hospital in Milfield in that time as well, and there she had learned the proper way to launder linens. It had quite shocked the sisters and nurses that she, a fine lady in the largest house in the area, would perform so menial of tasks, let alone be willing to actually get her hands dirty in her volunteering. They soon learned, however, that she was not the usual sort of fine lady, and eventually put her to use quite often.

She was grateful for that now. She might not have all of the attributes or talents that a lady of quality should possess, but she did not need those anymore. All she needed were the skills she had attained in her life, for they were what would enable her to make any sort of living and perhaps one day, provide for her and her son.

But for now, she had nothing. Absolutely nothing except for an impossible mountain of debts and her relative anonymity in this massive city. She was invisible to just about everybody, and that was exactly how she preferred it.

She knew full well that the debt collectors would not rest until they were settled, which would take many years, if ever. She knew that they would soon be in London to look for her, if they were not there already. She fully expected that they had sources in London looking for her, or waiting for the merest hint or rumor of her.

Time was not on her side, so all she had, for the present, was her invisibility.

Oh, Colin, she thought, as she often did and had so often done before, *what do I do?*

But, as always, there were no answers from him, and she was on her own to formulate a plan.

So focused on her situation and lost in her thoughts was she that she did not notice the bustling of the streets, nor anything except the path before her, and she quite suddenly found herself slammed against another person, one much larger and stronger than she. It was all she could do to avoid toppling over, and his hands on her arms was the only balance she had.

"I beg your pardon, please excuse me," said the man, and she felt her stomach clench in apprehension of the face she was about to see.

Colin.

Against her will, she looked up, her hands very innocently resting on his forearms for balance, though she was now quite steady in that respect.

The power in his blue eyes caused a fire to sear her hands, seeming to burn through the thick gloves where she touched him.

His eyes were wide as they met hers. "You…" he finally breathed.

She swallowed a cry and prayed her composure would remain intact. It was sheer agony seeing him in the flesh now when she had just been clinging to her memory of him. But the reality of him… She could not move, could barely breathe.

"I knew it was you," Colin said softly, his hands still at her arms, ignorant as to her torment. "I knew I had not imagined you."

She could not bear this. "Excuse me." She dropped her hands and tried to go around.

He held her fast in place. "No, you are not excused, wait a second."

"No, sir, you are mistaken, please let me pass." Panic was beginning to rise within her. She was not yet able to steel herself against him, had no defenses, and absolutely no strength to draw upon.

Still he held her. "I am never mistaken. I know you and you know it."

"No, sir, you do not, now please!" Her voice was becoming shrill and they would draw attention soon. He would not let her go, she knew it, so she closed her eyes and stomped with all of her might, driving that slight heel of the too-small shoe into his toes.

He grunted in pain and released her, and she dashed around him.

But he recovered quickly, and called after her, "Susannah Merritt, whatever are you doing in London after all these years?"

She halted suddenly and whirled, horrified at his volume, his identification of her, and how her name on his lips still made her heart dance. Her traitorous heart pounded against her ribs, an unsteady cadence of pain and fear, worrying at who might have heard, and what sort of emotions the man before her was engulfed in.

Without thinking, without even considering it, she rushed forward and stopped a hair's breadth from him. "Do not call me that. Do not even speak to me," she rasped fiercely, her words more of a sob than anything else. "Forget you saw me. Forget everything. Please." That last word had come out as a plea, begging him, and herself, to forget him, and them, and all possibilities that had ever lain therein.

His face was one of utter confusion, anger, surprise, and yes, curiosity. But his eyes were pure ice in their assessment of her, and she could not bear it.

She took advantage of his frigid silence, and whirled around again, dashing between people and buildings and carriages, desperate to disappear into their depths. She was grateful for the crowds, for the inability of London's finest to notice anything, and for her invisibility.

On and on she ran, tears burning her eyes. She was panting, hardly able to catch her breath, and her legs ached furiously. She did not hear any sort of pursuit, but she did not stop until she had reached her building.

Rather than enter, she moved to the alley just beside, leaned against the brick, and let her sobs finally be freed, covering her mouth to stifle the depth and despair of her cries.

Colin walked back towards his house slowly, every step dragging as if weighted down by chains. He had stood there in the street for so long he had begun to draw comment, but none of those even remotely registered in his mind. He could not acknowledge a single person, let alone their questions or teasings or flirtations.

He could not do anything except stare at the place where Susannah had disappeared.

Eventually, he had come to himself and turned around to go back the way he had come, whatever his purpose or errand had been entirely forgotten. And was now completely irrelevant.

So. She *was* here. He had not imagined her the other day. That was a slight comfort, as he had never before devised her appearance so vividly. But it was also the single most disconcerting thing he had ever known in his life.

He was angry. How dare she invade his life in this manner when he was already experiencing so much turmoil. And with her return into his world, she brought along painful memories that he had spent years burying. But all was forced to the surface now, the wounds as raw and exposed as the day he sustained them.

Anger had never been a sensible thing for him, and that had just been made evident again. His rage outstripped his good taste and behaviors, and bared its fangs in the light of day. Perhaps it was for the best.

What angered him the most was how beautiful she still was. Why could she not have grown ugly and old and fat and wrinkled in the intervening years since they last met? It would have given him a righteous sense of justice to see her so altered, and he would have felt no qualms whatsoever about hating her all these years. But no, she was not so altered. She was more beautiful than she had been at sixteen, which seemed so impossible to comprehend that he was sure he had conjured that by sheer imagination.

The pounding of his heart still informed him that he was not immune to her looks now any more than he had ever been, despite his current emotional cacophony. And for that, he was livid with himself.

In the midst of his overwhelming anger, there was also, he had to admit, a hint of curiosity. Perhaps confusion would have been a better word, but he was curious, as he usually was. The woman he had just seen had been on the verge of a torrent of emotions that he did not dare attempt to filter through. He had seen it in her eyes, in the shaking of her frame, the change in her tone... Even now, he could read her as easily as he had before. And her expression when he had called after her, impertinent and juvenile as it was on his part...

It had been the look of sheer and utter terror, and it had frozen his heart in his chest. And *never*, in all the years he had known her, had she ever spoken to him in that way.

What in the world could possibly have caused such fear in her? What had happened to make her change so? Why was she hiding? He could very well understand hiding from him, as she certainly had to know that seeing her would give him no pleasure. But she seemed to be hiding from everyone and everything, and Susannah had never been particularly shy or retreating.

The contradiction between the two versions of her had his mind reeling.

But then, fifteen years was a long time. A great many changes could have occurred.

Not that it mattered to him, he insisted to himself as he re-entered his home. He could not have cared less about Susannah

Merritt, or whoever she was now, and had absolutely no interest in her being in London, in her life for the last fifteen years, or in what manner she had changed.

She was nothing to him now.

But he could not keep from wondering.

He was distracted for a time by Bitty, whose merry greeting of him prompted further questioning, leading to the admission that she had lost Rosie's comb and would pay dearly for it if she could not find it quickly. Dutiful as ever, Colin considered himself recruited for the search party.

Having sisters was proving quite a trial. Thankfully, he discovered he had a maid in his home who had many younger siblings of her own, and she was more than happy to look after the girls until they settled on a more permanent solution. They were adjusting well, and Rosie claimed to only have gotten lost four times in the house, though he suspected it was closer to ten. Even so, he was surprised at how much he wanted them to feel as though they belonged, as if this were truly their home now.

He let Bitty take his hand and they began to walk from room to room in search of the troublesome comb, avoiding Rosie when they had to, and looking high and low for their quarry. Bitty chattered animatedly the entire time, and it surprised Colin that never once did he find himself bored or irritated by it.

It was an entirely new world that he had entered, and as yet, neither he nor Kit had ruined anything. Even so, he thanked the heavens that his friends would arrive in a few days, and was even more grateful that their wives were coming. He needed guidance on these children, and there was no way he and Kit could do this alone.

In spite of his current desperate search for the comb, and in spite of his chatterbox little sister, yet again his mind wandered, and wondered, and the topic of his mind's occupation made him more curious than the fact that he was curious did.

And that, indeed, was a curious thing.

Chapter Five

"Can I help you with something, sir?"

He barely heard the question, and had a bit of trouble processing the words.

"Sir? Do you require some assistance?"

Now it was firm, and a little louder.

Daft little bird, he was hardly deaf.

"Erm… are you lost, sir? I can help you with whatever you are looking for."

Colin finally looked up at the soft, rather confused tone of the young woman who had approached him. She was a pretty little thing. He would have noticed that a long time ago, had he been the man he once was. He would have already flirted with her, complimented a dozen or more of her features, spoken words of semi-original poetry, made her giggle, and have her doing him all sorts of favors, some of which might have gotten her fired from employ. Not for indecency, mind, but because it was bad for business.

Now, however, all he could do was smile very blandly and respond, "No, thank you."

Her smile was rather quizzical, and she gave him a look, no doubt a chance to change his mind.

Impertinent chit, he thought rather harshly when she finally turned and walked away. Why did it matter to her that he did not need help?

He scowled and moved to another part of the shop, looking without really seeing.

Then it hit him. She was perfectly right to repeatedly ask if he needed assistance, and to question his answer. Here he was, a grown man of thirty-two, perusing the items for sale in a modiste shop. And he had been doing so in the stocking section.

With no care for who might see, he clapped himself very soundly on the forehead. He had been completely unaware of where he was or what he was doing, and was two paces short of losing his ruddy mind! What in the world had gotten into him?

An involuntary glower darkened his features as he was brought back to it, yet again, for what had to be the thousandth time today.

Susannah.

Even her name, the mere thought of it, made him bristle and it was all he could do to keep from snarling.

Three days since he had seen her, had spoken to her, and in those three days, she had become his obsession. He had hardly slept, and when he had managed it, his dreams had been plagued with images of her, as she had been and as she was now, and imagining all that had lain between the times. His curiosity bordered on lunacy now, and the secret was dangerously close to coming out.

His sisters had noticed his moods, and the poor things had been confused by his sudden darkness and indifference. They had grown used to his cheerful, teasing, carefree self; they could not reconcile that brother with the one before them. He'd even heard that Bitty had gone to Kit the next time Rosie threatened her. Kit, of all people! It was madness, complete and utter madness.

His guilt knew no bounds where they were concerned. He owed them all his attention and all his efforts, not some mindless and useless lump of a man that ignored them. They already had that in a father, and no one needed to be reminded of that, least of all girls so young.

For pity's sake, even Tibby had noticed his change, and that was something he did not need at all. It was quite the blessing that she was so involved with the girls and their needs and desires and making them feel at home, or else she might have focused on him entirely and that was one inquisition that he would be powerless against. If England ever needed aid in interrogation, they would have no greater asset than Lady Tabitha Raeburn.

So irritated had she been by his behavior this morning, when he was supposed to be watching and appreciating the girls' newly acquired dancing skills, that she banished him from the house, his *own* house, to fetch the new clothing items from the modiste. And so out of sorts was he that he did not fight her, could not even muster up the effort to protest.

That, he was sure, terrified his sisters. Rosie watched him go, wide-eyed and gaping. He could hardly meet her gaze. Bitty had been close to tears, and he had been sentient enough to reach out and tousle her curls in some show of comfort. And Ginny had latched onto his leg and asked if she could come. He had picked her up, kissed her nose, and said no, which she had not cared for at all.

Even Tibby, quite the consummate actress herself, had been aghast. He could see she had not meant to be serious, the dresses were due to be delivered by carriage later that day, along with the items from the milliners, haberdashers, and who knew where else. She had never expected him to obey her now when he never had before. Her worried expression, unabashed and open, showed him just how dire his situation was.

It was hardly his fault he was so tossed about. Everything, every single pang of guilt and twinge of conscience, could lie squarely and completely upon the slender shoulders of Miss Susannah Merritt, as was. And he would quite happily layer each and every one upon them.

Except some small, but mighty portion of whatever semblance of heart he possessed pounded a steady cadence of betrayal quite angrily against his ribs. Lies. It was all lies, and he knew it.

Oh, he was furious, and quite rightly so. Anybody in the world would side with him on that one, he could safely say that. Anyone who had ever thought themselves in love, or found themselves spurned, or both, would have handed him pitchforks and cheered for his cause. He suspected it would be at least two-thirds of London, and that did not count those in various other parts of the country currently hiding from such pain.

No, he could be angry. He could be angry, upset, and confused. He could demand answers or some sort of explanation. He could refuse to see her, not include her on guest lists, and be undeniably cold when unfortunately confronted by her.

All of that he could do.

What he could not do was entirely blame Susannah for being the chief occupant of his thoughts, and the sole topic of his focus. Hadn't she always been thus? It was her rightfully earned place within him.

It was not her fault he was going mad because of her. That was his own doing.

And blast his interfering curiosity, and his indomitable will, he could not let it go.

He growled in frustration and rubbed at the place on his brow he had hit. What was he doing here again?

Right. The dresses.

He looked around the room, trying to discern if that sweet little assistant was still fluttering about, knowing he would get far more out of her than he would the proprietor of this fine establishment. Older women never cared as much for his charm, despite his best efforts.

The bell of the door chimed as it opened, and he looked around again to see if the girl would reappear. Surely for the sake of good service, she would have to.

He frowned when nothing happened.

He moved towards the large counter and shelves he saw in a rather poor position in a far corner of the room. Really, whoever constructed the layout and positioning of this place had a very pitiable idea of natural flow and ease of access. Why, he would never have found it at all if he had not been as tall as he was and diligently searching with his keen eye for detail. Not that it mattered, there was no one at the desk to assist anyone at all, let alone the only other patron, who was now heading towards it.

Her plain bonnet was cast down a bit, so she could hardly have seen where she was going well. If she did not mind her footing, she was going to topple over a rather trim mannequin. Suspicious and ever watchful for potential moments of heroism before young ladies, he made his way to possibly intercept the imminent disaster.

Sure enough, she barged headlong into it, and down it began to fall, destined to crash into yet another poorly placed item, a display of ribbons and lace. But, thanks to his fast reflexes and impeccable timing, Colin was instantly there to catch said falling mannequin and thus save the hopefully fair maiden from distress and humiliation.

"That was close," he said softly with a laugh, his easy rakish demeanor sliding perfectly into form.

"Thank you, sir," came the relieved reply.

His heart skidded to a halt as he righted the mannequin, straightening himself and stiffening his spine.

Fate was truly unkind.

Slowly, he turned his head only, coldness enveloping him like fog. "Susannah," he said with all the tautness in his being.

Her blue-green eyes widened and she mouthed his name. If it were possible, she was paler than the last time he had seen her, and she paled still before his eyes. She turned and ran, but this time he was ready for her flight, and caught her arm in a firm grip.

"No," he growled darkly. "No, you are not getting away that easily."

"Please, Colin," she replied, her voice hitching on his name in a way he tried to ignore. "Please. Let go. Let me go."

He held her more firm. "No."

Her shoulders sagged, and slowly, she turned to face him. "Colin…"

He shook his head, and gave her the slightest shake. "You are going to start talking to me, and you are going to do it now."

A steely coldness entered her eyes and her chin lifted. "My life is not your business anymore."

There was his Susannah. He shouldn't have been so secretly thrilled about it, and he definitely should not be referring to her as "his." He cocked his head a touch, giving her a serious look. "Then why are you afraid of me?" he asked softly, his hold on her relaxing.

"What?" she asked in return, her tone higher.

"You are shaking like a leaf. You are frail, tiny, much smaller than you should be. In fact, you look ill." The closer he looked, the worse it got. Her eyes bore heavy, dark circles and were tinged with a painful sort of red. Her cheekbones were almost harsh in the setting of her face. The lock of hair that had always and ever fallen out of place over her left temple now did so, and he had to clench his free hand to keep from reaching for it, as he had done so often before.

But he was the only one living in the past. Susannah's jaw tightened and she somehow snatched her arm out of his hold.

"If you are just going to insult me," she bit out, "I will leave." She turned on her heel and strode purposefully for the door.

The dark anger that had flowed through him so freely for fifteen years roared to life in his ears. "Don't you walk away from me again!"

With that, she stopped in her tracks, as if she had come to a wall. Her hands clenched and unclenched at her sides. There was no sound at all but their breathing.

Then he saw it. The slight tremor he had felt when she'd been in his grip now became visible as it coursed through her frame. From her head to her toes, she shook. Then her breath suddenly hitched loudly, and she clamped a hand over her mouth to stifle the sounds.

Something broke inside of him at that. What, he could not have said, but it sent his feet moving and his throat working absently. He slammed closed the cage around his heart and tried for a stranger's unaffected air. Awkwardly, his hand patted at her shoulder.

"Come, come, that's quite enough," he forced out, his voice uneven with the forced coolness.

She turned from him, unwittingly forcing his hand to settle more firmly on her.

He nearly gasped in shock at what his touch was telling him. She was not only frail in appearance, she was altogether feeble in frame. Her dress, what he had thought so well fitted, even if she were thinner, actually hung fairly loose on her. She was nothing more than skin and bones, and with the faintest pressure, he was sure she would break beneath his hand.

He forced back a swallow and patted her again, his touch far gentler. "There, there, come on."

She shook her head, her breathing growing more and more frantic.

Colin looked out of the windows and saw more potential customers approaching the store. He exhaled in exasperation. Whatever his feelings, he did not want a scene. He gripped her shoulder and put his other hand on her arm. "For heaven's sake, come here," he muttered, steering her in the exact opposite corner of the store, behind some very ugly tartan fabric that no one would want.

Susannah went to put her face in the corner, but he turned her back to him.

"Face me," he ordered, his tone brusque.

She hiccupped and trembled a bit at the command, then winced and rubbed at her eyes.

"Pull yourself together, woman." He looked around again, praying that idiotic assistant would stay away.

"Go ahead," Susannah finally grumbled. "Say something else. Twenty lashes, am I right?"

He gave her a quick look of surprise. "What are you talking about?"

Her tears were nearly gone, save for the tracks on her cheeks, but her breathing was still unsteady. "You are punishing me. Exacting revenge. Eye for an eye."

"Don't be ridiculous," he scoffed, looking away. But she was right, wasn't she? Was that not exactly what he had been doing?

She snorted softly and leaned her head back against the wall with a soft thud. "There is no need to keep me trapped here, Colin. No customers, no scene." Her voice was laced with a deep sense of fatigue, almost resignation. After what he had just witnessed, it was chilling.

His eyes slowly slid back to her. He couldn't let her go, not yet. She would disappear for good, and he would never have answers. And yet… He didn't want to press her. Not like this.

"Can I…" He fumbled for words, still playing the barely polite gentleman. "Can I help you find what you were looking for? A dress, a wrap, whatever you came here to get?"

She raised a brow at him. "Why? So you can tell me how ill it suits or poorly it fits?"

"It would fit poorly," he said at once. "You're even more fragile than I thought. What the devil happened to you, Susannah? Or can I call you Susannah?"

She closed her eyes and sighed. "You can call me Susannah. Or Miss Hart."

"Miss?"

One eye opened. "Yes. Not a real name, so don't bother asking."

He frowned, opened his mouth, then closed it when he heard the rustling of fabric. He glanced up and saw the assistant organizing something in the back. They were quite out of her sight, and she would never notice them. He looked back down at Susannah to find both eyes open and staring at him without emotion.

"Why are you here?" he asked in a low tone, not bothering to hide his irritation.

"You do not own London, Colin," she said softly.

That was beside the point. He shook his head at her. "You cannot go until you answer my questions, Susannah."

She folded her arms across her, which only emphasized the shocking slightness of her frame. She looked down for a long moment, swallowed once, then brought her eyes back up to his.

"I did not come here to purchase something," she informed him calmly. "I came to ask for work."

Had she said she were royalty, she could not have stunned him more. He blinked, then blinked again. Work? Her? In a place like this?

"Work?" he repeated aloud, the word feeling odd in his mouth. "Why work? Why do you have to work, Susannah?"

A small muscle in her jaw ticked. "I just so happened to inherit my late husband's debts. I need the resources to fulfill them."

Late husband. Late. Husband.

His teeth ground together for a moment. "Who?" he asked darkly.

She shook her head firmly. "No. That I will not tell you, and you can keep me here until dawn, if you wish, but I will not budge."

Still as stubborn as that girl from Seabrook. Why did that satisfy him?

He grunted and pretended it made no difference. He gave her a careful, thorough look, and she returned the gesture.

"What happened to you, Susannah?" he asked again, his voice no longer harsh, and suddenly he was not asking just about the years of pain, but more.

The slender column of her throat worked a few times. "Life," she finally said, the word almost an expletive. "Life happened, Colin."

He sensed that there were several layers to that response, and very few of them pleasant ones. This woman, the one he had hated for so long, had been through something, or several things, and in one way or another, had suffered. She might have broken him, but she was not whole either. Somewhere in that, he also found satisfaction.

And pity.

"Why London?" The question was bitter, as was he, for he did not want to feel pity or sympathy or any sort of connection between them. He did not want to understand, wished to God that she had never crossed his path again. Now that she had, he felt… duty-bound. Was it not the mark of a gentleman to help those who were suffering?

How much of a gentleman was he?

Susannah shrugged against the wall. "I needed a place to be anonymous, a fresh start, and the best opportunity for work would be here. Far better than in Bath."

"Is that where you've been?"

Her eyes had no expression as they stared back, and she made no reply.

Colin closed his eyes and ran a hand through his hair in agitation. He exhaled slowly, then gripped the back of his neck and looked at her again. She was so calm, so composed staring back at him. It reminded him eerily of the same attitude she had that day fifteen years ago. And yet… she still trembled slightly. Her knees shook beneath her skirts, and it seemed the only thing holding her up was the wall. And if he looked closely, she was not as calm in her breathing as she was in her looks.

Susannah was very, very nervous. And worried. And no doubt a hoard of other emotions.

Again, that same something broke and he groaned a small sigh. "What kind of work?" he mumbled.

She blinked once. "I beg your pardon?"

What he wouldn't give to ask her to repeat *that* phrase a few hundred thousand times. He pushed the impulse back and put his hands on his hips. "What kind of work are you looking for?"

She looked at him as if he had sprouted a spare set of arms.

Impatient and not understanding himself, he made a slightly dramatic gesture for her to tell him.

She swallowed. "Well… Anything, really. I thought… to try for a companion or a governess. I have some skills and education. But those are harder to come by, particularly with so few references. I can sew and launder, so that opens up a different set of options. I worked in a hospital before, but when I asked here I was told they cannot pay at this time." She shrugged again and sighed heavily. "At this point, I would be a scullery maid if it came to it."

Colin pulled his head back a touch, surprised yet again. Her words should have been dramatic, and as they replayed in his head, they certainly sounded dramatic. But the tone of her voice and the complete lack of emotion told him quite the opposite.

She was perfectly honest.

"You are desperate, aren't you?" he murmured softly, almost against his will.

Her look said all he needed to know. *Would I be here if I wasn't?*

He suddenly cleared his throat, decision made before he could think back on it. "All right. I will help you find work."

She slid a bit on the wall in surprise, and he ought to have smiled, except he felt the same way. "What?" she asked in a too-loud voice.

He steeled himself, and repeated, "I will help you find work."

Her lips tried to form words, and eventually, only one made its way out, "Why?"

"Why what?" he grumbled, looking away. He did not need her thinking this was an emotional thing, or that she was forgiven, or that he was being nice. He was simply being a gentleman. Or polite. Or something.

"After what I did to you, why?"

Ah, so she did see the irony here. He ought to say something clever, something cold, something with a sneer. But there had been quite enough of that. She had been candid with him, at least in part, and he would do no less. He offered a rough sigh and met her eyes steadily. "Because in spite of everything, we were friends once. And that young man would have helped you."

Hours later, Colin sat alone in his study, his mind more a mess now than it had ever been. The day's events unfolded before him over and over, and still they made no sense.

Had he really offered to help Susannah find work in London? Why?

His own answer to the same question from her kept repeating, and he knew that they were true. But he was not the young man he had been then. When he had loved her so blindly, so naively, so hopelessly. She had ruined him. She had broken him. And yet he was helping her.

It was no comfort to know that she was just as surprised. They had arranged to meet in a few days in Hyde Park to go over what he had found, and any success that she had had. Hopefully, that would be the end of it. If he did this good deed, this bizarre and kind thing, he might be able to let her go. He would do what he could to see that she would not be completely without resources in London, and what she did with his help would be on her head alone.

She had left the shop without speaking to the owner, looking back at him several times as if he had been an apparition that would soon vanish before her.

He thought it was a very distinct possibility himself.

Somehow, he had been polite and coherent with the assistant and modiste, had collected all the necessary frocks, and delivered them safely home again, to some very excitable sisters who immediately insisted on a fashion display for him. He politely accepted the invitation and showered each of them with accolades and praises. He truly had been impressed by the modiste's work and confided to Tibby the same. She gave him a smug reply about doubting her, but her eyes asked a hundred questions, none of which he answered.

He owed his sisters some attention, so the rest of the evening had been devoted to making up for the past few days. Now, however, they were all in bed, presumably asleep, and his mind could unravel at will.

What was he doing?

Never had his actions ever given him this much cause for distress. Never had he questioned a single thing he had ever done; he had always been strategic and precise in his actions. But now?

Now he questioned everything.

"Colin?"

His brother's voice broke his reverie and he looked up to see Kit in the doorway, watching him with uncertainty.

"Colin, why are you sitting in your study with only one candle lit?"

Absently, he looked and saw that the rest had gone out at some point. "Oh…" he murmured slowly. "I didn't notice…"

Kit made some noncommittal noise and leaned against the doorframe. "The girls tell me you have been a bit different lately."

"Yes." Really, what else was he supposed to say about that? There was so much… too much…

The silence wore on, and only the ticking of the clock could be heard.

Kit exhaled sharply. "Colin, what is wrong with you?"

He slowly dragged his eyes to meet those of his twin, and saw, beneath the furrowed brow and glower, worry. Kit should never worry about him; it was always the other way around, and had been for years. Not that Kit had any idea, nor would he ever, but Colin had always been perfectly situated and content, with nothing particularly distressing outside of his wardrobe or bad rumors.

He could not pretend there was not some cause for his brother to be concerned now.

After all, he was becoming quite concerned himself.

It was time Kit knew.

"Susannah is here."

Kit actually jerked from his position and took a few steps into the room. "I'm sorry, what did you say?"

"Susannah," Colin repeated without emotion. "Susannah Merritt."

"Yes, I know who you mean, but… Are you sure?"

He snorted once. "Quite sure."

Kit began pacing in the room, which was a rare sight indeed. "You've seen her?"

Colin nodded. "Three times."

"Have you spoken to her?" Kit was watching him intently as he paced, as focused and intense as if this were some criminal examination.

Again, Colin nodded in response. "Twice."

Kit stopped pacing and set his hands at his hips. "And…?"

Slowly, Colin shook his head. "I have no idea."

"About what?"

He shrugged. "Anything. Anything at all."

In one fluid motion, Kit grabbed the chair nearest him, swung it around, and set it directly in front of Colin's. Then suddenly he was sitting there, hands folded before him, leaning forward. "Talk."

Numbly, Colin related all of the events of the last few days, leaving out only the dreams. His twin did not need to know how long those had been going on. Kit had been there with him when Susannah had gone off to marry whoever she had, and he had done everything in his power to set Colin back to rights. It had taken ages, and Colin was indebted to him eternally for it, but Kit would never know that Colin had never been completely whole again.

Not now, not ever.

When all was told, sometimes repeated, Kit sat back in his chair, looking a touch winded. "Damn," he said softly.

That shocked Colin immensely. Kit, by a general rule, never swore.

Yet another sign that this was grave indeed.

Kit ran a hand through his hair. "Well, why would you offer to help her?"

"I don't know."

"Not good enough, Colin. We are not going back there."

Colin knew only too well not to be impertinent enough to ask where.

"I couldn't help myself," he murmured as if in a daze.

Kit's eyes widened. He wet his lips quickly, and then leaned forward again. "Colin," he began carefully, "do you... do you want to help Susannah?"

He thought about for a moment. A very long moment. Then, eventually, he met his brother's eyes. "Yes."

Kit stared at him, then got to his feet and moved to the sideboard. "I think we need a drink."

Colin quite agreed.

Chapter Six

$\mathcal{I}$t was hardly dawn three days later when Susannah made her way towards Hyde Park. The streets were silent and still, no one about to see her, which was much to her liking. She preferred the silence and solitude. It gave her ample opportunity to reflect upon her actions, as she had avoided doing in recent years.

What in the world was she doing?

Even in her mind, she knew it was a foolish thing she was about to do. She ought to be retreating into the darkness from which she had come, but instead of doing what was wise, she was venturing into the madness before her, ignoring every warning currently coursing through her.

Seeing Colin the other day, feeling his touch upon her, speaking to him, all had weakened her resolve and she had been helpless to confess what he wanted to know. She was only relieved that she could keep the details from him, dark and ugly as they were. At least she had some strength left.

He was too much of a gentleman to completely abandon her when she was in need, so there was still some heart to him, however small or hidden it might have been. She did not flatter herself that what he was doing was anything more than a sense of duty, long-instilled in him and his brother, to help those of their acquaintance. She remembered him saying his father had been a very generous man once, before his nature had turned and he had become the creature he was at present.

It would have been so easy for Colin to have followed the same path.

She shook her head at herself as she walked the cobblestone towards the park. She thought as if she knew him still, as if they were still friends. She knew no more about him than he did of her. For all she knew, he could have been the chilling and somber man who had lashed out at her and spoken so harshly against her.

But in her heart, she knew that couldn't be true. It was a good man who had offered to help her, though it could not be of any benefit or consequence to him how she lived or suffered. In spite of her injuries towards him, in spite of the complete betrayal of their young but fervent friendship, he was willing to help her.

She did not expect kindness. She was ready to accept more thinly veiled anger and insults, more buffeting about by his bitterness. She ought to have insisted to find work on her own, to keep her sense of pride and honor and not let him interfere in her matters.

She had no pride left and no honor to speak of.

If it were herself alone, it would be one thing. But for her son, she would travel into the very darkest depths of humility and mortification so long as it saved him. She would endure whatever she must to see his suffering ended.

Colin had connections that could prove valuable to her, if he would use them in her stead. All of this could be a rather intelligent move on her part, and could be the thing that saved her and Freddie. Or it could be the final straw that broke her weakened and brittle will.

But she wanted to go, wanted to see him again, despite everything. Because even an angry, bitter, cruel Colin was a soothing balm for her shattered soul and aching heart. He had been her dream every day, and now he was here, in the darkest, bleakest abyss of her life. She had been in such darkness before, when living with her husband. However, even in that nightmare, there was at least hope for the future, and she knew her place. But now, the darkness stretched on as far as she could tell, as far as she could imagine, and, as it was then, all she could do was cling to Colin. Even if he despised her. Even if it killed her.

It could not be worse than living without him.

But he couldn't know that. He needed to live in a world where right and wrong were clear, and hearts should not be broken, and old loves would never resurface. The past remained in the past, and did not haunt the present nor the future. The villains were never good at heart, could never be redeemed, and all suffering they endured was deserved.

He couldn't know the truth.

She flexed her fingers, scolding herself for not having brought the gloves Sasha had loaned her. The mornings were beginning to be cold and brisk and she was going to have to figure something out if they were to remain here. Her clothing would not sustain her for a winter.

Nor would Freddie's.

Right, that must be her focus. Not just repaying debts or keeping herself from a debtor's prison, which was undoubtedly where this would all end if she did not find work soon, but her son. Her poor and innocent son, who still assumed this was all an adventure, and had no idea that she never knew where dinner was going to come from, or that the meager earnings she received from doing the linens and mending at the inn only paid for their lodging and the occasional hot dinner. For one.

Her head swam a bit and she forced herself to place one foot in front of the other. She could not remember the last time she had a full meal herself. She did fair enough hiding it from Freddie, he was young enough that distraction still worked every time, but eventually he would notice.

Eventually, they all would.

The park was just ahead and a dense layer of fog lay like a shroud upon it. She shivered, wrapping her arms around herself tightly, wishing she owned a thicker coat. It would be embarrassing to recall how long she had spent poring over which of her dresses she ought to wear to this meeting, and she only had four, including the finer one for parading. The jacket, however, was the only one she had, worn and threadbare though it had become.

Why she cared, she refused to think on. What she wore had very little significance to her, and even less, she was sure, to Colin. But this was her best fitted one, and while that did not say much, it should keep him from being so shocked at her appearance.

Or at least commenting on it.

But then, Colin usually said whatever he wanted, polite, appropriate, or not.

And in case she had forgotten that, the last two meetings with him should have reinforced it enough.

She crossed into the park and looked for the bridge at which they were to meet. She'd only been to the park twice since she had arrived, and she promised Colin she knew where it was, but that had been a little fabrication. She had an idea, but nothing was certain…

Her breath caught painfully in her chest when she saw it, and the shape of a man standing upon it could just be made out through the mist.

She moved close enough to be able to make out his features, taking this one moment to watch him unobserved. This was the last time she would ever see him, he would undoubtedly make certain of that. And he would be right to do so, she would only ever bring him lower. The less he had to do with her, the better. For him, for her, for all of them. The ugly truth of her past would resurface soon enough, and she could deal with it by and by.

But Colin…

He was the only good thing in her past. The one thing that had not been tainted.

If she stayed, that would not remain the case.

So for now, she would take a moment and look at him, without any defense at all.

How could a man have grown more handsome in fifteen years? He was still as lanky as the boy she knew, but had filled out in the muscular form of a man, and it quite suited him. His hair seemed darker in this morning light, and it was longer than she remembered, and as he ran a hand through it, mussing it a bit in the process, she had to hide a smile. He had never maintained a neat appearance by his hair, no matter how perfect his brother's had always been. But where Kit was solemn and serious, Colin was easy and relaxed. Warm smiles, infectious laughter, and twinkling eyes that spoke of mischievous thoughts.

At least, that was who he had been.

She watched as he leaned forward against the railing of the bridge, his eyes focused on something across the water. He seemed tense through his face, neck, and shoulders, but then he released a sigh and his features relaxed. He rubbed his hands together lightly and his eyes narrowed slightly as his focus intensified.

What if she never approached him? What if she pretended to forget and never saw him again? She would always have this, knowing that he was alive and well, with at least moments of calm and peace, and she could content herself with that knowledge and this memory. Why should she force more pain and affliction on herself by this torment?

As if her thoughts were said aloud, Colin suddenly turned his head and his eyes found her, in spite of the mist. He did not move otherwise, his expression did not change, and no trace of distaste or disapproval could be seen. He stared at her, as she did him, and she felt the connection somewhere behind her navel. She could not look away, not for a moment, and she dared not even blink for fear it would all vanish before her.

He watched her steadily, his face devoid of all emotion, good or bad. No hostility or resentment, but no hint of smile or welcome either. He simply watched and waited.

He exhaled again, a small puff of fog dancing from his lips, and she echoed it herself, the tightness in her chest abating just enough to breathe once more.

She couldn't avoid it now.

Susannah swallowed once and made her feet move, heading directly for the bridge. She sent a brief, but fervent prayer that she might remain composed. He must never know of her turmoil.

"I wondered if you would even come," he said in a low, cold voice as she approached, that maddening vacant expression still on his face.

Her mouth tightened at his clipped tone. "I might have had a long walk." She had unwittingly matched his tone and she exhaled in frustration. He was helping her, and she needed to be grateful. She softened her stance and tilted her head a touch. "And I might have wondered the same thing myself."

He grunted softly, whether in satisfaction or irritation she couldn't tell, and straightened. "Well, what has happened since we last met? Any success on your part?"

All business, then. It would suit her better, pretending this was not an old friend helping another, but a stranger doing a good turn. Reluctant thought it might be, help was still help. And if she had to tell him just how far she had sunk…

She winced at the flash of pain in her chest and looked away towards the trees. "I have an interview with a family on Tuesday for a position as a governess."

"Very good. Who?"

"The Tarletons, I think."

"Never heard of them."

"And you know everybody?"

"Everybody worth knowing, yes."

She tried not to laugh. He was so sure, so certain. And yet she could hear the curiosity in his smart responses. "They are new to Town. Visiting relatives."

"Ah, so a temporary position?"

She wrinkled her nose up, and looked down at her shoes. "Yes, so it seems."

"Well, that won't do." He tsked clamping his hands behind his back. "It may pass for the time being, but not if you want to pay off those debts soon."

"Thank you for that lovely reminder," she muttered, tucking her blasted strand of hair behind her ear and scratching at the straw bonnet.

He huffed and took two steps towards her. "Look at me."

The order sent a habitual shock through her system and she craned her neck at the sensation, hating herself for the reaction yet again. But she did as Colin directed, and met his gaze.

His eyes searched hers for a moment, and he looked as if he would speak, but then he exhaled slowly. "Who is the relation these Tarletons are visiting?"

"Lady Greversham, or some sort, is what I was told."

Colin snorted a laugh and covered it with his hand.

"What was that for?" she muttered, folding her arms. "If you are going to be disapproving again, I promise I…"

"No, not at all," he interrupted, sounding too much like his old self for her comfort, "I just dearly hope that crone is not a part of your interview process, or you'll never survive."

He stopped himself then, and cast a harsh look at her as if she had been the one to say something indelicate.

She arched a brow at him, but ignored whatever sentiment he had been trying for. "I also have appointments with a milliner, a companion interview for a blind woman in Cheapside, and they're looking for a laundress in the Seven Dials. I thought I might try my hand at that."

His brows snapped together and his jaw tightened. She was goading him, and he knew it. But it seemed he could not bring himself to ask if such claims had truth to them, no matter how curious he might be.

Unfortunately, they were all true.

"Well," he said with a turn of his back, "I have three other opportunities for you, which makes me wonder what in the world you have been doing with yourself."

She chose not to comment, though a great many replies ricocheted in her mind. She merely waited for him to inform her of his great work and let him feel his duty fulfilled.

"There is a family near Trafalgar named Hayes with three children who need a governess. Not high quality, but well enough to set you up." He did not look at her, but kept his eyes fixed across the water again, as he had before. "Also a businessman in Piccadilly wants a female assistant so as to encourage ladies into patronage of his shop; I seem to recall you were fairly good with numbers, thought it would be worth trying. And lastly, the modiste that you tried for last week says she could use some spare help, her assistant is apparently useless, but she is a relation so she cannot terminate her."

He turned and looked at her then, utterly superior, and she was not prepared for it. She had been gaping at his speed and agility with the words, but she could follow clear enough. He seemed amused by her shock and he smirked.

"I have also," he continued, still smirking, "taken the liberty of procuring some items for you."

He had done *what?*

"I beg your pardon?" she stammered, watching in bewilderment as he reached down and picked up a parcel.

He gave her a rather frank look of appraisal. "You're never going to find work if you dress like that."

She felt her cheeks flame and put a cold hand to one.

"Here are three dresses, all needing work done, and all will be very ill-fitting as is. The modiste has no use for them, cannot sell them, and was rather glad to be rid of them." He hefted the parcel in his hands and held it out to her. "See what you can make of them."

Susannah took a few steps back, her other hand suddenly clutching at her jacket. "No."

Again his brow furrowed. "No?" he repeated slowly. "No what?"

"No, thank you."

He frowned in earnest. "Stop that. These are decent quality, they are not new, and they are certainly not fancy enough to offend or give you airs. Come on and take them."

She would not take anything from him, not like this. She shook her head, not trusting her voice at the moment.

He rolled his eyes and thrust it out again. "I am not being kind. I told you I would help you to find work, and in order for you to keep your end of the bargain and obtain the aforementioned work, you need to not look like a worn out scarecrow."

"There's no need to be cruel," she finally said, perhaps a touch loudly, for his eyes widened in surprise. She turned her hand over against her cheek, the freezing skin soothing the embarrassment. "I'm quite humbled enough, I don't your help there."

"I apologize, I did not mean to be."

She scoffed and gave him a brief look. "Yes, you did."

He twisted his lips, still watching her, and his shoulders relaxed a bit. "I only mean that you need to look your best."

"What do you think I meant when I said I had not the resources to pay the debts?" she barked, not willing to be patronized by him, not now.

He looked utterly bewildered. "I… I assumed…"

"You assumed wrongly," she replied, her indignation fading, yet again, into fatigue. "This is the best I have."

"Not anymore." He stepped forward and opened the parcel so she could examine them.

She could not resist; she looked down and saw that the fabric was sturdy, muted, and entirely suitable for a woman in her position. She could not pretend that she was not in need of clothing, particularly if she were to not appear desperate. She had barely managed to gather clothing for Freddie to wear in the next few months, she had not time nor funds to do the same for herself. This would relieve a burden, there was no question.

But did she dare take it?

She looked up into Colin's blue eyes, still fixed unnervingly on her. "Don't be kind to me, Colin," she said quietly. "I am not your pity project."

"I already told you, I am not being kind," he replied in the same tone. "And this is no charity."

"What is it, then?" she asked, feeling helpless and awash in far too many thoughts and emotions.

"An investment," came the simple answer.

She held up a warning finger. "I will not be in your debt, not for anything."

"I am not keeping a tally," he scoffed, though his eyes were serious.

She gave him a hard look. "Aren't you?"

He did not reply to that.

She sighed, swallowed her ridiculous pride, and took the parcel from him, rewrapping it. "Thank you for your help, Mr. Gerrard, and for these. It was very good of you to help me. I will make sure to look into the posts you have mentioned, and you may be assured that your efforts have not been in vain. And now I must get on with my day, and I am sure you have very many things to do. Good day."

She turned without looking at him and hurried back the way she had come.

"Susannah?"

His voice was too soft, too familiar, and not at all the cold and short tone of late. And it stopped her just as surely as if he had bellowed. She closed her eyes, willed herself to care just a fraction less, and turned around.

He had come forward maybe ten paces, but was still a bit of a distance away. His expression was now uncertain, confused, and cloudy. "Will you… will you come back on Monday?"

That took a moment to sink in and she could not understand it. "Why?" she asked bluntly, ignoring the tingling in her toes.

He rested a hand on the railing once more. "I think I need to make sure that my investment is worthwhile. You know, that my help actually means something."

She laughed in disbelief, and it was the oddest sensation, for she actually felt lighter at his uncertainty. "It already means a great deal, I can assure you."

"I highly doubt that," he replied with a small half-smile.

"No, it does." Why should he doubt it? Was her need not obvious?

"I don't know," he mumbled, running a hand through his hair again.

She tilted her head slightly, watching him. "Colin, it really does."

He met her eyes and dropped his hand. "No, I mean… I don't know." He swallowed and shook his head. "I don't know what I am doing and I don't know why."

She let the words hang for a moment, carefully considering them, before responding. "I understand," she finally said.

"Do you?"

She nodded once, keeping her eyes on him. "More than you know."

He stared at her for a long moment, then softly asked, "Will you come on Monday?"

"Same time and place?"

He nodded.

"Then I will be here."

She thought he might have smiled, but he only nodded again, then turned and walked across the bridge, casting a very quick half look over his shoulder at her.

She released a heavy sigh when he was gone and took a moment to collect herself. She needed to be stronger, to steel herself against him. She ought not to have agreed, but she needed the help so desperately. And she wanted to see him again, despite his bewildering mood shifts and unspoken accusations.

But she needed to mind herself, or she would begin to hope.

Someone was crying.

Or, rather, someone was most desperately trying *not* to cry and was failing miserably.

Colin groaned as he heard the noise in his study and set his work aside. He was hardly going to accomplish anything while someone was so distressed. It was far too early for such feminine emotions. It was probably a maid, they tended to be overly emotional when they thought no one was about.

Or it could have been Bitty, he reconsidered. That made him push out of his seat. If Rosie had been teasing her again, at this hour of the day, he was going to have to turn strict disciplinarian sooner than he thought. Or, more likely, he would make Kit do it. Kit could be the mean one.

He searched for the sound, a bit muffled now, and room by room his confusion grew. Where in the world was it coming from? It was too old a person to be Ginny, and she did not hide her cries. She wailed them for all to see and hear. And he was beginning to doubt Bitty as well, for she would seek out comfort when it was needed.

That left him with either a maid who would need to be sent down to Mrs. Porter for a cup of tea, or…

He stopped when he reached the doors to the ballroom. There, sitting under the end table between the two sets of doors, was the crying person.

Rosie.

She had her face buried in her knees, arms encircling them, her dark curls spilling over them like a blanket. Her little girl frame shook with her cries and she was trying her hardest to make as little noise as possible. Poor thing had no idea that in this part house, all noise carried elsewhere.

He approached slowly and sank onto his haunches before her. "Rosie?"

His sister jerked up, eyes wide, cheeks streaked with tears, and her lips quivering.

It was the saddest sight he had ever seen.

He smiled softly at her. "What's wrong, poppet?"

She sniffled and ran a sleeve under her nose, which amused him. "Nothing," she said moodily, swiping at her cheeks.

"Doesn't look like nothing," he quipped with a bit of a smile. "You look quite distressed."

Her stubborn chin lifted and she was no doubt building up quite the retort, but then it crumpled and her lips quivered again. "I got lost again," she whispered in broken tones.

Was that all? He sighed softly and squeezed her arm. "That's all right, it is a rather large house for just us, and I did not give you a very good tour of it. I'm not a very good host."

"No, you're dreadful at it," she replied instantly, though there was no force behind her words.

He smiled softly. "What were you trying to find?"

"The library."

That surprised him. Rosie was such an active, mischievous girl, he would not think the solemnity or solitude of the library would suit her. "You like to read?"

She nodded, sniffling once more. "Mama used to read to me after the girls were asleep." Her jaw trembled and more tears began to roll down her cheeks. "I miss my mother."

He had to swallow his own lump at that and he tugged his little sister out from the table. "Come here," he urged, relieved at her complete lack of resistance. He pulled her against him and tucked her under his chin. She shuddered against him and still tried to keep from crying, even as her little arms latched onto him.

"You can cry, Rosie," he murmured, kissing her head. "I won't tell a soul."

It was as if a dam broke in his strong and willful sister. She cried against him, soaking his shirt with her tears, and he could not have cared less about it. He simply held her close, occasionally stroked her hair, and carried her into the library so that her cries would not carry. He settled them into a chair, soothing her with whatever words came to mind.

When she was at last calmer, Rosie began to talk about her mother, about her memories, about what life was like before they had come here. While the other girls had forgotten, Rosie recollected everything. She watched her mother wither away into nothing, watched over her sisters, and wondered when or if Loughton would ever come for them.

He never did.

"I didn't care," Rosie said now with a shrug, her tears gone. "He had never been a father to us before, so why should he now? But someone would need to tend us, I couldn't raise Bitty and Ginny, and then that man came for us…"

Colin frowned and cursed Loughton silently. Leaving his daughters alone and only sending a man of business to pack them up and move them to London? It was unimaginable, and yet it had happened.

Rosie sighed and rubbed at her eyes. "You can't tell Bitty about this. I'm the older sister, I have to be strong and make sure she doesn't miss Mama or home either."

"I won't tell Bitty," he assured her, meeting her eyes. "But I will tell Kit. You understand why."

She nodded once. "I know. You are our brothers and you must take care of us, but…" She shrugged and gave him a sad half-smile. "It is very strange."

He laughed and hugged her quickly. "'Course it is, Rosie. We're Gerrards."

She snickered and pushed back with a smile. "Can you show me the books?"

He nodded and scooted her off of his lap. "Absolutely, assuming I know anything about them. I can barely read myself."

"Well, that figures."

They scanned the shelves and he started a pile for her based on her suggestions and insistence. She became quite animated as they did so, and he was entertained by her antics as she gave him abbreviated accounts of stories he pretended not to know. She had quite the memory for details, strong opinions on how things *should* have gone in the story, a vivid imagination, and an understanding of characters and themes that was rather impressive for anyone, let alone a girl of nine.

He decided that when she was older, she would either become a scholar, an author herself, or a spy for the Crown.

They sat down to begin looking through the books together when a commotion was heard from the front of the house. He heard Bartlet's staid tones greeting someone, servants shuffling about in their duties, and a few distinct voices echoing their way to his ears. Then, without warning, his name was called with no respect for any others in the house.

He grinned in relief and delight.

His friends had arrived.

Chapter Seven

"Oh, but you all are a sight for sore eyes!" Colin nearly gushed as he walked down the hall towards his four friends.

Duncan snorted. "You are never delighted to see us, Colin, so either you are terribly bored or things are far worse than your cryptic note said."

Colin shrugged. "There wasn't time for specifics, Duncan, and I know how you all love a mystery." He sobered a bit as he looked at them all.

His four best friends, all married, starting with their families, and yet they all still came when he needed something. He'd have done the same for any of them, and had done, in some cases. They had each been in the country for the summer and he was surprised at just how much he had missed them. And how much it meant that they had come.

"Are your families well?" he asked, asking with more sincerity than he probably ever had.

Derek grinned at him. "You already know they are well, though Kate is very upset you did not come for Helena's birth."

Colin shuddered playfully and shook his head. "Your wife cannot stand me in usual company, Derek. To visit her when she is in the utmost pain and distress? I would be dead in five minutes."

"Well, you did not come for Lizzy either," Nathan reminded him. "And Moira is most disappointed in you."

He clamped a hand to his chest and staggered back. "No, not Moira! I shall have to buy her a flower."

His friends laughed and Colin turned to the last two. "Well, what about you lot? Do Mary and Annalise want to butcher me as well?"

Geoff smiled, his eyes crinkling. "Mary sends her regards and asks after the gossip."

"And Annalise is actually rather fond of you, for some bewildering reason," Duncan added with a rueful grin. "I suppose she has yet to know your true character."

Colin smiled at that. While he truly adored all of the women his friends had married, Annalise would always be of special regard to him.

"So what was so important, Colin?" Geoff asked when Colin forgot to laugh.

He cleared his throat, suddenly a bit anxious about what he was about to tell them. He had been too hesitant to tell them via letter, this was something they needed to know in person. Now they were here, he had no idea how to begin.

How could he possibly tell them how drastically his life had changed in the course of a week? How his heart was somehow expanding, his empathy beginning to flower, and his ability to hear tears so incredibly heightened? His current plans had all been uprooted, his finances needed desperate rearranging, and he was more terrified of the future than ever before.

And that was just what he had felt the first day.

"Good heavens," breathed Geoff suddenly.

Colin looked at his friend in surprise, but saw he was not looking at Colin, but behind him. He turned to see Rosie making her way towards them hesitantly. She bit her lip and looked up at him, silently asking permission.

He winked at her and held out a hand. "Come on, then. It's all right, these are my friends."

She raised a brow in surprise and he gave her a mock warning look, which made her smile. She took his hand and stood beside him, smiling at the men before her by way of greeting.

Only then did Colin turn back to face them himself.

They were all staring fixedly at Rosie, eyes wide. Duncan was openly gaping, Derek had staggered back a few paces, Geoff had a hand at his chest as if he were about to have a fit, and Nathan was pale as a ghost. Very telling of each of their natures, that.

"Go on," Colin murmured, squeezing Rosie's hand a little. "Tell them who you are."

Rosie, who was no doubt spending too much time with Tibby, gave the horrified quartet a most perfect, if slightly dramatic, curtsey. "Pleasure to meet you. I'm Rosie."

"Charmed, I'm sure," Geoff replied faintly. He looked up at Colin. "If this is a joke, Colin…"

Colin shook his head. "No joke, but it is a bit funny, actually."

"Still waiting for the funny part," Nathan said unsteadily, running a shaking hand into his hair.

"Someone get me a drink," Derek muttered, flagging down a sniggering maid in the hall.

"Explain," Duncan growled, his eyes flitting between Colin and Rosie.

Colin straightened and smiled. "It's quite simple really. Rosie should have said this, but she is my…"

There was a series of insistent knocks at the door at the same time the bell rang.

"Who could that be?" Colin wondered aloud as Bartlet moved around the group to answer it.

"You're not this popular," Rosie informed him, looking confused. "It's probably for Kit."

Geoff barked a laugh and smothered it quickly.

Colin looked down at his smart-mouthed sister with a frown. "I am far more popular than Kit, I will have you know."

She shrugged. "So you say, but where is the proof?"

Now his friends were beginning to smile outright.

Bartlet opened the door to reveal four beautiful and very finely dressed women.

"Well, I didn't expect that," Rosie muttered under her breath.

"Hush," he hissed, grinning himself now.

"Colin Gerrard, you have some serious explaining to do," Moira, Lady Beverton, scolded loudly, her sapphire eyes flashing dangerously.

"Oh, no," Nathan moaned, covering his eyes.

The other men echoed the sentiment as each of their wives entered the room and handed their things to the waiting servants.

"Good morning, darling," Kate, Lady Whitlock, cooed in a rather offhand manner to her husband, patting his cheek. "Nice of you to tell us where you were going."

"Good morning, love," her husband dutifully replied, looking sheepish.

The women stood on one side of the hall and the men on the other, females all righteous indignation as they looked at Colin, males as uncomfortable as anything he'd ever seen.

"What's this about?" Duncan finally asked of the women.

His wife spared a brilliant smile for him. "Colin has a secret."

"We know," Geoff replied, absently pulling at his ear. "That is why we are here."

"Yes, but *we* know what it is," Mary retorted smartly, her eyes still on Colin.

"Start talking now, Colin, or I will lose my considerable patience," Kate ordered, arms folded, tapping her foot against the marble floor in agitation.

He smiled in utter relief at the women. "Thank God you're all here."

"What?" his friends all cried out in unison, and with good reason. He had never claimed to enjoy seeing the women before, but now he had never been more grateful in his life. Had he been less controlled, he might have actually gotten emotional.

He wanted to hug them all. "I can't tell you how much it means to me that you came. I assume Tibby told you?"

Annalise nodded, smiling fondly. "I had a letter from her last week."

"Tibby did what?" Duncan asked, no doubt feeling more than a bit surprised.

Colin ignored him. "Just a moment." He turned and cupped his hands around his mouth. "Molly!" he yelled up the stairs. "Bring them down, would you?"

Rosie shook her head in disapproval. "Shouting like that in your own house and before company? Such poor manners."

"That is quite enough out of you, little tart," he tossed back at her.

She shook her head and looked up at his friends. "I can't see why you're all friends with him, honestly, and I haven't known him long."

"Honestly, neither can I, at the moment," Nathan replied.

Molly appeared at the top of the stairs with Ginny on one side and Bitty on the other, and they obediently made their way down the stairs. No one spoke, not even Rosie, though the women did gasp softly.

"Come on, come on," Colin encouraged with a wave as they reached the bottom. He set Bitty next to Rosie, and Ginny next to her. Then he took up position on Ginny's other side, and looked at his friends and their wives. He opened his arms to indicate the three, looked directly at the women, and said, simply, "Help."

"Oh, please," Rosie said with a snort, even as Bitty giggled to herself.

"Oh, my," Moira murmured as she took in the girls.

Colin gave a helpless smile. "These fine girls you see before you are my sisters. Surprise."

His friends nearly fell over as evident relief washed over them. The women were wide-eyed, but smiling.

"Present yourselves," Colin murmured, nodding at Rosie.

She stepped forward and curtseyed. "Rose Marie Elizabeth Gerrard, age nine." Her accent, mostly gone now, rang out proudly here.

Bitty tangled her fingers and curtseyed, a bit wobbly. "Louisa Amelie Claire Gerrard. Oh, and I'm six." She, too, displayed her accent perfectly.

Colin saw Mary cover her mouth, but it did nothing to lessen her smile.

Ginny watched her two sisters, then looked at the people gathered, and tucked herself behind Colin, latching onto his leg and burying her face against him.

He smiled and reached behind to touch her head. "And Genevieve Sophia Anne Gerrard, age three." He looked up and gestured to the girls in order. "Rosie, Bitty, and Ginny."

No one spoke a word. They each looked from the girls to Colin, back to the girls, and occasionally at each other.

He quite understood.

"Who are they?" Bitty asked Colin in her best whispering tone.

He grinned and quickly made the introductions.

Ginny still kept herself tucked against him. He bent down and softly asked if she would meet his friends, but she shook her head and only clung closer.

"She's very shy," Bitty explained.

"That's all right," Mary replied, smiling at her. "I'm a bit shy as well."

Annalise surprised Colin by coming forward and sinking down to Ginny's level. "Pleased to meet you, Ginny," she said softly with smile. "My name is Annie and I'm friends with your brother and with Tibby. I would very much like to be your friend as well."

Colin looked at Ginny, but she would not move her face from his leg.

Annalise was not deterred. She smiled and reached out a hand. "Would you come and play with me, sweet? I don't know my way around this house, and I could use a friend to help me."

"I can help!" Bitty cried with a raised hand.

"Hush, Bitty," Rosie hissed, watching her younger sister with interest.

Ginny turned her head and looked at the outstretched hand, then up into Annalise's face.

"Go on, Ginny," Colin murmured, his hand still soothing her hair. "You can do it. Don't you want to see such a lovely person?"

Annalise looked up at him with a sardonic grin, then looked back at Ginny.

It seemed the entire room held their breath.

Ginny considered Annalise for a long moment, then detached a tiny hand from Colin's leg and placed it into Annalise's.

Bitty and Rosie gaped and Colin grinned, not bothering to hide the sigh of relief. Annalise closed her hand around Ginny's and slowly led her towards the others, though Ginny looked back at Colin a great deal.

"It's all right, Ginny," he told her, still grinning. "I'm still here."

"Like that's a comfort," Rosie muttered, even though she smiled.

"I think you are the best girl I know, Rosie Gerrard," Derek announced with a grin at Colin.

Bitty pouted. "What about me?" she asked with a serious look at the powerful marquess.

He chuckled and put his hands on his hips. "Except for you, of course, Miss Louisa." He bowed very deeply to her.

She giggled and looked at Rosie triumphantly.

"What's all this?"

Colin glanced up the stairs to see Kit descending.

"Oh, it's you lot," he said, answering himself. "Thank heavens, we are in desperate need of reinforcements." He bowed to them all and took a second look at Ginny as she stood with the women, being fussed over. He looked at Colin in surprise, but he could only shrug in response. How else could he explain their youngest sister's miraculous actions?

"They've come to meet the girls, Kit," Colin said with a pat on his brother's shoulder. "Nice of them, eh?"

"Very nice," Kit replied, nodding at his friends, and smiling, which Kit so rarely did that it surprised them all. "We really are most grateful."

Mary smiled back a bit wryly. "As if we would have missed this?" She scooped up Ginny, who let out a surprised giggle that nearly floored Colin.

"Colin, Kit," Moira said suddenly, completely forgoing propriety by calling his brother Kit when she'd never been encouraged to do so, and it made Kit twitch slightly. "Would we be able to take your adorable sisters into another room and get to know them?"

Colin looked at Nathan in bewilderment, then back at Moira. "When do you ever ask permission, Moira?"

"When, indeed," Kit murmured, looking interested.

Rosie was not impressed by their lack of answer. "Well, she just did! Now can we go with the ladies or not?"

Kit smiled at her, and chuckled. "Of course, little tyrant. Go off and learn proper manners, if you can. Lady Whitlock, please…"

Kate grinned rather deviously. "Oh, I think not, Mr. Gerrard. I like this one just as she is."

Colin and Kit groaned as Derek laughed out loud.

"Go on, Bitty," Colin sighed, waving a hand. "The ladies want to play and the boys need to have a talk."

Bitty did as she was told and skipped along with her sisters and new friends.

"God help us if they turn out like them," Colin muttered.

"Which set of females are you talking about?" his twin replied.

"I'm not entirely sure." Colin sighed and gestured down the hall. "Let's go, there's a lot of details we'll need to fill in for you."

"This might be the best story yet," Derek mused aloud as they followed.

Colin smiled, but held his tongue. There was a good story here, it was true. And yet, at the heart of it all, Colin found himself wanting to reveal another secret with them entirely.

He shook his head. *No.* Not only was he not prepared to discuss her, but he was not prepared to talk about what it meant for him.

Mostly because he did not know.

No, for now he would simply have to focus on the girls. That was his most pressing matter, at any rate. Rosie needed some more time to adjust to being here, but she would also need structure. A schedule of some sort. Perhaps a nursemaid, a tutor, a governess…

He knew someone who could be a governess.

"No," he muttered, shaking his head fiercely. "Absolutely not."

"Pardon?" Kit asked as he walked beside him.

Colin only shook his head again.

"Are you going to tell them about…?"

He shook his head firmly.

"You should."

"Not yet," Colin hissed.

Kit gave him a hard look, but shrugged one shoulder. Disapproval flashed in his eyes, but he wouldn't say anything Colin did not want him to. That was Kit's way. He might not have agreed with Colin, but he would respect this decision.

For now, at least.

He could not tell them about Susannah. Not yet.

"So, Colin… Kit…" Duncan drawled as he took a seat. "I think there are a few things that we need to discuss."

"Yes, quite," Kit replied smoothly, giving Colin a brief flash of a warning glance before taking his own seat. "It has been… an eventful few days."

Colin snorted, reverting back into character. "That is one way to put it, yes."

"I need to hear all of this from the beginning, if you don't mind," Geoff laughed with a raised hand.

"Oh, of course you do," Derek scoffed as he sat down. "You'd never figure it out unless they spelled it out for you all specifically like that."

Colin snickered helplessly at Geoff's outrage. It was bizarre for Kit to be here for the antics of his friends, but he was glad for it. He ought to be part of them, now more than ever.

"Yes, but first I have a question." Nathan looked between the brothers carefully, his dark eyes serious. "About Rosie."

Colin exchanged looks with Kit, then turned back to his friend. "Go on."

Nathan settled his gaze on Colin. "Are you *sure* she's not yours?"

The others laughed in agreement. Kit looked rather smug and folded his arms, raising a brow at Colin.

Colin smiled and tried to be his old, relaxed self, but it was not possible. "Quite sure, but I would claim her in an instant."

"Absolutely," Kit murmured softly, his eyes suddenly distant.

The others were silent, until Duncan suddenly cleared his throat.

"All right, you two," he began, his tone warm, but serious, "you cannot go warm and fuzzy like that without sharing. So tell us. What happened and what can we do?"

Colin smiled, but looked at Kit and gestured for him to tell it. Kit looked surprised, but pleased, and began the tale of their rather unorthodox beginning to guardianship.

Chapter Eight

Susannah made it a point to arrive earlier on Monday to the bridge, to see that Colin had not yet arrived. She was grateful for that, she was far more nervous than she would ever admit. There had been something in his eyes last time that she was hesitant to remember, for fear of becoming fanciful. And there was far too much that she needed to focus on now than whether or not Colin Gerrard might actually enjoy seeing her.

Freddie was restless in their little flat and Sasha was growing busier with her… clientele, though she was always willing to help with him. She needed to find a better solution for them all, and quickly. A run-in with debt collectors yesterday had her rattled, though they had not harmed her, and a strong stranger with an impressive glower had cut off most of their threats. She'd tried to thank him, but he only said, "The Gent keeps his word, ma'am."

If only the Gent could find her a position that would provide enough for her and Freddie while satisfying the debt collectors' demands. That would solve everything.

"You're early this morning."

She jumped a bit at Colin's voice, nearer than she expected, and turned to see that he was coming up the bridge towards her. She swallowed her nerves and tried for a smile. "It was easier to find the second time."

He raised a brow. "You didn't know where it was the first time?"

What was the point of lying to him? She shrugged. "Not really. And the fog did not help much."

He smiled easily. "You could have told me."

"No," she replied quietly, "I couldn't."

His smile faded, and sighed. "Well, there's no fog this morning."

She looked up at the clear morning sky. "No, and I think it will be a beautiful day."

He said nothing for a moment, and then, "You look thin, Susannah."

She bristled at his words, but his tone was not the cold, superior one he had used with her before. It was almost warm, and concerned. She turned to look at him and found his eyes fixed on her, watching, examining, but not harsh.

She had to swallow again. "I know."

He stepped closer and the blue of his eyes was all the more vibrant in the morning light. "Are you eating?"

"Of course," she replied simply, the back of her neck warming.

He gave her a look. "Susannah…"

She sighed and pinched at the bridge of her nose, a headache beginning to form behind her eyes. "Money is a problem, Colin, or else I would not be needing help to find work." She looked back at him, waiting for his response.

"Are you eating?" he asked slowly, every word carefully emphasized.

"What I can," she answered with reluctance. Then she swallowed, and corrected herself. "When I can."

His eyes widened and he reared back just a bit, his eyes quickly raking over her. "Susannah…"

Susannah exhaled sharply. "Colin, not everybody in the world can afford to put food on the table. I do well enough with what I can, so may we please move on?"

He did not look convinced in the least, but Susannah clenched her jaw and gave him as steely a look as she could manage.

Eventually, he sighed, but his eyes were still troubled. "How is your search going?" he asked, trying for light conversation.

She nearly laughed. Where last week it was all business, now it was almost a passing thought, much like the state of the roads or the gossip from Brighton. "Not as well as I should like," she said, folding her arms.

"How so?"

"Well, I saw the family you found for me, the Hayes." She shook her head at the memory. "I was turned away at the door once the wife saw me."

"What?" Colin asked, jerking to look at her. "Why?"

"According to her, I was too young to have any sort of education worth sharing and too pretty to be any sort of sensible creature." She rolled her eyes. "Too young, indeed. I am older than she is, and I doubt her limited education has done her any good."

Colin chuckled and inclined his head to indicate they walk, which she responded to with a nod. "Well, we can't all have been brought up by scholars at Seabrook."

She laughed, a strange thing for her these days. "I have not thought about them in years! Oh, that was miserable. I was so bored!"

"I remember." He sighed and gave her an apologetic look. "Well, I am sorry that did not suit. I like Mr. Hayes quite a lot, but I had no idea his wife was a shrew."

Susannah shrugged. "Perhaps she is not; one encounter need not dictate her entire personality. If that is how she feels, then I would not wish to work for her any way. I may be desperate, but I'll not be ill-treated."

Colin smiled a bit too proudly as he looked away towards the trees. She could almost hear the old Colin murmur a soft *"That's my girl,"* and it shook her as she moved beside him.

"And the 'too pretty' comment?" he asked in a would-be innocent tone. "What of that particular complaint?"

Heat suddenly infused her cheeks as she sat. "Surely you cannot expect me to comment on that."

"Modesty? Really?" he responded, the first hint of a bite to his tone.

She raised her eyes to his at once and glared. "I cannot help what I look like, can I? I am trying everything I can to make myself as undesirable as possible to avoid that very thing, and if it's not enough for dear Mrs. Hayes, that is not my fault."

Colin's mouth hung open at her words, then suddenly he took her arm and stopped. "I'm sorry, did you say you were *trying* to make yourself look undesirable?"

Susannah snorted softly and looked down at her hands. "Don't think me a vain creature. I've never been a pretty girl, and I know it, but once I was at least considered fair. I had thought my age would change that, but it seems I will age well, unfortunately. Plain women always get work because no one will notice them. I do the best I can, all right?"

"You misunderstand me, I think," Colin said too roughly for her comfort.

She looked up to find him watching her with a sort of bewilderment. "About what?"

He shook his head quickly, as if shaking off water from rain. "Never mind. So, the Hayes family is out. No great loss to us, but tragic for their now hopelessly dimwitted children."

Susannah let out a brief burst of laughter, which she muffled slightly.

Colin grinned and shrugged as if he did not care. "What else have you discovered?"

She quickly and without much detail related her other experiences, none of which had proven successful, save for the modiste, who could only offer her occasional work at this time.

"But there is that appointment with the Tarletons tomorrow," she finished, "so that could be promising."

Colin scoffed, shaking his head. "Forgive me if I do not hold my breath for that one. I would not wish anyone to work for a relation of Lady Greversham." He shuddered and made a face.

Susannah could only shrug. "I've never heard of her, and perhaps her relations are not as tiresome."

"Perhaps…" But he did not sound convinced. "Nothing else has worked?"

Susannah shook her head. "Not as yet, no."

He winced. "I am sorry."

"Why are you sorry?" Susannah asked, smiling. "It is not your doing, and they were under no obligation to consider me. And I am the one, if you remember, that found a position as a laundress in the Seven Dials."

Colin groaned and managed a weak smile, a bit more at ease. "Please tell me you are not serious."

She shrugged. "Probably not, but you never know."

"I do know, and the answer is no."

He knew no such thing. She knew very well what sort of place the Seven Dials was, and it was not that much worse than where she was living now. Working there would be far more convenient to her location than anything he could suggest, proper or not.

"And you said something about a blind woman in Cheapside?" he asked, navigating them around a puddle. "What of that?"

She had to smile now. "Mrs. Rogers is probably eighty-three, and is more able than I am in her apartments. She needs assistance when venturing out, and I will be helping her there, at least until I have something else. She just sends for me when she wishes to go out."

He made a noise of assent, but no further comment.

Susannah did not tell him that Mrs. Rogers could not promise much pay, but she was very gifted with knitting, even without her eyesight. The fruits of Susannah's labors there could help them get through the winter, but would do nothing to feed her poor boy.

Colin surprised her then by asking after her family, and she barely managed to avoid striking out defensively. No one asked about her family, no one ever knew about them, and she certainly did not want Colin Gerrard to know their situation.

Nevertheless, it seemed he asked in kindness, so she swallowed and assured him that, yes, her family was well. He surprised her with the details he remembered about her siblings, and asked after each in their turn. She was as brief as she could be without being short, avoiding sharing the details of George's shocking death, Felicity's ill-fated elopement, and passed off her parents' descent into utter poverty as "living in quiet contentment."

"I always liked Charles," Colin commented as she finished. "The most sensible of your brothers, and the most athletic."

Susannah smiled at the mention of the one family member who did not plague her. "Yes, he is quite happy in Sussex, I think."

He raised a brow in question. "You think?"

She shrugged lightly. "We do not communicate much. You

forget, we were not that close a family."

He hummed a noncommittal noise she did not trust, but he said nothing else on the subject.

She slowly wet her lips, then as carefully as she could, asked, "And how is your family?"

To her astonishment, a slow smile spread across his lips. "Rapidly expanding, actually."

She frowned in confusion. "How's that? Don't tell me Kit married a Society lass and is breeding an army somewhere in the country."

He threw his head back and barked a laugh. "No, heavens no. Kit is as single as any bachelor ever was. No, he is in London, rather wealthy, and the subject of far too much speculation for my taste. But mystery is always a source for gossip, and you know Kit, he won't address it, so there it is." He shook his head, still smiling fondly.

"Then what do you mean by expanding?" she asked, still at a loss. A sudden fear seized her chest. Had *Colin* found love? Had he married and produced children? Were they staking his reputation in this dangerous rendezvous game of theirs?

"What in heaven's name is going through your head right now?"

The tone and manner were so like the Colin of her past and her dreams that she choked on a swallow as she looked up into his face, hints of a smile dancing at the corners of his lips. He looked so much younger than he had only moments ago, so easy and warm. It was almost as if no time had passed at all.

But it had. And she painfully recalled each agonizing second.

She tried for a smirk. "Lost in my thoughts. You were saying?"

He looked confused for a moment, but mercifully, he did not press her. "The Gerrard family has expanded by three. Three very small and decidedly feminine creatures bearing the unfortunate curse of being our sisters."

Susannah's mouth popped open with an audible sound.

Colin nodded at hearing it. "Yes, quite. Loughton, it seems, has been quite the busy fellow."

Relief cascaded over Susannah like wave after wave upon the shores at Seabrook, and her heart was near to skipping out of her chest. She cleared her throat and tried to think of something to say in response. But thanking him for her present relief seemed rather inappropriate and nothing else was coming to mind.

But Colin had always been a clever fellow, and he pressed on, thus sparing her the trouble of formulating words. He quietly spoke of what had happened, and his sudden fondness for the girls, sharing far more with her than she'd ever expected from anyone, let alone Colin.

"So," he finished with a sigh, "I suppose the next thing to do is to find a governess."

The words hung in the air between them, and Susannah glanced at him in disbelief.

Surely he did not expect her to… *Surely* he was not saying that…

She was shaking her head before the words were even thought. "I can't do that."

He looked as surprised as she felt. "I would never ask you to."

"You weren't saying…?"

"Absolutely not." He shook his head frantically and ran his hand through his hair again. "I couldn't ask that of you, not given our relationship. And you certainly deserve better work than a madhouse of Gerrards."

Susannah managed to smile, both touched and amused. "I see. Thank you, I think."

"You are welcome." His look turned rueful. "Do you think you could help me find a suitable governess for them? Not right away, they are still adjusting, but it should be soon. I have no idea about these things, and as you are looking for such work yourself…"

She tried not to smile, but failed. "I could ask around," she relented, her cheeks beginning to ache. "And I shall be most discerning about it. No Gerrard girls can have a pitiful or lack wit governess."

He grinned in relief. "Thank you."

Susannah released a small sigh and looked up at him, feeling open and honest for the first time. "What are you doing, Colin? I mean really, what is this?"

He shrugged lightly, though his expression was anything but. He knew exactly what she was asking. "Haven't the foggiest. Don't really want to think about it either. Do you?"

Did she? Did she really?

"All I know," Colin said, his voice suddenly low and serious, "is that I'm not done with you yet."

She could not tell if the words were meant to be ominous or encouraging, but she felt somehow both fearful and hopeful.

This serious and somber Colin, this darker Colin, this more emotional and mysterious Colin… He quite terrified her. And she did not think she was done with him either.

"Can we meet again on Wednesday?"

She looked at him curiously. "So you can see if I've eaten? It won't show by then."

Something almost like a smile lit his face. "True, but humor me. Besides, I will be curious if you meet Lady Greversham tomorrow, and you promised to help me with finding a governess."

"So we are using each other?" The words were said with too much bite, but there was nothing for it now.

He gave her a serious, but thorough look. "Something like that. Do I need to see you home, or…?"

"No, no," she replied too quickly, panic welling up inside. "I have several errands to run before I return home. Thank you, though. For the offer and for the conversation. It was… very kind."

"I'm not kind, Susannah," he reminded her.

She now appraised him. "So you keep saying," she murmured. Heat rose in her cheeks and she bobbed a curtsey. "Good day, Mr. Gerrard," she said, rushing past him without looking back.

"Good day… Miss Hart."

Her breathing picked up as she moved away from him, and she scolded herself for being such a fool. She *had* to be more controlled. She *had* to find strength where he was concerned.

He *was* her strength. For fifteen years, he had been all she could keep for herself.

Now her strength was her weakness.

So what could she cling to now?

Chapter Nine

"*How* dare she! High and mighty troll, no sense or manners, how did she ever manage to become anything of importance?"

Muttering under her breath was all that kept her from tears as she marched away from the Tarletons' rented townhome. Mrs. Tarleton had been nothing more than a mouthpiece for her aunt, Lady Greversham, who had wasted no time at all in coming in herself and tearing Susannah apart piece by piece, without knowing anything about her. Not that she cared, she simply insulted everything she could find and then dismissed her.

She wouldn't have wanted to work for such a family anyway.

Lady Greversham had spoken to her niece the entire time as if Susannah were not in the room, though she stared at her while doing so. Her looks were all wrong, she was too skinny, yet too voluptuous, too dark, and yet sickly, and her hair was unnaturally colored. She had claimed Susannah was a conniving social climber trying for positions to which she was not qualified for.

She had accused her of being a carrier for infidelity, illegitimacy, and blackmail, who would destroy the family and twist the minds of the children. She was undoubtedly a cast-off daughter who had ruined herself and her family, possibly broken the heart of some deluded chap, reduced to using a false name, and now unsuitable for any sort of proper society.

If only that last hadn't been true.

Susannah walked faster, shaking her head as her eyes began to burn. Why was there truth in her attacks? Why could she somehow cut Susannah despite knowing nothing?

It would never match what Susannah thought of herself, but it was enough.

"Susannah?"

Her breath hitched on a painful hiccup.

Colin was suddenly at her side, matching her pace. "What's the rush? What are you…? Good heavens, Susannah, what's wrong?"

She shook her head, knowing she could not trust her voice. She could barely breathe without bursting into wild sobs, and that would not do.

Colin moved in front of her and stopped her movement, hands firmly gripping her arms. "What's happened, Susannah? Are you ill? Are you in danger? What?"

She shook her head again and looked down at her toes. She could not meet his eyes. Colin had always had too much power over her; one look at him would ruin her. She swallowed hard and her breath caught on a shallow exhale.

His hands were suddenly on her face, cupping the back of her head, his palms at her jaw. He tilted her face up and she closed her eyes rather than look at him. She trembled more dangerously in his hold than she had yet.

"Look at me."

She twitched at the gentle command, her hands reaching up to wrap around his wrists for support, and her eyes opened of their own accord.

His expression was soft, concerned, and curious. "What's wrong?"

Her grip on him clenched and a weak, distressed sound escaped her lips.

His eyes widened at it, and his face tightened. He moved his hands from her face to her arms. "Come on," he urged, moving her off of the path and into a thick stand of trees, out of sight of anyone who might pass.

She held his wrists still, knowing that without that hold, she would not be able to stand. Everything was rising too fast, too powerfully, and she was so tired, so weak. There was no strength left to fight it.

Colin's hands suddenly moved to wrap around her and pull her tightly against his chest. She stiffened at it, her hands freed of their support and now suspended in the air awkwardly. "Let it out," he whispered, his mouth dangerously close to her ear. "Let it go. I won't tell a soul."

Swallowing repeatedly, fighting the comfort being in his arms afforded, she hesitated.

His arms tightened. "I've got you. Let it out."

Her trembling increased and her heart could not take it. She wrapped her arms around his waist, her fingers clutching at his coat, and she buried her face into his shoulder as tears and sobs exploded from her. Her slight frame was wracked with cry after cry, and Colin held her steady and sure for the whole of it. His hold never wavered, his warmth never faded, and the soothing words he murmured settled as a balm on her unseen wounds.

When at last she was coherent, which took some time, she eased herself away from him, reluctant but determined. "Thank you," she murmured, her voice a rasp in her throat. "I'm sorry for being a watering pot."

Colin, however, was not finished. He kept a hand at her back, his eyes still fixed on her face. "What happened?"

She looked up at him, thought up a hundred different things she could say to avoid it, and then gave up. What was the point of resisting him any longer? She sighed and let him pull her into a walk beside him, his hand moving at last to loop her arm through his. To anyone watching, they might have been any couple having a pleasant walk in the park. They would never see how much she allowed him to support her in this fashion.

She softly relayed the entire story of her interview and what Lady Greversham had said. When she had finished, her hold on Colin tightened again, tears rising anew. He was furious; she could feel it in the steely tension of his arm.

He suddenly released an expletive of such a horrid nature that she looked up at him in surprise. He shook his head and covered her hand with his own. "Apologies. But I can't think of a more polite way to describe her."

Susannah almost laughed in spite of her tears. She swallowed hard and whispered, "What hurt the most was how close she was to the truth. And how violently she spelled it out."

"No, Susannah," Colin urged, gripping her hand tightly, "there is no truth there at all."

But it was too late, Susannah could not stop herself from telling him exactly how she felt. "I may not fit her mold exactly, but you must admit there is a certain parallel there. Particularly with regards to men and hearts."

"Don't."

She brushed angrily at her fresh tears with her free hand. "I have to, Colin. I need to… to tell you how sorry I am. I knew I had hurt you, I was well aware that I was destroying what we had. I have lived with that guilt, have been haunted by it…"

"I don't want to live in the past, Susannah," Colin interrupted, his own voice rough. "It is done, it happened, it's over."

Could he not see? It would *never* be over. She shook her head. "I won't ask for your forgiveness because I do not deserve it. But I want you to know that I am so very sorry. I have been sorry every day for fifteen years." Her voice broke and she could not say another word.

"Susannah…"

She looked away, biting down on her lip hard.

"Did you have to do it?" he asked softly.

She nodded just once.

"Then I accept it."

She jerked in his hold and her eyes flew to his. "What?" she gasped.

He seemed surprised by the words himself. "I am… actually not sure what just happened, but suddenly that doesn't matter anymore."

"You're joking," she managed in a squeaking voice.

He slowly shook his head. "I'm afraid not."

"That's not possible." It came out as a whisper, her entire body somehow both hot and cold, and all she could feel was his arm beneath her hand and the heat of his hand on hers.

He smiled, his thumb absently stroking her hand. "I know. Believe me, I know. And yet…" He shrugged, his smile growing.

This was no smiling matter. She wet her lips and slowly tried, "Colin…"

He sobered at once. "I don't know what it means, not yet. But… I want to see you more, not just for business or by coincidence. I want to intentionally see you, talk with you, plot Lady Greversham's mysterious demise with you…"

A startled, yet delighted laugh escaped her and she covered her mouth, her heart swelling at least twice its size in her chest.

Colin's smile returned in all its glory, and he held her hand more tightly. "I want to be friends again. In truth, not just for old time's sake. Can we do that?"

Could she? Could she really take the chance to glimpse heaven, even if it could not last?

Slowly, very distinctly, she nodded. Then nodded again.

His smile impossibly grew, the corners of his eyes crinkling. "Good," was all he said, holding her eyes captive with his. Then he abruptly cleared his throat and tore his gaze away. "Now, here's what I propose: I have a great many friends in London, each with their own valuable connections. I may have only given half effort before, which is careless on my part, but it will have the full measure of my attention and influence now."

"You don't need to ask everyone," Susannah insisted, her voice finding its usual strength and tone at last.

He chuckled. "Oh, I will talk to exactly one person and that is all I need to."

"Who?" she asked, tilting her head slightly.

His smile turned devious. "Lady Tabitha Raeburn. The most terrifying woman in England, Ireland, Scotland, Wales, and I'm quite certain a few countries on the continent as well."

"Oh my," Susannah murmured, swallowing nervously. "I should have thought that title belonged to Lady Greversham."

He snorted. "Lady Greversham has all the mannerisms of a cross between a troll and a gargoyle, and the only reason she has not turned to stone yet is that all forms of stone take great affront to that idea."

Susannah snickered helplessly and clamped down on her lips as a few men on horseback tipped their hat at Colin.

"No," he went on as if he'd said something normal, "Lady Greversham will never even half match Tibby, in influence, popularity, good taste, or splendor. Plus, Tibby adores me. She'll find you a position that will be beyond perfect, I am quite sure of it. Good housing, excellent pay, high-quality family, and most importantly, close to me so I can keep an eye on you." He grinned raffishly at her.

Her heart had begun pounding a steady, but fervent cadence against her chest. He was making plans already, she could see it in his face. She adored him, loved what he was suggesting, admired his determination to watch over her, but…

"I have something to tell you," she said slowly, unable to return his smile.

He caught the serious tone and he stopped their walking. "What?" he asked, looking closely.

She released a slow, soft exhale, swallowed, and met his eyes steadily. "I have a child."

Colin stared at her for the space of seven heartbeats, only able to blink, his mind seeming to move backwards at a snail's pace. He could not seem to understand the relatively simple words that had just come from her mouth.

A child? How was that even possible?

He swallowed as his mind laughed at him. Of course, he knew it was possible, and he knew how, but he had never thought, for one moment…

"A child?" he asked, his voice not nearly the steady, unaffected air he would have liked.

Susannah seemed to sense his turmoil. She gave him the slightest smile and tried to pull her hand away again. He wished she wouldn't do that. He was not going to let her go, and at this moment, her hand was the only thing anchoring him to the ground.

Her eyes widened at his increased hold. She swallowed and wordlessly tilted her head in a question.

He somehow managed to hold her gaze. He might be tossed about, might not know what to think about her being a mother, but he was not so far gone that he was stupid enough to let her pull away now.

"Yes," she said at last, her smile returning with a quizzical curve, "a son."

A son. His Susannah had borne her husband a son. An heir, if they were at such a height in Society. Faintly, it occurred to him to wonder if this boy looked like his mother or his late father. At least six different faces sprang into mind as he imagined this lad, some looking like Susannah, some looking like various men he had seen around London, and one that looked too much like him for comfort.

He fought the urge to shake his head to dismiss that one. That, at least, was one he knew did not exist.

The twinge of disappointment at the thought was something he was entirely unprepared for.

"Tell me about him," he asked, suddenly having the most intense desire to know everything.

He was not so polite as to have entirely innocent motives. He felt this churning in his stomach, something bitter and snarling that wanted to hate her for daring to have another man's child. But his better nature tamped that urge down and kept the beast contained. He may not know what he would do with this information once he had it, he might harbor some resentment that was irrational and immature, but he did know that Susannah was his friend, was rapidly becoming more important to him, and if she had a child to think of, that meant he would deal with that as well.

Susannah looked as though she would refuse to tell him, as her eyes searched his, still uncertain and untrusting. But eventually, she relaxed once more in his hold and he felt her fingers curl around his arm in an unspoken expression of gratitude.

"His name is Freddie," she said softly, unable to keep from smiling. "He is seven years old, and already too smart for me to keep up with."

Colin found himself smiling with her. "Seven?" he asked, quickly doing the simple math. "That seems…" He trailed off as he realized there was no polite way to say what he was thinking.

But Susannah caught his meaning and her smile turned fixed. "He was an accident. My husband let me know very early on that he had no intention of producing children with me, though he was eager enough with others. He went to great pains to prevent a child on those occasions he was bored enough to visit his wife. One night he had too much to drink, and…" She shrugged lightly, but Colin saw the coiled tension in her frame.

There was far more to the story than she was sharing with him. Now was not the time for further exploration into it, but he would not let this go.

"So Freddie was born after that?" he asked, shifting topic away from her husband.

She nodded. "My husband was… less than pleased. He wanted me to get rid of it. Always calling him 'it,' even after he was born. He paid him no mind, except when he had to, and we liked it that way. Freddie has no real memories of his father, and he is far better for it."

Colin's bitter and snarling monster was threatening to roar to life for entirely different reasons. He found himself disappointed that this man was already dead, because he would dearly have loved to put him there himself. Any man who wished to rid the world of an infant deserved to have the world rid of him. And to treat Susannah with apparently no more interest was the most idiotic and blasphemous thing he had ever heard.

"So you see how this complicates matters," Susannah moved on with a sigh. "It is not only me to think about, but my son."

Colin looked at her and realization dawned. "That is why you are so thin," he murmured, his eyes widening. "You've been sacrificing yourself for Freddie."

Her eyes were moist as she looked back at him. "Can you blame me? I've had to make do with what I could, knowing debts had to be paid and my son fed, clothed, warm… I could manage well enough, but I could not see him want for much."

He found himself swallowing with difficulty. He reached out and brushed away a tear that rolled down her cheek. "I understand," he said, allowing himself to give her a small smile, though his body seemed turned to ice at the prospect she was painting.

And he did understand. Before, he never would have considered such a thought. It would have been a completely foreign concept. He probably would have laughed at it. But since the day the girls had come into his life, everything was changed.

He was changed.

"You do, don't you?" she murmured in wonder.

He could only nod.

The relief in her smile was palpable. "Then you can see why I have to be more selective in my employment. I cannot bring Freddie with me, not if I am to pose as a single woman."

He would not have thought of that. Now his mind whirled with every conceivable disaster that could occur. A bewildering sense of panic welled up. "What if you had been hired on with someone who wanted you in-house?" he cried, releasing her and running his hands through his hair. "What would your son have done then?"

"Don't you think I worried about that?" she replied only slightly calmer than he was. "I was terrified of what he would have to endure. Of having to be parted from him. Of trusting his care to others long-term, as I have had to just to find interviews. But a widow with a son has very little respectable options, unless she is willing to make significant sacrifices. I will not give up my son, unless I have sunk so low he would do better without me."

Colin stared at her in horror. "Surely it is not so bad as that…" he managed slowly.

She gave him a hollow, almost empty look that was destined to haunt him. "It is every bit as bad as that. I had even thought about becoming a mistress."

His stomach plummeted to his toes. "What?" The word was hardly a breath, his lips forming around it with difficulty.

She would not look at him. "It would allow me to be well provided for, as most gentlemen would not care about the baggage with a mistress if it does not affect him. I could stay with Freddie and earn substantial funds in the meantime. And I have been married, after all…"

Images flashed into his mind of nameless, faceless men putting their hands on her. Darkened rooms, secret liaisons, Susannah wrapped in finery while leering eyes made a meal of her. "No," he growled darkly.

Susannah looked at him then, brows raised. "Excuse me?"

He shook his head very deliberately, his frame the slightest bit tremulous with his rage. "No. No, no, and *hell* no."

Susannah opened her mouth, but Colin shook his head again, grabbed her shoulders, and pulled her flush against him.

"Don't think that, don't speak of it again, and don't ever wonder about it. I would steal the Crown jewels and be hanged before I would let you do that to yourself. Or to Freddie." He wanted to bury his face against her until he was calm once more. He wanted to pull her tighter, closer, until she was part of him, always safe and where he could see her.

Undoubtedly confused, Susannah patted his back awkwardly. "I won't, Colin. I promise."

"Thank you." He sighed and felt some of the tension leave. He slowly let her move out of his arms, but was quick to loop her hand through his arm and begin to walk again.

An idea formed in his mind, an insane, crazed, ridiculous idea that made absolutely no sense at all. And yet, it was the most brilliant idea he'd ever had.

"All right," he said in a matter-of-fact way, "send your son to live with us and he can run around with my sisters until we find you something suitable."

Susannah stumbled a step, but he caught her with ease. "What?" she nearly shrieked. "No, Colin, what would people say?"

He shrugged one shoulder, but gave her an honest look. "I haven't a clue, but they don't know how many siblings I've inherited or what genders, so we could easily pass him off as another."

Susannah made them stop and took both of Colin's arms. "You would… You are willing to claim Freddie as one of them?"

He copied her hold and stroked her upper arms softly. "Who is going to ask? I would be more than happy to claim guardianship if it came down to it. And it would do the girls some good to have a boy around to keep them from getting silly."

She did not smile. "Colin... You don't have to."

One side of his mouth curved and he stroked her arms once more, then turned her so they could walk again. "I know. But you are trying to do the best for your son. I can help you with that. Lord knows he will do better if his mother is in his life."

Chapter Ten

$\mathcal{M}$uch later that evening, Colin walked slowly to the study he shared with his brother, whenever Kit opted to use it, which was a rarity, as Kit spent more time out of the family house than he did in it. But lately, they had crossed paths in there more often than they had in the last ten years, and he'd just had it confirmed that Kit was, in fact, at home. He was glad for that. There was much to tell him.

He'd spent much of the day with Susannah, rekindling the friendship they had lost, laughing and smiling and reliving the best days of their youth. The gaunt and hollow look she had been wearing of late was finally beginning to dissipate, and it soothed his heart every time he brought a smile to her face. There were no words to describe what was happening to him, and he had been absolutely stunned by his admission to Susannah that the past no longer mattered.

What had been even more shocking to him had been that he had meant it.

Somewhere, somehow, that resentful and bitter corner of his heart that had flared to life sporadically over the last fifteen years was suddenly gone. He was not perfectly content with how things had played out, and he still had more questions than he could contemplate, but his anger was gone. His hatred was gone. All that remained was curiosity, concern, and an inexplicable budding excitement somewhere in the pit of his stomach.

It was the most unfathomable transformation, one he had long thought impossible.

He rubbed at his eyes and sighed as he hesitated outside of the study door. How in the world was he to explain any of this to his brother? He could not manage to explain it to himself.

And if he was to be spending more time with Susannah, and bringing Tibby into the fray, then he would have to include his friends. There was no predicting what a melee of insanity that would bring forth.

But what could he tell any of them? How could he give them any information when he had none?

At what point did his long-hidden past need to be brought to light?

"Colin, I can hear you breathing," Kit called softly from within the room. "Don't skulk, I have already had to deal with Rosie doing that."

Colin sighed and pushed the door open, a half smile on his face. "That sounds interesting," he said as he came in, rubbing at his hair sheepishly. "What did she do?"

Kit was surprisingly relaxed as he sat behind the desk, his coat off, cravat loosened, and waistcoat unbuttoned. He quirked a brow and a corner of his mouth curved up. "She managed to confuse four maids, two footmen, and Bartlet himself into thinking that there were several small creatures skittering about the house, that clothing had gone missing, and that Ginny was only speaking in French."

Colin could not help but to bark a laugh, and he covered his mouth quickly when Kit gave him an exasperated frown. "Why did she do that?"

One imperious brow rose. "She is your sister."

That explained it.

"You sure she isn't yours?" Kit asked with a hint of a mischievous grin.

Colin snorted. "Positive."

Still, it was rather uncanny just how like him she was turning out to be.

"Bartlet was livid," Kit continued, leaning back with a sigh. "I only just got him calm enough to stop talking about the south of France and some cousin with a farm…"

"Bartlet on a farm?" Colin snickered and sank into a chair, covering his eyes. "Can't you just see him in his evening wear behind a plow?"

"No," Kit laughed, shaking his head. Then he sighed. "I had to scold Rosie. I'm afraid I was a bit harsh with her, and she didn't take it well."

"I can imagine not." Colin dropped his hand and rolled his gaze to his brother.

Kit was watching him. "Perhaps if someone else had been here to help…?"

Colin sobered and sat up in his chair. "I know. I had only meant to be gone for an hour, perhaps two, but…" He trailed off, wondering just how to do this.

"Colin, what is going on with you?"

His twin's voice was calm, but the hint of concern was clear.

Colin paused, trying to collect his thoughts. "There are a few things I need to make you aware of. Some situations that have arisen. And I have decided something that will in some ways directly involve you."

"Me?" Kit asked with wide eyes. "What are you talking about?"

In low tones, Colin told him everything that had happened in the last few days. His meetings with Susannah and his attempts to find her work, his concerns of her frail figure, how extensive he believed the debts to be. Then he ventured into this morning's surprise meeting, and all that Lady Greversham had said, the decision to involve Tibby in the search for work for Susannah, and last of all, the revelation of the existence of her son.

Kit listened quietly, his eyes fixed on Colin with their usual intensity, never saying a word. When Colin had finished, Kit's mouth was parted in surprise, and his eyes were wide.

"I don't know what came over me," Colin said as he gripped the back of his neck. "I thought of that boy being in some random hovel in London all alone while Susannah tries to find work, and I just thought of the girls. I couldn't imagine them in such a state, it was too horrifying, and she has nowhere else to go."

"So you thought we would be the best place for him?" Kit asked, not sounding particularly fond of the idea, but neither was he making any refusals.

Colin huffed in irritation. "I know. It's not ideal, but…"

Kit scoffed. "When has that ever stopped you?"

Colin managed a wan smile.

His twin eyed him closely, then sighed. "Colin, of course I don't mind if the boy comes here. He can stay forever for all I care; it might do the girls some good. You said you wanted to help Susannah, and that is certainly something we can do, by all means. My concern is you."

Colin snorted and averted his eyes. "What about me?"

Kit flashed a tight smile. "What are you even doing, Colin? You want to take in the boy of the woman you have despised for years, the one who broke you and left you in pieces. You are bending over backwards to help her, and it makes me nervous. I am concerned that you are being too quick to jump, too eager to please, too…"

"Too nice?" Colin asked with a sneer. "I thought I was supposed to be the nice one."

Kit only looked at him. He knew Colin too well to think his petulance anything but a defense.

Colin leaned his head back. "I don't know what happened, Kit. Every time I see her, the past grows foggier in my mind. I can't hate her, not anymore. I see her now, the fear in her eyes, the weakness in her body, how she struggles, and I cannot stand by. In spite of everything, I still care. Far more than I ever thought, it seems, and I don't want to go on as I was. I want a fresh start with her, Kit. I don't understand, but the past is irrelevant now."

"Enough that you want to pass her son off as one of our siblings?" This was said without rancor, but Colin winced.

"I know, and I am sorry. I just…"

Kit waved a hand. "I have concerns, but I am ready to do it if I must. So long as you have your intentions aligned properly. I won't see you hurt again, and I refuse to let you become a master of vengeance. You would be far too good at it, and not even I could save you then."

Colin was oddly touched by his words. He knew his brother would be unfailingly loyal, but he had never understood how deep their bond was on his end. Kit was a puzzle to all, and while Colin knew him better than anyone, he was still a puzzle.

"You don't have to be involved if you prefer not," Colin said softly, leaning forward and folding his hands. "I'll do all of it."

"You'll manage the boy *and* finding Susannah work *and* the rest of your life? And *still* have the ability to be a stable adult influence to our sisters?" Kit scoffed. "Highly unlikely. You'll bungle something up, if not multiple things."

Colin grinned. "Well, I can try, at any rate."

Kit returned it briefly. "I cannot be here all the time, you know, to mind the girls while you run circles around your youth. I have obligations. And I am not sure you know this, but I have a house of my own. In London."

Now it was Colin's turn to raise a brow. "Have you?"

Kit looked a bit sheepish. "Yes. It seemed appropriate. A man of mystery must have mysteries, after all."

"I figured you had something of the sort, but I never tried to investigate it."

It made sense, now that he thought about it again. Kit was always disappearing without a word, supposedly to lands unknown, but he would suddenly reappear. Letters to him would get answered far too quickly for someone out of the city, but no one could verify where he was within the city. Colin trusted his brother enough not to ask questions, but that did not mean there were none.

"It's in St. James," Kit told him. "I can be a perfect recluse there and no one cares. Why didn't you look into it, if you suspected? I know you have the resources."

Colin shrugged and gave him a frank look. "I thought you deserved privacy, even from me. Who was I to invade that?"

"Thank you," Kit said with a faint smile. "But with the girls being here, and now gaining Susannah's son, I will spend as much time here as I can."

Colin nodded and sat back in his chair once more. "What do you think of all of this, Kit?" he finally asked, feeling drained. "I mean honestly, what?"

Kit watched him for a long moment. "I think… I think you are in trouble. Possibly great trouble." He tilted his head as if considering

Colin from a new angle, and there was the barest hint of a smile in his face. "And I am not sure if I want to help or simply watch."

Susannah arrived in the middle of the morning, as they had discussed the day before, and it took Colin a few minutes to settle his nerves and anxieties before he could venture out into the hall. Kit had been sitting with him and he watched Colin carefully, silently giving his support to whatever Colin decided. It was ironic, Colin had been the one to suggest all of these things, yet he had not slept the entire night, second guessing his decisions, and second guessing his second guesses.

It was four in the morning before he made his final decision, which was that Susannah needed him, and everything else was just details.

The hours that had passed between then and now had been an entire lifetime. He had sent the girls off to Tibby's for their very first music lesson, as much to have them out of the house for all of this as anything else. Besides that, it did make sense to do so, as they had no instruments here, which was shocking and nearly scandalous, according to Tibby. They would remedy that, he vowed to her, but that seemed of little consequence at the moment. There were far more pressing matters at hand.

In his opinion, Susannah was late, and he was irritated about it. But as she was here now, was here at all, he supposed he could live with that.

His irritation faded into excitement as he rose and went to exit the study, Kit following him silently.

Susannah was dressed very simply today, in a grey frock that had seen better days, but fit her far better than anything she had worn when he had first seen her. Her bonnet and cloak had already been taken, and her honey-colored hair was fixed tightly at her neck, highlighting her flawless bone structure. If she were not quite so fragile, she would have been the picture of an ideal woman.

As it was, she was still the closest to perfection he had ever seen.

Next to her, clutching her hand and looking around at the entryway in awe, was a small boy with dark, curly hair, though in every other aspect he was the picture of his mother, right down to those delightful green-tinted eyes. He made no secret of his delight with the house, craning his neck this way and that in an attempt to take it all in.

Colin felt the urge to smile at the sight, which was as unexpected as it was amusing. He was seeing Susannah's child, something he had never wanted, never thought about, and the boy was so like what Susannah had been it was uncanny. He had the sudden idea that this could all be more fun than he thought.

"Good morning," Colin greeted them as warmly as he could. "Welcome to our home."

Susannah smiled at him, and he could see the touch of nerves. She curtseyed properly. "Good morning."

Colin glanced at Kit, who had come just behind him to his left. He was staring at Susannah in the sort of stunned astonishment that did not encourage anything except insecurity, and were Kit a man of less control, there was no doubt his mouth would be gaping wide. Colin knew exactly what had him so shocked.

Colin had grown used to Susannah's wasted and sunken appearance. Kit had only ever known the healthy and active girl she had once been.

The discrepancy between the two versions was enough to scare one senseless.

Colin cleared his throat, still watching Kit. "Susannah, you remember my brother?"

There was a slight shuffling. "Of course. It is very nice to see you again, Mr. Gerrard."

To Colin's eternal astonishment, he saw Kit fight at least two swallows, and his eyes held a suspicious sheen in them. "Call me Kit. Please," his brother said, his voice surprisingly unsteady and hoarse. "And it is my pleasure to see you again."

Colin found himself fighting a lump at the utter sincerity in Kit's tone. He turned back to Susannah and found her looking embarrassed, but holding a steady gaze at Kit. She managed a weak smile that showed a surprising amount of understanding. "Thank you, Kit," she murmured softly.

Kit gave a short, half-bow of acknowledgment that made Colin bite back a grin. Ever the polite one, his twin.

"May I present to both of you," Susannah said proudly, looking down at the boy, "my son, Frederick? Freddie, this is Mr. Gerrard, and Mr. Colin Gerrard."

The boy looked at them both, eyes wide as he looked between them, then he swallowed and gave them a perfect bow. His form was even better than Kit's had been, which meant the lad could already be presented at court. "Pleased to meet you," Freddie said without hesitation. Then he looked between them again and said, "Erm, which one is which again?"

Colin chuckled and gave Susannah a smile. She had been just as confused about the whole twin thing when she had met them both. "My name is Colin, Freddie. And that's Kit. We hope you'll make yourself quite at home while you are here with us."

Kit said nothing as he stared at Freddie, but neither was he foreboding as he had been when he'd met the girls.

"Would you like a tour of the place?" Colin asked, trying to draw attention away from Kit. "The library, perhaps?"

Freddie's eyes lit up and he gasped without shame. "Library? How many books do you have?"

Colin grinned. "I can't even count them all. And you are welcome to any of them."

Freddie tugged on his mother's hand. "Come on, Mama! Let's go see!"

Susannah smiled at her son and let him pull her towards them. "Which way?" she asked Colin softly.

Colin turned to the side. "Bartlet?" His butler appeared from one of the rooms. "Would you show Miss Hart and Master Freddie to the library? And have a tray of refreshments sent up. I'll be along momentarily."

Bartlet clicked his heels in a bow and gestured the way for Susannah and Freddie.

Susannah mouthed a "thank you" as she passed. Colin offered her a wink, which brought a touch of color to her cheeks.

When they were out of earshot, Colin released a sigh and turned to Kit, who stared after them without speaking. Slowly, Kit looked back at him.

"What I said the other night?" Kit murmured roughly. "I take it back. All of it. Whatever you want, whatever you need, I am with you. I'm all in."

Colin sobered at once. "It is quite a shock, isn't it?"

"Worse than I could have imagined." He looked down the hall again, and shook his head. "We need to fix this, Colin. Whatever it takes."

Colin nodded and opened his mouth to reply when Kit was suddenly heading for the door. "Where are you going?" Colin asked in surprise.

Kit turned, finally regaining his calm. "I am going to fetch my tailor. Freddie needs new clothes and I refuse to let him go without them for long."

Colin reared back. "Now?"

Kit gave him a look. "You would prefer next week? Yes, now. Don't tell Susannah. Make something up, will you?"

And then he was gone.

A slow, satisfied grin spread across Colin's face, and he spun on his heel and hurried towards the library. And Susannah.

He entered the library to find Freddie fairly skipping along the shelves, too excited to speak coherent or complete sentences. His young eyes were wide and his grin threatened to split his face in two. And Susannah watched him with raw, emotional delight. Colin went to her side immediately.

"I take it this is a success?" he chuckled as he reached her.

She looked up at him with a smile. "Oh, Colin, it's wonderful! Look at him!"

He did and grinned when Freddie yanked a book from the shelf and plopped himself on the ground to begin reading it. "I think he will do quite well here."

Susannah nodded, one hand going to her throat. "He certainly will. I don't know…" Her voice broke and she swallowed hard.

Colin rubbed her arm soothingly. "It won't be for long," he assured her. "I am going to see Tibby today and she'll find a position close by in no time. You can see Freddie any time you wish. And Freddie will have lessons with the girls once we secure a governess, so he will be learning and growing every day."

Susannah nodded, a soft hiccup escaping her. "I know that. I know all of that, but… But I won't be there to tuck him in at night," she whispered. "To hear about his day and what adventures he had, to hug him, to tell him a story…"

"You can do all of that here." Colin tightened his hold on her a bit fiercely. "We can arrange an outing for you every day, just you and Freddie, away from Kit and me and the girls. You are his mother, Susannah. You have complete access to your son, we are merely watching over him for you."

"I know." She sniffed and straightened out of his hold, causing a flash of disappointment in his frame. "I would like that very much." She gave him a half smile. "How is the search for a governess going? Did any of the names I secured work?"

Colin sighed and made a face. "Not really. Nobody wants to work for us, for some reason. And that is just before they met the girls, who knows who will stay afterwards?"

Susannah smiled. "How seriously did you look at them? Two of them, at least, were quite desperate to work."

Colin smiled sheepishly. "Not so very. I did look into them each, and nothing seemed to fit. Perhaps my expectations are off base, or perhaps I just don't know what to look for."

Susannah glanced at Freddie, and smiled at his complete absorption by the book in his lap. She waved Colin over to the set of chairs nearby and sat, and he was quick to follow, taking the other.

"Well," Susannah said, smiling on a sigh, "perhaps I can help you there. I should have done before, it just never occurred to me."

Colin waved that off at once. "You have been somewhat occupied with your own concerns, there was no cause for you to fret yourself over mine."

She inclined her head in acknowledgement. "So what do you

have in mind? We can see if there is a way to align your expectations with what is available to you and begin there. If I cannot recommend someone, perhaps your friend Tibby can."

Colin sat back and thought about it. "Well, for starters, she must get along with the girls."

"Naturally."

"I think they would be fairly easy to accommodate, they are so desperate for attention, anyone with a heart should do. But she should be young."

Susannah immediately shook her head. "No, older."

He frowned. "I don't want the girls being taught by a crone."

Susannah sighed in exasperation, though a light smile touched her lips. "Really, Colin, I don't intend for them to be taught and minded by the woman who raised you."

He shuddered at the memory of Miss Layton and his neck burned from the memory of her lash. "Young. Please."

There was a long silence as Susannah watched him. "Not too young," she finally relented, giving him a firm look.

He tilted his head, curiously amused. "Why are you insisting on that?"

She gave him a thin smile. "You can't have the poor thing falling in love with you."

He jerked in shock. "What? Why would you even think that?"

Susannah snorted, smile genuine now. "Please, Colin. It's you."

"Meaning…?"

One brow rose. "Everyone falls in love with you. You know that."

"Not everyone," he replied in a much lower voice than he had intended.

Her eyes turned wary. "Colin…"

He couldn't stop, not yet. "You never did."

She looked away at once. He saw her throat work in a swallow, and then in a hoarse whisper, she said, "You don't know that."

If the heavens had started raining fluffy white dogs and old crones, he could not have been more stunned. He could not feel his heart anymore, or his toes, and his ribs seemed to be constricting his lungs in the most disconcerting way. He stared at her in abject wonder, the way her color was suddenly heightened, her breathing unsteady, her graceful neck strained with the slightest tension.

Could she really mean…?

He had always assumed the worst, that he had been a fool of unrequited love in his youth, played into the naïve dream of friendship turning romantic, while she had not seen anything of the sort. His heartbreak had been as much of his own making as it had been her actions, if not more. Was it possible, then, that his assumptions had been completely false, even unfounded?

Could his heart have been right after all?

The silence stretched on and on as he attempted to process these revelations. Susannah began to look more uncomfortable, so he cleared his throat and folded his hands together. "So, older, then?"

She kept her gaze down, but he saw the tension ease. "I think that would be best."

"Right. I'll have Tibby look into that, she knows everyone."

"Excellent idea."

Chapter Eleven

$\mathcal{I}$t only took two days for Tibby to find work for Susannah, and it was far more convenient than Colin could have hoped. She was hired as a companion for one of Tibby's oldest friends, Lady Cavendish, who lived in Grosvenor Street, even closer to Colin than Tibby was.

Tibby had been so delighted to have something to do that she had not even managed to properly interrogate Colin as to the nature of his relationship with the lady in question. She had to be curious about her and why he was so insistent on finding her a good and respectable position. He had even told her that there was a boy to think about, but that he would be with Colin. Uncharacteristically, Tibby had not even blinked at that. She merely waved that off and agreed with him, and loudly bemoaned any friend of Colin's suffering so harshly when she could help them.

She'd been equally as devoted and determined with finding an appropriate governess for the children, and not two days after that, Mrs. Creighton had been appointed, moved into the family home, and begun her instruction. It was a week into it now, and it was better than Colin had hoped for. Mrs. Creighton was somewhere in her forties, a widow, had grown children of her own, and had just the right mixture of severity and charm. The children both adored and feared her, and finally a sense of order was prevailing in the house.

Tibby had been remarkably quiet of late, which was suspicious. She still offered her home for the girls to use for their music lessons, and Kate was helping there. Other than that, Tibby said nothing about Susannah, about Freddie, about any of it.

Colin knew it would not last long. Tibby would come to her senses soon enough and then he would have to answer all sorts of things. In the meantime, however, he would enjoy the respite and begin preparations to build up defenses and rebuttals. And distract her with the three very precocious and opinionated young girls he was attempting to teach the finer points of pall-mall to at this moment.

Freddie heaved a sigh from beside him. "This will take forever," he moaned, rolling his eyes up to look at Colin.

Derek chuckled from Freddie's other side and patted his shoulder. "Get used to this, Master Fred. You will spend the rest of your life waiting on women, and it does not get any easier."

Freddie shook his head. "I don't like it, Lord Whitlock. Not one bit."

"I'm afraid you're not supposed to, mate," Colin sighed, folding his arms. "Long suffering gentlemen and all that."

Freddie sniffed. "Come on, Rosie!" he called down the green. "Just hit it! It is right there in front of you!"

Colin and Derek shook their heads in unison. "Freddie..." they warned at the same time.

Rosie's head snapped up and she pointed her mallet directly at Freddie's throat as if it were a sword. "One more word, Frederick, and you will eat this mallet."

"If she could aim it right," Freddie muttered, scratching at his ear.

Rosie, thankfully, did not hear him. "Once more, Mr. Bray, if you please," she called to Duncan in her sweetest voice.

Duncan brought the ball back to her again, and again, Rosie sent the ball in almost the opposite direction of where she meant, causing another round of muttering from Freddie as Geoff stepped in to adjust Rosie's form.

Derek nudged Colin's side. "So I take it that the girls have grown used to Freddie now?" he asked quietly, minding Freddie's attention.

Colin snorted. "You could say that. They are as thick as thieves. He's such a bright lad and challenges them in lessons. Mrs. Creighton says he is smarter than any seven-year-old she's ever seen."

Derek chuckled and folded his arms over his chest. "I bet Rosie

112

loves that.”

That drew a smirk. “Rosie just loves having someone else who likes to read. Bitty is too impatient and knows so little, and Ginny only likes books if you do the voices. Rosie and Freddie would spend hours in the library if I let them.”

Kit suddenly appeared on the terrace and took in the assemblage with one quirked brow. He looked over at Colin with mild interest. “What is going on here?”

“Pall-mall lesson,” Colin called back. “I should think that obvious.”

Derek stifled a laugh into his fist, and Freddie looked at him with concern, but it faded when Derek winked at him.

“For girls this young?” Kit replied sardonically. “Does Mrs. Creighton approve?”

“Of course, I do!” Mrs. Creighton called from her chair on the far side of the green, where Ginny was picking flowers for her.

Kit frowned and muttered something that sounded suspiciously like “Wonderful.” Then his expression cleared and he looked back at Colin. “Colin, it’s half past. Time for Freddie to go meet his mother.”

Freddie cheered and raced into the house and up to his room to change his jacket. They had not managed to find the appropriate way to tell Susannah that they had refurbished her son’s attire, and as most of the clothing was not done yet, it was not deemed necessary. So for his daily outings, he wore his old jacket. He never minded, so long as he was with Susannah.

Rosie came over to Colin and was pouting.

“What’s the pout for, poppet?” he asked, putting his hands on his hips.

“I’m not very good at pall-mall,” she said, a furrow forming between her brows. “It’s too hard.”

He smiled and ruffled her curls, his smile growing when she hugged his side briefly. “That is why you practice, Rose. And I will bet, if you ask nicely, Kit will help you while I am gone.”

She snickered into his shirt. “I can’t see Kit being any better at pall-mall than I am.”

Colin clamped down on his lips to keep from laughing out loud.

Derek, still nearby, had to walk away to hide his own laughter.

"I will have you know, Miss Rosie," Kit announced as he approached them at a surprisingly relaxed stroll, "that I am an expert at pall-mall. Much better than Colin. I can teach you tricks that will have you running circles around everyone else."

Rosie gave him a disbelieving look. "Really, Kit?"

He shrugged, which Kit never did. "Try me and see." He shucked off his jacket and set it on the terrace steps. "Come on, let's have a go."

Rosie looked at Colin in shock.

He was as bewildered as she. "I think you had better do it, Rose," he said with a pat on her shoulder. "It could be a ruddy miracle."

She nodded and hurried over to Kit.

Colin made his farewells and went to meet Freddie before the boy could rush off on his own. One of the footmen accompanied them, dressed as commonly as any man in London. He did not usually travel with a servant about London, but with Susannah and Freddie under his care, he was not above such measures.

He had come to crave these visits as much as Freddie did. Initially, he had meant for them to be at his home, but Susannah had adamantly refused to do that. She insisted on meeting on what she called "neutral ground," a phrase he did not care for at all. It was hardly a battlefield they were dealing with. He had asked her why, and the answer changed every time. Concerns about his sisters, involving his friends, disrupting their lifestyle, and something ridiculous about potential impropriety; he did not understand the lot of it. But she was stubborn enough that not even he could move her on the subject. He did not mind bringing Freddie wherever they settled, not at all, but he was growing tired of her imposed distance.

Each visit was entirely private and he would hang back and observe as an outsider, content to let mother and son have their precious time, but more and more he was being drawn in. He loved it, the delight on Freddie's face when he saw his mother, though he saw her daily, and the delight on Susannah's when he spoke to her, all were enough to make Colin's heart lighter than air.

Susannah was happier, he could see that much. Her eyes had life to them again, and the gauntness was leaving her face. There was not time enough to see if her figure was improving with her situation, and he could hardly examine her closely without being scandalous. But he would settle for the color in her cheeks and the smile on her face to set his heart at ease.

Although, being with Susannah was not putting him quite as much at ease as it had been before. No, now it was exciting and thrilling and almost uncomfortable, though their conversation was always light and easy, and they were already better friends than their childhood had allowed. It was a rather promising beginning, although where it would lead was a mystery he would not face.

Today's outing was to a quiet corner of Hyde Park, and the number of people milling about outside of it was small enough that Colin signaled to the footman to stay further back than normal.

"Excited, Freddie?" Colin asked of his young companion, who was obviously restraining the urge to run.

He nodded. "Very. I miss Mama."

Colin smiled and put his hand on the boy's back. "I know you do." An errant thought prodded him, and before he could quash it, he said, "Freddie, what is your last name?"

Freddie became thoughtful, then shook his head. "I don't know."

Colin frowned and leaned a bit closer. "What do you mean you don't know?"

Freddie heaved a sigh. "We've had so many last names, I don't know which one it is now. I used to be Master Frederick or Master Freddie, but that was a long time ago." He looked up at him. "Is that all right?"

Colin immediately smiled. "Of course it is, my friend. I was only asking. Look, isn't that your mother?"

Freddie brightened and dashed forward at once.

Colin exhaled slowly. Freddie's answer unsettled him. Too many unanswered questions, even for the boy. He would never pressure him, he was not that ruthless. But to be addressed as such at one time could indicate a certain level of wealth or prosperity.

What implications could that have for their current situation?

He shook his head and smiled at the joyous reunion before him, and eased his way over to them, careful to not intrude on their moment.

Susannah smiled warmly at him when he approached, and the burst of heat in his chest echoed it.

"Good day, Colin," she said, ruffling Freddie's hair. "I hear you have been teaching pall-mall today."

He grinned. "Indeed, we have. And Freddie was most distressed at the slow speed of our instruction."

"Mama, Rosie took *forever*," Freddie said, gripping at her skirt. "I thought we would never get back to my turn."

Susannah smiled and brushed his hair back. "I am sure Rosie was doing her best, love, same as you were. I saw a very lovely pond not far from here, shall we go see it?"

Freddie nodded and ran on ahead of them.

Colin chuckled as he and Susannah fell in behind him. "Does he run everywhere?"

Susannah smiled and shook her head. "He certainly does it a great deal. Everything must be done straightaway, as soon as possible, whether it is walking or reading or eating."

Colin nudged her with his shoulder. "Reminds me of someone else I know…"

Susannah pushed back at him. "Oh, stop that. I was never so hasty."

"You were!" he insisted. "We ran absolutely everywhere, I was panting like mad every time I went back to the house. You try hiding such physical distress from Aunt Agatha."

Susannah giggled and looked up at him. "You never complained at the time."

He shrugged lightly. "It never bothered me that much. I didn't care if I ran to France and back, so long as I was with you."

She smiled in a bemused sort of way, having grown used to his referencing the past in such terms, and it no longer made her blush. "We were inseparable, weren't we?"

He nodded, holding her gaze steadily. "And delighted to be so."

Her fingers brushed against his lightly as they walked, and his skin burned with it as if by flame. She must have felt the same, for she gasped softly and stepped a little away. He tamped down the urge to bring her closer, and was profoundly grateful when Freddie called out to them about ducks in the pond.

Soon enough, however, they were alone again as Freddie wanted to explore the entire outskirts of the pond. Colin sent the footman to follow and he and Susannah walked along the edges slowly, reminiscing about their glorious summers of youth at Seabrook. Stories and memories he had not thought of for years and years were suddenly fresh and bright in his mind. Names and faces of villagers and short-lived friends sprang into recollection, as if the days had been weeks ago and not decades.

Her hand absently brushed his again, and this time he captured it in his. Her breath caught on whatever she had been saying, he had long lost track. Other memories had started to blossom in his mind, one of which was suddenly brilliantly before him.

On a day just as fresh and cool as this one, near a body of water somewhat larger than this pond, he had walked with her just as he did now. And he had taken her hand, just as he had it now. And after that...

Susannah stopped, looking down at their joined hands, her breathing unsteady.

Colin looked around quickly, scanning the relative seclusion of their location, and decided it was not enough. He tugged Susannah quickly behind him into a small stand of trees nearby, giving them the perfect obscurity from anyone else.

No less sensitive to her touch, Colin swallowed hastily as her fingers curved in his hold. He set her before him, her back to a tree to further shelter her from any other eyes, and looked at her.

Her eyes were lowered, apparently still fixed on their hands, and her chest moved rapidly with unsteady breaths that he faintly echoed. She was beautiful, in the most healthy and purest of ways. The natural curve of her cheek was perfect, the exact color of her complexion divine, and she had the most adorable ears he had ever seen.

He could have stared at her for ages of time and never seen enough of her.

As if time were repeating itself, that lock of hair of hers broke free and danced across her face. Helpless against the temptation, Colin reached out and tucked it behind her ear, taking the same opportunity to stroke her cheek softly, just as he had done then. This time, however, he waited. He caressed her cheek over and over until she raised her eyes to his, her face the slightest bit flushed.

He drew his fingers down to her chin, his thumb dipping ever so slightly beneath her bottom lip.

She stilled beneath his touch, her eyes fixed on him.

His heart was the only thing he could feel, pounding an unsteady beat against his ribs.

A soft breath passed her lips, tingling against his fingers.

He matched it and ducked his head to press his lips to hers, gentle and sweet, again as in the past. But it was so much more now. "Better than I remember," he murmured, his lips grazing hers with his words.

"Definitely better," she replied faintly, tilting her head up to kiss him again.

Encouraged, he took the kiss deeper, his hand sliding to the back of her head, her hands fisting into his jacket, and suddenly it was as though the past never happened. There was no pain, no resentment, no question, just this extraordinary woman in his arms. She sighed against him then, as if she felt it too, her hands pulling him closer. His heart surged at her response, and though he kept his attentions light and caressing, the feelings coursing through him were anything but.

When they finally broke apart with faint gasps, they stared at each other, breathing heavily. Then Colin swallowed hard. "I had no idea," he rasped.

"Of what?" Susannah asked, her voice hoarse, her hands still at his sides.

He shook his head. "No idea... how long I have wanted to do just that."

Susannah's eyes took on a light that made him feel weak. "Me neither." She exhaled sharply and stepped safely out of his embrace, her color delightfully heightened, her eyes averted.

Colin smiled at it. She had been the same way after he had kissed her fifteen years ago, suddenly shy and retreating.

He was not about to let her retreat now. He kept his hold on her hand and when it became evident he would not relinquish it, she sighed and shook her head, allowing him to lead her into a slow and leisurely walk once more.

But he caught the curve of her smile that she attempted to hide. And it made his grin impossible to remove.

Eventually, they were fit to converse again, and he let her go on as if they had not shared the most stirring kiss of his life. She spoke of her new position and how easy Lady Cavendish was to please.

"She enjoys being read to, but it usually ends with her wanting to debate whatever the author says, or reminds her of a story from the days of her youth." Susannah laughed and gave Colin a gleeful grin. "There are some stories, Mr. Gerrard, that would shock even you."

He chuckled. "I do not doubt it, particularly if she was friends with Tibby in her younger years."

Susannah narrowed her eyes and looked up at him. "I have yet to meet her, you know. I am inclined to think you made her up."

"Not even I could make up such a person. I shall have to introduce you soon."

She smiled softly. "I would like that very much. I owe her a great debt of gratitude."

He shook his head at once. "She won't see it that way. You'll just have to be forever in awe of her like the rest of us. And once she's brought you into her circle, there is no escaping it."

She laughed and looked across the pond at where Freddie was explaining something to the footman, who was doing his best to keep his composure. "I don't think I would want to leave it, to tell you the truth. I don't want to leave any of this."

Colin watched her for a long moment, different responses and questions and thoughts whirling around him. "I want you to meet my sisters," he said suddenly.

Susannah turned in surprise. "What? Why?"

"Because…" He trailed off, fumbling for the words he hadn't

articulated in his mind yet. "Because it's time. Your son plays with them, no doubt he tells you stories, so I think you should."

"Colin..." she murmured uncertainly, trying again to remove her hand from his.

He took it more firmly in both of his. "I want you to, Susannah. I want... I want you to be in their lives."

She bit her lip, and her blue-green eyes blinked rapidly. "I'm not sure that is a good idea."

He straightened and released her hand slowly. "You're right," he sighed.

Her jaw tightened. "Am I?"

He nodded once and continued to walk, clasping his hands behind his back. She trotted after him and was immediately back at his side, looking curious. "Yes," he told her. "If they knew who I spend my time with when it is not them, the person who occupies more and more of my thoughts every day, the reason I am becoming more and more absent... Why, they would get so jealous, and then you would feel guilty, and spend more time with them and less time with me, and that does not suit me at all."

Her mouth popped open and he grinned mischievously. He picked up her hand and kissed it once, lingering.

She swallowed once, then again, her throat working to speak. Finally, she said, "You are far too persuasive for your own good."

"I know," he replied cheekily. "So you'll come?"

She sighed and nodded, sliding her hand from his as they neared Freddie. "Tomorrow."

"Not today?" he asked with a frown. "We could go right now, there is plenty of time."

She shook her head, looking away. "I have business to attend to today. Tomorrow will be good enough."

He did not like her evasiveness, but he let it go and pretended to accept it.

When the time came for their departure, he removed himself to stand near his footman so Susannah and Freddie could make their farewells in private.

Colin turned his back on Susannah and Freddie to appear as

though he were looking behind where he and the footman were. "What is your name again?" he murmured to the young man.

"Nick, sir," he replied, a corner of his mouth ticking.

Colin smirked slightly. "I've asked you that before, haven't I?"

Nick shrugged, which was answer enough.

Colin nodded. "Nick, no doubt you've been informed that occasionally, my servants do unusual errands for me. Don't indicate, just blink once if this is true."

Nick blinked once.

"Very good. Do this for me: follow Miss Hart on this errand she is tending to, just a precaution for her safety, you understand. But stay out of her sight. When she has safely returned to Lady Cavendish's residence, come back to the house and report to me. You'll receive some sovereigns for your trouble. Blink once if you understand and accept, Nick."

Again, Nick blinked once, very determinedly.

Colin nodded and murmured, "Very good." Then he turned back with a bright smile as Freddie skipped to him. "Ready?"

Freddie nodded and smiled up at him. "Mama says she's coming to the house tomorrow."

Colin looked up and met Susannah's eyes, letting her see just how delighted he was at the same prospect. "That's right, she is."

Susannah colored under his gaze, and he could see her fighting a smile.

He grinned and nodded in farewell to her.

She wrinkled her nose up a bit and waved to Freddie as she left.

Colin watched her for a moment longer than he probably should have, then turned to her son. "Well, shall we go and see if Kit and our friends have turned the girls into pall-mall experts while we were away?"

Colin's friends were still at his house when he arrived, and they had some comments to make about his recent behavior. He was smiling too much, he was too warm with his sisters, too happy to see their wives and children, too eager to help wherever he could. In short, he was everything they had grown accustomed to being the exact opposite of him.

"I am telling you," Derek was saying to the group as they were preparing to leave, at last, "something is wrong."

"I can see that," Nathan allowed. "Colin is a bit... Well, he's a bit mawkish lately."

"What?" Colin said with a laugh. "I am not."

"Softer than a pillow," Duncan said with a sad shake of his head.

Geoff snorted. "I've eaten puddings harder than Colin."

Colin gave him a hard look. "Have not, unless your fool of a cook made it."

"Yes," Derek said slowly, eyeing him carefully. "I do believe he is glowing a bit."

"I'm a robust fellow," Colin scoffed. "I cannot help but shine."

Nathan shrugged back into his jacket, still watching him. "You aren't going to tell us, are you?" he finally asked.

Colin turned to him fully, expression as curiously blank as he could manage. "Tell you what? What exactly do you think has happened to me?"

None of them had an answer for him, and he was certainly not inclined to let them into his private thoughts at this time. Not when he couldn't manage to make sense of them himself.

They departed then, all looking back at him with curious stares.

He sighed and went to his study, putting his head into his hands. Eventually, they would have to be informed. When there was something for them to be informed of.

Right now, all he had were feelings... and questions.

A knock at his study door brought his head up, and Nick stood in the doorway, posture every inch the footman, though his apparel was still common.

"Nick," he said, waving him in. "Come in, good man, and shut the door."

Nick did so and presented himself before the desk silently.

Bartlet always trained the footmen so well. Colin had the urge to smile, but refrained. "Go on, then. What did you find?"

"Miss Hart went directly from the park to the financial district, sir," Nick reported stiffly, eyes fixed out of the window. "To the office of a Mr. Samuel Jacobs, who is a solicitor, but not a well-known one, hardly used but for tradesmen and the like. She was there half an hour, and then went to Lady Cavendish."

Colin sat back, hand near his mouth as he thought. "How did she look?"

Nick glanced at him in surprise. "Sir?"

"How did she look?" he repeated more clearly. "When she exited the building. Was she distressed, was she pleased…?"

Nick frowned in thought. "She did not look pleased, sir, but I could not say she was distressed. Perhaps… disappointed?"

That was not what he wished to hear. His brow creased as he glowered and he reached into his desk drawer for some coins. "Thank you, Nick," he said, handing the coins out. "You may return to your duties. I may have need of you again in the future, if you don't mind."

"Yes, sir. As you wish, sir." Nick left the room silently, leaving Colin to his solitude.

He did not like that Susannah had secrets from him. He understood her reasoning for it, of course. They were only newly friends again, and the trust they had lost would take time to rebuild. He had no reason to know her secrets, her past, or how exactly dire her straits were.

But he was troubled, and he could not deny that. Between still not knowing her last name or her husband's identity, and Freddie not knowing what to call himself anymore, her starving herself to feed him, and now this mystery solicitor… Not to mention her fear, her weakness, and the way she hid from everyone and everything. There were far too many questions, and a creeping sense of unease was starting to swirl within him.

He wanted to help her. Not just to find a position or to take care of Freddie, but he wanted to help remove the shadows she lived with. He wanted to soothe her fears, fend off her troubles, and know every deep, dark secret she was hiding from him. If it was money, he could take care of that. If it was law, he had friends and power enough to take care of that. He could take care of everything that troubled her, if only she would let him in.

He shouldn't have had Nick follow her today, that was probably going too far. He had absolutely no intention of having her followed all around London, he was not that protective or desperate. And there was the value of her privacy that he would respect. He would never force her into confines he set out. He could not. She would have resisted with every fiber in her frail being, and he would lose all that he had gained by having her in his life.

But he could not let this go, either. He would go mad without something to settle his mind.

He pulled out a sheet of paper and jotted a quick note down before he could reconsider it. He sealed it per his usual manner, and left it unaddressed, as the case called for. He quickly rose from his desk and went into the hall. "Bartlet?" he called softly, looking around.

"Sir?" Bartlet replied, sticking his head out from one of the rooms, his hair slicked over his baldness, as usual. He came out and started towards him.

Colin met him halfway. "Take this to Jim, if you please, and tell him to deliver it, same as usual."

Bartlet nodded and took it. "Wait for a reply?"

Colin shook his head. "If he wants to reply, he will make it happen."

Again came the nod, and Bartlet bowed with a sharp click of his heels and disappeared.

Colin shook his head and went back to his study, grateful that the children were in lessons and Kit had gone out. He was a mess at the moment, going to extreme lengths just to settle his own nerves and conscience. It was hardly the behavior of a gentleman, and there would be no explaining this all to Kit. If there was anything that the Gerrard twins had in common, looks aside, it was their decidedly gentlemanly traits. There might be rumors and mystery, and a good bit of eccentricity to make things interesting, but no one would ever deny that they were both gentlemen. To their faces, at least. Who could tell what was said in the forgotten corners of drawing rooms and ballrooms of London?

He sank his head into his hands with a groan. He was going to go mad.

Colin did not recognize himself anymore.

He stood by what he had said all along, that he had no idea what he was doing. He was just as clueless now as he had been from the very beginning. He knew he was going to help Susannah in whatever way he could. He knew he would do everything in his power to help her son.

He knew he needed to have her in his life.

And therein lay his greatest danger.

There was a very real probability that this was no mere friendship rekindling. The feelings were too deep, too intense, too hungry to ever be anything less than… than…

Saints above. He was in love.

With her.

Again.

"Oh, lord," he muttered, eyes wide, shaking his head. He sat back into his chair with a snort, feeling completely ridiculous at his sudden epiphany.

But he knew it was true. He couldn't deny that any more than he could refrain from letting a wild, breathless grin spread across his face.

Well, how exactly was he going to explain this?

Chapter Twelve

"*M*ad, mad, mad, mad…"

Susannah shook her head as she hurried towards the Gerrard house in Bruton Street. There was no reason in the world why she should still be clinging to this mad fantasy of Colin, letting him bring her closer and closer, all the while knowing she should be fleeing in the opposite direction. For his own good. But she couldn't resist him, not now, not ever. He had always had power over her and she was just weak enough to submit.

For now.

The memory of his kisses the day before still seared her lips, and she smiled to herself yet again. What wild and reckless feelings had surged within her then, making her bold and brave, pressing herself more tightly against him, clutching his clothing like a madwoman in her passion. There had been no thought or logic in it, only the heady sensation of his very essence swirling around her, through her, stealing the very breath from her lungs…

She faltered slightly as she lost her footing, her heart racing far too unsteadily. She cleared her throat and forced her mind into safer paths. Colin Gerrard was dangerous in general, and for her in particular. The more time she spent with him, the more dangerous the situation became.

Which made her actions now entirely idiotic. Imagine, going to his house to meet his sisters and to spend more time with him, knowing their relationship was changing more and more every day, and knowing how she longed to be in his arms again. Everything made perfect sense there, and what did not make sense was simply not there. No evil existed, no fear prevailed.

But the harsh reality of her life crashed down more painfully about her ears when those moments ended.

And she was determined to keep a level head.

She bit her lip as she looked up at the house. It was far easier to say such things than it was to do them.

She had avoided this for as long as possible, knowing it would be harder to turn back once this began. London was far and away safer, as a whole, than Colin's home and Colin's family. She could hardly maintain an appropriate distance when she was enveloped within his life.

After what she had allowed, and enjoyed, yesterday, there was very little distance anywhere he was concerned.

She shouldn't be doing this. Her business with Mr. Jacobs had not gone well, and she could not afford distractions. Her family needed money badly, and she had very little to share as yet. Charity of the family neighbors would only go so far. She ought to be finishing her work from the modiste, and finding other small tasks she could do while staying with Lady Cavendish. Anything to earn money.

Not spending her free time for exquisite moments of sweetness with a man she could never have.

She was shown into the house at once and her things were taken by a rather somber-faced butler, who then handed them off to a pair of apparently fatigued maids. He then directed her to the back terrace, where both Misters Gerrard were currently situated, and where children were playing. Susannah wanted to ask questions, but uneasiness oozed from the butler as if it were cologne. She felt bad for the man, sensing that order and composure were essential not only to his position but to his nature. Such an upheaval of normalcy must have been very distressing for him.

And it appeared that the newest Gerrard siblings, for all that Colin sang their praises, had not won over the *entire* household.

Outside, she saw Freddie running around with three little girls, one of whom wore a blindfold and was trying desperately to chase the others. All four were laughing uproariously, and Freddie and another girl were helping the youngest to evade the blindfolded one. When she nearly caught the youngest again, but missed, they all laughed once more. Freddie and the other girl helped the little one onto his back, shushing each other as they did so.

"Careful now," an older woman called in a pleasant tone as she watched from one side of the green. That had to be Mrs. Creighton, from the fond, yet protective way she observed them.

"What are they doing?" the blindfolded girl demanded, reaching for her eyes.

"Don't!" the other children shrieked, still laughing.

"Rosie, don't cheat!" her sister insisted.

"If you are tricking me, Bitty…" she warned, leaving the blindfold where it was.

"Just play!" Freddie yelled, adjusting the smallest onto his back more securely.

Susannah stepped forward and cleared her throat. "Freddie, be nice," she scolded, though she was smiling all the same.

All present turned to look at her in surprise. Freddie grinned and waved gaily, then quickly replaced his hand on the small girl he bore on his back. The girls looked confused, and the blindfolded one pushed the fabric up to look at her.

"This is a surprise," Colin said, coming towards her from where he and Kit had been watching on one side of the terrace. "We were not expecting you for a while yet."

Susannah shrugged, unable to help smiling warmly at him. "Lady Cavendish is visiting friends this morning and had no use for me. I thought I would come early."

Colin grinned and gently took her arm. "I'm glad for that."

Her cheeks warmed under his earnest gaze, and his eyes danced at it. He turned a bit so Kit might see her.

"Good morning, Kit," Susannah murmured, curtseying in greeting.

Kit curved a half smile and bowed. "Susannah, a pleasure, as always. Should we interrupt the game for introductions?"

She waved a hand and laughed. "Let them play, for heaven's sake. Only tell me who they are, and I shall get to know them later."

Colin squeezed her arm softly and Kit nodded, apparently ignorant as to his brother's actions. Kit turned and pointed at each girl in turn. "The tall one is Rosie, she is nine. Then Bitty, over there by Freddie, she's six. And last is Ginny, on Freddie's back, she is three. Girls, this is Susannah, a very old friend, and Freddie's mother."

They greeted her in chorus, though Ginny looked uncertain about it.

Bitty put her hands on her hips and looked Susannah over speculatively, then turned to Kit. "She's not very old, Kit. That wasn't nice."

Kit looked back at Susannah with a bemused smile, shaking his head, then turned to face the children once more. "I meant that we have been friends for a very long time, Bitty, not that she was old."

Her mouth formed a silent *O* and Rosie rolled her eyes with a laugh.

"Not to be impolite or anything," Rosie called, putting her hands back onto her blindfold, "but can we get on with our game?"

Colin chuckled and said, "Yes, Rosie, if you call your random flailing about a game."

She made a face at him and was quick to right her blindfold and set after the others with a roar.

Susannah rapped Colin sharply with a laugh. "You should be nice too," she scolded.

He grinned at that. "Going to punish me, as well, Mother?"

She scoffed and looked at Kit, watching them with real interest. "They are beautiful girls," she told them both. "And just as I imagined them, from how Freddie talks about them."

"Bitty is the little mother of the group," Kit explained as he turned to lean on the balustrade and watch the game. "She wants us all to be nice all the time, and points out any impoliteness. As you can imagine, she has quite a time with Colin."

Susannah snickered, which earned her a mock severe look from Colin.

"Ginny is shy," Colin took over, moving to the terrace railing once more, "and it is nearly impossible to get her to speak more than a few words at a time, even to Kit and me. But she makes her point well enough."

Kit snorted softly in agreement.

Susannah watched the two brothers as they considered the children. Their warmth and genuine affection for their sisters was plainly evident, and they could not seem to help smiling as they spoke about each. She wouldn't have thought these two, knowing them as she once had, would ever have been so soft-hearted towards three little girls, but the proof was before her.

"And Rosie," Kit said, looking at his brother mischievously, "is a handful. Rambunctious and daring…"

"Sweet and stubborn," Colin added.

"Outspoken and headstrong," Kit finished. "In a word, she is…"

"Colin," he and Susannah said at the same time.

Colin looked mock-outraged as the other two laughed heartily. "I beg your pardon!" he said, looking between the two.

Susannah wiped at the tears of mirth. "Oh, Colin, she is your very likeness. Are you sure she isn't yours?"

Kit scoffed loudly and covered his mouth at once.

Colin glowered at them both. "Positive. And that joke is getting really old."

They all continued to watch the children for a bit, when Susannah suddenly noticed something about her son. Not just something, but something rather important and almost shocking as he ran around gleefully with the girls.

"Wait, wait," she said, interrupting whatever Colin had been saying. "What is Freddie wearing?"

The men said nothing.

She looked more closely, and sure enough, he was wearing new clothing, of a far better quality than he had worn since his early days at Pavel House. And not only was he wearing them, he was romping in them. Getting them dirty. Completely at ease in them.

"Where did Freddie get new clothes?" she asked, whirling to face Colin. "How much did you spend on him, Colin? Why would you exert yourself like that? I never intended for you to have to go that far for him, it was enough that he should be tended to, but to provide him with such excesses? Colin…"

"Don't yell at me," Colin said, raising his hands defensively and shaking his head with a smile. "That was entirely Kit."

Susannah turned in surprise to Kit, who was smiling without shame.

"Kit?" she asked softly, completely baffled now.

He shrugged, still smiling. "We couldn't have a pretend Gerrard not matching the real ones, now could we?"

She swallowed with great difficulty. "I will never be able to repay you."

"Who is asking you to?" Colin murmured behind her.

Kit nodded in agreement. "Call it our dues, Susannah. We are happy to do this and more, without question. And without restitution." His last words were said with a very severe look of warning at her.

She could only nod, tears welling in her eyes, her chest beginning to burn with emotion.

Kit smiled and put a hand on her arm, which she covered with her own. Colin encircled her shoulder with his arm and pulled her in close. "Don't cry," he murmured with a soft laugh. "You'll set Bitty off, and then Ginny will cry because Bitty is, and then Rosie will yell, and all hell will break loose."

Susannah managed a watery chuckle and dabbed at her eyes quickly. "I'm sorry," she said, finding a handkerchief suddenly at her disposal. "It's just too much…"

"Stop that," Colin insisted. "You heard Kit, we're happy to do this and more. And you know I always agree when Kit is working in my interest."

They all laughed and continued watching the children until they were exhausted from the game. She met Mrs. Creighton and found her to be far more suited to the eccentricities of the house than any other woman she had ever met. She handled the children, and the grown men, with ease and candor that was refreshing and amusing, and never so much as batted an eyelash when Ginny ducked under the table at luncheon to hide.

"Someone slide her plate down there, if you would be so kind," she had simply asked the others. "She throws the most frightful tempers when she is hungry."

Colin seemed to sense Susannah's awe and amusement, for his eyes met hers with a knowing light on a regular basis. He always seemed to be on the edge of laughter, and she wondered what it had to be like to live in such a joyful place.

The girls themselves were delightful, if a bit overwhelming. Bitty wanted to show her the new song she was learning, but there was no pianoforte yet, at which point she glared viciously at her brothers, who looked sheepish. Rosie animatedly described the book she was currently reading, with some help from Freddie, who seemed to view all of the girls with a wondrous sort of amusement and delight. She had always wanted siblings for her son, but not as things had stood before, and not with his father, or in that life.

But this was perfect for him.

Even Ginny had warmed to Susannah by the end of her visit, sitting on her lap and chattering away as they played with two of her stuffed dolls. She had not needed to see the openly gaping expressions of Ginny's siblings to know that this was a rare thing indeed. And she had nearly cried again when the sweet child yawned and cuddled against her for warmth.

All too soon, it was time to return to Lady Cavendish, and extensive farewells were required, along with a promise for a quick return and a storytelling next time. Colin offered to walk her home, and she was only too delighted to accept the invitation. As charming and warm as she found his family to be, she wanted to have time with him as well. Alone.

"I cannot imagine anyone being so well received by my sisters," Colin praised as they walked. "You were the epitome of a triumphant success!"

Susannah smiled and gave him a wry look. "Oh, I imagine Tibby does better with them than I."

He shook his head immediately. "No, they are fascinated and terrified by Tibby and are more like her puppies than anything else. You were their friend and their playmate and their confidante… Susannah, you were the closest thing they have had to a mother since they lost theirs."

She sighed and had to look up at the sky to avoid tears. "I'm sorry."

"Why in the world are you sorry for that?" he asked, stepping closer so their arms would brush.

"I didn't mean to become so attached." She shook her head, forcing the tears back. "I know how hard it must be for them, adjusting to life here without her, and then to have someone else come in and make things muddled and confusing…"

"Sweetheart, I couldn't be more delighted by what just happened," he gently overrode. "I am glad for it. Beyond glad. And so is Kit, if you could not tell."

She looked up at him with a frown. "No, I'm sure you are wrong."

"I am positive I am right," he insisted. "He has not smiled that much in one day in years. He adores the girls and anything that makes them happy makes him happy. We try our best to fill the gaps in their life, Susannah, but we are two bachelors with no idea of anything much. The cards are stacked against them. You brought light into their day, and we are all desperate for more."

It was too much, too difficult to breathe in the idea of more with him, with them. She exhaled a dry, half sob and put a hand to her chest looking away. Faintly, she wished that Lady Cavendish lived closer, not for nearer proximity to Colin, but for a quicker escape. Her heart could not take these glimpses into a heaven she had craved so desperately her entire life.

"Is it too much?" he asked softly, still too close for her sanity.

She nodded rapidly, her breathing beginning to settle. "I loved every moment of today, Colin. I am sure I won't be so overwhelmed once I get used to it. I just… I never thought I would have this. Even for a day."

Colin groaned and moved to pull her into his arms, but she hastily skittered back, holding up a hand.

"We are in public," she laughed, giving him an apologetic smile. "Though I appreciate the thought."

He looked disconcerted, but he dropped his arms, his hands

becoming fists, and he nodded. "How is life with Lady Cavendish?" he asked, his voice carefully polite as he continued walking.

She smiled in relief, and in amusement. "It's wonderful, now that you mention it. But I am entirely useless to her."

He gave her a look. "I refuse to believe that."

"I'm not being self-deprecating!" she insisted with a laugh. "I mean she literally has no use for me. I see no reason why Lady Cavendish has a need for a companion at all. She has many friends, rarely sits down for more than ten minutes, and is not at all interested in slowing with age."

Colin chuckled. "I should have known that Tibby would have friends just as independent as she is. Do you get to see much of London? The shops, or calls, or anything fun?"

She smiled thinly and raised a brow. "A bit. But we have been a little occupied the last few days. Lady Cavendish is expecting her nephew any day."

Colin slowed his step and exhaled slowly. "Idiot," he hissed to himself. Then he turned his head just enough to look at her. "That would be Miles Cavendish, yes?"

Susannah nodded, biting the inside of her cheek. The sudden tension in Colin was practically visible. He was perfectly coiled, as if ready to fight at a moment's notice. She knew he would not like this, but a sudden mischievous streak had lit her mind, and she wanted to see where it led. "And she is most anxious for me to meet him," she added for good measure.

"You are not to go within twelve feet of that man, do you hear me?" he growled, sending a shiver up her spine.

The order made her twitch slightly, and again she had to crane her neck in response.

Colin did not notice. "It would be entirely improper, Lady Cavendish has to know that. Her nephew… and her companion? No, absolutely not." He shook his head frantically. "I'll tell Tibby, she can talk some sense into her. Difference in station, in fortune, in temperament, everything. Wrong, wrong, wrong…"

Susannah almost gagged at the sudden flash of pain that lit her chest and her throat at his words. He was so fierce and determined, his words harsh and his manner almost violent. She had not expected this reaction from him. He had been so good to her, so thoughtful, and he had said it was all behind him now. But this?

"There is no need to point out the discrepancy," she snapped, putting as much distance between them as possible. "I already did that, I can assure you. And I am well aware of the distance between Mr. Cavendish and myself, I have no expectations or designs."

She turned and started to walk briskly ahead, but he caught her arm.

"Hold on, there," he said roughly, pulling her back. "Come back."

She exhaled sharply and stopped, her lips compressed tightly together. Colin put both hands on her upper arms and bent a little to meet her eyes.

"You know why I am upset, don't you?"

Susannah shrugged and looked away.

He reached out a hand to cup her cheek and turn her face back to his. When she met his eyes again, he smiled and stroked her cheek softly. "Miles Cavendish is a young and attractive man of considerable means, which means he can have any woman in the world. And if he spent five minutes with you, there would be nothing in heaven or hell that would keep him from proposing to you."

Her jaw went slack at his words, and her knees shook as he continued to stroke along her cheek.

"And I just can't let that happen," he admitted, his smile turning curious and warm.

She needed to think clearly, needed to be away from his tantalizing touch. She swallowed hastily and forced a laugh as she stepped back and started walking again. "Don't be ridiculous, Colin. No one would propose to anyone that fast."

"Well..." he said slowly as he followed.

Something in his voice clenched her stomach and she half-turned, but kept walking. "Well what?"

He met her gaze, his eyes clear and bright. "Marry me."

She nearly stumbled backwards and coughed her surprise. "Excuse me?" she managed to get out.

He raised his chin a little higher. "Marry me, Susannah. I've been up most of the night thinking about it, and I want you to marry me."

Her mouth worked without sound, and she stopped to face him completely. "You can't be serious."

"I am serious. Completely."

"Colin," she said in exasperation, wildly looking around for any witnesses. "You can't propose that fast, we just got to know each other again."

He shrugged. "I can if I love you."

All of the air in her lungs rushed out in one breath. "Wh-what?"

Slowly, he shrugged once more, now smiling. "I love you. Again. Still. Always. And I don't see the point in drawing things out."

He could not, *could* not understand what he was asking of her. What he was saying. He couldn't mean any of this, not really. She slowly shook her head. "Colin…"

He took two steps forward and seized her arms. "Tell me you don't love me."

A small, stray fragment of air hitched in her throat. "I…" she choked, her voice disappearing entirely.

"Go on."

She shook her head. "It's too soon. I… I need more time."

He gave her a look. "It's been almost twenty years."

She returned the look coldly. "You know what I mean. We have just barely been friends again, and we were only children before, we did not…"

"Don't," he interrupted. "Don't trivialize what we had. That was as real as anything, and we both know it."

She shook her head, unable to think about that. "And you're ready to marry me already?" she went on, as if he hadn't spoken.

He exhaled in irritation. "People have done so for less."

"We are hardly just any people, Colin." How could he not see that? But she could not walk away from him, not yet. She held her breath, pleading with her eyes for him to understand.

His eyes narrowed a little. "So… no?"

Without breathing, she repeated, "No."

He made a noise of consideration, tilting his head a bit. "More time, you say?"

She nearly wept with her relief. "Definitely," she said, smiling for effect.

He grunted and released her arms, putting his hands on his hips. "All right, I can be patient. But you had better kiss me or I shall think myself actually rebuffed."

Willing and able, and glad to do so, she looked around, then quickly stepped forward and took his face in her hands to give him a brief, but fierce kiss. He smirked against her lips and extended the kiss, lingering. When he had her toes trembling in her boots, he broke off and whispered in her ear, his lips dancing lightly across the skin, "I just want you to be assured that this conversation is far from over."

She shivered as he pressed a light kiss to her ear, no doubt scorching the delicate skin.

Mercifully, he stepped away and laced his fingers with hers, his eyes daring her to deny him. Then he pulled her along and they slowly walked towards Lady Cavendish's house together.

Susannah breathed in her relief with every step they took, feeling both strengthened and weakened by the feeling of his fingers with hers.

That had been too close for comfort.

It was too close for sanity, let alone comfort.

That could not happen again.

And yet… Colin said he loved her. Whether or not that was really true would remain to be seen, he could hardly understand the value or impact of those words as yet. Perhaps he never would. Perhaps the closer he got, the more he would see that she was not fit for him. She couldn't be, not anymore. Not with her past and history, her current troubles and danger.

But for now, this beautiful, extraordinary, maddening dream of hers held her hand and thought he loved her.

She could live with that.

For now.

Much later that night, Colin silently made his way through the dark London streets. The note had arrived, as it always did, with clear and direct instructions, no signature, and no indication of what would come.

It didn't matter. After his missive yesterday, he knew exactly what it was about.

Colin reached the alley he was supposed to, and he leaned against the brick, looking down at his boots, pulling his cap down lower.

He should have known Susannah would have refused him. His proposal had been rash, rushed, and entirely ill-timed. He stood by what he said, he loved her, he wanted to marry her, and he was tired of waiting. But he was not the one who would need convincing that this was right. Susannah had obviously had a hard time of it, and she had every reason to wonder if he was in his right mind.

He needed to court her, prove to her that this was real. He was not reliving his youth at this time, he was very fully and conscientiously in the present. And he loved the woman she was here and now.

And that was what brought him here to this alley in the middle of the London in the dead of night.

Love. And Susannah.

"Care to tell me what business you have with Miss Hart?" asked a familiar yet unfamiliar voice.

Colin sniffed a laugh and looked down the alley, where his companion remained in shadow, as he always was. "Shouldn't that be my question to you?"

He saw the other man shrug. "I have an interest in everybody. Ergo, my letters about your brother and Miss Bray."

Colin considered that for a moment. "Fewer letters of late, there."

"Fewer things to say. Why are they so quiet?"

"Well," Colin sighed, leaning his head back, "Marianne has been surprisingly reserved since that incident with her brother's wife in the winter. She hardly made a peep all Season. I think she is making restitution."

There was a faint snort. "It won't last."

"Never does," Colin agreed.

"And your brother?"

"A bit occupied with our new sisters, I think."

"I heard about that."

Colin grinned and looked in his direction. "Yes, I suppose you would have." He laughed once. "Beyond that, I think there is a problem with one of the estates that has him distracted. Cheshire, I think."

"Yorkshire."

Colin laughed. "Braggart. At any rate, he should be back to normal soon as well. Back to Miss Hart, if you please."

The man laughed softly. "Very well. I happened to meet Miss Hart in London myself a few weeks ago. We've been keeping an eye on her ever since, so you could say I have a personal interest."

"You what?" Colin asked jerking up. "What was she doing? What were you…?"

"I am not here to talk about that," he said brusquely, effectively cutting him off. "There is not time, and it doesn't matter to the present situation. You want me to look into her past?"

Colin did not like being dictated to, nor having his questions dismissed, but considering the man he was dealing with and the potential severity at hand…

"Her real name is, or was, Susannah Merritt. Her family lived near Seabrook in Devon. She was married around the age of sixteen, or so I think, and I do not know who or where, or anything beyond that. But she has a son, Frederick, and he is seven. Also, yesterday she was seen going to visit a Mr. Jacobs, a solicitor for tradesmen in the financial district. I don't know what for."

"And why do you need the information, Gerrard?" There was no accusation in the tone, he was all business, but Colin had enough dealings with the man to know his hints of concern.

"She is in trouble," he said softly. "Possibly a great deal of trouble, and I need to know about it."

There was a faint hum of discontent. "I knew there was something about her, and my men have reported things to me that don't add up. Why haven't you tried to find something out yourself?

You have the resources and the ability."

"I did. Years ago, before I had the resources I do now. And now that I have them, and she is back in my life, I cannot be the one to do it. I can't." He shook his head quickly, and swallowing was difficult. "I need you to do this."

"Are you sure you want to know?" he asked cautiously. "Who knows what I may find."

Colin nodded, swallowing at last. "I know. I am sure."

There was a moment of hesitation. "All right," he said finally. "I'm on it. I will be in touch." He turned to go.

"Gent?" Colin called softly.

He turned only slightly. "Yes?"

"Thank you. For watching out for her."

The Gent gave a light chuckle. "It has been my pleasure. And I mean that this time."

Colin glowered. "I hope you mean that platonically."

He could almost see the suddenly quirked brow. "She's yours, then?"

Colin stiffened and his jaw tensed in defense. "No…"

"So, yes."

He heaved a sigh of resignation. "Yes."

The Gent chuckled heartily and it echoed off the alley walls. "Well played, Mr. Gerrard. Good night."

And as he always did, he disappeared silently into the night, just as he had come.

Colin shook his head with a smile. The Gent was one of his greatest allies, but he never knew what he looked like or who he was beyond that. It didn't matter now, but someday…

He shoved his hands into his pockets and walked home, whistling a jaunty tune to himself.

Perhaps this was high-handed of him, and probably a waste of the Gent's time and abilities. But his motives were sincere, and the information crucial.

Susannah was his.

And he needed to know everything.

Chapter Thirteen

"Colin Gerrard, I do not like secrets being kept from me."

Colin looked up from his breakfast into the flashing eyes of Lady Raeburn, wreathed in emerald green, a matching feather, and a golden brooch so large it was ostentatious. Her eyes narrowed at his lack of immediate response and she tilted her head dangerously.

He cleared his throat and attempted to form thought. "What secrets, my lady?"

When she sniffed indignantly, he tried frantically to remember what he had not told her. He had slept horribly and was only barely conscious now, which meant it was far too early to face her inquisition. He had no strategy and absolutely no defense.

"I saw you walking with Miss Hart yesterday morning, Colin."

He was likely to revisit his partially digested breakfast at any minute.

"You were holding hands in the most intimate of fashions. And neither of you were wearing gloves."

That was it? That was all she saw? His stomach settled noticeably and he could force a smile. "I never wear gloves, Tibby. You know that."

"And her excuse?"

He shrugged. "Perhaps she does not have any. Not all ladies wear gloves, you know."

"The lack of gloves is hardly the important part," Tibby said, sniffing again and raising an auburn brow. "I have eyes, my dear boy, and I know a secret affair when I see it. Believe me, I have been in my fair share."

The urge to be sick flared once more at that thought.

"I will not advertise my findings," she informed him, as if that were a kindness, "because I am just too delighted to see you so deliciously pummeled by any woman, and that was not even my reason for coming to you so early."

"No?" he asked, dabbing at the corner of his mouth with his serviette carefully.

She narrowed her eyes again. "No. I am collecting your sisters and Mrs. Creighton, as you are still incapable of procuring an instrument for them. Really, at this rate, they shall have no accomplishments whatsoever."

"You would never let that happen, Tibby," he commented with a grin. "Take Freddie, too. He would love your house."

Tibby hummed dangerously. "What does Duncan have to say about your little liaison with your ward's mama?"

Colin chose that moment to yawn, stretch, and look at the ceiling with a great deal of interest.

"He doesn't know?"

The floor was also very interesting at the moment. He ought to consider a new rug for it, the old one was a bit worn in places.

"I revise my threat," Tibby said at once.

Colin looked at her immediately. "What threat?" he barked.

Her smile was bordering on the menacing. "You tell Duncan, and the others, about what you have going on. Or I will."

He slowly rose from the table and leaned forward on it. "You wouldn't dare," he murmured.

She matched his pose and expression. "Try me."

"Tibby!" shrieked two very high-pitched voices thundering their way down the stairs.

Tibby gave him a very dangerous warning via the regal quirk of a brow, and turned from the room. "Darlings! Ready to go and make the world sing anew?"

"If Bitty's playing, there will only be squawks of protest," Rosie said in her matter-of-fact way, sending Bitty and Freddie into a fit of giggles.

"Master Frederick, it is lovely to see you again," Tibby said as she smiled down at the lone male in the group.

He bowed, perfectly as always. "Lady Raeburn."

She trilled a bit like a bird. "Sweet boy, you may call me Tibby, as the girls do. Though I applaud your excellent manners and form. Must be that wonderful mother of yours," she added tilting her head slightly to bellow the words to Colin in the dining room.

He fisted his serviette in his hands and forced himself to take a steadying breath. He pushed out of the room and into the entryway where they all stood. The girls grinned up at him, and he nearly smiled back.

"Come on and hug me farewell, then," he grunted, going to his knees.

All of them, even Freddie, hugged him tightly, and Bitty went so far as to kiss his cheek, which instantly smoothed away his agitation.

Mrs. Creighton took Ginny by the hand and smiled down at him. "Nice to see you have the ability to be on your knees, Mr. Gerrard, despite all evidence to the contrary."

Tibby looked at the governess in a whole new light that Colin did not care for at all. Tibby's approval for independent thought and brash speaking was never something he applauded. He got to his feet with a grunt of disgust. "Well, why don't the two of you go off and vaunt my flaws amongst yourselves while you corrupt the children? I'll wait here for my ears to burn."

The women gave him a pitying look and were soon gone with the children in tow.

Colin rubbed the back of his head for a moment, considering what Tibby said. He knew he ought to tell his friends about Susannah; the real story, and they ought to meet her. And then he really ought to tell them that he was in love with her and had asked her to marry him…

Those were fairly important details.

But after everything that he had said and done concerning his friends and love and the like over the years, he would be in for a very rough confession indeed.

He did not want to do it, but he knew better than to tempt Tibby. She would not only carry out her threat, she would expand upon it and worse. If she had her way with it, not only would Duncan know, but all of London as well, and none of them would have the correct details. No, Tibby would create all manner of scandal just for spite and to fan the flames of Colin's reputation, which would mean he would either be forced into marrying Susannah to save them all, or...

He grinned and chuckled. That alone was a tempting enough reason to let Tibby run with it. But he would not go there. Susannah had reasons for her secrecy and discretion; he ought to act with the same decorum. His friends would understand, and, undoubtedly, would be able to help.

After they had finished laughing at him, of course.

He leaned back against the wall with a heavy sigh. "Bartlet!" he called.

For the first time he could recall, he heard the tread of Bartlet's shoes rather than his voice. Colin turned his head at the approaching steps. Bartlet stopped just before him. "Sir?" he asked calmly, expression as devoid of emotion as ever.

His butler sounded fatigued, which had to be distressing, as Bartlet was never anything but perfect. Further proof that life was changing for all of them.

"Bartlet, I need you to send for the troops," Colin said returning his gaze to the ceiling.

He heard Bartlet exhale, but whether it was from relief or irritation, he couldn't tell.

"Very good, sir. And what shall I tell them?"

Colin bit back a smile at the imperious, yet curious tone.

"Tell them they were right."

Bartlet said nothing.

Colin looked over and saw his butler gaping at him. He grinned at the sight. "That should get them running, don't you think?"

Bartlet snapped his mouth closed and cleared his throat. "Indeed, sir." He clicked his heels, and was gone in his usual, vanishing manner.

His friends were even more efficient than he had predicted they would be. Less than thirty minutes after he'd dispatched Bartlet with instructions, all four were in his drawing room, looking as eager as young boys with the prospect of a holiday.

"What," Nathan began with a gleeful note in his voice, "was the meaning of that message?"

Colin sat on the couch behind him and gestured for the rest to do so, but they remained standing. He mumbled a curse under his breath, ran his hands through his hair, and clasped his hands before him. This was going to be more difficult than he thought.

"I… have been dishonest," he started slowly, his palms beginning to sweat.

"Well, there's a revelation," Derek muttered.

Colin ignored both him, and the snickers from someone else. "I never told any of you about it because it was too embarrassing, too painful."

"An embarrassing Colin story I don't know?" Geoff snorted and moved to sit. "I am all ears."

"Shut up," Colin snapped more viciously than he meant, glaring at him.

That stopped Geoff in his tracks and he raised his eyebrows in shock.

Colin swallowed and looked away. "I am going to tell you the story now, late though it is, due to the threat of exposing my status now…"

"Threat?" Nathan asked at once.

"What status?" Duncan broke in, looking suspicious.

Colin sighed. "Tibby thinks she knows something, and maybe she does… it is Tibby, after all. She threatened to tell what she knows if I didn't tell you first."

Duncan made a sympathetic face, and told Colin his suspicion had merit.

"Why didn't you tell us… whatever this is?" Derek asked, gesturing with his hands.

Colin gave him a look. "Would you come forward to you lot with something so personal that it could eviscerate your soul to relive it?"

Four sets of widened eyes met him, but no one said a word.

"Susannah Merritt was a girl I met during my summers at Seabrook," he said, rubbing his face. "We were best friends for those few months at a time, and we wrote back and forth the months we were away. I…" He swallowed harshly and pushed off of the couch, pacing a bit. "I fell in love with her when I was fifteen. Didn't tell her, didn't understand what it even meant at that age, but I knew it. I finally worked up the courage to kiss her when I was seventeen, and that was my first kiss."

"Not Clara Maxfield?" Derek broke in suddenly, looking a little windblown.

Colin shook his head. "Clara was a distraction for the rest of the world. She was obsessed with me and I was content to let her be. I led her on a bit, it was good for my ego and took away the anxiety of Susannah. I never actually kissed her, or did anything else, for that matter. I just let the world think so." He saw their frowns and he added, "I felt horrible about the way I treated her, and apologized a few years ago. She says she enjoyed every minute and knew full well it would go nowhere. She's very happily settled in Kent now, so wipe those expressions off of your faces."

They looked at each other, then back at him.

"The day after I kissed Susannah, she asks to meet me, tells me she is engaged, and vanishes. I didn't know who or when, and I never found out. I never saw her again." He exhaled slowly. "Until… a few weeks ago. I saw her here. In London. That friend that I told you I was helping? The one who needed work? It's her. I've seen her so many times since then, and suddenly it's not enough. None of it is. I cannot do enough, extend myself enough, help her enough. I brought her son into my home because I couldn't think of what else to do."

"Wait, wait," Duncan overrode loudly. "Freddie is her son?"

He nodded and pinched at the bridge of his nose. "And somehow, even though he is the son of the woman I hated bitterly for years, the son of a man I have wished out of existence more than I care to recall… I am growing as fond of him as I am of my sisters. Much longer, and suddenly I'll love him, just as unexpectedly as I found myself loving her."

"Them," Nathan said.

Colin looked at him in confusion.

Nathan's eyes widened. "You… you mean them, right? Your

sisters?"

Colin slowly shook his head. "No, Nathan. No, I mean Susannah. I still do. I never stopped."

Derek fell sideways and had to grip Duncan for balance, Geoff gasped out loud, Nathan's mouth hung open and slack-jawed, and Duncan looked as though lightning had struck him.

Colin smiled slowly, oddly savoring this sight. He shrugged his shoulders and scratched at the back of his neck. "I tried to tell her that when I proposed to her yesterday…"

Derek sank into a chair, staring at Colin in horror, while the others merely maintained their bewildered expressions in a paler shade.

"… but for some reason, she thinks that is a bit hasty," he finished, shaking his head as if he did not understand. "She kisses me with enthusiasm, so I must be rusty in all things finesse. I'll need some help there."

Geoff fumbled for the couch opposite him and sat heavily.

Colin waited a long moment, watching his friends. Then his amusement faded into a somber reality and he sighed. "Look, I know it is hard to believe, considering it's me, and I…"

"Wait, wait, wait…" Nathan interrupted, waving his hand. "So you're… you're in love with her?"

Colin folded his arms across his chest. "Yes," he said simply.

Derek cleared his throat. "You've been in love with her?"

"Yes."

"All these years that we've been friends?" Geoff asked, looking winded.

Colin nodded. "Yes."

Duncan grunted. "And you've never told us."

"Yes."

Nathan had a finger to his lips, and it now pointed directly at Colin. "You have been in love with the same woman for fifteen years, even while the rest of us were falling in and out of love and marrying and having children, and you played the fool and mocked us for the whole of it?"

"Again, yes."

"For heaven's sake, Colin!" he cried out. "Why?"

Colin sighed and winced, but met Nathan's eyes steadily. "Because playing the fool is easier than feeling like one."

They seemed to digest that for a moment, and then Duncan and Nathan took seats as well.

He exhaled slowly, hands on his hips, looked down at his boots, then back up. "I love Susannah. Senseless and wild though it is, I can't deny it. It has always been her. It always will be her. She is... she is the one for me. You all have your one and only. So do I." He swallowed with some difficulty, then he flashed a roguish grin. "And I pride myself on finding mine first."

Geoff cleared his throat. "Technically, Derek was first."

Colin shook his head at once. "No, Derek did not find Kate until much, much later. All he had was Katherine, and nobody was looking for that."

"Excuse me!" Derek cried out as the others broke into laughter.

Colin grinned in earnest, and finally took a chair with them all, feeling lighter than he had in some time. Perhaps things would turn out right after all.

"So, when do we meet her?" Geoff asked as the laughs faded into smiles. "You've been keeping her a secret for so long, now I'm desperate to know what she is like."

"As soon as it can be arranged," Colin said. "But I'll warn you, she won't like it."

"Won't like us?" Derek looked a bit offended.

"Well, that goes without saying," Colin informed him. "Nobody likes you, they simply tolerate you."

Derek snorted and waved a dismissive hand at him.

"No, she won't like the attention." He shook his head. "I haven't figured out why yet, but she is determined to be unnoticeable to anyone or anything. She is hiding from everyone, even me, on occasion. All she wants is to earn money to pay the debts and to see that Freddie is well and safe. Mingling with you lot is likely to put her on display a little, and she'll detest that, no matter how charming you or your wives happen to be."

Nathan hummed in thought. "So we do this carefully, then. You all know Moira, once she gets word of Colin being in love, she will be over here in three seconds, if that."

"Kate, too," Derek agreed with a nod.

"Mary would want to meet Susannah, and find out all of the details of Colin's misspent youth," Geoff pointed out.

"And Annalise will want to adopt her and become instant friends," Duncan said with a sigh. "I won't keep a secret from her, Colin."

"I would never ask you to," he told them all, shaking his head. "I want them to know. I want Susannah to have friends, to know you and your wives. I just think Nathan is right, it will have to be done carefully. She works for Lady Cavendish at the moment, so no grand parties or invitations with other people. It would have to be just us, our families, our women. That's it."

Derek nudged Geoff in the side. "Did you hear that?" he whispered loudly. "Colin said 'our women.'"

"Colin has a woman," Geoff replied, sniggering like a child.

Colin rolled his eyes. "Yes, you are very mature, both of you."

Duncan scoffed. "After what you have put us through over the years, Colin? Please, you have earned this and tenfold more."

He grinned cheekily. "Indeed, I did. And I fooled you all in the meantime."

They each cried out in protest, claiming they knew something at some point, or other nonsense, but Colin knew the truth. They never suspected anything. How could they? He hadn't suspected it himself.

He sat back and smiled with ease. His worries were alleviated for the present time. The Gent was investigating for him, his friends knew all, and his sisters were happy and thriving here with him.

All he needed now was Susannah to be his.

Then he would be content.

"Lady Raeburn to see you, ma'am."

Lady Cavendish looked up from her embroidery in surprise.

"Thank you, Simms," she replied. "Send her up."

Simms nodded and bowed, leaving them again.

Susannah felt her throat tighten in anticipation. Did she stay in the room with the ladies? Should she gather the needlepoint and make herself scarce? She was not prepared to meet Lady Raeburn, not dressed like this, and not without Colin. Lady Cavendish was very good and liked her creditably, but she could hardly give the woman a glowing reference after less than two weeks of work.

Before she could ask what she ought to do, a woman in brilliant green silks was in the doorway of the drawing room, sweeping in grandly as if she were an exotic empress. Her fiery red hair was wrapped in matching green ribbon, and her lips were painted the color of rubies.

"Lady Cavendish," she chirped with a waggle of many ringed fingers.

"Lady Raeburn," the other replied with a knowing smile. "What brings you to my humble abode?"

"You have never been humble a day in your life, my dear, and you know it," Lady Raeburn said with a snort, sitting regally in a nearby chair.

Susannah nearly gaped at the bold frankness of this woman. To speak to Lady Cavendish in such a way was beyond daring, and ought to have earned an affronted reaction. But Lady Cavendish only offered a smile that was as genuine as anything.

"True enough," she admitted. "You are here for gossip, aren't you?"

Lady Raeburn inclined her head in a nod. "Is there ever another reason? I had to hear from my haberdasher that your nephew is coming? Really, I thought we were closer than that…"

Lady Cavendish tittered a little. "It was a surprise, to be sure; I've not had time to tell anyone yet. Miles will be here next Wednesday, and I plan on showing him off in grand style, now he is come back from Brighton. I also have the keenest interest in introducing him to Miss Hart, here," she added, giving Susannah a devious little wink.

Susannah blushed and ducked her chin.

"Indeed?" Lady Raeburn asked, turning to her with interest.

"And how do you like being companion to Lady Cavendish, Miss Hart?"

Susannah looked up into the bright eyes of the woman and stammered out, "It is delightful, Lady Raeburn. I greatly enjoy Lady Cavendish's company and hope I have been of some use to her."

"Essential, my dear child, essential," Lady Cavendish crowed in delight. "It is so much better talking to a person rather than a tapestry, I can assure you. And I think Miles will find her as delightful as I do."

Lady Raeburn pressed her lips into a thin line and glanced in Lady Cavendish's direction. "Did you receive an invitation to Lord Cartwright's soirée? I heard it was to be terribly exclusive, only the essentials of Society will be there."

Lady Cavendish gasped and her hands began to flutter. "I had not heard that! I hardly know, Simms has not brought the cards up."

Lady Raeburn hummed as if that answered the question, and not favorably. "Well, perhaps they overlooked you by mistake."

"I cannot see how," Lady Cavendish sniffed. "No one forgets me. I shall go and check the cards for myself. Excuse me." She rose and hurried from the room.

Lady Raeburn watched her go, then turned to Susannah. "That should occupy her for a few minutes, if not longer. The Cartwrights have only just thought of a soirée, invitations won't go out for a week at least. I have been meaning to speak with you, Miss Hart, for some time now, and I certainly was not about to do so in front of that woman."

Susannah nearly choked on a laugh and looked to the door in shock, but there was no one there. "Me, Lady Raeburn? Whatever for?"

Lady Raeburn smiled broadly. "Because, my dear, I adore your boy, and I like what I hear of you, and I had to know you myself."

"You know Freddie?" Susannah whispered, eyes darting to the door once more. Lady Cavendish had no knowledge of her son, and she wished it would stay that way. "I thought... only the girls were..."

"Do you think I would ignore that sweet boy just because he was not a real Gerrard?" she interrupted gently. "Heavens, no. And let me tell you, Miss Hart, I also adore the grown Gerrards. I am excessively fond of them both, always have been; it is unspeakable, I like them better than my own niece."

Susannah giggled and covered her mouth.

"And I know that Colin is a particular friend of yours," Lady Raeburn continued, "and his sisters were singing your praises this morning at music lessons. As the center of gossip and influence in Society, I could hardly ignore such things. Now I look at you, I see a very pretty young woman with exceptionally good taste, a fine figure, though you could do with more crumpets in your diet, and significant potential."

"Potential for what?" Susannah asked, tilting her head.

"To become my companion."

Susannah gaped openly. "But... but I am already employed. You were so good as to help Colin find me this post, and I am ever so grateful, but I could not do Lady Cavendish the injustice of..."

Lady Raeburn tossed her head in a firm shake. "You most certainly can, it is no injustice to her to give you to me. It is vastly more suitable position, a better house, better wages, comes with a complete wardrobe of new clothing of your choosing, and best of all... your son will live with us."

There was no restraining the gasp that escaped her. "You would... let Freddie live with us?"

Lady Raeburn smiled and took her hand. "I would insist upon it, my dear Miss Hart. At this point, I know him better than you, and I generally never take in strangers, but I am prepared to make an exception, because I have a sneaking suspicion that I will like you very much."

"But..." Susannah sputtered, "but Lady Raeburn..."

"Tibby, my dear, I never stand on formality with my friends unless it proves a point."

She gave her a look of complete exasperation. "Tibby, then. It is too much!"

"Well, why should that stop either of us?" Tibby huffed. "I usually have too much, and it has done me a world of good. I insist upon having you, Miss Hart, but I shall not force you. I can promise you this, however," she looked back at the door, then leaned forward.

"I will give you a far better situation myself than what you have here. When you tire of me, I can give you reference and recommendations beyond your wildest dreams. Think of the possibilities, and to have your boy with you all the time. I will find the best tutors for him, and give him any opportunity you wish. And I certainly have better taste in men for you than Eloise Cavendish and the record to prove it. What do you say?"

Susannah only thought for a moment. "I accept. Provided Lady Cavendish will not be too upset."

Tibby grinned in a manner that was too devious for words. "Oh, I will see to it she is not. It shall be her idea, and no doubt the first good one she has ever had. Give me a few days, and I shall make it so. Not a word to Colin, you understand? Not until it is done."

She did not like the idea of secrecy, particularly not when it involved Colin directly. There was no telling what he would do when he found out. But surely he would be happy for her. And he adored Tibby; he had told her himself.

And to be with Freddie… that she craved most of all.

She smiled at Tibby and sat back. "You really are as devious as Colin says, aren't you?"

Tibby matched her pose. "Worse, darling. Far worse. He has no idea what I am capable of."

Chapter Fourteen

Tibby was better than her word. Within the space of one week, Lady Cavendish had given Susannah over to Tibby, which allowed for a very quick and efficient relocation of Susannah, and ultimately Freddie, to Tibby's home in Hanover Square, which had caused some tears from the children, and the promised new wardrobe had been ordered, fitted, and delivered. It had been a bit of a blur, but now, at last, they had settled into a rhythm of normalcy that set Susannah quite at ease.

She still did the odd work for the kind modiste, Mrs. Randall, in her free time and was getting to have so much work there that it would supplement Tibby's generous payment quite well.

She would need all the funds she could get. Her recent meetings with her solicitor, Mr. Jacobs, revealed that her family was not doing well at all and were growing nearly as desperate as she was, and she cursed their inability to properly manage funds. Mr. Goulding was not much of a comfort either, as her visit with him the other day only disclosed that the creditors were growing vastly impatient with all of the waiting and no significant payments. He feared she would be in danger if she did not produce money soon.

He, obviously, had no idea that she had already been nearly attacked four times.

Neither did Colin, nor would he ever.

The Gent's contacts had helped her three of the four times, and she had saved herself the last, her slight frame and quickness making disappearing into the bustling crowds far simpler than it would have been otherwise. They always had caught her at different points, never lying in wait outside of either solicitor's office or near her favorite shops. There was no rhyme or reason or pattern to their sudden appearances, which made avoiding them impossible.

She would have to be more careful, now she was further from the dirty and crowded heart of the city.

Freddie had adjusted well to his new home here, though he missed the girls and Mrs. Creighton, as well as Colin and Kit, very much. For that reason, he still continued lessons with Mrs. Creighton and there was a specific play time every day, either at the Gerrard home, at Tibby's, or at some other location outside of them. Only yesterday they had all gone to the home of the Marquess of Whitlock to meet the young Lady Helena, now two months in age, and a beautiful addition to her family. The girls had been understandably delighted by the infant, while Freddie was more content to entertain the only slightly older Earl of Lambert, otherwise known as Harry.

Susannah would never get used to moving in circles with a marquess and an earl and the like, nor wiping the tears of a very small earl, despite being in possession of a title herself. But it was not the same thing by any stretch. These men were good and honorable and kind, while anyone her husband had brought around...

Well, there was no comparison.

She hadn't wanted to know Colin's friends personally, but he had insisted and so she bore it. The men were altogether too pleasant, too friendly, and too attractive for the appropriate distance, which was as maddening as it was entertaining. And their wives were worse. They had descended upon Susannah in droves when she had first met them last week, and already they were the closest female friends she had ever had.

Mr. Bray's wife Annalise was, perhaps, her favorite, as she was more reserved than the others and was far less intimidating. Lady Whitlock and Lady Beverton were very bold, but delightful, and Mrs. Harris was charming and warm, but with the sort of grace that spoke volumes of her character. Annalise was softer and gentler than the lot, and from what she had learned in the last few days, her past and upbringing had been the stuff of nightmares. Only recently had she embraced the life of Society, but still she clung to her friends and her husband for assurance and comfort.

It did not escape Susannah that the lady of smallest stature and personality had the husband with the one of the largest and most intimidating personas she had ever encountered. The strong connection between the two was palpable and, though neither spoke of it or were particularly demonstrative, all could feel its intensity. Once she had caught them staring at each other from across a room, and it rather felt as if she had invaded the most intimate of moments.

And then there was Tibby.

Tibby was the single most magnificent woman Susannah had ever met. She spoke frankly, acted independently, and gave generously, all to a fault, except there was no fault in anything she ever did. She was above all criticism and negativity, and she never listened to anything anyone protested. She adored that Colin's friends and their wives had adopted Susannah, tsked audibly when Susannah chose simple garments instead of finer ones, and actually attempted to make her feel useful, which was more than Lady Cavendish had done. Yet Susannah still suspected that Tibby had no more need for a companion than she did a golden hat stand, though she would not be surprised if there was one of those hiding in a closet somewhere in the house.

But Tibby allowed Susannah anything she wished, even the simpler dresses, though she did insist on a very fine quality, and Susannah was just selfish enough to want that for herself as well. Tibby adored Freddie beyond anything he had ever received from her own family, and she had even seen them holding hands and skipping down the gallery two days ago after luncheon.

Her one sanity and stability in all of this had been Colin. He had not been at all upset when Tibby's plan was revealed. In fact, he delighted in it, and had been her staunchest supporter. He saw her every day without fail, regardless of when the children gathered, and sometimes multiple times. He had said no more about love or marriage, but he had been doting on her with looks and smiles, touching her hands, her shoulder, her cheek, and stealing a kiss whenever he could. She felt like a young girl in the bloom of first love, anticipating every moment with feverish delight. He was spoiling her with presents and attention, and she was beginning to worry at how much his little gifts had cost. She'd already been forced into dealing with one man's squandered finances, she could not endure seeing that again, and certainly not from Colin. But he never worried, always soothed her nerves, and brought her smiles and laughter that chased away the secret shadows of her mind.

She was living in a fantasy world, and it was a heady thing indeed.

"My goodness, you are a long way away."

Susannah looked up suddenly into Annalise's kind face as she watched her over her teacup. She smiled and lifted her own cup, having momentarily forgotten her friend in her reflections. "I'm sorry," she murmured after a small sip. "Just reflecting."

Annalise smiled and set her cup down. "Yes, I can imagine you have done that quite a lot lately."

Susannah nodded and put hers down as well, though it rattled.

"There is no need to apologize, you know," Annalise murmured, her green eyes soft. "I remember what it was like to be thrust into this life. It is quite taxing."

Susannah sighed and relaxed a bit. "Yes, very. I'm still trying to catch my breath."

Her companion's smile turned wry. "Tibby takes some getting used to."

That drew a smile from her. "Indeed, she does. How did you do it, Annalise?"

"Well, I didn't really have much of a choice," she replied, pushing a golden curl behind her ear. "Tibby quite took over my life; I was a little puppet for her until I found my feet. But she was a most skilled puppeteer and I loved every minute of it," she added hastily, her eyes taking on a hint of panic.

Susannah patted her hand. "I know exactly what you mean. She is extraordinary. I adore her."

Annalise smiled with relief. "She truly is, and I love her dearly. And I had some help, you know. Duncan was always there with me, ensuring my comfort and helping me find my way. And Marianne, of course, was essential."

Susannah frowned as she thought back to Colin's descriptions of each family. "Marianne is Mr. Bray's sister, yes?"

Annalise's gaze suddenly sharpened. "Yes. What have you heard of her?"

Susannah shook her head. "Not much, beyond her great beauty and popularity. Also that she was apparently unwell this Season."

A small, sad smile flickered on her friend's face. "No, she was not unwell, only more reserved. She had a trying time with my venture into Society, and then the events leading to my marriage…" She sighed and took a biscuit. "She is a complicated woman, with more heart than she would dare let anybody know, but I love her all the same."

Susannah offered what she hoped was a reassuring smile. "I shall remember that, Annalise."

Annalise tilted her head a bit, her complexion enhanced by the rich cream gown she wore. "You know, you may call me Annie, if you like. I don't feel the need to stand on ceremony with you, for some reason, and it's far easier to say."

That took Susannah so by surprise that she gaped.

Annalise giggled. "When you look at me that way, I feel as though I have done something worthy of Moira or Kate."

Susannah snapped a grin in place. "I cannot picture that for you."

She shrugged, still laughing. "Give me time, you never know. Although that would terrify Duncan." She actually seemed to consider that for a moment, then shrugged again. "Ah, well. I mean it, though. Call me Annie."

"Very well, then," Susannah replied, her smile fading into sincerity. "Annie. I wish I had something I could share with you in return, but…"

Annalise waved her hand impatiently. "No matter." She looked her over briefly, then smiled. "You are looking very well. That gown suits you perfectly."

Susannah looked down at the simple blue muslin and her cream shawl, and she adjusted it slightly. "I'm afraid that Tibby was disappointed that I did not want something more elaborate, but I couldn't do it."

She looked up at Annalise to find her biting her lip.

"What?" she asked suspiciously.

The corners of Annalise's mouth quirked. "If Tibby disapproved of your simplicity, and still let you do as you wished, it would only be because she is doing something behind your back. She will have her way, you know, at least once. You might as well accept it and embrace it now."

Susannah gaped again. "But… but I am her companion! And I don't wish to be over-trimmed or ridiculous!"

Now Annalise took her hand and rubbed it soothingly. "She would never make you ridiculous. She actually has quite the eye for fashion and keeps your tastes in mind. But your being her companion is not going to stop her. I was less than that, and she sent me to a ball."

A cold sweat threatened to break out on her forehead and palms, while a sudden tightness seized her chest. Surely Tibby wouldn't do that to her, not without warning. She could not have expensive things, or be forced out into Society. It would ruin her, and ruin everything.

She opened her mouth to say more, but the sounds of little girl voices were suddenly heard from the hall and little feet were dashing about.

The door to the salon was thrown open as three little girls raced into the room and went straight to Susannah and Annalise, gleefully bouncing up and down and chattering wildly about everything that had occurred since they had seen her the day before. Rosie had found a book of fairytales from when Colin and Kit were small and had been reading it ever since. Bitty was gleeful about conquering a piece of music, and Ginny's favorite doll had torn a seam, which could be easily mended.

"Yes, darling," she soothed, cupping the girl's face. "I will mend it, not to worry."

Ginny nodded once, then went over to Annalise and settled herself into her lap.

Susannah and Annalise bit back smiles as they exchanged a look. Ginny might not be as vocal as her sisters, but she had more than her measure of the same will.

"Where is Mrs. Creighton?" she asked Bitty, now sitting beside her.

Bitty helped herself to a biscuit and shrugged as she munched on it.

"Mrs. Creighton has today off," a warm voice drawled from the doorway.

Susannah looked up to find Colin leaning casually against the doorframe, cravat loosened, crooked grin in place. And his eyes on her might well have been fire for the effect on her skin. He was far too attractive as it was, but when he looked so easy and unaffected, and his eyes held such intensity? Breathing seemed fairly unimportant under such circumstances.

"What have you two been doing today?" he asked, as if he were speaking only to her.

Susannah flicked her gaze to Annalise and found her watching her with far too much interest. She struggled to swallow as she felt her cheeks flame, returning her gaze to Colin. "Oh, this and that. Annie and I have just been chatting, and…"

Colin straightened very suddenly, hands on his hips, glaring at Annalise.

Susannah stopped talking in disbelief, and found Annalise surprisingly unmoved by Colin's apparent distress.

"Why does *she* get to call you Annie and I have to call you Annalise?" he asked, or rather demanded, pointing at Susannah.

"Colin," Susannah said, smiling just a touch, "it would hardly be proper for you to call her…"

"Only my particular friends may call me Annie," Annalise broke in gently, as if Susannah hadn't spoken.

Colin huffed and folded his arms. "And I am not your particular friend?"

Annalise giggled lightly. "Not yet," she replied, smiling fondly at him.

He narrowed his eyes and pointed at her. "I will get there, Mrs. Bray. Mark my words."

She gave a slight tilt of her head at him. "I look forward to it."

Colin finally smiled, laughing softly and relaxing entirely.

Annalise wrinkled her nose in a hint of a laugh and returned her attention to Ginny in her lap and Rosie at her side.

Susannah had watched the exchange with interest, wondering at the warmth between them. It spoke of sincere friendship, and the gentle sparring was like the interactions she had seen with Colin's other friends and their wives, although much subdued by comparison. And Annalise had rarely participated in the sparring there, though she had been willing enough just now. Colin could be an overwhelming man in his charisma, but Annalise showed no fear or trepidation. She trusted him enough to open up, and that said volumes about the man that Colin was, despite what he showed the rest of the world.

"Where's Freddie?" Rosie asked around a mouthful of biscuit, smiling as Annalise handed her a serviette for her crumbs.

"With the tutor," Susannah told her. "You were a bit early, he should be finished soon."

"What tutor?" Colin asked suddenly.

Susannah gave a soft moan of apprehension. Colin hadn't been told about Mr. Townsley yet, and she'd just blurted that out like anything. This was neither the time nor the place to discuss it, but there was nothing for it now. And he would not like it. "His new tutor. He… started yesterday."

Colin gave her a searching look that was far too thorough. "A young man?"

She swallowed hastily. "Not too young. Perhaps thirty. He is a scholar from Oxford, and Tibby said he came very highly recommended."

"Tibby said that," he commented, his eyes tightening just a touch, though his expression remained blank. There was something in his voice she did not trust, and she bit her lip at the sudden tension she felt.

"And is he a handsome, not-too-young scholar from Oxford that came so highly recommended?" he asked, his voice dipping lower.

Susannah looked at Annalise quickly, and her wide eyes were full of warning.

"Yes," Susannah murmured softly as she bent her head closer to Bitty. "I daresay he is."

Brisk footsteps exited the room and she exhaled in relief as she looked up to find him gone.

"What was that about?" Annalise asked as she helped Rosie break a biscuit for Ginny.

Susannah only shook her head, exhaling slowly once more.

"Any idea where he went?"

She bit her lip again, and winced. "Tibby," was all she said.

"Why did you bring that man here?" Colin demanded as he barged into the sitting room where Tibby sat.

She looked up at him through gold-rimmed spectacles, open book in her lap, one brow raised. After a very long moment of staring at him, she removed the spectacles from her nose and said, "My dear boy, you are going to have to be more specific than that."

He was in no mood for her games. "You know perfectly well who I am talking about," he snapped.

She pursed her lips and closed her book, setting it on the table near her. "From your shocking rudeness, I can only assume you mean the very intelligent and charming Mr. Townsley. A most delightful gentleman. And so very tall!"

"I could care less about the scarecrow's perch," he snarled coming over and setting his fists on a table near her. "Why is he here?"

Tibby tilted her lace-capped head to give him an incredulous look. "To teach Freddie, of course. Why else would I hire a tutor? I can assure you, my personal tastes are not so scholarly."

He slammed an open hand on the table. "Stop making light of this. Why wasn't I informed of a tutor coming in for my ward?"

She snorted and her eyes turned cold. "Mr. Townsley happens to be one of the leading scholars in London, highly respected and very hard to come by. You should be grateful I was able to snap him up."

He gawked at her for a moment, his mouth working. "Grateful?"

he managed. "That a young and apparently handsome idiot is floating around your house who knows how often and…"

"He is helping Freddie to prepare for when he goes to school," Tibby overrode, putting out a hand as if to stop his words herself. "Mrs. Creighton has told me that while Freddie is quite brilliant in many respects, the girls outstrip him in some areas. All I am doing is helping, which, by the way, you asked me to do." Her cold eyes turned less so as she looked him up and down, and a corner of her mouth ticked. "The fact that Mr. Townsley is young and handsome, and remarkably available, not to mention quite perfectly suited for my new companion is merely advantageous."

His brows snapped together and he curled his fingers into a fist. She was teasing him, playing him, and he knew it. Worst of all, it was working. He was in a rage, jealous beyond expression, and barely reigning in his control. He hissed a breath through clenched teeth. "Tibby, you are meddling."

She gestured faintly with the spectacles she still held. "Well, of course, I am. That is what I do."

He would have laughed had he not still been seething. "Stop."

Tibby actually looked surprised for a moment, and her hands moved to her hips. "Stop? Colin Gerrard, when have you ever known me to take orders from anyone?"

He looked down at his fist and uncurled his fingers one by one as his anger started ebbing into a grumpy irritation. "Never," he muttered.

She sniffed once. "Exactly. And I do not mean to start now."

He shook his head and clenched his jaw. "Tibby…"

"What?" she asked with a bit of a bite to her tone. "What exactly do you protest, Colin? And why?"

He felt a muscle tick in his jaw. He stared at Tibby with a surprising amount of hardness, his mind conjuring all sorts of rebuttals for her extraordinary lecture, none of which he could bring himself to verbalize. He could not explain himself to Tibby, not really, and not to the extent he should.

He understood Duncan's complaints of her all too well now. And the helpless devotion that followed.

"Townsley can tutor Freddie," Colin said slowly.

"Thank you," Tibby said drily, her lips quirking.

He ignored that. "But he is to have nothing to do with Susannah. I mean it."

"They have to interact, Colin." Tibby had suddenly gained a very suspicious gleam in her eye. "Freddie is her son."

"Does he know that?"

She nodded once. "He also knows to keep it quiet. I would hardly hire an idiot I could not trust. And I have no plans of setting him with Susannah. I am no matchmaker, she is free to make her own decisions."

And that was what frightened him. Being with Colin would be a complicated affair for her, given the past and their current situation. Some fresh young scholar who had ties to her son would be a convenient solution, and Colin could not be here constantly to ensure that he was in her thoughts and in her heart. She received his attentions with pleasure, but seldom returned them. She was carefully staying within restrictions that he would have torn aside but for his determination to win her by patience.

The lack of information from the Gent as yet was frustrating, but so long as he minded his time with her and did not press further than she would allow, he would be safe.

Susannah was not about to reveal things to him on her own; she was too proud and stubborn for that. And heaven help him, it was one of the things he loved most about her.

Tibby gave a soft clearing of her throat and smiled genuinely when he met her eyes at last. "There's a story here…"

He shook his head, exhaling a heavy sigh. "Not yet, Tibby. Not now."

She lifted one brow. "I have eyes, darling. You don't have to tell me anything."

He was afraid of that. He pointed a finger at her. "Keep Susannah away from him."

"I am not her keeper. I won't push, but I will not pull either." And by the firmness of her stance and the determined set of her jaw, he knew the conversation was over.

He shook his head and grudgingly gave her half of a smile. "I love you, Tibby. You know that. But right now, I hate you."

Her lips twitched and she shrugged. "Love and hate are two lines on the same palm. You'll thank me later."

He snorted and moved around the table towards her. "Provided I don't kill you, right?" He leaned down and kissed her on the cheek.

She patted his chest fondly. "That is a risk, yes."

He smiled in earnest now and turned to leave the room, then looked back over his shoulder. "Gold-rimmed spectacles, Tibby? Really?"

She tittered in her usual manner. "I was not about to let fading eyesight turn me into an old woman. Very fashionable, yes?"

He shook his head with a chuckle and went back to the girls. He wanted to walk with Susannah for a while. He wanted to do a great many things with her, but for now, a walk would suffice.

Thankfully, the girls had already gone off to collect Freddie and play, with Annalise volunteering to mind them for the time being. Susannah took very little convincing to take a stroll, and he was thrilled with that. Her color was heightened, and her figure looked healthier than he had seen her yet. Still too thin for his taste, but it was progress. And she smiled so easily now, each one catching in his chest.

"Are you all right?" she asked softly as they left the house, still tying her bonnet ribbons.

He shook his head and fought for calm. "No. But I am better than I was." He looked over at her and felt the tightness in his chest loosen. "I am much better now."

She opened her mouth to say something, but then only smiled and took his arm. "Bitty tells me you've finally procured a pianoforte for them."

He shook his head. "Yes, and the monstrosity has taken over the whole of the house. It will never be a quiet place again."

Susannah laughed softly and squeezed his arm. "You have three little girls living there, Colin. It was never going to be a quiet place again regardless."

He smiled at that. "Very true. Bitty is delighted by it. I think she

165

will be our musical one, though I fear she has a long way to go."

"She was telling me about it, how pretty it is and the carvings on it…" Susannah hesitated, and Colin watched her, transfixed by the play of emotions on her face. "Colin, why did you spend so much on it? You could have easily purchased a simple one. I know they have shops in the city for it. There was no need to be extravagant."

He gave her a searching look when her eyes met his. "I wanted a quality instrument for them, one that would last for ages and that they would want to perform on one day. That sort of thing costs more, and I have the funds for it, so why shouldn't I have given them the best?"

She gave a short sigh and shook her head. "Forgive me, I am in no position to judge."

"You're forgiven, of course," he assured her, reaching into his pocket. "In fact…"

He pulled out the locket he'd purchased for her and dangled it in front of her face.

She gasped and looked up at him, curiously upset. "What? Why would you do that?"

He reared back a bit in surprise. "Do what? Buy you a pretty trinket?"

"Yes!" she screeched, pulling away from him. "Colin, you can't just keep buying me things! You spend too much money! You buy expensive pianofortes for your sisters, you buy me dresses, you bribe shopkeepers to interview me, you buy my son clothes…"

"Kit did that," he interrupted hastily, though he had no defense for the others, as they were true.

"…and you are constantly buying me things I don't need!" she rambled, throwing her hands up. "I can't see how you can afford any of this and maintain your usual lifestyle. Colin, tell me the truth: are you a spendthrift?"

He widened his eyes as he saw the real concern and fear in her eyes. "A spendthrift?" he echoed faintly. "Why should you…?" He trailed off as realization dawned. "Your husband mismanaged money."

She folded her arms grumpily. "He didn't manage money at all.

It went out faster than it came in. He threw it away and he was constantly buying things we didn't need with money we didn't have. He gambled all the time, badly and recklessly, and there was nothing anyone could do about it. He ruined us, Colin. Beyond any hope of repair. So I need you to tell me if you are going to go the same way."

He considered her words carefully and took a moment. Then he took a measured step towards her. "I am not a spendthrift. I do not spend money recklessly, though I do spend it. I know exactly where every farthing is going at all times. Kit and I learned a lot from our father, not the least of which were mistakes to avoid. We have each made some very lucrative investments and have several estates in the country that we manage in Loughton's absence. I have far more money than anybody thinks and I do that intentionally so no one will suspect. I am careful with my money, Susannah. And I never gamble. Well," he amended with a small smile, "almost never. But I'm smart there, and very good at it."

She did not return his smile as she searched his eyes with a slight sense of panic.

He put his free hand on her upper arm. "I do not waste money. Ever. Everything has a point, place, and purpose. Including my gifts to you. So please, will you take the locket now?" He held it up for her to examine again, swinging it just a little.

She bit her lip, her eyes finally darting to it. One side of her mouth began a slow, almost imperceptible curve, and he almost grinned. She wanted it. Despite her argument, she wanted the pretty little trinket.

He chuckled and turned her around, draping the locket around her neck and fastening it for her. Too tempted by her skin, he stroked two fingers along her nape and she shivered, then turned to face him, her eyes scolding.

He grinned and shrugged unrepentantly. He would not apologize for wanting her.

Susannah took his arm once more and tucked a pleased smile into her cheeks as they commenced their walk once more. She inhaled the brisk air and looked around at the trees, now changing color with the fading temperatures. She leaned against him slightly with a sigh.

"Don't you just love London in autumn?"

He smiled down at her. "Not particularly."

She pulled back and looked up at him, laughing. "What? Why not?"

He shrugged and made a face. "I hate London."

Her step slowed and her brow puckered adorably. "You love London. You live here. You've always lived here, you said so yourself."

He hadn't intended to reveal this yet, or perhaps ever, but now it was upon him, he'd see it through. He held her gaze steady. "We always said we'd meet again in London."

She stopped completely, her eyebrows nearly to her hairline. "Wait..." she said slowly. "You... you're not saying..."

He smiled softly and turned to face her completely. "I love autumn. In the country. I have not really seen an autumn in the country in almost fifteen years. I have spent those fifteen years in London, or travelling from place to place, but mostly, I was in London. Waiting. Hoping. Wishing that we would truly meet again in London."

"But..." she stammered, shaking a bit, "but you couldn't know..."

He shrugged one shoulder. "I didn't care. I loved you." He stepped forward and cupped her face in his hands, despite their being in public. "I love you. And right now, you are in London in the autumn. I love *you* in London in the autumn. But I would love winter, spring, or summer in London so long as you were there."

Susannah stared at him for what seemed an age, not moving save for the slight tremor coursing through her. Then suddenly, she took one of his hands and pulled him quickly from the street to the side of a building, beyond where wandering eyes would see. She went up on tiptoe and laced her fingers behind his head, and pulled him down for a kiss that was slow, long, and maddeningly delicious. He wrapped his arms around her and pulled her closer, wondering faintly when he would get used to this thrilling rush of pleasure he found in her, the effect she had on him, the growing need he felt for her.

Never, he decided as her hold tightened on him, her fingers curling into his hair just enough. He would never get used to it. And there was nothing at all wrong with that.

Chapter Fifteen

"*A* musical evening? But she's not at all musical, she said so herself."

Colin chuckled and leaned back on his hands in the grass. He looked so easy out here behind Tibby's house in the garden, jacket off, cravat loosened, hair tousled. It might have been his house instead of Tibby's. In fact, if it weren't for the fact that Mr. Townsley was chatting with Mrs. Creighton on the terrace, they might well have been at Colin's.

Susannah smiled faintly and was tempted to push a lock of his hair out of his face. But the children were playing not far away, and Mrs. Creighton was directly facing them.

"Tibby loves music, despite her lack of ability," Colin said on a sigh, bringing her back to the conversation at hand. "She hosts one or two of these soirées a year and they are a favorite for all. Except for the year she invited Isabelle Compton to sing." He shuddered dramatically. "My ears have never been the same."

Susannah still felt a faint clutch of nerves in the pit of her stomach. "But... why would she want me there? I'm just her companion, I'm not supposed to associate with society."

Colin gave her an incredulous look, half of his mouth curved up. "Do you think Tibby actually pays attention to conventions, Susannah? She defies them with flare. And she wants you there because she likes you, sweetheart."

As always, the endearment from his lips caused a warm tingle somewhere in the base of her spine. She fingered her locket with one hand, the cold metal on her skin a constant reminder of Colin's warmth. She had not removed it even once since he gave it to her three days ago, and she didn't think she ever would. She had long given up the idea of distance between them. How could she distance herself from the man she loved more than life? He was everything to her, always had been and now and forevermore would be. She might never have him, her past was too muddled and murky for him to become involved in; and knowing his penchant for heroism, he would fully invest himself in solving every one of her problems, and that she absolutely could not allow.

So long as he never proposed again, she would always have him.

But he would propose again.

And it would all be over when he did.

She glanced over at Mrs. Creighton and Mr. Townsley, completely absorbed in conversation and not minding them at all. Slowly, she moved the hand on the grass towards Colin, not stopping until their hands were touching, little fingers overlapping.

His skin was hot to the touch, and his sudden change in breath told her everything she needed to know.

"I like Tibby, too," she said, pretending as though there was not a fire building between their hands, "but I hardly think I need to be there."

Colin swallowed and curved his finger enough to interlock with hers. "No one refuses Tibby, especially not an invitation. And she is not making a grand spectacle of it, just a few friends. Nathan and Moira, Derek and Kate, Geoff and Mary, Duncan and Annalise, Marianne, me, Kit… Perhaps Miss Arden, Miss Templeton, Lord Blackmoor, Thomas Granger, maybe even the Beckhams, if she's feeling adventurous."

Susannah gave him a wry look. "And that's just a few friends?"

Colin snorted. "You should see the spring musicale at the beginning of the Season. Packed in so tightly you can't breathe unless you're fortunate enough to have an end seat."

Susannah shook her head slowly, wondering what it would be like to enjoy such a plethora of friends.

"Maybe even Lady Cavendish and that rather charming nephew of hers will be invited," Colin said with a grin, his little finger sliding along hers in a faint caress.

Susannah rolled her eyes and laughed. "After what you went through about poor Mr. Townsley? I had better write to Lady Cavendish to warn him off."

Colin glowered just a bit as he looked back at the man in question.

"You probably should apologize to Tibby," she prodded gently. He shook his head at once. "No, absolutely not. I have never apologized to anyone and I will not start with Tibby."

"You apologized to me," she murmured softly.

He froze and a soft smile appeared on his face. "True," he murmured, caressing her finger again, "but I love you. That's the difference."

She swallowed the lump that had formed and had to look up at the sky to blink back her tears. "You're not supposed to say things like that to me."

"Well, who else should I say them to?" he asked with a warm chuckle. "I've loved you since I was fifteen years old, and that's not something I take lightly."

She swallowed and exhaled slowly. "You said before that you accept that I did what I had to do when I... that day I left."

"So I did, and I still do."

Susannah opened her eyes and looked at him, his face taut, but his eyes warm. She fought for control and removed her hand from under his. She couldn't touch him when she talked about this. She angrily swiped at the remaining tears and murmured, "I couldn't even cry that day. My parents found out about us, you see, and... They knew your family's reputation as it stood in those days. And they..."

"Susannah, don't."

"They made me agree to a marriage of their choosing," she said, her voice dangerously shaking. "I was supposed to send you a letter, but I... I had to see you."

"Susannah..."

She bit her lip and looked at the sky. "I was cold and brusque, because I couldn't do it otherwise. I was shaking with terror on the inside. And then when I left... When I left, I wanted you to call after

172

me. I wanted to look back for one last look at you, but I couldn't turn around. I couldn't do that to myself. Or you." She glanced over at him, and he still watched her steadily. "Why didn't you call after me?"

Slowly, he shook his head. "I couldn't," he said softly. "I couldn't even move."

Susannah's eyes filled with tears as she held his gaze. "I'm so sorry," she whispered.

Colin reached over and took her hand, squeezing it tightly. "Don't," he said, his voice low and raspy. He brought her hand to his lips and held it there for a long moment. "Don't," he murmured again as his lips brushed her skin.

She reached out and pushed back his hair a little, letting her fingers trail along the side of his face. He leaned into her touch, his eyes still on her.

It would have been the perfect time for her to tell him that she loved him. She could feel the fire burning in her veins, the faintest hint of tingle in her lips, the words rising up within her chest.

But that was where they stayed.

And all she did was sigh and nod once.

Colin generally did not enjoy Tibby's musical events. Oh, he could admire fine musical talent and certainly there were moments of great genius, such as Mary's stunning performance a year and a half ago. She'd set the room aflame and even Colin had considered calling on her after that, but it had quickly faded back into normalcy.

What he hated generally were the people that thought themselves so very capable of performing when they were absolutely anything but. Tibby had learned from the events in the past and now only those who had been invited by her specifically were permitted to perform. Suggestions could be made, of course, but she had final approval.

It was her way of ensuring that she would reign supreme at her own event.

And then there was the parading of young ladies who had only come to feign an interest and snag a husband, the gentlemen who came to find talented potential wives, and the older women who could only croak and fawn about the days when they were performing at such events.

Society as a whole was idiotic, and when one threw music into the mix, it only got worse.

Tonight's event was destined to be better, though. Tibby had kept the list remarkably short, it being well into autumn and many families having left London. As he looked around the room, he thought he could enjoy it immensely. Everybody here was a friend of his, in one way or another, and while he was generally thought of as being the most affable and pleasant of fellows, and a friend to all, the truth of the matter was that it was a select few indeed that he would have put into that category.

Another benefit from the small numbers was the more casual attire they were permitted to wear. Instead of the grander set of clothing he would have worn for her usual musicale, or a ball, he had simply donned some fine evening wear, and all the other gentlemen were dressed similarly. The women looked well indeed, but a more reserved sort of fashion than London generally saw from them at an event.

It was perfectly suited for Susannah, though she sat relatively off on her own. Moira and Annalise had been speaking with her while Kate and Mary had gone into another room to prepare for their turns at performing when they were inevitably invited. He would have liked her to also become acquainted with Miss Arden, who was an unassuming, sweet tempered girl with a furious skill for the pianoforte, though she did not sing at all. But she, too, was preparing for the evening. Perhaps later, at one of the intervals, he might make the introductions.

Susannah simply had to accept that her position had very little to do with who she could be friends with.

He sighed a little to himself as he looked at her now, as she smiled at something Moira had said. Susannah was lovely, in every respect, and the gown she wore tonight only heightened the richness of her complexion, and its pale green color accented the green of her eyes to a maddening degree. She was bewitching and he was only grateful that she would not be prevailed upon to participate tonight. If his memory served him, and it usually did, she was a talented musician and vocalist, and though his taste for music was middling at best, he would have been caught in a tide of emotions and impulses that he was not entirely certain he had the strength to combat.

"Stop that, you'll make a scene."

Colin turned to find Derek standing nearby and grinning at him a bit like a wolf.

Colin snorted and gave him a look. "Oh, and you were so reserved when Kate was looking pretty?"

"I didn't know you thought my wife was pretty," he replied as he came to his side. "She'll be delighted to hear it."

Colin shook his head and returned his gaze to Susannah.

"She is looking very well, indeed," Derek told him. "Not half so gaunt as she was, and her color is improved."

Colin nodded, though he thought Derek's words a pale comparison to what she was.

Derek watched him for a moment, then chuckled and clapped him on the shoulder. "You are a lovesick loon, my friend."

The doors to the music room opened and Kate and Mary entered, followed, rather grandly, by Tibby, to polite applause. Colin glanced over, then looked at his friend. "Oh, look, Whitlock, it's your wife. Run along, little puppy, and see if she will give you some meat or a pat on the head."

Derek raised a very ducal brow. "Better scraps from her hand than always waiting to be noticed." He gave a polite bow, then went to his pretty and charming wife.

Colin glowered at his friend's back as he retreated. Derek had always been an impertinent man, least of all because he was the highest ranking of them, but his aim had been true. And he bristled at it. He was going to have to propose to her in all sincerity again soon, and she had better accept him this time. His control was wearing thin.

Tibby greeted them all with her usual dramatic effusiveness, and the evening took off at breakneck speed, with a charming duet between Mary and Kate that might have been the most delightful thing he'd ever heard. Everyone in the room seemed to agree, for the applause was rather extensive, enough that Kate rolled her eyes with a grin while Tibby begged them all to be quiet so Miss Templeton could begin her violin performance.

Colin relaxed as much as he could while standing against a pillar. Susannah was enraptured by the music, smiling and clapping, and looking quite lost in it. She might have been carried away by it, and he longed to be carried away with her.

His gaze slid to his brother, standing in a corner and focused upon the performances with his usual intensity. He had not thought Kit a great admirer of music either, it being so frivolous compared to other accomplishments Kit valued highly. He would never have said such things, but Colin suspected he thought that.

Or, rather, he *had* suspected. Up until this afternoon, he would have been quite convinced of it.

But there had been a bit of a surprise when he had returned from seeing his solicitor. He'd heard the pianoforte and a shaky melody that told him Bitty was practicing again, but this time she was singing along, and her sweet little voice brought a smile to his face. He'd heard her sing before, but only little nursery songs to herself. This was a new development indeed. And then, as if that was not enough, there was a second voice joining in with hers.

A male voice.

Curious, and a little concerned, he headed straight for their new makeshift music room, only to find Kit, of all people, at Bitty's side and singing the song with her, keeping his surprisingly rich baritone voice in check to keep from overpowering her. They made for an exquisite duet, and Colin had been so close to tears his eyes had burned suspiciously.

He had stood in the doorway, watching until their song was completed, and then slid out of sight as he tried to process what he had just witnessed. After thirty-two years with his brother... his twin, for heaven's sake!... how had it never come to his attention that Kit was musical?

Kit had come out and seen Colin at once. He'd only raised a

brow in a silent query.

"I didn't know you could sing," Colin had said.

Kit had straightened up a bit, curved one side of his mouth, and replied, "Despite what you may have heard, Colin, you do not know everything."

He'd seen very little of Kit since then, and they had come separately. Looking at him now, he could easily have assumed that his brother was only being polite with his interest. But knowing what he did now, there was undoubtedly some further appreciation. He praised each performance with polite applause, and when Gemma Templeton had been asked for an encore of three more songs, which never happened, Kit had smiled.

Smiled! In public! Thankfully, no one had seen it but Colin, or else the whole world, or at the very least London, would have gone into complete disarray.

Colin fought to smile himself, and returned his attention to the performances, feeling rather bemused about the whole thing.

When Miss Templeton had completed the last of her three additional songs, each as accomplished as the last, Tibby called for another surprise of the evening.

"In a quite shocking and rather pleasant turn of events," she trilled as the applause for Miss Templeton faded, "and certainly the first time it has occurred at one of my events, I am pleased to announce that the next performance will be by my own niece, Miss Bray."

Colin nearly slid down the column. Now he *knew* there was no way that Marianne was musical. She had so often said that she had no talents at all and was simply a pretty face and capable dancer. If she had musical abilities, she would have paraded them about for all to admire and see.

He glanced around the room to see similar expressions of shock and disbelief on every face, except for Duncan and Annalise, who merely looked surprised, although they smiled. He chanced a very slight glance at his brother, who suddenly looked as if he was considering throwing himself out of Tibby's very fine windows.

Colin groaned internally as Marianne made her way up to the

pianoforte. She was among family and close friends, so she had very little airs or flirtation, but she could hardly be entirely without them. Her dress was too bold, but not shocking, and he strongly suspected she had used a bit of eye paint to enhance her eyelashes, though he would never be so crass as to accuse her of it.

Marianne smiled shyly as she sat at the pianoforte and flicked a look over in the direction of Kate, Mary, and Annalise, then exhaled silently and began.

The music from the instrument was pretty, but hardly as accomplished as Kate had been, or as Miss Arden would undoubtedly be when she performed. Skilled, certainly, but not particularly impressive. Nothing that he should have thought good enough to induce a woman such as Marianne to be prevailed upon to perform for a gathering.

Then she began to sing. While not as captivating as what Mary Harris was capable of, she was not too far behind. Where her speaking tone was usually full of false lilts and coldness, her voice when singing was as natural as the breeze and just as refreshing. Clear and pure, her tone was everything she was not, but every bit the little girl he had once known.

If she ever performed for a gathering with her usual following and members of society, she would be more fawned upon than royalty and no other young woman would compare in the least.

Which begged the question: why hadn't she?

Suddenly someone seized his arm and he turned to find Kit standing there, looking wild and furious. "Where did she learn to sing like that?" he hissed, his grip on Colin's arm rather painful.

"I don't know, it's a usual accomplishment for females," he murmured, trying to reassure his unnerved twin. "Perhaps Mary helped her? They are friends."

Kit clenched his teeth as the song continued, reaching higher and purer notes from Marianne's voice. "Tell her to stop helping her," Kit managed, perspiration forming on his brow. "Tell her... Make it go away."

Colin gaped at him. "How do you expect me to...?"

Kit did not mark him at all. He looked down at the ground,

shaking his head slightly. "I can't do this. I can't…"

Suddenly, his arm was released and Kit left the room, still walking, but only just. Nobody noticed, as they were so captivated by the song, but Colin had lost interest. His brother was in sheer agony, beyond what Colin thought he was capable of. He might not understand it, but he could certainly sympathize.

Kit did not leave entirely. Colin could still see him just outside the door to the room, listening to every note, no doubt against his will. When at last Marianne had finished, the last note still ringing softly through the room, Kit was gone and applause rang out from every quarter enthusiastically.

Tibby called for a reprieve and some refreshments, and general talk and praise filled the room with indiscernible murmurs.

Geoff came to Colin, looking curious. "Where did Kit go?"

Colin forced a light smile. "Oh, Bitty has been under the weather today and he wanted to go check on her."

"Is she all right?" Geoff asked in concern. "Should I send Mary over? Or perhaps Susannah should go? She has experience in hospital, you know, and might be of use."

Colin shook his head, biting back a laugh. "No, no, Bitty will be fine. A little cough and some sniffles, nothing to get worked up about."

"And Kit left for that?"

Colin shrugged, as if he did not understand it either.

Geoff hummed and his brows furrowed. "A bit overprotective and rash, isn't it?"

Rash? Yes, Kit was being rash. And ridiculous and mysterious and drastic. But it had absolutely nothing to do with the girls, or anything else. It had everything to do with Kit's secret, and the too-pretty young woman that had taken them by surprise.

Kit, by a rule, hated surprises.

Colin smiled at his friend. "Kit is a very attentive guardian. And Bitty is his favorite, I think."

Geoff chuckled. "Can you have favorites in this?"

Colin clapped Geoff on the back as his friend went to procure refreshments. He leaned his head back against the pillar and released a sigh. He was used to making excuses for Kit, he had done so for years. But those had always been in grand circles when rumors ran rampant. Never before had he lied to his friends about it. They always accepted that Kit was reserved and did as he pleased without reference to Colin, and there had never been questions raised by any of them.

If this kept up, there would be several questions, and he would not have a single answer, made up or otherwise.

"You look distressed. What can I do?"

He smiled and opened his eyes to look down into Susannah's pretty blue-green eyes. Her honey-colored hair was pulled back fairly simply, but some blessed maid had given her just a bit of a ringlet behind her ears, and he reached out to play with one a little. Her eyes widened in surprise, and her color heightened a little, making the temptation to kiss her a rather unholy one.

What could she do? The words "marry me" came to mind, but he held them in check. He could hardly do a proper job of proposing in Tibby's ballroom with these people around, no matter how they ignored them at present.

He let two fingers stroke her jaw as he considered the incomparable woman before him. "What can you do?" he repeated softly.

She nodded, taking his hand in both of hers, taking care to hide it between their bodies.

"Smile, love," he murmured, stroking her jaw again. "All I need in the world is in your smile."

She blushed, but rolled her eyes at the compliment. He made a quick scan of the room, then quickly brought her hand up to his lips and kissed it twice. She slapped his arm with her other hand, but he felt the fingers he held flutter against his skin.

Susannah was his for the taking now. She might not have said the words, but he knew it.

She gave him an impish smile and a wink as she left to return to Annalise and Moira, who had now brought Lily Arden into their midst.

Colin watched her go with a bit of a predatory look that was matched by the growing fierceness within him.

Susannah was his.

And he was not going to wait anymore.

Chapter Sixteen

*C*olin was in a rather strange mood as he walked Susannah around Hyde Park, and she could not account for it. The musicale the evening before had been a great success, according to Tibby, and he had been so very handsome in his finery, even if he preferred the casual wear of daytime. He'd said nothing unusual then, had been charming and sweet, just as he had been of late.

When he had shown up at Tibby's this morning just shortly after breakfast and asked for a walk, she'd been confused, but not concerned. Now that she had seen the evidence of some agitation… he spoke too fast, his walk was too clipped, his hold on her too tight… she was growing more and more worried by the moment.

Various scenarios and schemes worked their way in and out of her mind as they walked, neither of them speaking much. Had he been distressed by something at home? He'd had that moment of unease last night that he did not discuss; was it perhaps something more serious? It could have been something to do with the girls, but surely he would not have left them if it were so very bad. And he would have told her of them by now.

A cold fear lurched her heart. Had he somehow found out about her? Had Sir Martin's identity and history somehow reached him? Or perhaps the debt collectors had discovered her and were making threats against her friends. It could not have been about her family, their once haughty view of life had long since vanished, and where they had once been appalled at the idea of the Gerrard family and fortune, now they would have welcomed it with open arms on bended knee.

The irony in that idea still left a very bitter taste in her mouth.

Whatever it was, Colin had made it perfectly plain that he would not tell her until he found a secluded spot for them. Such was his luck, the day was so fine that many had come out to the park, even at this early hour. The further they walked, the deeper Colin's glower became.

Susannah chewed her lip anxiously as her heart pounded. Could this, perhaps, be the end of everything? It was too soon, she was not prepared to go back to the way things had been. But then, she might not have a choice.

She had survived it once, she could do so again.

Colin finally stopped in a secluded stand of trees far away from anybody or anything, and only then did he seem to relax. "I'm sorry," he said on a sigh as he looked at her. "I just had to get you alone."

Susannah tilted her head to look up at him with a small smile. "Why?"

He returned her smile. "Well, for starters…" He cupped her face with one hand and brought his lips to hers for a warm, teasing kiss that made her toes curl in her boots. She sighed against him and raised up to meet his eager mouth more fully, his other arm latching firmly around her as she did so.

She loved kissing Colin; from the very beginning, she had loved it. It was more than she had ever imagined a kiss could be, and it was also a tantalizing amount of fun. She had been kissed a few other times in her life, but there was something about Colin's kisses that made her feel wild and giddy, that tasted of spice and heat, that sent her pulse pounding everywhere.

And she could cling to heaven a bit longer.

She raised a hand to the back of Colin's neck while the other clenched at his jacket, her senses awash in the heady attentions of his lips. Her fingers tightened into his hair and he raised her higher, closer, his kisses turning into something deeper, darker, far more dangerous, and far more enticing. She wanted this, she wanted *him*, she wanted…

She broke off with a gasp, her head falling back as Colin moved to her throat, nuzzling and spreading soft kisses along the column.

She inhaled slowly and moved her hand to Colin's face, forcing him to look at her. His eyes were dark, serious, and very focused.

Oh, no…

He lowered her until her feet touched the ground, then touched his forehead and nose to hers. "Marry me, Susannah."

Her breath caught in her throat and her hand fluttered from his face to his shoulder, as if she needed him for balance.

"I love you," Colin said softly, stroking her cheek with one hand, keeping her close with the other. "I've loved you for so long, I don't know who I am without it. But it's more than that, because ever since you have come back into my life, I feel whole again. I didn't know what I had been missing all these years, I only knew something wasn't right. Now I know." He brushed his lips across hers again. "It's you."

She shivered in his hold and clamped her lips together to keep from crying.

Colin shook his head against her, laughing softly to himself. "I thought I knew how I loved you when I was seventeen. But it is nothing compared to how I feel about you now. I love you. I love your stubbornness and your sweetness, your generous heart and unconquerable will. I love that I want to spend every minute of every day with you, I love that you are the last thought I think at night and the first every morning. I love…" He pulled back and grinned broadly. "Oddly enough, I love that I have become the sort of lovesick loon I used to mock, all because of you. So marry me, my darling love, and let me worship you until the end of time."

She stared at him, breathless and unsteady, tears beginning the slow trickle down her cheeks. She longed to say yes, the words were there on her lips.

But…

"I can't," she forced herself to say, her breath hitching.

Colin's brow furrowed and he pulled back a little. He swiped away one of her tears. "What do you mean you can't?"

She swallowed and sniffed sharply. "I mean that I can't marry you."

Stung, Colin let go and stepped further back. "Why the devil not?"

"There are things…" She shook her head and fought for control. "Too many things. I can't marry you, or anyone. It would destroy you."

"I doubt that."

"You don't know!" she insisted, wanting to grab his coat and shake him. "You can't possibly…"

"I've tried!" he interrupted, his voice rising. "I have tried to get you to tell me, but you won't! How can I know without you opening up once in a while?"

She let out a sound that was half of a moan, half of a whimper and put her face in her hands. "I can't. I can't…"

"Why won't you trust me?" Colin asked, his voice pleading.

She looked at him, agonizing over what he must be feeling. "I do trust you! Would I have done any of this if I didn't trust you? I should be hiding in the middle of the darkest corner of the city, and here I am out in the open with you."

"Hiding from what?" he exclaimed, flinging his arms out. "What is so horrible?"

Again, she shook her head. "I can't tell you."

Colin scoffed and put his hands on his hips. "You trust me. But you can't tell me. Do you see why I am having trouble here?"

"Yes, I see it!" she cried. "And I am asking you to trust me that I can't tell you!"

He shook his head, his eyes pleading. "I love you! I want to marry you! Is that not evidence enough? I don't care!"

"You would care," she vowed, suddenly very fatigued. "When it was all brought to light, when there were no more secrets, you would care very much. And I couldn't bear that."

His eyes narrowed at the catch in her voice. "You couldn't bear it," he repeated.

She nodded, swallowing with much difficulty.

He stared at her for a long moment, his shoulders heaving unsteadily with his breath. "Tell me now why you won't marry me," he said in a soft, almost dangerous voice. "And don't you dare say a word about your past or our past or your ridiculous husband's debts or anything else because I don't care. I want to know why *you* won't marry *me*."

Would he never understand? Could he not see that she was all wrong for him? She had proven it time and time again, but he refused to accept it. She bit her lip and exhaled shakily. "A goose will never be a swan, no matter how fervently it is wished," she murmured softly.

His mouth opened and his brows shot up. "What? Don't be ridiculous!"

"I'm not being ridiculous! That is the best way I can think to illustrate it."

He laughed one mirthless, cold laugh. "So you're... you're turning us into birds? Geese and swans, is that what we've come to?"

She wanted to cry, she wanted to hold him, she wanted to run... She caught at her trembling lips with her teeth and pled with her eyes, begging him to understand. "Colin, I can't!"

He snorted once. "Yes, you've said that. Let me just tell you one thing. I love you. And I thought that was all that mattered."

She looked down at her boots, willing her tears back. If only that were true. "You were mistaken."

He seemed to fall back a step, and she looked up, catching the half-furious, half-horrified expression on his face. Then it all turned dark and a glower appeared. He inhaled through his nose and started past her. "I need to go, I need to think..."

"Colin, please," she cried, reaching out for him.

He jerked away and held out a hand. "You can't... you cannot expect me to stay with you right now. Not after this. I need time, I need to..." He trailed off, shaking his head. "I need to be away from you. I need time."

"I understand," she whispered.

He looked at her for a moment, and his hand raised just a bit, as if he were to touch her face. But then he pulled it back, and fisted his hand at his side. He nodded once, and then stormed out into the main of the park.

Alone and exhausted, Susannah slumped back against a tree, hand clutching at her chest, where her heart threatened to burst. Her tears were gone, but her breathing refused to settle. She would break

Colin all over again, and it would be more painful the second time than the first.

Because his words were true for her as well. She thought she knew what love for him felt like when they were young, but now? Now she loved him with a full woman's heart, grown and mature and full of deeper meaning than she'd ever thought she could have. He was everything to her, more than he'd been before. He was her heaven and her hell, her salvation and her damnation.

And it would be better for him, for all of them, if she were gone.

But she couldn't go.

Painful as it would be, she had to stay.

For now.

Colin seethed the entire walk back home, his fists clenching and unclenching at his sides. He walked passed his house and continued for several blocks, then walked down to St. James, then wandered as his feet carried him. He really didn't care where he went.

So long as he didn't have to see her.

What did she mean by refusing him? He loved her, and he *thought* she loved him. But now, just as it had been then, he didn't know. She'd never said it, despite what her smiles and her eyes and her kisses might have led him to believe.

She'd said she needed time. She had never said that she could not marry him, or anyone. What did she mean by that? Did she really consider her situation so bad that she could not marry at all? Or had her marriage been so bad that she refused to enter into such an agreement again?

The latter he could understand, but it was still a ridiculous notion. Her marriage, by her own account, had been set up by her parents, and she'd had little choice in the matter. A marriage of her choosing with someone she trusted or loved would hardly be comparable.

She claimed to trust him, but he failed to see how that could be true. If she trusted him, she would confide in him. He would move heaven and earth to save her, if only he knew where to begin.

And the Gent had yet to give him any sort of details.

He could do it on his own. He could march down to the financial district and get Mr. Jacobs to talk to him, despite whatever agreement of secrecy they might have had. Colin did not know any man who could not be tempted by the right amount of money. There was not that much honor in anyone.

Well, all right, there were a few, himself included, that still had scruples, but his were crumbling at a rapid rate.

The tension in his neck and shoulders eased a bit as he thought about Susannah.

She had been in distress today, he was not so blind as to miss that. He had seen the battle waging within her, and had willed her to his side of things. But it was not to be, and he saw the cost of it in her face. It had angered him, had cut him quite deeply, and echoes of the past had sprung into memory. But what about her? They'd had so many delightful days of late, and still she hid. Still she refused him.

Still she was afraid.

And he couldn't do anything about it.

He found himself back in Bruton Street without realizing it, and he leaned against the brick façade of his home. He was supposed to have come home in unfettered delight, whistling jaunty tunes, ready to spread the news far and wide of his impending nuptials. Now he was feeling rather devoid of any emotion at all. The anger had faded, the embarrassment had ebbed, and now he was weary beyond anything.

Where did he go from here?

Did he continue to court her? At the moment, he was not even sure he wanted to see her again, let alone give his heart another chance. But could he leave her alone?

That sent a cold chill through him.

A mother and her two daughters walked past, the girls smiling invitingly at him as their mother greeted him.

He nodded absently in their direction, and he saw the flash of disappointment in their faces as he turned and entered the house.

He didn't care.

Colin Gerrard had a heart, contrary to popular belief, and at the moment, it ached like hell.

A note sat on the desk in the study in familiar handwriting and he seized it at once, breaking the seal so hastily the paper almost ripped with it. His eyes scanned the short missive multiple times, and the information gave him as little pleasure on those attempts as it had the first time.

Two solicitors, it appears. Tracing what I can. Reply only if you wish me to stop.

Colin scrunched the paper in his hand and tossed it into the corner of the room with a sigh. He had not expected a full report, the Gent would hardly put such details onto paper. Gossip was one thing and this was entirely different. But he had expected to hear *something*. This was nothing, this brought only more questions, this…

He grunted and sat down at the desk roughly.

He hated not knowing what he needed to.

Another paper caught his eye, and his jaw tightened as his stomach roiled. He grabbed this paper more gently than he had the Gent's note, but he was quick to shove it into the nearest drawer and close it tightly. He did not need that now, though this morning he had been keen enough to look at it. What use was a special license to a man without a bride?

Breathing was suddenly too hard, perspiration was beginning to form, and the room was much too hot. He couldn't stay in here, when everything would remind him of her. He couldn't stay in the house, where her smell seemed to invade everything. He could not go to the garden, where the laughter of his sisters brought her smiles to memory.

No, he needed to escape and to work. Something to burn off his agitation and keep him from going completely mad.

Dressed as he was, he left the house through the servants' entrance and made his way to the mews, knowing he would shock anyone there, but also knowing it was one place he could let out whatever he wished without consideration to anybody.

His servants greeted him, and then ignored him as they

continued with their work. He was rather pleased they were so disinterested in him at this moment. He headed directly for a chopping block and a large pile of wood that could serve his purposes quite nicely. The sky, once cloudy before, now began to sprinkle light drops of rain, but he did not care. In fact, he liked the day better for it.

It should rain again, on this day of all days.

Nearly an hour later, he would surmise that he had not gone completely unnoticed from the house. Kit must have seen something, and acted upon it, for Colin's four friends had now appeared at the mews, dressed as he had been, though his coat and cravat had long been tossed aside. His shirt was drenched, from the now steady rain and from his sweat, and it clung to his skin in an irritating way. He had split almost twice the amount of wood that was needed, and his servants had told him that. But he ignored them, and they let him be.

Just as he ignored his friends now.

They stood near him, watching, no doubt waiting for him to greet them in some fashion.

They would wait quite a while.

"Colin?" Geoff finally tried.

He chopped another piece of wood, a bit askew this time. He swore and kicked it aside, picking up another one.

"Are you… perspiring?" Derek asked, trying to tease him.

Colin grunted as he swung the axe again. "Yes."

"Voluntarily?" Nathan asked, and he could hear the smile in his voice.

Again, he swung the axe. "Yes."

"Are you quite well, Colin?" Geoff sounded the slightest bit concerned. "Do you need to lie down?"

"No," he bit out as he picked up another piece.

"No?"

"No what, Colin?"

He swung the axe, but said nothing.

"Colin?"

"What I need," he ground out harshly, picking up the wood pieces and setting them in the pile, "is for someone to figure out what

190

she wants. What I need is for her to not be so blasted tempting and addicting." He snatched up another piece of wood and set it on the block. "What I need is to push myself to my limit and beyond so that I can still be a gentleman in public and not some wild animal. What I need is to not feel as though my entire life has been a waste. What I need is for my so-called friends to get out of my face if all they are going to do is pester me with inane questions on a subject they know absolutely nothing about!"

With a harsh cry he slammed the axe down and split the piece into perfectly even halves that careened off of the block.

Breathing heavily, he waited there, axe down, unmoving.

No one said anything. No one made a sound at all.

Then Duncan bent down to pick up yet another piece of wood, set it in the middle of the block, and waited.

Colin gave a short exhale and dislodged the axe with a brief nod at his friend.

Duncan returned it, then put his eyes back on the wood at hand.

Without a word, the others removed their coats and hats, set them in the relatively dry stables, and went to the woodpile themselves, stacking the wood neatly beneath its shelter, and finding more pieces for Colin to split.

No one asked questions, no one told him he was mad, and no one complained that it was raining.

He might not be able to understand Susannah's reasoning for her refusal, he might not be able to make sense of his own life, he might be a complete idiot when it came to love, but here, at least, were men who could sympathize, some in very real ways. They were his friends, his allies, and men who understood that there was no understanding anything in the realm of one's heart.

When he had exhausted the woodpile, and himself, he let his friends lead him back home, and once they had seated themselves in the kitchen with a hot fire, warm blankets, and warmer drinks, they sat in silence there as well.

In some cases, such as this, words were unnecessary.

One by one, his friends drifted off, each clamping a hand on his shoulder as he left, returning to their houses and wives, to their children in some cases, and to their relative comfort. He was grateful for each of them, and for their happiness and contentment. And he was envious of it.

He was oh so very envious.

And that burned just as fiercely as anything else.

Chapter Seventeen

*T*hree long and torturous days later, Colin and Mrs. Creighton ventured to take the girls around London, and while he tried to feign attentiveness, he was irritable and sallow. Rosie kept looking back at him with concern, but she mercifully kept her mouth shut, although whether that was from her own intuition or Kit's threats about their behavior on this outing, he couldn't have said.

Bitty was enraptured by London and its finery, gawking and gasping at ladies on horseback in the park and riding by in carriages. She waved gaily at all and received a surprising amount of responses in kind. Whatever Colin's popularity had been, his sisters were going to outstrip him very smartly. It struck him that this guardianship would send more females flocking his way than anything of his own merit ever had; and the irony there was not lost on him.

He didn't want more females.

He only wanted one.

Colin sighed and winced a little bit, forcing her back from his thoughts for the thousandth time this morning alone.

"Colin sad?" asked a little voice with great concern.

He looked down at the tiny girl clutching his hand with all of her might. Ginny was terrified of being out here, her eyes wide and her steps hesitant, and only Colin's touch had soothed her. Now she looked up at him with those sweet eyes, the smallest of puckers between her brows.

He tried to smile as his heart tugged a little. "A little sad, Ginny."

The pucker gathered a few more furrows and her lower lip stuck out. "No sad, Colin. Sad means you go home."

He almost laughed and squeezed her hand a little. "Don't you want to go home, Ginny?"

She shook her head at once. "Stay with Colin. Make you happy."

Now he smiled and wanted to hug her. "You make me happy, poppet. I won't be sad."

She beamed up at him, then went back to her usual somber observance of the world around her.

His sisters looked a picture today, each in their matching blue coats and bonnets. Tibby had known enough not to give them much by way of matching, but in this case, she had been quite right to do so. Any artist with an eye would have begged to paint them just as they were now, with their vibrant blue eyes and dark brown hair, all of them looking more perfect than the finest porcelain dolls. They would be a credit to their family in looks, if nothing else.

But he and Kit were determined that they be smart, accomplished, and well-mannered as well. And so far, they seemed on the perfect course for it.

Well, Rosie could have used a little more polishing, but at nine, they were not too worried. Yet.

Kit had been remarkably present over the last three days, and they had shared precisely one conversation on the topic of Susannah, wherein Colin had revealed everything to him, including writing to the Gent and his two refusals. Kit had listened quietly, offered some bland sort of counsel that really didn't mean very much, and then asked Colin what he wanted to do about it all.

"You mean to let me have my way?" Colin had asked in surprise.

Kit had given a small smile. "I am not your lord and master, Colin, and it is your life. Provided you do no injury to yourself or anyone else, if you think it best, I will go along with it." Then he'd snorted and leaned back. "'Let you.' Me letting you do something. Most ridiculous thing I've ever heard."

And that had been the end of it. But more than Kit's words, his presence had meant a great deal. His silent show of support and strength had bolstered Colin, and the girls had loved the last three days of having their brothers so much around them. Kit had taken them over to Tibby's for their lessons with Freddie, ensuring that

Colin wouldn't have to see anyone he did not wish to, and had actually taken up the entertainment of the girls, which was a refreshing change, as that was usually something only Colin really did.

Just yesterday Colin had come upon the four of them in the library, sitting on the floor, all three girls piled on and around Kit, while he read aloud from the fairytale book, using the most extraordinary range of voices. There were pauses for tickling, giggling, surprised screams, and a general sense of merriment that Colin wished he had been a part of. He had been tempted to join, but opted against it. It had been a precious moment for Kit to share his true nature with his sisters, and for them to enjoy their eldest brother alone.

Colin could not distance himself forever, nor would he wish to. He felt more himself today than he had in days, and as such, he had volunteered for the outing, knowing he owed it to the girls, but also knowing that his lack of being seen would soon give rise to comment. And comment was the last thing he needed at this time.

"Rosie, stay close, please," he called as the streets became more crowded.

Rosie came to him at once and tucked into his side, looking a bit uncertain for the first time this morning.

Colin smiled and nodded at a passing woman and her daughter, who stared at the girls in shock.

"Nervous, Rosie?" he murmured, keeping his smile fixed.

"Trying not to get trampled," she replied. "We never had crowds like this at home."

He chuckled. "This isn't a crowd, Rosie. This is usual foot traffic for this time of morning."

She looked up at him with wide eyes as Bitty's gleeful cries met their ears. "You can't be serious."

He nodded slowly. "Welcome to London."

"And when are we going home?" Rosie asked faintly, looking around again.

"Look!" Bitty cried loudly, waving with more excitement. "It's Freddie and Susannah."

Colin stiffened and looked where Bitty was indicating, and

suddenly he echoed Rosie's question. Susannah looked just as enthused about seeing him. Her eyes were wide and her face faintly echoed the pale gray shade of her dress. Freddie strained against his mother's hold, waving back at the girls, but Susannah held him fast.

"Colin, can we go? Can we? Please?" Rosie and Bitty asked in unison, Rosie's inhibitions suddenly gone.

His eyes were fixed on Susannah, anger and irritation swirling throughout him, as well as a startling flash of pain. She was lovely, even looking as drawn and uncomfortable as she was.

Mrs. Creighton came to his side. "Mr. Gerrard, I can handle the girls myself if you would prefer to…"

"Go on, girls," he murmured, "but behave."

Bitty and Rosie dashed ahead the short distance to their friend and his mother, while Ginny stayed near him. He spared a glance for Mrs. Creighton, whose expression was composed, but a hint of concern was evident.

"It's all right," he said quietly. "I can… It's all right."

She nodded once and went ahead to mind the older two, while he and Ginny slowly moved forward. Susannah murmured something to Mrs. Creighton, who nodded and distracted Bitty and Rosie with an older woman's dog nearby.

Colin looked at Susannah, who met his gaze steadily, and he wished he could rage at her, as he had so often done in his mind. He felt it, along with a hundred other things. But despite his turmoil, he was, above all else, a gentleman. And he would remain composed.

He looked down at Freddie, who was watching him with concern. It struck him that he had not seen the boy in three days, which was not a significant amount of time, but it felt much longer. "Good day, Freddie," he said, trying for a smile.

Freddie looked at him for a long moment, looking uneasy. "Colin, are we not friends anymore?"

Colin's brows rose sharply. "Why would you say that, Freddie?"

"You never come to see us now," Freddie replied, looking as though he might cry.

Colin closed his eyes for a moment, and then lowered himself down to be at eye level with the boy. "Listen up, lad, there is nothing on this earth, the heaven above, or whatever is beneath that could make us not be friends anymore. I am sorry I have not come by lately, adults get a little distracted sometimes. To make amends, if it is all right with your mother, we will all go to Dennison's Stables and see the horses."

Freddie gaped. "Can we really?"

"Really?" Susannah faintly echoed, looking at him in wonder.

He swallowed and nodded, rising to his feet, and staring at her with far too much intensity than he should have. "It is the very least I can do, I assure you. If I had more time and a more creative mind, I would come up with something better."

She shook her head. "This will be more than enough."

Colin nodded and gestured to Mrs. Creighton, turning from Susannah so he would not have to look at her anymore. "Besides," he said roughly, "I happen to be on rather good terms with the owner."

As much as he enjoyed visiting Dennison's, and seeing his friends, he wished fairly quickly that he had not said anything at all. Nathan and Mr. Grant, the manager, were pleased to see them and took great care with the children. Ginny had ventured off with Mrs. Creighton to see the foals, which left Colin alone with Susannah.

He was less than pleased about it.

Everything about her drove him mad. Her scent, her manner of breathing, her slight smile as she watched her son laugh and ride around the paddock, the way her eyes sparkled against the cloudy skies… He hated how much he wanted her, and that she would not give him the relief of admitting her feelings and accepting him. He wanted to be patient, he wanted to trust her, but a bitter seed was growing within him, and far too many echoes of his painful past were constantly on his mind.

"Thank you for this," Susannah said softly, glancing over at him. "It is very kind, and you did not have to. I… would have understood if you'd done nothing."

He grunted and watched his sisters giggle as they pet a horse on the nose. "The girls see Freddie every day, he is a great friend of theirs and a good boy. I don't see why they should suffer simply because we cannot see eye to eye."

Susannah flinched a little at the bite in his tone and she frowned. "Colin…"

"Don't frown," he ordered sharply, forcing himself to appear at ease. "The children are watching."

Susannah suddenly craned her neck as if a shiver had run up her spine. He had noticed her react thus on occasion, but had never questioned her on it, and her bland smile for effect did nothing to remove the sudden hollowness in her eyes.

"Why do you do that?" he asked in a low voice.

Her eyes widened and she looked back to the paddock, swallowing sharply.

"Any time someone tells you to do something," he continued slowly, "whenever an order is given, you react similarly. Why?"

She exhaled slowly and he could see the play of emotions across her face as she forced herself to remain composed, and her color heightened. "I didn't know it was obvious."

"Why?" he demanded, tired of her evasiveness.

Again came a slight twitch, and her mouth tightened as she looked down at her hands folded before her. "A habit from my marriage. One that I would much rather forget."

Colin felt a wave of surprise hit him like a wall, and swarms of questions flooded him. He waited, watching her, but when she brought her head back up, she fixed her eyes away from him and on the children.

And he wanted her still.

He nearly growled at himself. Enough was enough. He took her arm and forced her out of sight to the closest stables. She went without resistance, gasping a little, and the noise stirred him. He backed her against the wall of the building, kissing her before she could say anything to enrage him further.

She moaned and softened beneath him, her fingers curling into his coat. He cupped her face in his hands, worshipping her with his lips and his heart.

Susannah broke off and shifted her mouth from his. "Let me go, Colin," she gasped weakly, her voice choked with tears. "Please let me go."

He pressed against her more fully, his lips almost frantically dancing across her skin. "I can't," he groaned in a low, harsh tone. "Don't you understand? I can't…"

His lips found hers again and words were meaningless. Need and hunger clamored within him, and he wished that she would let go, would give herself up to this, to him. Longing for her to be his in truth.

She arched her neck, gasping for air, then pressed her hands, which had become trapped between them, into his shoulders, trying to force him away. "Colin, no…"

The finality in her tone, despite the breathless quality, sent a chill through him and the hollow look in her eyes cooled his desire in an instant, and he stepped away. He shook his head and fixed his eyes on the horses in the paddock beyond them, carefully avoiding her captivating eyes.

He was through. For his own sake, he had to be.

"Apologies," he said, his voice rough but somehow managing to keep it polite. "I would hate to continue to plague you when you find my attentions displeasing."

"Colin…" she whispered, his name sounding painful to his ears.

He shook his head once, very firmly.

"Please."

"You aren't going to tell me, are you?" he asked darkly.

She kept her face firmly away from him, but he saw her throat work for a swallow.

"Geese and swans," Colin muttered, moving back into plain sight of everyone. He met Nathan's eyes and raised his chin in acknowledgement, then turned from the stables and began the walk back home, resentment and anger leaving a foul taste in his mouth.

Susannah closed her eyes on her tears as Colin walked away. She couldn't say a word to him, couldn't bear to look at him. He would grow to hate her at this rate, and perhaps it would be better for him to do so. She knew what he wanted, and she also knew how desperately she wanted the same thing, if her life were any other life. But the secrets of her past were too much, too shameful and horrifying for her to relate to anyone. The debts themselves were mortifying, but the darker secrets, the ones she fought daily to forget… No one would look at her the same way after that.

Memories of cold voices, darkened rooms, sneering orders and insults assailed her. Revulsion welled up within her and she clung to the paddock for balance as she swayed under the weight of it. She would never forget the faces, the leers, the superior and callous expression on her husband's face as he criticized every aspect of her existence…

A cold shiver ran up her spine and she bit back a soft cry as she forced a smile, moved back into the sunlight, and waved at her son, riding so happily on the large horse. He looked where Colin had been and his face fell, but she could fix that. She could be sure that he would never think less of Colin for his absence. She ought to have done so before, but she had not known how.

Mrs. Creighton would be back with Ginny soon, and Susannah would have to create an excuse for Colin that would be believed by all.

She could hardly tell them that Colin could barely stand to be in her vicinity because she could not admit how she loved him, and had rejected his offer of marriage.

Twice.

"Susannah! I didn't know you were going to be here; I would have come earlier!"

She closed her eyes again as Moira's cheery voice reached her. She could hide her distress from the children, they were easy enough to distract. But Moira would be another matter entirely.

She forced herself to open her eyes and smile at the woman as she approached, her copper hair partially hidden beneath her bonnet, sapphire eyes brilliantly sparkling. Moira was a very striking woman, and her independence only added to her attractiveness.

"Good morning, Moira," Susannah said, mentally wincing at

how rough her voice sounded.

Moira gave her a searching look, her smile fading. She looked beyond her, where Colin had left some time ago, and then back to Susannah. The longer she looked, the more Susannah felt tears rising. Moira had that effect on people, she'd heard. It was as if she could see into her heart, and draw out the emotions she so valiantly tried to contain.

Moira's expression softened. "Oh, darling," she murmured, coming to her and giving her a tight hug.

Susannah resisted at first, only half returning the hug, as was polite. But Moira held firm, and whether it was the warmth in her nature or the steady comfort of her heartbeat, she didn't know, but suddenly she had to wrap her arms around her fully. Her frame shook with the restrained cries she would not let loose, her breathing erratic and unsteady.

"Come see me tomorrow and we'll have a chat," Moira whispered. "I insist."

Susannah shook her head slightly. "The Cartwright masquerade is tomorrow." It was to be one of the finest events in London, given that the Season had ended, and Tibby had been talking of nothing else for days.

"Yes, it is," Moira said, pulling back to look Susannah in the face. "But that does not mean I cannot talk with you beforehand. And don't worry, I won't press. Colin has already told us you are very private and to respect that, and for once I agree with him. But you could use a friend, couldn't you?"

Susannah nodded, unable to vocalize anything at the moment.

Moira smiled and took her hand. "I'll have the other ladies come, too. We'll all go to the ball together. There is strength in our numbers, Susannah, and we can help you sort out whatever the matter is."

Susannah sniffed and looked up at the sky. "Oh, I cannot let them see me cry!"

"The children?"

She nodded, blinking quickly.

Moira shrugged. "Tell them it was me. I am a very emotional person, I cry all the time for no reason at all."

Susannah laughed and her first genuine smile of the day appeared.

Moira squeezed her hand. "There, that is much more like it."

Susannah looked at Moira for a long moment, digesting her words. "Colin... told you not to press me?" she finally asked, trying to keep her voice light.

Moira nodded as she waved at her husband and the girls. "Yes, he was most insistent. Generally, I never listen to anything Colin says, as he is simply ridiculous most of the time. But in this case, he was the most serious I had ever seen him, and said if we could not behave properly around you, he would not let our association continue."

Susannah gaped openly, no sound possible. "He... he said that?" she finally managed.

"Something of the sort, the implications were the same." Moira smiled at her then, a mischievous light in her eyes. "He is very protective of you, you know. I thought he'd been so when Annalise had her troubles, but with you?" She shook her head. "It is so much more. I did not know this version of him existed."

"I did," Susannah murmured softly, turning to look back at the children. "That is the Colin I knew."

Her voice broke a bit on the end and she scolded herself, clearing her throat.

Moira watched her for a moment, then put a hand on her arm. "I must get home to my children, but do come tomorrow. We'll talk if you wish, and if not, you can help me figure out what to do for my gown for the masquerade. I know absolutely nothing about such things, and Tibby said you have quite the eye for it."

Susannah offered a small smile. "I should be happy to offer my services, my lady."

Moira looked quite severe. "Stop that right now, Susannah. I am no fine lady to you, I am your friend. And you had best remember that, or I shall be quite vexed."

Susannah smirked as Moira walked away, and she wondered what on earth a vexed Moira would even look like.

It was probably quite terrifying.

She turned back to the children, and was relieved when Mrs.

Creighton appeared, seeming not at all surprised at Colin being gone, and she asked for no explanation. She carried on a conversation with Susannah as if all was normal, and when the time came, it was she who made the excuses for him, saving Susannah the trouble of having to do so.

There was no telling how long she could continue in this sort of life, with Colin's friends and family surrounding her. She could not change her mind in this, not if she wanted to save him from what lay ahead for her, and especially not with the law and debt collectors getting closer and closer by the day. Who would wish to remain connected with her then? If they knew her, if they knew all, who would stand by her?

She valued the friends she had found, but she could not confide in them completely. Their loyalties were with Colin, as they should be, and they saw Susannah as an ally there. They had no idea she was also the villain.

Time would tell when things would end here.

She only hoped she could get out before the worst happened.

Chapter Eighteen

"There," Susannah said as she snipped the last of the thread and removed the pin from her teeth. "I think that should do for you, Moira. Have a look."

Moira stepped off of the stool she had been standing on and went to the mirror in her dressing room, turning to see the back of her dress. "Perfect! The detailing is just what it needed! Susannah, you are a wizard! I have no idea how you could take a disaster and make a masterpiece in one sitting!"

"I have no idea how you allowed yourself to let Susannah work on your gown," Kate said with a snort as she watched from the bed, where she was leaning comfortably. "Really, Moira, the poor girl is down on the floor working on your gown when she could very well be getting ready herself."

Moira gave Kate a dirty look. "Don't be churlish just because she was willing and able to make my dress prettier than yours."

Kate gaped in mock-offense and looked at Mary on the other side of her. "Is her dress really prettier?"

Mary raised a brow. "I thought you were more concerned about the fact that Moira had Susannah down on the floor toiling on the fabric than your appearance, Kate."

"That, too," Kate sniffed, looking down at Susannah with a wink. "Vastly talented though she is, I cannot condone my sweet friend being forced into manual labor for your vanity."

Susannah rolled her eyes as Annalise laughed and helped her up. "I offered to help her, Kate."

"See?" Moira smirked at her friends and joined them on the bed.

"Susannah likes me well enough to use her accomplishments for my benefit."

"If only you had some accomplishments to give her in return," Kate sighed, patting her hand fondly.

Susannah watched with interest and leaned closer to Annalise. "Are they always like this?" she murmured.

"Always," Mary and Annalise replied together.

Susannah grinned and pushed back the lock of hair that had dislodged itself in her work. It had not been hard, she had rather enjoyed the challenge, and being able to be of use was always refreshing. If she needed to turn her hand to more laborious work than the current demand from Mrs. Randall, she enjoyed knowing she could do so without difficulty.

Her particular skill set would not be of much use in those whose sole demand in life was to populate ballrooms and carry on family titles. But they just might save her, if she employed them correctly.

"Are you sure you won't join us?" Kate asked suddenly, looking at Susannah with a sad expression. "You have such a pretty figure, I should love to see you in a ball gown."

For what had to be the fourth time in an hour, Susannah shook her head, smiling. "No, I am not suited for a ballroom. Despite what you all say, I am Tibby's companion, not her relative, and my place is elsewhere."

"What a load of rubbish that is!" came a very familiar trilling voice from the hallway.

Susannah turned to the doorway in shock to find Tibby entering, her gown and turban entirely of gold and her glittering mask in hand. She also wore a sheer cape of gold, for whatever reason, and lace half-gloves were cluttered with her well-famed rings. She bore a very imperious expression that Susannah had come to know well, and it terrified her.

"Moira, my dear, your directions were monstrous," she sniffed, sparing only half a glance for the now grinning countess. "I should have been here half an hour ago."

"You know where I live, Tibby," Moira replied with a laugh.

"I cannot be bothered to remember such things, darling." She entered the room fully, and Marianne followed, looking rather impish for what Susannah knew of her. She had only met her twice, and had hardly conversed with her at all, but she seemed very kind, if a bit conceited.

Tibby greeted the others, gave a fond kiss to Annalise, and then focused in on Susannah once more. "A load of rubbish," she repeated firmly.

Susannah swallowed and stammered, "I beg your pardon?"

Tibby folded her arms and looked severe. "Your place is with us, darling. I have had quite enough of your insisting on distance, though I completely respect privacy."

At least three of the women present chortled at that, but Tibby ignored them all.

"You have not been yourself lately, and I must have you smile." She looked around the room briefly. "We all must."

Every head in the room nodded, even Marianne, who smiled gently at her.

"So we have been very mischievous little mice," Tibby continued, grinning now, "and put together the most perfect ensemble for the masquerade tonight, which you *will* be attending, and the more you struggle, the more outlandish we shall make it out to be."

Susannah stared at Tibby in shock, then at the others, her mind feeling as though it was working backwards.

"I couldn't possibly," she whispered, her breath hitching in her chest. She wanted to go, she had not danced in years, but she would not belong, she could not pretend that much.

"You can," Annalise said softly from behind her.

She turned to look at her, knowing she, of all people in this room, would understand. But Annalise only smiled in encouragement, nodding.

Susannah sighed and a hint of excitement started in her stomach. "All right," she said softly, allowing herself to smile

The women sprang into action, squealing in delight and hugging her, then stripping her completely and bringing in new undergarments, stockings, and a corset, while someone let her hair out of its pins and began brushing it out.

It was an odd feeling to be fussed over so, to have someone else adjusting her garters and pulling at her chemise, tugging on her corset laces, and for two maids to be working at her hair at once. She'd only had one maid, and only for the first few years of her marriage. She'd forgotten how it was, but to now have two of them aiding her? It was absolute madness.

But the giddy delight the others shared was infectious, and she found herself laughing and relaxing with them as they debated over her hair and whether or not a bit of rouge or eye paint was necessary. Thankfully, they listened to her when she said she would prefer not, but they refused to heed her about simplicity in her pins. No, they brought out ornamental pins with pearls and glittering stones, and several different ribbons were tried as well.

Then the dress was brought in, and Susannah's breath caught at it. She had never seen anything so beautiful, and the entire room hushed as she stepped into it. It was as white as snow, with a sheer silver overlay and the finest details embroidered out of a shimmering silver thread. The sleeves came to her elbow and were entirely of the same fabric as the overlay. The bodice gathered the white with the silver in the most elegant of ruches, while a fine band of thick silver ribbons lay just beneath it.

It was the most exquisite garment she had ever set eyes on, and she could hardly breathe as the buttons were done on her back. She wanted to touch it and toy with it for ages, but she was too afraid to touch such a fine thing, for fear of it dissolving beneath her fingers. It was as if the clouds and the stars had combined in one glorious moment and formed themselves into this dress, and why it should possibly have come to her was unfathomable.

"Susannah," Kate breathed, looking her up and down in awe.

She could hardly breathe but for her excitement, and tears began to prickle at her eyes.

"Don't cry!" Marianne laughed, coming over to take her hand, while Annalise took her other. "You'll set the entire room off."

"I can't believe…" Susannah shook her head, her jaw quivering. "Thank you," she managed.

Moira grinned. "Perhaps you should look at yourself before you thank us, dear."

She took a breath in, and turned to the mirror

Her breath vanished suddenly. The woman in the mirror was breathtaking, every aspect of her striking yet demure, her complexion glowed warmly, and her eyes sparkled as a mixture of sapphire and emerald. The gown was perfectly fitted to her form, hugging every curve flawlessly, and her hair seemed rich and luxurious with its curls and styling. This woman had no flaws the eye could see, nothing to haunt her nights, no worries in any part of her days. This woman could hope and dream at will. She could have whatever she wished.

"Two things more," Tibby said, her voice surprisingly choked, though she tried for her usual air.

She stepped up behind Susannah and set a necklace of diamonds around her neck, bringing a gasp of pleasure from all in the room.

"Tibby!" Susannah tried to shriek, though it was rather breathless.

"Don't get excited, my dear," Tibby scolded with a pat to her arm. "They look brilliant, but they are not real diamonds. I know what offends you, silly though it is."

Susannah was not entirely sure she believed her, but she would not argue.

"And the second?" Mary asked, grinning from ear to ear.

Tibby flicked two fingers at the maids, who sprang forward and attached a small, simple white mask to her face.

The effect was so perfectly enchanting, so beyond anything she had ever imagined, that Susannah smiled at her reflection.

"There," Tibby said with a firm nod of approval. "Now you are ready."

The ballroom at Lord and Lady Cartwright's London residence was packed with people, some in the most extraordinary of ensembles. Apparently, all one needed was a mask in order to have societal restrictions and inhibitions completely removed. Susannah had never been to a masquerade, even in her younger years, and now she could see why. But there was a contagious air of excitement and anticipation floating about in the room, and even the sound of the musicians tuning was delightful.

She entered with Tibby and Marianne, no escort for any of them, and due to the mysterious nature of the evening, there was no announcement of those entering. Some of the guests were fairly easy to identify as it was, such as Mr. Bray and the Earl of Beverton, and Lady Cavendish, having apparently tried to match Tibby's public displays, was arrayed in some ghastly purple ensemble with more feathers than fabric.

"Rather like a rather plump canary I saw once," Tibby murmured, seeing where Susannah looked. "And the poor bird has been doused in blackberry wine."

Susannah and Marianne snickered into their gloves, and then Marianne left them for a collection of men nearby. They anticipated her arrival with eagerness, and considering the vision she was in vibrant blue and the natural grace of her gait, Susannah could see why. Apparently, not everyone wished to hide at a masquerade.

She quickly spotted Mary and could only assume the man standing close to her was her husband, it was difficult to tell under the circumstances.

Mary smiled at her as she came to her side. "You are magnificent, dear," Mary said, taking her hand. "You were born for a masquerade."

Susannah laughed, knowing her friend had no idea just how true that statement was in her life. She lived a masquerade.

"You look very well indeed," Geoffrey said with a smile that she immediately recognized.

"Thank you, Mr. Harris." She curtseyed playfully.

"Formality?" he asked, tsking a bit. "Not fond of that."

"Under the circumstances, I beg you would excuse me," she replied, twisting her mouth.

He considered that, then nodded. "Perhaps you are right. But just this once."

She inclined her head, and turned to watch the dancing that was beginning.

Geoffrey murmured something into Mary's ear, making her blush a bit beneath her mask, and then he left, walking over to the punch table.

Mary giggled softly to herself, then caught Susannah's eye.

"What did he say?" Susannah asked, unable to resist smiling at Mary's expression.

"Oh, he was just telling me how he loves masquerade balls," Mary said with a wave of her hand.

Susannah raised a brow that Mary would only barely be able to see over her mask. "Does he really?"

The skin of Mary's neck suddenly turned pink. "We, erm… we had a rather significant turning point in our relationship at a masquerade ball. It is still one of his favorite memories."

Susannah turned away quickly, focusing on the dancing at hand. Her question had been too personal, though Mary had answered with both politeness and candor, which she did not deserve. And to know something so intimate about her friends made her ache with sudden longing.

A tall gentleman with a small smirk asked her to dance, and she obliged him, enjoying the anonymity on both sides of the mask, able to converse without wondering at the other's impressions, and a sly bit of innocent, playful flirtation that made her feel years younger. And knowing that she would never know this gentleman if she saw him again, be he rogue, scholar, or peer, was vastly entertaining to contemplate.

That dance was followed by two others in quick succession, with young lads who complimented her effusively, danced energetically, and had absolutely no sense between the two of them. But they amused her, and she did so love dancing. There had been no dancing, no balls of any kind during her time at Pavel House, and only in the infrequent solitude of the house, alone in the ballroom, had she even imagined such things.

She had a respite after, allowing her to take in the elegant furnishings of the room. So many candles and windows, such tall and grand ceilings, and the artistry of every aspect of the majestic space was a masterpiece alone. But when all combined together, it was breathless beyond reckoning. Lord and Lady Cartwright were very kind, very generous people, and there was not a soul in the room who did not think most highly of them.

Well, perhaps one.

"Have a care," that one individual said as Susannah walked passed her, blocking her path with a thick walking stick. "You nearly trod on my gown, you impertinent chit."

Susannah turned back to face Lady Greversham, giving her an apologetic smile that she did not feel. "My apologies, madam. I meant no trouble."

Lady Greversham stared at her with narrowed slits for eyes. "I do not care what you mean, you daft creature. You must mind yourself in a place such as this, or people will think that you *do not belong.*"

Susannah inhaled silently, forcing herself to remain calm, though her heart skittered to a halt. There was no mistaking the meaning in her words, but it was not possible for the woman to know her. Or was it? The glint in the older woman's eyes, the sneer in the curve of her mouth, all indicated a particularly sinister intention.

But Susannah had spent enough time around liars to always suspect a bluff.

"I beg your pardon?" she asked with a bit of a sniff, her hands curving into fists at her sides.

"Don't play at airs you do not have," Lady Greversham hissed, beginning to draw the attention of those nearest her. "I know you. I shall place your name soon, but I know your face. And you should be most grateful for the lack of announcement, you gilded strumpet, or you should have been cast out into the street where you belong."

Susannah stiffened and stepped back. "Excuse me, my lady." She moved around the walking stick and would continue on with her head held high until she could find a private moment to calm herself. Then something came in contact with her ankles and she tumbled forward, but was caught in a moment by a rather strong set of hands before she even came close to the ground.

She looked up into an unfamiliar face, angular features and the palest eyes she had ever seen, beneath a simple black mask. He steadied her in an instant, keeping his hold on her, then turned his hard gaze to Lady Greversham.

"Have a care, Lady Greversham," he growled in a deep voice that was laced with venom. "The lady might have received injury at your hand, and I would not take kindly to that at all."

Lady Greversham retracted her outstretched walking stick, and gave a toss of her awkwardly turbaned head, sending the beaded material of her bodice jingling. "What care you for her, Blackmoor?" she scoffed, looking at him with as much displeasure as she had Susannah.

His glare turned harder still, his eyes ice cold. "A great deal more than I care for your presence, madam, and if I hear of you mistreating her again, I shall take a most personal offense." His clipped and menacing tone widened Lady Greversham's eyes, and she looked uneasy for the first time.

Susannah did not know why his most personal offense should make anyone blanch so, but she quite enjoyed the sight.

Lady Greversham swallowed, her complexion now pale, and she pulled her fan and began speaking to the shocked woman next to her as if nothing had happened.

"Well," Blackmoor said, returning his eyes back to Susannah, "now that is settled, will you dance the next with me?"

She nodded quickly, letting him remove her at a rather fast pace. "Thank you, sir," she murmured softly.

"Never mind Lady Greversham," he instructed in a surprisingly gentle voice. "I never do."

"And you are?"

He almost smiled. "Lord Blackmoor, at your service," he replied with a nod as they went into the dance. "Though you may have heard me referred to as 'the Viscount Blackmoor'."

She hadn't.

"And how came you to be in my service, my lord?" she managed, her heart still pummeling her ribs painfully.

"I am a friend of Kit Gerrard," he said softly. "And I trust him implicitly. When he instructs me to act, I do so."

She looked back at him in surprise. "He sent you?"

Again, the viscount's lips quirked as if he would smile. "Technically, though he didn't have to. I was already coming. Now, for your own sake, smile as if the harpy cannot touch you. It is a dance, not a funeral."

Seeing the reassurance in the man's eyes, Susannah found herself relaxing at last, and the smile she bore was not as forced as she had anticipated. Her friends had rallied to her defense, silencing the old dragon, and now she was dancing with a particularly powerful viscount who had also taken up her cause.

Faintly it occurred to her to wonder where Colin had been for all of that. Had he seen it? Would he have been upset by it?

Lord Blackmoor turned her as part of the dance and her eyes caught sight of something in the corner that immediately drew her attention. Duncan and Geoffrey were bodily restraining a third man in a mask, whose shoulders heaved unsteadily, and whose vibrant blue eyes Susannah knew in an instant.

Colin.

Beneath his mask, his eyes clashed with hers, and they were wild and enraged. After a moment of contact, they eased into hardness, and his jaw tightened as his breathing became steadier. He straightened up, no longer fighting his friends, and he kept his eyes fixed on her. Then, almost imperceptibly, he nodded. Just once.

She clamped down on her lips as she was turned again, away from him. He was not unmoved by what had happened, and he was not indifferent to her.

But she could not encourage him. Not anymore. Not like this.

Lord Blackmoor was not a talkative man, but he maintained a fairly consistent line of questioning, even if there were several breaks where nothing was said. It was not awkward, or uncomfortable, and she enjoyed not being forced to speak. He was considerate and the utmost of a gentleman, and when the dance was done, he turned her into Derek's care with a kiss to her hand and a deep bow.

"Fresh air?" Derek asked softly, taking her by the elbow.

She nodded, putting a hand to her brow where a throbbing headache was beginning to form. "Please, my lord."

He steadied her with a hand on her back and Kate suddenly flanked her other side, and without a word, and without drawing any sort of attention, they escorted her out to the terrace and into the night air.

Colin released a heavy breath as he saw Derek and Kate take Susannah out to the terrace. He had not been able to breathe properly for about an hour now, and this was the first time his chest did not ache with the action.

Susannah was tormenting him with the vision of loveliness she presented, and it was all he could do to remain upright. His teeth had been grinding together so hard that his jaw throbbed as if he'd been in a particularly vicious brawl. He had not known she would be here. He would have to have a word with Tibby later, and perhaps with the others, but he knew full well that Tibby was the ringleader. She adored Susannah, it was true, and he could hardly ask her to stop liking her so readily, but this was madness.

His eyes had been on Susannah all night, unable to look at anything else. He knew every man she danced with, every person she spoke with, noted every time she laughed. And each and every minute that passed only caused his stomach to clench more than it already had. His control was paper thin and getting thinner rapidly. He could hardly have said if he were more tempted to cause a scene by raging at her or ravishing her, but he was not coherent enough or calm enough to speak to anyone.

And apparently it was obvious, for no one even tried to approach him.

He did not know what Lady Greversham had said, but he had started towards her the moment she'd stopped Susannah. He remembered all too clearly the last time that creature had interacted with Susannah, and he was not about to let it happen again. Duncan and Geoff had grabbed him and pushed him back into a corner, away from the notice of most everyone, and their combined strength kept him there, though the more he watched, the more he had strained against their hold.

When Lady Greversham had stuck her cursed walking stick out into the folds of Susannah's dress to trip her, he'd thrashed so hard against his friends he'd nearly broken free. But Duncan's growled command, laced with his authoritative tone from the army, had settled him enough to watch as Lord Blackmoor had saved her and then taken Susannah into the dance as if nothing had happened.

He would owe the viscount a debt of gratitude if he'd thought the man would take it.

Duncan and Geoff were far more sensible than he was, knowing he had not been in any kind of state to properly defend Susannah, and certainly not in a way that would help matters. He might have made things worse. And he might have done something he would have regretted.

His breathing was calmer now, and he was regaining his now usual irritated airs as he saw Susannah enter the room once more with Kate, looking much refreshed and so beautiful he hated her. He should be going to her and whispering in her ear, making her blush with his praises, promising better things to come when they married. He should have her on his arm, declaring to everyone in attendance, including her, that she was his and his alone.

But instead he was relegated to glaring from across rooms.

She was not indifferent to him. She wanted him, or at least had made a good show of it. It was entirely possible that she had been lonely, simply longing for human touch of any kind, and he had been there and convenient.

Had she ever loved him? She had never said so, not before and not since. She had been encouraging, yes, but she had never given him any expectations herself. He had assumed them all.

Perhaps he had been mistaken in her. Perhaps she did not care for him beyond what he could offer her without commitment.

He hated that he considered the thought. It was hardly like Susannah to be that way, he did not suspect she had the nature to be anything but sweet and charming.

And stubborn.

And confusing.

And captivating.

He ground his teeth again and took a sip of the punch he was holding, only to find it was empty. He growled and thrust it at Geoff, who still stood next to him.

"What am I supposed to do with this?" Geoff asked with a snort.

"I don't care," Colin snarled, walking towards the other end of the room.

His arm was grabbed and he whirled to see Duncan glaring at him. "You need to pull it together, Colin. If you want any sort of discretion at all, you need to mind yourself."

Colin inhaled and exhaled through his nose in agitation, staring at his powerful friend for a long moment. He swallowed once and nodded, then moved about the edge of the room until he was calm once more. That was not to say that the feelings fled, for he was as resentful and angry as he had been before, but he no longer wanted to tear the room apart.

Which was just as well, for now Susannah was headed in his direction, and such was the crush of masked individuals at the time that the only way for him to escape would be to go past her.

He clenched a fist and kept his gaze straight ahead, as if he were intent on the dance. He forced the muscles of his face to be relaxed and at ease, and curved one side of his mouth up. To anyone looking at him, he would be the very picture of an amused rake at a London soirée, more at ease in a mask than without one.

At this moment, it was true.

Out of the corner of his eye, he saw Susannah stutter a step when she neared him. He nearly smirked. So she had not intended on coming to him, then. Was that supposed to make him feel better or worse?

She took a glass from a passing footman and turned to face the window behind her, though her rigid posture told Colin everything he needed to know.

"Are you all right?" he asked in a low voice, knowing he should have asked more gently, but not managing to find patience at the moment.

She offered a shaky nod. "Just pretending."

Her voice sounded steady, despite the trembling of her hand as she sipped her drink. He turned just enough to speak to her. "So is everyone else. We all wear masks tonight."

She looked down at the glass she held. "Some of us wear more than one."

Colin stiffened at her words and his jaw tightened. Whether the words had been a barb for him or a reflection on herself, he couldn't have said. It burned as if she had slapped him, and his fist tightened at his side. And given the way her eyes shifted, she had noticed.

He wanted to ask her what Lady Greversham had said to her. He wanted to know how she was. He wanted her to leave and take her tempting sight and scent with her. He wanted to grab her hand and take her out to the gardens, away from the noise and the people and the moderately respectable atmosphere. He wanted her alone and in his arms. He wanted to shake her and demand to know why she wouldn't love him. He wanted to know why he would never be good enough for her, after everything.

He wanted…

"Colin…" she whispered.

He shook his head once, very firmly.

"Please."

He turned finally to look at her, and he let his rage show, enough that she took a small step back.

"Unless your feelings have changed on the topics we have previously discussed," he clipped in a low, dangerous tone, "I do not care to hear. Have they?"

Susannah stared at him, her eyes starting to shimmer with tears. Then she swallowed and looked down at the floor.

Colin huffed impatiently and moved past her, his shoulder brushing hers as he did so. He ignored her fragrance, her faint sniffle, and the way his fingers itched to linger against her skirt. He pushed passed several other members of society, none of whom marked him, and he kept his gaze fixed on the doors. He was not going to stay in this stifling environment any longer.

All these masks and costumes, all of this pretending and

entertainment, he was done with all of it. He wanted what was real, something he could hold onto and trust. He was through with wishing for something that would never come, yearning for some far off dream like the foolish young boy he had once been.

Colin stormed out of the room, yanking off his mask and tossing it aside. He nodded wordlessly when a servant asked if he wanted his carriage called and paced in the entryway while he waited for it.

He was done with all of this madness.

Chapter Nineteen

"*They are looking for you, Lady Hawkins-Dean. I was able to hold them off last time, but they begin to threaten me.*"

Susannah hurried through the rain, the skirts of her gown in hand. Mr. Goulding had looked very concerned, and much older than she had seen him before. She had given him what she could and he had been satisfied, compared with her usual amounts, but then he had set it aside and said those words to her. She promised that she would take care of it, and begged to hold them off as long as possible.

He had not been pleased, but he had given her his word, and he had never treated her wrongly before.

She had known for some time that the men she owed were looking for her; the thugs she had run into on the streets before had given her that indication. But according to Mr. Goulding, now the collectors themselves were getting involved. And if she could not give them the amounts they demanded for their patience, they would see her in a debtor's prison and force her son into indentured servitude.

She need not give them the full amount, he had assured her, for they knew very well the complete balance would be impossible for now. But the payment they wanted was more than she had earned at this point, considering she'd had to give some to Mr. Jacobs for her family.

She should ask for help. A loan, perhaps, to keep herself out of prison and to keep Freddie safe. But who could she ask? Tibby was already so generous with her, to ask for more would be impossible. Colin and Kit claimed to have plenty, but considering the strain on their relationship, she could hardly ask for anything from them. And

Colin would demand that she explain, and he already knew she had debts. If he knew the extent of them, and the rest of the story…

A loud crash of thunder made her jump and she turned to cut through Hyde Park, rather than going around. The trees would provide her some shelter, though not much, considering her hat had proven useless. She needed to get home as soon as possible, she could still take whatever money that remained to Mr. Goulding. Perhaps this close to the payment requested would satisfy them until she could get more. She could go to Mrs. Randall and ask for more work, her niece was apparently worse help than she previously thought.

But would any of it be enough? No one had dared to threaten Freddie before, and the merest hint that he should be in danger…

She jerked at another flash of lightning and accompanying thunder. The rain picked up its intensity, sweeping sideways and pummeling her clothing and skin. Her feet were slipping in the damp grass, and she was going to do herself injury if she were not careful. The raindrops were becoming painful as they hit her, and she winced as there was another crash of lightning and thunder.

She spotted a gazebo not far off, and hurried towards it. She did not need to be reckless, even if she did wish to be expeditious.

She would be no good to anyone injured or worse.

The rain picked up even more as she made her way over there, and she breathed a sigh of relief when she was at last beneath it. She removed her sopping hat and tossed it aside. Her spencer was absolutely drenched, so she unbuttoned that and removed it, wringing it and shaking it out. Then she hung it on a railing and shivered. It was a cool day, and while there was no possible way the jacket would be dry by the time she would leave, it might at least be less sopping.

She rubbed her arms quickly, trying to restore some warmth to her, when she heard someone else arrive in the gazebo just as the rain began coming down in torrential sheets, and the wind whipped the drops around viciously. The air blew through the gazebo, drawing another shiver from her and she tucked against a pillar to attempt to shield herself more.

She laughed a bit shakily. "It seems you've made it just in time," she said, turning to the other person. "You would be swimming if you still…" She broke off with a faint gasp when she saw the person she was now sharing the gazebo with.

Colin stared at her as if he had been struck from behind, eyes wide, mouth slightly parted, and his expression spoke of the temptation to turn and run, despite the storm.

The thunder and lightning picked up in their volume and intensity, and Susannah felt her heart echoing them. She could not look away from Colin, no matter how her heart and mind told her to. His chestnut hair was clinging to his face and dripping visibly. His cravat hung limply against his soaked linen shirt, which clung to his skin. His fine waistcoat and jacket were drenched, as were his fawn-colored breeches, while his boots were caked with mud and blades of grass.

She realized she could not have looked any better. She felt her hair dripping on her neck, and damp tendrils stuck to her cheeks and forehead. Her green muslin, though fine and impressive usually, was now limp and faint, not to mention filthy, considering her traipse through the park. Her petticoats were clinging to her legs, and the long sleeves of her gown had become a second skin to her. She dared not look at her bodice, but thankfully, she had folded her arms across it before she had seen who it was.

She swallowed hastily as she continued to look at Colin, and saw him do the same. His eyes left hers to take her in, as she had done with him, and her cheeks flushed as she saw his gaze darken. His lips pressed together in a thin line, and his eyes came back to hers, but he said nothing.

He moved to one of the posts and leaned against it, eyes still trained on her, as if he were waiting for something.

Suddenly nervous, Susannah broke eye contact and moved to the furthest part of the gazebo from him. She pushed a dripping lock of hair behind her ear with shaking fingers. Her face was warm to the touch, or perhaps her fingers were chilled. She glanced surreptitiously at Colin, who watched her still, and she looked away, swallowing again.

She could not feel her knees at the moment, and it really was, quite suddenly, fairly warm out. She brushed at the tendrils clinging to her brow and tried to wring out some of her hair without letting any of it tumble down. That would not help matters at all. An odd coiling sensation was building somewhere in the vicinity of her stomach, yet she felt it down to her toes and in the tips of her fingers.

She shivered again, and rubbed her arms, looking up briefly.

Colin had not moved. He leaned against the post still, just as he had with the doorjamb at Tibby's that day. He looked perfectly at ease for all his posture, yet there was a visible tension riding through his entire frame. His face was taut, his eyes focused, and she was not entirely sure if he were angry or callous or intrigued. She could see traces of all of them, along with something else.

Something that terrified her.

She looked out at the rain, still coming down impossibly hard, lightning and thunder rolling on. She would never be able to make it back to Tibby's in this, and there was not a thick stand of trees in sight. She could not escape. She bit her lip and moaned softly, then caught herself and covered her mouth at once.

Somehow, her eyes went back to Colin. His jaw had tightened more, his throat worked once, and his chest moved unevenly with each breath.

He should not be here with her. But she could not find it in her heart to wish him away. He was so alluring in this manner, as if the elements could not affect him, as if he had been perfectly disordered by nature to grace him with sinfully attractive airs. His eyes were so dark now, their blue depths captivating in their strength.

Her hand fluttered from her mouth to her throat, where her pulse throbbed painfully and every breath caught. He watched her for so many heartbeats she lost count, his eyes measuring every breath she took, as he if knew exactly what turmoil was raging within her. He barely blinked as he stared at her, nothing moving but the increasingly unsteady rise and fall of his chest and shoulders. The coiling in her swirled and rose, threatened to consume her, and all she could do was exhale a soft, gasping breath.

Colin shoved off of the wall and came towards her, brows narrowed, eyes focused on her lips, and before she could move or breathe, his mouth was on hers, hungry and insistent. There was a fury that drove him, his hands seizing the sides of her head as if in a vice, locked in his hold, captive to his desires.

The tension within her burst into a thousand pieces as a sob of relief and agony escaped her. She latched her hands into his hair, pulling herself closer than she thought she could, pressing herself along every inch of him, her need suddenly overwhelming and consuming.

He tilted her head for a better angle, and his groan of satisfaction seem to catch in her own throat as her fingers clenched more tightly into his hair. Suddenly he forced her back against the post, the rough wood pressing and catching on the back of her delicate dress. She gasped and pulled him closer, wrapping an arm around his neck as her other hand rubbed and stroked along his stubbled jaw.

He bracketed one of his hands against the post, leaning more fully into her, while the other still held the side of her face, his fingers clenching slightly into her skin as his lips devoured every coherent thought, every fluttering sensation now coursing through her in waves. Their breath mingled as one, panting and gasping, a new tension rising between them as the thunder roared around them.

It was not enough. It was too much.

It was everything.

She felt her tears flowing, could taste the saltiness of them in their impatient and frenzied kisses. Colin was wild and unrestrained in his passion, thrilling her with his strength and the force of his emotions, the strength of his hold, and the desperation in his lips. She was no match for him.

His mouth suddenly slid from hers to her cheek, his breath rasping against her skin as his lips wandered across her face. He grazed her jaw with his teeth, then whispered, "How can you kiss me like this and refuse me?"

Her heart stopped in her chest at his harsh words and just as suddenly, he shoved off her, backing away, his chest and shoulders heaving, his eyes wild. His expression was cold, and bordered on disgust, despite the trembling now visibly coursing through them both.

Susannah clamped a hand over her mouth as her desperate

emotions recoiled into sobs.

Colin shook his head slowly, eyes hard, then turned and walked out of the gazebo, back out into the still raging storm, head held high.

Susannah inhaled sharply as her knees gave out, and she collapsed to the floor, her sobs coming at a frantic pace. She was drowned out by the noise of the storm, and she clawed at the wood, wishing she could sink herself into it, that she could expunge any and all feelings out of her soul. She had destroyed Colin, and he held all power to destroy her.

He wanted her, and he hated her for it. That was what she had tasted in his kisses. Anger. Seething, burning anger that consumed him just as much as his desire did.

She had wounded him beyond reckoning and he was not going to stand idly by this time. He was not going to be made a fool the second time. He would exact his revenge, knowing that she was not immune to him.

And yet, she would cling to this just as fiercely as she had her other memories of him. This feeling of being wanted so madly, so desperately, even if it killed her, would live with her forever.

She had to be strong, to move forward, to go on and face her future. The future she always knew she would face. Alone. Without him.

Broken hearted or not.

But for now, while the storm raged outside, and within, she curled up into a ball on the floor of the gazebo, and sobbed.

Colin sank into a chair once he was alone, after having forbidden Mrs. Creighton to let the girls near Susannah any more, and put a hand to his head. He was never going to be able to face the world if he could not find some control. And every time he closed his eyes, he was back in that blasted gazebo, heart and soul and body aflame.

He ought to have had more control than to assault her in such a way, particularly when he was furious with her. When she wore more masks than he had the patience to reveal. When she had apparently gone the way of her family and found him lacking in every respect that mattered.

His heart still leapt in excitement when he recalled her eager response to his kiss, the fervor in her arms, and tears of relief. He'd not meant to be cruel, he'd been helpless in the face of his love, his need, his yearning for all that she was. His mind had been obliterated by the thrill of having her in his arms again, in surrendering to her, in grasping whatever glimmer of hope she would give him. Only at the end had his thoughts been clear, and the dark, bitter monster within him had roared in the indignity of once more being ensnared by her. Those words, harsh and cruel and biting, yet poignantly true, had been ripped from him, and he found he did not wish them back.

He wanted her to hurt as he did.

He wanted her to suffer.

He wanted her to understand just how deep his feelings for her went.

He slammed his hand down on the desk and cursed once more. Why could he not be rid of her?

The storm had done nothing to cool him, and it had taken him a full day to be able to speak anything of sense to anybody, and even now, he was tormented with an inferno of rage unlike anything he had ever experienced. Mrs. Creighton felt the force of it just now, the girls avoided him as if he was the devil himself, and the servants were hesitant and cowering in his presence.

His upending the tea tray yesterday may have had something to do with that.

Quick, brisk footsteps brought his head up to see his brother entering the study and closing the door, his jaw and neck so tense Colin could see it from where he was.

He glowered at Kit's back, knowing he was in for another pompous speech from his always-perfect brother.

"Colin, I need to say something to you," Kit said slowly, hand still on the door, his voice remarkably calm.

Colin snorted. "Spoken with Mrs. Creighton, have you?"

Kit turned and looked at him with marked coldness. "And

Bartlet. And the maids. And Rosie and Bitty."

"Oh, yes, you've made the rounds, I see," Colin retorted, propping his feet on the desk and crossing his ankles. "A few more people, and you could hold a trial for me."

Kit's brows snapped together. "You would not speak to me after the ball, but so help me, you will speak with me now."

"I thought you said you were not my lord and master," he sneered.

"That was before you were being an imbecile."

"Go to hell."

Kit exhaled slowly through his nose, hands on his hips. Then he looked at Colin once more, apparently calm. "Colin, you are losing yourself in your hatred and anger towards Susannah. You are going to suffocate everything good about you and her. I don't think you are being fair with her. In fact, I think that…"

Colin held up a hand, his jaw working a bit. "Kit, you are my brother and my friend, and I value your opinion in all things. But just this once, shut up. I will hit you, if I must. I mean it. Stop."

Kit's eyes widened. "Don't be ridiculous."

Colin pushed to his feet, temper rising further. "Kit, I have never said a word about your obsession with Marianne Bray, mostly because I generally trust your judgment and Lord knows you deserve a lapse of it now and again."

Kit slowly straightened at that, any warmth disintegrating from his features.

Colin allowed himself a cold smile. "Because I have not said anything and you have been very kind about Susannah all these years, I will remain calm. But if you push me on this and do not shut up this instant, you will find yourself flung out of that window and landing on the unfortunate side of the stables."

"I am not obsessed with Marianne," Kit growled.

Colin tilted his head. "And I am not an idiot. So who is lying here?"

His brother pointed a deadly finger at him. "Do not talk about Marianne. Ever. You have no idea what you are talking about."

"Then it appears we are both clueless," Colin sneered with a shrug, folding his arms tightly.

Kit raised his chin, his eyes frigid. "I have a clue. Several, in fact. And I will employ them as I see fit. And because I am your older brother by forty minutes, I will tell you now that if you ever mention my feelings for her, whatever they are, again, I will see to it that the unfortunate side of the stables will be your warmest thoughts of home." He bowed as if Colin were nothing more than a guest in his home, turned on his heel, and stormed from the study, the door slamming against the wall with the force of his exit.

Colin stared at the open door for a moment, then turned and punched the bookshelf with a violent curse. He had never said anything like that to his brother, and had never intended to, but he had never been so riled and unhinged in his entire life. For Kit to mistrust his judgment was unsettling. Though they might not see things the same way, he had never been so directly attacked or questioned. And he had certainly never lashed out in the way he had.

It felt good. In a horrible, vindictive way, it had felt as thrilling as he always imagined a victory in battle would be. His blood still burned as it coursed through him like fire, and his breathing was ragged.

So people were curious about him, were they? Concerned about his behavior? Well, that was all well and good. They had no idea what had seethed beneath his surface for his entire adult life. They could not begin to imagine what his heart endured daily.

A shuffling sound met his ears and he turned, looking back towards the door, but nothing was there. He glanced around the room, unable to place it, and then he saw a small, dark, curly head appear from beneath his desk.

His breath caught as Ginny turned to see him there, her blue eyes wide, shining, and terrified.

He nearly swore again, but caught it in his throat. He swallowed and said, "How long have you been there, poppet?"

It was a stupid question, she had obviously heard everything that had transpired in here for at least an hour. He should not have been surprised, Ginny hid in the oddest places at will. But for her to have been witness to what had just happened…

He held out a hand and started towards her. "Come here, little one," he murmured, keeping his voice as gentle as he could.

Ginny skittered back immediately, her back coming in contact with the sideboard loudly. A soft, childish whimper escaped her trembling lips and his heart shattered.

"Ginny," he whispered, unable to move.

She turned and shuffled quickly out of the room, never once looking back at him.

For a moment, he did nothing. He could not move, or breathe, or think.

He ran his hands through his hair, not surprised at how they shook. He was in tatters, nothing left of respectability or goodness, and no good to anybody.

He had to get out, before he hurt anyone else, before he was entirely consumed by his wrath.

Colin grabbed the jacket he'd thrown on the floor and was out of the house before he'd managed to get it completely on. The evening was upon him, and the chill in the air suited his mood too perfectly. The sky above was blanketed with clouds, no hint of stars or moon, which was also too appropriate.

People milled about, no doubt leaving for fine events about Town, hopes high and energy spirited. They paid him no mind, which he was grateful for, considering he might well have snapped their heads off, and that would not have done at all. He needed to be alone. He needed to go somewhere to cool off, to regain himself.

Or to forget himself entirely.

He was not prone to drinking strongly, he found it did not suit nor sit well. But at this moment, it was the only thing he wanted. And he would do so in the darkest corner of the world he could find.

Hopper's Tavern, known for its underhanded dealings, gambling with more than cards, and the ability of its proprietor to look the other way, was the perfect means to the end he had in mind. No one would suspect him of being there. No one would know him there.

And once inside, seeing the dank and oppressive scope of the place, he was quite sure he would not know himself either.

Darkness settled on his heart and he felt it seeping through him like an illness. He moved to a corner of the room, sat at an old, worn, suspiciously stained table, and signaled to the homely barmaid for a drink. She gave him a bawdy wink that made him shudder, and he promptly ignored her when she returned with the overflowing tankard.

Another replaced it before he was completely finished, but he did not mind. He would rather be insensible, and the faster he could get there, the better.

A man in dirty, common clothing approached him. "You ignored my message," clipped a familiar voice.

Colin looked up into a bearded, tanned face with imperious dark eyes boring down on him. Cap on head, the top of his face was slightly shadowed, but there was no mistaking the command of his tone. The Gent had found him, even here.

Colin shrugged. "It hardly seemed important."

The slight stiffening of his companion nearly made him wince. "Did you read it?" he asked in a low tone.

Colin shook his head slowly, focused more on trying to place the man before him, now he had seen his face. But it was just as unfamiliar as the voice had ever been. He would never know the identity, it seemed, and that irked him.

"Why not? You sent me on this errand, and now that I have results, you would want to know them, would you not?"

Colin did not care for the faint taunting in his voice, the hint of a sneer, though his face held nothing of the sort. He pushed himself back from the table and rose, moving to push past him. "I don't want to hear this," he muttered.

His shirt was suddenly seized and he was thrown back against the wall and into his seat. "I don't care," the Gent snarled, releasing him and taking the seat next to him. "You will hear me out, and then we will see what is left of your indignation."

The bite in his words left Colin stripped of resistance, his curiosity unwittingly aroused, and the dark feeling from before now flooding through him with sharp pains. Something was not right, he could see it in the Gent's face. A strange tingling prickled the back of his neck and started making its walk down his spine.

The Gent gave him a hard look, disapproval wafting off of him. "Do not ask me how I know this, I will not share my methods or my sources. And none of this, I repeat, *none* of this is to be shared beyond those of the utmost discretion and trustworthiness, if you choose to include anyone at all."

Colin swallowed and nodded only once, involuntarily inching a bit closer.

The Gent released a soft exhale. "Your Susannah Merritt was indeed married at sixteen years of age. To Sir Martin Hawkins-Dean. Heard of him?"

Colin shook his head quickly.

There was a low grunt. "That does not surprise me. He was, in life, the most vile, depraved, pathetic sort of bottom dweller that ever slithered on this earth, and I have known a great many villains. Her family married her off to save their fortune, which was rather efficiently milked away by poor management and poorer investments. They knew of the rumors surrounding him, but so desperate were they for monetary salvation, they practically sold their daughter to him."

His now-constant companion of rage burned fiercely and he curled his hands into fists as he stared at his associate.

"Sir Martin was a simple knight, nothing worthy of honor or acclaim, but it did not stop him from trying," the Gent continued, shaking his head. "His holdings are in one of the furthest points in Northumberland, a little place called Milfield that most people have never heard of, which was perfect for his means. He squandered his fortune regularly and without a care for its effects. He left the management of his wife's family to her and the allotment of funds that had been agreed upon in the marriage negotiations. But it did not take long for him to lose so much that those funds were no longer available. His lands were sold off, piece by piece, until only Pavel House and its immediate gardens remained in his care. And then he partitioned that off as well, the staff dwindling into complete nothingness. And do you know who served him then? As footman, butler, housemaid, cook, and valet?"

Colin's eyes widened and his throat worked absently in an

attempt to formulate some response.

The Gent nodded slowly. "He owned her, so he used her. He ran up debts upon debts, keeping up the appearances of his wealth and prestige. No one suspected that he was so in want of funds that he rid himself of the responsibility of his son's inheritance in order to attempt to satisfy a portion of it."

He looked at Colin with an increased intensity, and Colin sat back hard against the wall. "What did he do to Freddie?" Colin whispered.

The Gent's eyes shuttered and his mouth tightened. "He declared the boy illegitimate, provided apparent proof of the lady's indiscretion, and thus negated the terms of the will. The house was mortgaged over to the creditors as part of his debt."

Colin put his head into his hands with a hiss. Then he looked over at the Gent as he replayed the words. "Part?"

The Gent nodded slowly. "A mere percentage of what was owed. And somehow, Susannah managed to set aside some meager amounts to send to her family."

Colin shook his head quickly. "But there must be some way to prove that Freddie was his son, that he can inherit…?"

"No," the Gent overrode with a shake of his head, "there isn't. It is as irreversible as it is false. Sir Martin went a step further and declared himself to be impotent, which no one would dare refute, as such a thing would never be admitted by any man of sense and title. But the claim was complete nonsense, as he had fathered several illegitimates over his lifetime."

Colin groaned and closed his eyes, leaning his head back against the wall. Never had he imagined it could be so bad, that anyone could be forced to live in such circumstances, that Susannah had endured such a life.

"The debts piled up continually during the course of Sir Martin's life," the Gent continued, "and when he died, courtesy of a violent fever, justice came to claim them. And the widow of Sir Martin had no idea how extensive they were. The house was seized, and all has been sold for a pittance of its value to Sir Martin's cousin, who wanted to claim the inheritance that is not his. Nothing was left to satisfy the creditors, and though Susannah was liked in Milfield for her service in the village, and with the nuns, and at the hospital, there was no one to help her. She gave over the funds she had, and began to work in the village she was once the lady of. And when that did not satisfy the demand, she took her son and fled rather than face the poorhouse or debtor's prison."

"To London," Colin rasped, running shaking hands through his hair.

The Gent nodded, waving aside the barmaid who was coming to ask after him. "She changed her name often, worked as she could along the journey here, and arrived in the heart of the city, where she worked for their boarding. And even now, she pays amounts to the solicitor for her husband, and to the one she hired for her family, who are now almost completely destitute and have no way to alter their circumstances without her."

"I had no idea," Colin whispered. He shook his head, attempting to swallow multiple times before he succeeded. "No idea." His eyes began to sting suspiciously and he pinched at the bridge of his nose.

The Gent said nothing for a long moment, then he sighed heavily. "There is more."

"How much more could there be?" Colin asked, his voice croaking.

"I have only spoken of money and situation." There was another long hesitation, and then, "I have not said anything at all about what life was like for Susannah. What horrors she endured."

Slowly Colin lowered his hand, his eyes fixed on the Gent in dismay. "What else?" he asked, his words scraping against his throat.

The Gent looked down at his hands on the table. "Anyone who ever went to Pavel House was going into a den of the foulest, most unspeakable sort of place. Ruination was commonplace. Nothing respectable ever entered or came out. There was no secrecy or discretion about it, rather it was on grand display. Reckless extravagance and wildness fueled behaviors that would scandalize even the darkest parts of London. Greed, deception, and lust were all that ruled there, and there was not any member of the house that was spared in the undertakings. Saving for one small child, whose father hated him with such ferocity that he was never mentioned and never allowed any sort of privilege." There was a very faint shadow of a smile. "But his mother found ways around that as well. He was remarkably sheltered for the hellhole in which he was raised."

"And Susannah?" He could barely get the words out, could hardly manage to speak her name.

The Gent looked at him now, expression and eyes hard and cold. "She was forced into whatever her husband saw fit. Commands and edicts were obeyed or she was punished, sometimes brutally. She was continually and publicly mocked, derided, and humiliated, and she had to bear it all with silence, for anything else was punishable. Abuse in every form was her daily promise, and every bawdy, disgusting event Sir Martin hosted she was forced to attend. To host alongside him. But never as his lady, he would never raise her to his level. She was less than a servant to him, and to all that attended there. Never a participant in what took place there, but she was forced to be witness to it, and refusal was impossible. She had to obey. She always had to obey."

Colin stared at the Gent without seeing him, his eyes unfocused as his body roiled with the revelations. His head swam and his fingers shook, and suddenly he was ill. He latched onto the table, and retched on the far side, emptying his stomach again and again.

Shame poured over him in unending waves, and still he felt sick. Why could he not see it? He had been so intent on what he wanted, what he could see, what his injuries had been, that he had missed what had been right before him. He knew that she had suffered, had seen it from the beginning, but never could he have imagined that it would have been so horrific, so beyond words.

And he had wanted to force her to tell him all?

He could barely stand to hear it from someone completely unattached, he would never have survived hearing it directly from her lips. And how could he have expected her to relive such horrors?

He'd thought it all about money. Such a simple, childish assumption. It might have been the cause of her desperation now, but it was hardly relevant by comparison.

He righted himself and set his elbows on the table, covering his face. How he had misjudged her. How he had betrayed her with his anger and his mistrust. He was hardly worthy of a woman who could endure so much and still find the autumn beautiful. Who could still hope. Who could love so tenderly.

"I trust you have all that you need to proceed as you will," the Gent murmured, getting to his feet. "If I can be of any further assistance, you know how to contact me."

Colin did not respond, his face in his hands, faint convulsions racking him.

A coin landed on the table near his elbow.

"Get yourself a hack and get home," the Gent suggested firmly. "You are in no condition to walk there, and this is not the place for you."

Colin heard the rustle of his clothes and the fading footfalls. "Gent?" he called.

The footsteps stopped. "Yes?"

He rubbed at his eyes. "How much?"

There was a pause, and then he heard the boots shift against the wood floor. "How much what?"

Colin dropped his hands, met his friend's eyes steadily, and swallowed hard. "How much money, exactly, remains to be paid?"

Chapter Twenty

S usannah did not even attempt to play at haughty airs with the assistant this time, or change her dress, or care at all about what anybody thought of her. She had run almost the entire way there, and her hair was a fright, her face and brow and back dripping with perspiration, and the shock on the assistant's face registered somewhere in the back of her mind, but not with any significance.

She was immediately shown into Mr. Goulding's office and he rose with a kind smile, but she ignored that as well as she set all of the money she had managed to scrape together, most of it rather frantically over the last three days, on his desk. The moment she had picked herself off of the floor of that gazebo, she'd had the sole focus of getting all the money she could, however she could, in the hopes that it would hold off the creditors and their threat of prison.

Susannah had not shed another tear since then, not for herself or Colin or her fears. She had worked her fingers to the bone for Mrs. Randall, hardly sleeping at all and almost completely neglecting her son, and Tibby had graciously given her an advance on her salary without any questions or raised brows. Three days and nights of emotionless, mind-numbing work and desperation, all for this.

All told, it was not the grand amount she had hoped to achieve for all her efforts, but it ought to have been enough to settle the feathers of those who hunted her now.

"There," she said with satisfaction as she pushed the money towards him. "Will that satisfy them, do you suppose?"

Mr. Goulding looked down at the money, then back up at her. "I don't understand," he finally said.

She gave him a look, her hands setting at her hips. "What is there to understand?" she asked. "They wanted more money, I have brought more money. Do you need further explanation?"

Mr. Goulding did not react to her sudden rudeness. He wet his lips, slowly drew his spectacles off of their perch on his nose, and exhaled. "Lady Hawkins-Dean, I thought you knew…"

Susannah was suddenly very uneasy. "Knew what?"

His expression remained placid. "The debts are paid. In full."

She must have been more sleep deprived than she thought, for the words she had just heard were complete and utter nonsense. She staggered to the side a little and caught the chair nearest her. "I beg your pardon?"

His eyes were curious, but kind, and his mouth curved into a small smile. "They are paid, my lady. All of them. Every bit. The creditors are all satisfied, no one is hunting you, and no one is going to a debtor's prison. You do not owe anything to anybody anymore. Not a farthing."

Her hold on the chair trembled and her head was suddenly swimming. "How?" she managed. "When?"

He picked up her money and brought it over to her, taking her arm and helping her into the seat she clung to. "It was all settled about an hour ago. I don't know how, or who; I was working with other solicitors and bankers. I just assumed it was your friends we have been speaking of, though I hardly expect that any one person could pay so much at once. Could they have done this in secret out of kindness for you?"

"I never told them," she whispered, finally admitting the truth of it. "I never told anyone how much it was, how bad it had gotten there at the end…" She shook her head. "No one knew. And I took great care not to be followed or accompanied when I came here. You understand why."

He nodded at once, seeming more comfortable now that she was speaking sense. "I do. And all I can say, my lady, is that someone very powerful, or several of them, must be looking out for you. It is the only explanation I can come up with for this miraculous turn of events."

Susannah would not contradict him, considering what had occurred, but there was no such person in her life. No one knew the truth, especially not her friends, and no one had those funds. Well, perhaps Tibby, but she had taken great care to completely avoid any hint of possibility that she would ever know.

"No more debts," she murmured softly, the reality sinking in. She ought to cry, she felt as though she *should* be crying, but there were no tears to be had. She was almost numb, in fact.

One thought found its way through the murky melee of her thoughts: what of her other debt that Mr. Goulding knew nothing about? Not a debt as structured or demanding as what was now apparently settled, but it was no less pressing in her life.

She rose quickly, and stammered out some sort of excuse that nobody in their right mind would have believed, forcing the money back into her reticule.

Mr. Goulding bowed as he took her hand. "It has been my honor to be of service to you, my lady, though the circumstances were abominable. If there is anything I can do for you in the future, please do let me know."

She nodded, thanked him, and swept from the office far more grandly than she had entered.

At which point, she ran, full tilt, for Mr. Jacobs' office. She had no reason to suspect that anything should have been done on that end, even fewer people knew of her family's destitution than knew of her husband and his ruin. But she had to know, had to be sure.

Mr. Jacobs did not look at all surprised to see her. And he gave her the second blow of the day.

"They are all taken care of, Mrs. Clarke," he said with a smile, using the alias she'd provided. "Your cousin explained that he had come into some money and thought he could help the family. They will not be well off, but it will be sufficient for their means. And he was particular to set up an annual sum for them. You don't have to supply them any more funds."

Susannah clamped her lips together to keep from letting a hoarse cry escape. Then she found her way through the shock and managed to say, "Cousin?"

Mr. Jacobs grinned. "Yes, he said you might be startled by it. Wanted it to be a surprise, I gather."

"Which cousin?" Susannah asked carefully, knowing full well she did not have any cousins living.

Mr. Jacobs thought for a moment. "Do you know, I don't believe he said? We only finally worked things out with him and his solicitor this morning, and with all of that, I did not get a name. I apologize."

She forced a smile she did not feel. "What did he look like, Mr. Jacobs?" she asked, hoping to at least get an idea of who might be setting out such money for her.

"Average height," he said, measuring with his hand. "Blonde hair, dark eyes, very finely dressed, stocky fellow, bit of an Irish lilt. Do you have Irish blood?"

"By marriage," she lied easily, feeling even more bewildered. She didn't know anyone matching that description. And if Mr. Jacobs didn't know who it was, or question the supposed relationship, she could hardly press the matter.

And at this moment, she didn't want to ask any questions at all.

Mr. Jacobs laughed at her expression. "It's over, Mrs. Clarke. Get on with your life."

She nodded, her chest tightening and her head feeling so light she thought it would fly off of her body with the slightest breeze. Somehow she made her way from the solicitor's office, and the business district, and eventually wandering back into Mayfair.

She walked towards Tibby's house, her thoughts awhirl, unaware of her surroundings. How could her debts be so easily paid? She refused to believe it, and yet her solicitors had said so. She was free. And yet her freedom did not sit well. Would the men who had been so ruthlessly pursuing her be so easily appeased? They wanted far more than the settlement, they wanted complete ruination. She was not ruined, only destitute.

She could not trust this.

Her desperation might be gone, but her situation was not much different. Her past was still her past, and the ties remained.

They could still come for her.

She did not owe money to anyone, which meant she could settle for less wages. More discretion. Less pain. London was perfect place to hide, and now she had more reason to. Or… there could be something more.

She heard her name called and thought for a moment that her fears had been right. Her heart, having leapt to her throat, now crashed to her stomach as she saw Colin and a very pretty young woman headed in her direction. Colin's expression was blank, but the girl on his arm was beaming.

Her name escaped Susannah at the moment, but that seemed inconsequential.

Colin was obviously close with her, and it was the final straw.

She tried for a smile, though the effort nearly killed her.

"Miss Hart!" his companion exclaimed with a genuine delight and too-perfect smile. "What a most pleasant surprise!"

Susannah licked her lips quickly and curtseyed. "Miss Arden," she murmured, relieved to have recalled the name at last. "I wonder if you might lend me Mr. Gerrard for a moment. Only a brief one," she added, seeing Colin stiffen a bit.

Colin shook his head, his jaw tightening further still. "I am sorry, Miss Hart, but I really must see Miss Arden returned to her aunt. She is late, and must not go unescorted."

Miss Arden looked confused, but said nothing.

Susannah tried for a swallow. "Very well. Perhaps another time then." But she doubted there would be another time. She needed to leave, and he obviously took no pleasure in seeing her. She had not forgotten their last encounter, and there was nothing in this version of Colin to recommend him.

"Indeed," he said with a nod, shifting closer to Miss Arden. He started to move, then stopped and gave her a too-polite look that she did not believe. "Is it of importance?"

"No," she heard herself say in a tremulous voice. "No, it is only the topics we have discussed before. I have… been giving them thought."

His eyes narrowed slightly, but were cold. "I see. I have been doing the same."

"Have you?" she asked, almost holding her breath.

He nodded once. "You were right." He gave her a tight smile that could have been a grimace. "Geese and swans and all that."

She could only blink as the air in her lungs was suddenly gone. "I... I see," she finally replied, her tongue and throat feeling parched and coarse on the words.

"Do you?" he asked, peering more closely at her.

She gave a brief nod. "Yes. Far better than you can imagine. I..."

I did not think you would feel that way. I thought I could... I thought... I thought...

Lord, what a fool she was.

She cleared her throat and somehow managed to force a smile. "I apologize for taking up your time, Mr. Gerrard. Miss Arden. Good day."

He inclined his head. "Miss Hart."

But she had already turned from him, nearly stumbling in her haste to be away from him. From them. From feelings. From memories.

She couldn't breathe, her lungs simply refused to take in air at all, and her knees quivered in their attempts to work properly.

She had spent so long dreaming of heaven, thinking she could never have it, keeping herself from touching it. And now that a way had been opened, heaven within her reach, she had found herself forbidden after all.

And consequently found herself in hell.

Scattered, panicked breaths eventually emerged from her and she clutched at her chest in agony, pain searing her. He didn't want her. He finally saw what she had been telling him, that he was too far above her for such a connection, despite their feelings. She had forced his feelings from him, turned him into a memory after all. He found her unworthy, lacking, perhaps even tainted.

Her head swam, her cheeks burned, it seemed every eye was on her as she staggered along the paths towards home. Her feet were as unsteady as her mind, too painfully focused on the loss of her one bright shining memory, the only thing Sir Martin could not steal, to do anything else. Her ears rang strangely, no sound audible but the frantic, scattered, agonized pattering of her broken heart.

What would she do without Colin? He could go on as he ever had, perhaps even with Miss Arden at his side, or some other nameless, faceless proper Society girl. He could be what she'd always assumed he would be. Happy without her, better without her, loving without her.

It was not supposed to hurt this much. She had been resigned to it before. Now…

She covered her mouth as a soft sob nearly broke free. She squeezed her eyes shut on the falling tears, every bone in her body suddenly on fire. She couldn't bear this. She was free to do as she wished and yet she had no direction. Nothing to hope for or dream of, nothing to wonder about or wish on a star for, nothing to take her from her reality.

Nothing.

She could not bear this.

Mayfair was suddenly a place of nightmares. Everything… every tree and horse and person… would remind her of Colin. The houses she was now seeing would remind her of the walk to Colin's. Hyde Park would be all memories of Colin. The dress she was wearing had been a gift from Colin. Even Tibby would remind her of Colin.

She had to leave. She had to take Freddie and go.

She did not know where, and she did not care either. Anywhere would be better than here. She was not desperate for funds anymore, she could work anywhere and do anything without worry.

But she could not wait. She would not.

Explanation and reason would be impossible.

She was leaving at once, within the hour, if she had anything to say about it.

And no one would dissuade her.

Colin slowly made his way home after escorting Lily Arden to her aunt's home. He'd happened upon her in the park by accident, and, finding her alone and unaccompanied, he had volunteered to see her there. He'd spent the entire morning finalizing the details of Susannah's debts and finances, and now it was done, he was finally starting to see a hint of his old self.

But then he'd seen Susannah, and he'd had a devil of a time containing himself.

She wanted to talk about *them*. He wasn't ready yet. There was too much left to do.

Yes, he had gone to extraordinary lengths for her, and he would have done more if he could, but he did not do any of it to win her. He was only doing what he could to ease her path, to do what he should have been doing for fifteen years. Instead of doubting her and hating her, thinking the very worst of her, and doing his level best to pretend she was nothing to him, he ought to have given in to his instincts, found a way to dig deeper, and trusted what his heart had been trying to tell him all along.

If he had, perhaps he might have saved her sooner. He might have prevented the horrors in her past, or at least relieved some of them. They might have found happiness. Had it not been for his wounded pride and obstinacy, he might have been worthy of her.

She was the single most remarkable woman in the world. And he loved her beyond all comprehension and reason, far more deeply and thoroughly than he thought he could bear. He loved her enough to know that marriage to him, as he was, while his wildest and most fervent fantasy, would never be a single percentage of what she ought to have.

Through the help of the Gent and his associates, and Colin's own, they had managed to make a start, and perhaps eventually he would be able to attain his heart's only desire. But while he was so unworthy, he couldn't presume such things.

He entered his house to find the strange solitude he had become accustomed to of late. He peered into a drawing room, wondering why the drapes had been pulled to make the room so dark.

He set about pulling back the drapes of the room, feeling as if he were starting to pull back the thick and darkening drapes of his own heart and soul as well. It was an apt analogy.

"Lady Raeburn, sir," Bartlet's voice intoned a bit breathlessly from the door.

Colin started to turn when he heard a very shrill voice screech, "What the hell did you do, Colin Gerrard?"

He smirked a little and raised a brow as he turned completely to face Tibby. "I thought you said a lady never swears," he replied cheekily.

Tibby's expression wiped his amusement away. Her face was contorted with rage, her lace cap askew, and all hint of her usual finery gone as she stood before him in a simple gray dress and plum colored walking coat. She snarled a bit at him. "Do you see a lady at this moment?" she snapped.

Colin took a moment, measuring Tibby's obvious distress and anger, something rather nervous unfurling in the pit of his stomach. "What's happened, Tibby?"

"What's happened is that I came home from the milliner to find my beloved companion packing her bags," Tibby snapped, something that looked too much like tears shimmering in her eyes. "It was quick work, as only her old and tatty things were packed. I persuaded her to take two of her newer gowns, but I am half convinced she will sell them, as I believe she did with the others. She did pack Freddie's clothes, not that he'll care about that, considering they'll be living like vagrants."

Colin marched over to her and seized her arms. "What are you talking about?" he demanded.

She met his eyes indignantly. "I couldn't stop her, not even when I begged. She refused to say why, only that she couldn't stay. She was distant and distressed and so pale I thought she was ill. But for all of that, she said she was well, she simply had to leave at once. I knew you had to be at the heart of it. The moment they left, I…"

"They're gone?" he whispered, his chest beginning to throb. "Where?"

Tibby blinked and was suddenly softer. "I don't know, Colin. I don't think she knows either. But yes, they are gone."

Colin released her arms and tore from the room, his heart in his throat as he ran from the house. She couldn't be gone, it was a misunderstanding, a mistake. She would never leave Tibby, she was devoted to her. And Freddie was well looked after, and his best chance for the future surely lay there.

Colin's feet skidded as he rounded corners, taking all sorts of shortcuts to get the few blocks to Tibby's house. People were milling about, staring at him like he was the wild man he was, but he ignored them as he moved around each, his entire being focused on his destination.

Tibby's house loomed before him suddenly and he burst through the front door, startling the aged butler, two footmen, and three maids in his mad haste.

"Susannah!" he bellowed as he charged the stairs three at a time. His voiced echoed in the entryway and hall eerily, the only sound in the entire house his voice and his steps.

"Susannah!" he cried again, rounding the landing towards the bedchambers. "Freddie! SUSANNAH!"

The door to her room seemed forever out of reach as he raced down the hallway towards it. "Freddie, Susannah, answer me!"

At last, he reached it, and he wrenched the door open. He barreled into the room, nearly tumbling over headfirst as he did so, gasping Susannah's name.

The room was empty, the bed perfectly made and pristine, and on the table beside the bureau, glinting in the morning light, lay a small, silver locket.

Half of his heart wanted to touch it, thinking it was an illusion, a hallucination, some horrid nightmare from which he could not seem to awaken.

The rest of his heart forced himself out of the room, his chest heaving with agonizing pants of air that sustained nothing. He collapsed against the wall, unable to support his own weight anymore.

She was gone.

How much she had already endured, and survived, and he alone had been what broke her.

A low, shuddering whimper escaped him as his eyes burned. He leaned more heavily against the wall and clutched at his hair, his fingers digging into his scalp.

What had he done?

Chapter Twenty-One

"*You stupid lout…*"

Kit's voice echoed in Colin's head over and over again, the same as it had done for the last several days. It was one of several insults and scoldings that had been doing so, but was the only one Kit had doled out. And it was, by far and away, the tamest of the lot.

It was nothing compared to what Colin had told himself.

How could he not have seen that his words, though honest enough in his mind, would have been taken in such a way? To use Susannah's own words against her? Though he hadn't seen it at the time, it was now acutely and painfully obvious that she had never meant him in her ridiculous analogy. And Kit had taken great care to point that out to him, which was when his one insult made its grand appearance.

Since then, he had been annoyingly considerate and involved, which was why Colin was currently sitting in his new favorite tavern with a drink in front of him. He could not quite recall which drink of the day it was, which was becoming a fairly usual pattern, but what else was a man to do when he had broken his own heart by being the thickest, most heartless imbecile that had ever walked God's earth? And not only that, but he had destroyed the finest creation of all: Susannah Merritt Hawkins-Dean. The only woman he would ever, or could ever, love.

There would not be anyone else.

Ever.

And the pain of that knowledge was only deadened when he was too soused to know his own name.

So here he sat, and here he drank, and while he was quite certain his brother knew where he was, he had never sent for him. Which he supposed was Kit's way of allowing Colin to do as he wished. Had he been permitted to drink fifteen years ago, he probably would have done the same thing.

It rather felt as if he were drinking for his sufferings twice over now.

At least his sisters were back to loving him now. Every morning was bright and sweet with their hugs, almost as if nothing foul had ever happened. But the pain came, as it always did, and not even Ginny's kisses or Bitty's giggles or Rosie's sharp wit could bring him out, and it was then that he left. He would not bring them down with his misery.

He could spare them that.

His head pounded and his chest burned and the room spun, and he felt terrible. But everything felt terrible now, so it suited him.

"What happened?" demanded a too-haughty sounding voice.

"Is that a beard?" said another.

"Colin can grow a beard? I thought he was perpetually twelve."

"He looks bad."

"That would be an understatement. Colin?"

"Sit," he ordered, his voice rough and slightly garbled. His head was swimming already, but he ought to have talked to his friends days ago. They should have been told what he'd done, what Susannah had done, everything. Perhaps they could have helped with the money situation. Not with the funds themselves, for he had managed that without trouble and he would never have asked them for it. But the details of it could have used their polishing.

It hardly mattered now.

There was an odd sort of buzzing, a bit muted, and the volume and pitch were changing rapidly. His arm was being shaken repeatedly, and then someone punched him in the face.

He jerked and shook his head rapidly, his eyes focusing once more. He looked around the table at his friends, who were all staring at him in various states of horror.

"Colin," Nathan said softly, eyes wide, "what happened?"

He was not entirely sure he could do this. Admitting his appalling behavior to people he respected as much as the men before him would crush him further than he already was. The shame would be too much.

Then again, he was unshaven, dirty, rumpled, drinking his umpteenth glass of whatever it was, and was not entirely sure his head was going to remain on his shoulders. It couldn't exactly get much more shameful than it already was.

So he told them, in a low, flat voice, everything. The secrets, the proposals, the money, the gazebo, the revelations from Gent, everything up to her coming to him the other day and his response; he told them it all. And they made no response until his voice trailed off to nothing.

And then it came.

A wave of noise, loud and magnified in his drunken ears, indistinguishable words from three different voices crying out in disbelief and shock. Gasps and groans, blinking eyes and wide-open eyes, and many frantic hand gestures all whirled together before him.

"You didn't!" he finally could make out from one of them.

He closed his eyes and rubbed at his temples.

"Are you mad?"

"I can't even... I don't..."

"Oh *hell*, Colin..."

"Colin," Derek finally said, the only one who had yet to make any comment at all.

All eyes, even Colin's, looked to him.

Derek seemed almost disgusted as he looked at Colin. "Colin... you're an ass."

Colin groaned and put his head into his hands, grinding his eyes with the heels of his palms.

Geoff gave an odd sort of laugh. "We all were."

Duncan cleared his throat. "I wasn't."

Nathan snorted. "No, you were just stupid," he reminded him. "You qualify."

"It's a miracle any of us got our wives at all," Derek sighed, leaning back.

"I didn't," Colin murmured, feeling the need to point out the obvious.

Derek looked back at him with a raised brow. "You didn't let us fail, despite your mocking and protests. We are not going to abandon you now that it's your turn."

Colin shook his head at once. "It's too late."

"That's not what Annalise says…" Duncan murmured.

Colin jerked sharply, which made his head spin. "What?" he croaked as he tried to look at only the center Duncan rather than the two on either side of him. "She's seen her?"

Duncan nodded. "She ran into her the other day while running around in Town. Now she meets up with her every other morning. They talk, shop, who knows what else."

Colin swallowed hard, his throat feeling filled with shards of glass. "How is she?"

"Hurt," Duncan said simply.

Colin groaned and put his head into his arms.

"But she won't talk about it," Duncan went on, speaking to the others. "Annalise says she's more skittish than ever. Always wants to meet in a different place, never lets her see her home, insists on walking everywhere and paying for herself… Annalise says she is not herself, but if what Colin says is true, she really has nothing to fear anymore."

"Except me," Colin mumbled into his arms.

"We can fix this," Nathan urged, grabbing Colin's arm. "You may have to grovel more than the rest of us did…"

"A lot more," Geoff murmured.

Derek hissed a wince. "I had to grovel a lot. Still do."

"I'm good," Duncan said, sitting back.

"Shut up, Duncan," everyone except Colin replied.

"…but nothing, not even this, is irreparable. Particularly if she is still inclined towards you," Nathan continued.

Colin shook his head again. "No. I've gone too far, I've done enough damage."

"Colin," Derek tried, leaning forward. "We can come up with a plan."

Again, he shook his head. "No. There is no plan. I am not getting her back. Don't waste your time."

"Come on, Colin," Geoff said. "Remember what you told me? Romantic heroes run after their women."

He could sense the attempt at humor, but it fell very flat indeed. He shook his head, making it throb more.

"You have to try," Duncan insisted. "You know you still want her, and I think she could still…"

"No," Colin barked suddenly, making his own ears ring. "End of discussion. Accept it, or get out."

No one moved even the slightest.

The room was feeling rather warm and he had to blink a few times to clear his eyes. He sighed and looked to Nathan. "How are the children?"

Seeming to accept his demands, they began to talk of common things, subjects which no one in a dark pub like this would have been discussing. It did not last long, as Colin was no longer feeling particularly talkative, and his friends eventually drifted away without him noticing. He rubbed at his head, coughed deep, racking coughs that burned his chest even more than it already was, and his stomach rolled and pitched like a sailing ship. How could he possibly have communicated with anyone like this? He ought to stop drinking, it made things so complicated.

He sat there for a while, as time became more and more irrelevant. Everything became irrelevant. He was irrelevant.

He was starting to talk and think nonsense. And he felt miserable, in mind and body. Perhaps he ought to go home, where servants could tend to him and he wouldn't have to think. And maybe then his head would regain its balance.

Colin pushed back from the table and stood, but had to grab onto it as the room spun and turned black before him.

And then he was falling.

Susannah rubbed at her eyes with a sigh as she left Mrs. Randall's modiste shop. She had been up most of the night the last three nights finishing the work she had given her, but it had been some of her best work. She ought to receive some very good wages for those pieces, and now that she had finished the commissioned items, she could set to work on the rejected ones that she could keep herself if she could mend them.

She'd never truly thought she would find satisfaction in employment, but there was something to be said for accomplishing work and then receiving pay for it. Particularly when something was done well and she was proud of it.

She had it on very good authority that she would soon be offered a full position there instead of just on the side, but she would have to be patient there. She would be grateful for that; it was tiresome to work so many small positions.

Sasha had let them stay with her until Mrs. Jones agreed to let them back into their old apartment. She still did the laundry for the boarding house, though she really did not have to do so to earn their meals the same way. Instead it simply took some of the amount for rent off. Freddie was miserable, but he tried not to show it. He never complained, and he continued his lessons as Mrs. Creighton and Mr. Townsley had laid them out. Soon, though, it would not be enough.

Though she could now provide for him, it was meager, and she did not have enough to hire a tutor. She could teach him what she knew, but beyond that, she was relatively useless for his education. He ought to go to school, to be with other children and receive a real education that might actually prepare him for the future.

Perhaps when she earned enough, they could move to the country. A cottage near a village with a school might be just the thing for him.

She looked up at the sun, peeking out from the clouds, adding some warmth to the surprisingly brisk day. It was still early, she ought to go and check in with Mrs. Rogers. The sweet woman had been so delighted to have her come back, it almost made Susannah glad for it herself. She was shocked at how far the woman had wasted away since her absence, and it soothed her a bit to help.

As much as she was ever soothed these days.

She could hardly sleep. Even when she could, sleep was more dangerous than being awake.

More than once, Freddie had woken her up, finding her in tears, almost inconsolable. But he never said anything about it. He just rubbed his eyes and returned to his bed, while she attempted to find a way back to sleep. In the mornings, Freddie went about as if nothing had happened, and Susannah was content to let him.

She sighed and started for Mrs. Rogers' apartments. Her head and heart ached constantly, but if she did not dwell on it, if she stayed busy, it faded into a distant annoyance that she could almost ignore.

Almost.

"Susannah!"

She turned in surprise, knowing Annie's voice before she saw her face. The woman was hurrying towards her, blonde hair bouncing loosely beneath her bonnet. Her green eyes were wide and worried, and her face was paler than normal.

Susannah rushed to her. "Annie? What is it?"

She'd meant to cut off associations with anyone who knew Colin or would remind her of him. But when she and Annie had crossed paths a few days ago, Annie had refused to let her. And Susannah was grateful for it. Annie never asked questions, never pressed her to come back, never once made her feel as though their friendship had been only on the surface. And Annie was not of a fine background or upbringing. She did not judge.

Annie grabbed onto her arms, as if she were steadying her and not the other way around. "Colin. It's Colin."

She had not said the name before, and Susannah had gone days without hearing or saying it herself, except for her dreams. Hearing it now made her heart lurch and she gasped audibly, the sound very nearly a sob.

"I'm sorry," Annie whispered, gripping her hard. "But I had to find you. I've been looking everywhere for you, Susannah. Everyone is so worried, Colin's been drinking himself into a stupor every day, all day, and we all thought he was just drunk. No one ever suspected that he was sick."

Susannah finally raised her head to meet her eyes. "Sick?"

Annie nodded, her eyes shimmering. "He's been in bed for three days now. They found him in a pub, burning with fever and almost unconscious. Doctors have been called for, he's been bled several times now, and between laudanum and his fever, he's so delirious he's incoherent. They say there is not much to be done, but I thought..." Annie bit her lip and tilted her head. "You worked in a hospital, yes? I know it is an impossible thing to ask, Susannah, but..."

Susannah was already moving, pulling Annie behind her, running towards Mayfair. Her heart pounded frantically within her chest as if she were the one suffering fevers. Colin was apparently lying at death's door; there was no question but that she would go to him. She was neither physician nor apothecary, and would never claim to be, but she had worked with some, and recalled their most useful remedies. Perhaps she could do something, though likely everything she knew had already been done.

Even if she could not help, she could be with him at the last.

"Susannah, are you sure you can...?" Annie tried, panting behind her.

"No," Susannah interrupted, shaking her head at once. "I am not sure of anything. But I have to go. I have to..." She shook her head again.

Annie did not say anything else as they ran to her nearby carriage, and kept pace with Susannah very well, never once voicing a word of complaint. She was grateful for that. She knew this was mad, but Annie had to know when she sought her out that she would not remain while Colin was in such a state.

The house was suddenly before them and she rapped on the door anxiously, biting her lip. She would beg, plead, apologize on her knees if only they would let her in.

The door opened and Bartlet's face was worn and lined, a clear indication of the attachment he had to his employer.

"Miss Hart," he said wearily. "Mrs. Bray."

"Bartlet," Susannah whispered, trying to look past him. "Is he... Is...?"

"Susannah?"

She stiffened at Kit's voice, steeling herself as he appeared in the doorway, Bartlet sidling aside.

He stared at her for a moment, so rumpled and disheveled that he hardly looked himself. Then he reached for her and hauled her into his arms. "Oh, thank God," he whispered, clutching her tightly.

Susannah's eyes filled with tears and she slid her arms around his slender waist. "Kit, is he...?"

He pulled back, his own eyes shimmering, and he shook his head. "He's resting, finally, but the fever is raging. He was bled again this morning, but I don't think it helps him. Whitlock sent his private physician, and he has done everything, but says all we can do is wait. I just... I can't..." He ran a shaking hand through his hair.

Susannah hugged him again, feeling a slight tremor through him. "Can I see him?"

He nodded against her and helped her inside. He turned back to Annie, who had tears running down her cheeks.

"I can't..." Annie said, taking a step back and shaking her head. "I want to, so desperately, but Duncan forbids it. I'm... in a delicate condition, and I..." She bit her trembling lip. "I'm so sorry."

Kit reached out to wipe a tear away and squeezed her hand. "It's all right, Annalise. I understand, and I agree. Go to your husband, let him hold you. I will send word as soon as I can."

She nodded hastily and turned from the doorstep.

Kit turned back to Susannah as he closed the door. "Let's go."

He took her arm gently and they started up the stairs.

"Is it infectious?" she asked, all business as they mounted the stairs.

"Doctor thinks so," Kit responded, steering her towards the rooms. "He told me to send the girls away."

"Did you?"

He shook his head with a heavy sigh. "I should have. But they were sent away when their mother got sick and never got to say goodbye. I couldn't do that to them again. Not when they adore Colin so."

His voice caught on Colin's name and he cleared his throat, shaking his head.

"He'll be all right," he murmured, eyes unfocused. "He's too stubborn to die in a sickbed."

Susannah felt her lips curve briefly. She needed to believe that, had to cling to it. This could be the last she saw of Colin, and she could not bear knowing he had...

Kit opened the door and let her in ahead of him. She rushed to the bed, where Colin lay sprawled, sheets damp with sweat, his skin almost gray in color, his breath rasping audibly.

"Colin?" she murmured, sitting on the bed and touching his face.

He twitched at the contact, turning his head away and mumbling under his breath.

"Colin," she said louder.

"He's insensible," Kit said from the door, his eyes taking in his brother's form almost dispassionately. "Has been for days."

Susannah shook her head and stood, stripping off her coat and rolling up her sleeves. "I can reach him," she said, going to the wash bin. "Get me rags and fresh water. Is Mrs. Creighton about?"

Kit stared at his brother, unmoving.

She understood, she truly did. She longed to sit and stare at Colin and will him back to health with her eyes. But while there was blood in her veins and breath in her lungs, she would fight for Colin's life. And she needed all the help she could get.

"Kit!" she called loudly, pouring every ounce of strength into her voice.

He jerked and looked at her with wide eyes.

She smiled softly. "Rags and water, Kit. And Mrs. Creighton."

He swallowed and nodded, glancing back at the bed as he left.

She washed her hands quickly and took a moment to go back to the bed and put her damp hands on Colin's face. She stroked his cheeks, brushed back his hair, and kissed his brow. "Stay with me, my love. Come back to us."

Hours later, Susannah wiped at her brow and glanced up at Mrs. Creighton. For the third time, she had been flung off of the bed and landed in a heap on the floor. It was a good sign, as Colin was no longer lethargic and unmoving, but he continued to resist anything Susannah tried to do.

"You do it," she muttered to Mrs. Creighton as she got to her feet. "He tolerates you."

Mrs. Creighton gave her a sympathetic look, but nodded. She spoke softly to Colin, who did not twitch or groan or react at all. He let her sponge his fevered skin with cool water, responding incoherently to her questions.

Susannah blinked hard as she mixed another tonic from the medicine the doctor had left and the herbs she had brought. It ought to have brought down his fever, and perhaps ease his breathing. Ideally, she could make a paste of it that should be applied to his chest directly. But at the moment, getting near him sent him thrashing and moaning violently.

She handed the glass to Mrs. Creighton and tried not to take it personally. Colin was out of his head with illness, he could not be blamed for what torment he suffered thus. And he was entitled to his feelings towards her, whatever they were.

Mrs. Creighton tried to get Colin to drink it, but he moaned and turned his head away, clamping his lips together. Mrs. Creighton sighed, and looked to Susannah.

Pursing her lips, Susannah marched over to the other side of the bed. She pinched Colin's nose shut and when he gasped for air, Mrs. Creighton poured the liquid into his mouth. Susannah released his nose as he gasped and sputtered, and she rubbed his throat soothingly. He settled somewhat, and she murmured a word of praise.

That riled him yet again. "Susannah," he moaned, swiping viciously to his side. "Damn it… damn it… No, go away…" His agitation grew and both she and Mrs. Creighton restrained him bodily.

His moans turned to whimpers and Susannah shushed him as best as she could. "Easy, love," she murmured, rubbing his chest gently. "Easy, now. Relax."

He stiffened, his face contorting. "No, Susannah. Not you... not... not you..."

She closed her eyes against tears. "What do you need, Colin?" she asked, her voice breaking.

"Away," he moaned, his head rolling from side to side against her. "Away..."

She raised a hand to his brow and looked at Mrs. Creighton as she felt the skin, which was markedly cooler than hours ago. It was far too soon for that to be the medicine's effect, but it was an encouraging indication for when it did begin to work.

"All right," she managed, torn between laughter and tears. "Whatever you like." She moved off of the bed, wincing at the flash of disgust that crossed his face.

He growled deeply. "Away!" he bellowed, coughing painfully. "Out... No more, no more..."

Susannah hiccupped on an exhausted sob, wringing out a fresh, cool rag.

"Pay him no mind," Mrs. Creighton ordered as she came to her side. "He is out of his head, it's the laudanum."

Susannah shook her head. "Not all of it." She clamped her lips together and wiped his face and neck and chest once more, silent in her ministrations.

"Not Susannah," Colin muttered, opening his eyes to look at her, but not seeing her. "Not Susannah."

She looked at Mrs. Creighton helplessly.

Mrs. Creighton gave her a long look, then called, "It's me, Mr. Gerrard. It's all right, it's just us."

He grunted and turned his head into the pillow. "Not Susannah," he muttered again, settling deeper and losing the stiffness in his frame.

Susannah stroked his face once and kissed his head, squeezing her eyes shut. This was it. He was going to be well, and he would never know she was here. He would never see her again.

She stepped away and handed the rag to Mrs. Creighton, feeling a few tears hit her cheeks. "His fever should break soon," she murmured. "I've left enough for another dose if he needs it. Ice chips and cool rags for the rest of the night."

Mrs. Creighton nodded, though Susannah suspected she already knew all of that. She took Susannah's hands. "Bless you, my dear," she whispered.

Susannah sniffed hard, willing her tears away. "Take care of him," she whispered.

"Of course."

She squeezed her hands and left the room quickly, not daring to look at the bed again.

Kit was pacing the hallway, looking somehow more disheveled than he had earlier. He looked up as she exited and went to her at once. "Is he…?" he asked, his voice rough.

Susannah took his hand. "He is improving. Still feverish, but much better. He has been fighting us for the last few hours and is strong enough to shove me from the bed three times."

Kit exhaled heavily and looked up at the ceiling, blinking rapidly. "Stubborn fool," he whispered.

Susannah swallowed hard. "He is, indeed. And Mrs. Creighton can manage him from here."

He looked at her then, eyes questioning. "You won't stay?"

She shook her head, sniffing again. "No. No, it is distressing to him to have me in there. He becomes violent and restless, saying all sorts of things about me and…" She shook her head. "He would do better without me."

"Seems to me that is what got him here," Kit said softly.

Susannah winced and looked away. "I am surprised you let me in."

"That was not a jab at you, Susannah," he said at once, taking her arm and forcing her back to him. When she finally looked up at him again, he gave her a serious look. "Colin is a stupid lout."

Susannah reared back in surprise, wiping at her eyes. "You told him that?"

"I did. Twice."

She bit her lip. "I don't blame him. I can't."

"Stay," Kit said softly. "Stay and see what happens."

Slowly, though it broke her heart to do it, she shook her head. "He hates me now, Kit. Violently."

He tilted his head a bit. "I do not think he does."

She sniffed once and raised her chin, the barest hint of a smile on her lips. "Oh, I am content with it."

"Are you?" he asked.

"Yes," she said with a nod. "He would not hate me with such passion if he had not loved me with the same. I can be quite content with that."

Kit sighed and put his hand over hers, squeezing tightly.

Susannah wondered at his tenderness, then realization dawned. "You know."

Kit looked at her curiously. "Know?"

Somehow, she managed to swallow. "You know about... my past. You know everything."

He hesitated momentarily, then nodded, just once. "I do. As does Colin. Stupid lout."

A watery, surprised laugh escaped her and she finally felt her knees again. "I can't stay," she told Kit, hoping she looked as apologetic as she felt. "And don't tell him I was here. Or that I know."

Kit did not look pleased by that.

"Please, Kit," she said, gripping his arms.

He sighed and looped her hand through his, heading for the stairs. "Oh, all right, but only because it's you."

"Thank you." She leaned into him a little as he led her down.

"I have done something that I will tell only you," Kit said suddenly, his voice serious again. "Even Colin does not know this."

Susannah swallowed. "That sounds ominous."

He hesitated just a moment as they turned on the landing. "I have set aside a sum of money with my solicitor that is for Freddie's education."

She stumbled a step but he caught her easily. "You did what?"

He chuckled softly. "I know your sensibilities, Susannah, and I promise you, it is not extravagant. It is enough for him to begin at Eton when he reaches eleven, and then Cambridge afterwards. What he does there is entirely up to him, and there is no money after, but by then he should have the resources to build quite a life for himself."

They reached the bottom of the stairs and she turned to him, a few tears falling still, her mind whirling. "Kit, why in the world would you do that?"

He wiped away her tears and smiled. "Because I am your friend, Susannah. Not as close as Colin, I grant you, but we are friends nonetheless. And I have grown quite fond of your son. I would do more if I could, but I know you, and you would not take it. But I am thinking of Freddie's future, and this much I can do."

She shook her head, taking his hand in hers. "I don't know what to say," she admitted.

He shrugged lightly. "Say nothing, then. It's already done and I cannot change it; no one can. And my motives are not entirely pure, I will have you know."

She looked up at him curiously. "They're not?"

He shook his head, looking sober. "No. I have high expectations of him, you see. He will either become the next me, a world renowned scholar, or marry one of my sisters."

Susannah grinned. "I would love all of those things."

He returned her smile. "I know."

She cocked her head at him. "Is there anything you don't know, Kit Gerrard?"

His grin spread and he suddenly looked mischievous. "Quite a bit, actually. But I dare say I know more than Colin."

Chapter Twenty-Two

$\mathscr{I}$t had been three days since Colin had been bedridden, and he had done his level best to make up for lost time with his sisters. His behavior had been abominable to everyone, and his selfishness had left him so close to death he would swear he'd actually seen the gates of heaven. He'd even heard Susannah's soothing voice, calling him her love and encouraging him softly. Out of his head with fever, he'd heard and imagined all sorts of things, and it had changed everything for him.

Apologies now flew from his mouth faster than compliments ever had, and he felt worlds lighter for it. Not that his guilt surrounding Susannah had lessened at all, but he was assured that where everyone else was concerned, he could be settled. He had made no attempt to find Susannah or to reach out to her. He probably should have, but what could he possibly say? Though he could admit to being wiser and more of a man for the ordeal he had just survived, he had no more answers there than he'd had before.

But he would live, and go on living, and would not think of himself alone anymore.

At this moment, in fact, he was not thinking of himself at all.

He sat next to Rosie's bed, clutching her hand, while the inestimable Dr. Howard, the private physician of the Whitlocks, looked her over. Two days ago, Rosie had complained of a headache and been unusually tired, yesterday the same and worse with a cough, and this morning she had been too weak to even rise from her bed. And she had refused breakfast. Since then, she had grown listless, pale, and had begun to burn with fever.

Colin and Kit had wasted no time in sending for the doctor at that point. They both knew very well that Colin's fever had been considered infectious and thus the entire house had been at risk, but as it had been five days since Colin had been declared out of danger, they thought the rest had been safe. But looking at the somber look on Dr. Howard's face as he listened to Rosie breathe and took her pulse, there was nothing safe about this.

He slowly shook his head, raising his eyes to the brothers. Kit stood behind Colin, his fingers rubbing anxiously against each other as they hung at his side. He would have been at Rosie's side as well, but one of them had to be composed.

"She is not doing well," the older man told them softly, glancing down at Rosie. "I have no doubt it is the same fever you suffered from, Mr. Colin."

Colin winced and moaned, leaning his head to touch the coverlet. Kit immediately put a hand on his shoulder and squeezed hard, pulling Colin back upright, leaving his hand in place.

"It was bad enough in a grown man of your robust nature and stamina, but in a child this young?" He shook his head and put a hand on Rosie's perspiration dampened brow. "It could be quite dangerous." He hesitated, then added, "It already is dangerous. It's taken such a vicious hold already, I'm not sure there is much to do."

"What *can* we do?" Kit asked roughly, his grip on Colin's shoulder tightening.

For a moment, Colin feared the good doctor would simply say "Pray." But he stared at Rosie for a long moment, his mind obviously whirling. "If she were older, I would suggest blood-letting. But as it has moved so fast and she is already having pulmonary distress, I dare not. Have you any of the laudanum I left for you?"

Colin nodded once, swallowing with difficulty.

"Dilute that significantly, as she is a child, but she will grow more restless and need it." He looked at her eyes, his mouth forming a thin line. "She's not to crisis yet, but it won't be long. I will go and fetch some things to help her. Is Mrs. Creighton still about? She was instrumental in caring for you, was she not?"

Colin nodded again. "Yes, she was. She is with the girls at the moment, but we can have her tend Rosie."

Dr. Howard hummed a noise of discontent. "Your other sisters are still about? I would send them away, sirs, for their own good."

"No," they said together at once.

Dr. Howard looked at them strangely.

"They lost their mother to illness," Kit explained in a stiff voice. "And were sent away without knowing it would be the end. They could not leave their sister the same way. And we would have us all remain together. As a family."

Colin nodded his "amen" to that.

Dr. Howard sighed and picked up his bag. "I stand by my recommendation, the girls should be removed. I will come back in a few hours. In the meantime, try to cool her, open a window, and turn her if she coughs too much." He nodded to them both and left the room.

"I'm so sorry," Colin whispered to Rosie, holding her hand tightly. "I'm so sorry, sweetheart."

"You cannot blame yourself," Kit said coming around to rest his hand on Rosie's brow, smoothing her hair back.

Colin looked at his brother, struck by how disheveled Kit looked. They'd been observing Rosie all morning and into the afternoon, but Kit looked as rumpled and untidy as Colin had ever seen him. "Who else is there to blame, Kit?" he asked, his voice cracking in agony. "It was my idiocy, my stupid, selfish behavior that got me sick, and now it has taken hold in her. I did this."

Kit gave him a severe look. "It is *not* your fault, Colin."

Colin shook his head. "You will never convince me of that. Not in a million years." He took Rosie's feverish hand and brought it to his mouth. "I've been such a fool. I've wasted the time we've had with the girls; I could have given them so much more of myself."

Kit made an impatient sound and grabbed Colin's shirt in his fist. "She is not dead, Colin. And our sisters adore you. They've forgiven you your moments of idiocy, and they love you. We've just gotten you back, don't you dare waste that."

Colin swallowed and gripped his brother's wrist hard. "I can't breathe, Kit. I can't think. I can't lose Rosie, not now."

Blessedly, Kit said nothing else, and the two of them watched Rosie's bedside, only leaving when the other two girls needed one of them.

Hours later, they watched with more anxiety. Dr. Howard had left again to tend to Lady Ralston's impending delivery, but Colin had known the look in the doctor's eyes. He had done all that he could.

Mary had come to help with the girls, and Geoff was on hand below if anything was needed. The girls were being distracted, but he knew it would not last long.

He needed someone to distract him.

Still he sat at Rosie's side, her hand in his, not seeing anything anymore. Mrs. Creighton had worked herself into exhaustion and had retired to rest for a time. Colin and Kit were alone in the room with Rosie, the only sound the crackling of the fire.

"What do we do, Kit?" Colin asked finally, wishing for the thousandth time that he were back in this bed and not Rosie. "We can't just let her…"

Kit, sitting on Rosie's other side, rubbed at his eyes. "Honestly, Colin? I have one idea. Just one."

Colin looked at him expectantly.

Kit stared back for a long moment. "Susannah."

Colin flinched, the sound of her name something he had somehow forgotten, the pain as sharp as his guilt over Rosie. "No."

His brother growled. "You have a better idea?"

"No, but I…" He swallowed and shook his head. "I can't. I can't ask that of her. I can't ask anything of her."

Kit got to his feet and put his hands on his hips. "She can help, Colin. She worked in hospitals and with doctors. She can…"

Colin shook his head fiercely. "No. I cannot ask her to do that."

His brother frowned at him. "Not even for Rosie?"

"She wouldn't come. She hates me, Kit. She wouldn't come." He had been tormented by Susannah every night since he had said those things to her, his sleep destroyed by every agonizing moment of joy and pain he had shared with her. He'd felt her pain at his hand, imagined thousands of scenarios where she was cool and dismissive of him, as she ought to be, and others where she raged, no matter how against her nature it was.

She would not come for him.

And she ought not.

"You don't know that," Kit murmured in a low tone.

Colin did not respond, could not. He looked down at Rosie's coverlet, her hand the only thing he could feel. No, Susannah might not hate him now. But she should.

He heard Kit sigh, and then move away from the bed in clipped steps. "Fine!" Kit snapped. "I will go for her myself."

Colin snorted softly. "You don't know where she is. I don't even know. She's vanished."

Kit gave a snort of his own. "Of course I know where she is. I knew that a few days after she left."

That brought Colin's head up with a jerk. "Why didn't you say anything?" he whispered.

Kit raised a brow. "You never asked. If you wanted to find her, you would have."

That much was true. But it did not explain how Kit had done so. Kit did not have Colin's network of connections. "How did you find her?" he asked, confused.

Kit smiled faintly. "Come now, Colin. You think you are the only one who has contact with the Gent?"

Colin looked at him for a long moment, stunned and more confused than ever. "You know who he is," he said slowly.

"I do."

"Who is it?"

Kit shook his head firmly. "I swore not to tell, though I am surprised you haven't guessed yet. But he's been watching over her for us, and I'm bringing her here so you can do that from now on."

Colin felt his heart leap at the implication in the words, but was just as quick to snuff the feeling. He shook his head. "She won't come, not for me, not after what I did."

"She loves you, Colin," Kit murmured.

"I know," Colin whispered. "I know she did, but…"

"No," Kit interrupted roughly, "she *does* love you. I would bet both of our fortunes on that. And you do not deserve her."

Colin glared at him. "I know that, don't you think I know that?"

Kit tilted his head, folding his arms across his chest. "So what is holding you back?"

There was no fair way to answer that. Colin couldn't even admit to himself his reasons. Again, he shook his head. "I can't… She will never forgive me."

"You underestimate her, Colin." Kit's voice was disappointed, and sad.

"I can't face her," Colin admitted with a hitch in his voice. "I can't."

"Then I will go, damn you. She is Rosie's best chance. And yours."

A knock at Susannah's door interrupted her nightly reading to Freddie. He was so close to sleep, he barely noticed as she slid from beside him.

"Miz Hart?" Sasha called, knocking again. "Gentleman at the door for you. An' he's a looker."

Susannah looked to the ceiling in distress. Sasha had been out of work, having found herself in a difficult and delicate situation, and she was desperately trying to get Susannah to pick up where she had left off, claiming there was good money and a bit of fun to be had.

She left the bedchamber, thanked Sasha, and went to the cracked door. "Yes?" she asked, opening it slightly.

Kit Gerrard stood there, looking disheveled, rumpled, and exhausted. "Susannah."

She gaped, then swallowed. "Who?" she asked faintly. Then she shook her head. "Never mind, one moment." She left him at the door, raced for her cloak and shoes, and told Sasha she was leaving, which earned her a cheeky grin and a wave. Susannah frowned at her. "Mind Freddie?"

"O' course, Miz Hart," Sasha replied. "Pleasant evening to you and your fella. Get your money's worth!"

Susannah shook her head and ran back to the door, surprising Kit as she exited, shutting the door behind her.

"You live with a...?" he said, fumbling for words.

"Prostitute," Susannah supplied, pushing a loose bit of hair behind her ear. "Yes."

Kit opened his mouth, then shook his head and gestured for Susannah to lead the way.

They hurried out of the building while Kit apprised her of the situation and gave her the pertinent details, helping her into the carriage. She made him repeat several things, her mind thinking quickly. She had them stop at the apothecary again, grateful she was on good terms with him, as it was far beyond his shop's hours, and then they barreled on for the house.

Rosie's situation sounded grave indeed, and she was not entirely sure what she could do to help, given the speed with which the fever was raging. But she could try. And she could be with the people she loved most in the world, except for Freddie. And if Rosie was destined to... She could hardly think the words, but if the worst should happen, then Susannah might perhaps be able to make the passing easier for the sweet girl.

Before disappearing forever.

There would be no remaining in London if she could not help Rosie.

She forced all of that aside as they reached the house. There was work to be done, and she would need all of her skills and abilities to do it.

"Where are Bitty and Ginny?" she asked.

"Sleeping, for now," Kit told her, taking her arm and letting her inside. "Mary Harris is with them. I doubt they will sleep for long."

She nodded, stripping off her cloak and gloves in the hall, dropping them on the floor as Kit had done as they moved to the stairs. They took the stairs two at a time, Susannah holding her skirts with one hand, her heart pounding hard in her chest.

Entering the room, she immediately felt the stuffy congestion of a sickroom, and the dim light of the fire cast distorted and miserable shadows.

"More light," she murmured to Kit as she entered. She saw Colin by the bed, clasping Rosie's hand with both of his, his head on the counterpane. Her heart was suddenly in her throat and she worked hard to swallow. What would Colin think?

"I need more light," she said again to Kit, whose hand was suddenly at her back. "And fresh linen and water."

Colin's head jerked up at her voice.

"Of course," Kit murmured. "I'll see to it. And Mrs. Creighton?"

Susannah nodded, pushing her sleeves up. "Unless she is fatigued. In which case, would you ask Mary if she would mind?"

She did not wait for his response as she went to the bed to check on Rosie, who was pale and far too still for her liking. Her pulse was soft and thready, not at all the strong, steady cadence it ought to have been. And she was hot to the touch.

She ignored Colin as best as she could, though he was just to her right, and she knew his breathing was uneven. The warmth from his body could have seared her had she been any closer. As it was, her right hip and leg were suddenly tingling in a strange sort of anticipation.

Whatever injuries he had caused, whatever their past had been, she could not feel anything for him but love and compassion. And she wanted him still, more than she ever had.

Kit murmured softly to Colin, though she could not make out the words. Save for these: "She didn't even ask. She just came."

She swallowed hastily, peeling away the high collar of Rosie's night gown to expose her throat more fully.

The door was softly shut, and she looked back to see that Kit had left. Which meant she was alone. With Colin.

For a moment, there was no sound at all but their breathing, and Rosie's rasping, shallow breaths.

"You came," Colin finally said, his voice rough and awestruck.

She looked down and found him watching her with the same awe she'd heard in his voice. His eyes were soft and full of wonder, and she gave him a gentle smile. "Of course, I came," she murmured. "Did you really think I wouldn't?"

He made a choked sound and his throat worked, then he looked away.

She covered his hands, then looked down at Rosie with a small sigh. "Are you sure she isn't yours?" she asked with the barest hint of teasing.

Colin looked down at his sister and swallowed hard, then shook his head. "No, I am not sure. It hurts like she is mine. I love her like she is mine. She…" He shook his head again, dropping his head.

Susannah moved before she meant to, wrapping her arms around him, though she stood and he was seated. He buried his head against her, his frame shaking with emotional tremors. She rubbed his back soothingly, forcing her fingers not to wander to his hair. She blinked rapidly to keep her tears from falling, and kept her breathing shallow to fight off her own distress at his state.

When she could, she said, "I am not going to make any promises but this: I will do everything I can for her."

Colin looked up at her, his eyes shining.

Susannah smiled and touched his cheek once. "Because she is mine too."

Colin's breath hitched at her touch and his eyes fluttered ever so slightly.

Feeling rather the same way, Susannah smiled again. "When this is over, we need to talk," she murmured, stepping out of his tempting hold.

Colin suddenly had a strange light in his eyes. "Let's talk now," he said simply, hooking his leg around another chair and pulling it over.

She looked over at Rosie, who was starting to shift restlessly. She put her hand to the girl's brow, shaking her head. "Rosie needs us."

"I need you."

Something in Colin's voice made Susannah go completely still. He was so earnest, stripped of artifice and pride, and all that was left was his heart. Which was all she ever wanted.

She wanted to look at him, but she couldn't bear to.

"Whether Rosie lives or… does not," Colin said in a low voice, his body canting towards her though he still clung to Rosie's hand, "I will be eternally grateful to you."

"I don't want your gratitude, Colin," she whispered.

"I know."

She looked at him then, and his eyes were full of such longing, such adoration that it stole her breath completely. There was only one thing she could say to such ardency. "You still love me," she said in wonder.

"I never stopped," he replied. "Marry me, Susannah."

She stiffened and tried to turn back to Rosie, but Colin caught her arm with his free hand. "Let me worry about your sister, Colin. We can…"

"We have waited long enough," he said firmly.

She sighed heavily and looked back at him. "What if I can't save her?" she asked in a small voice.

He kept his eyes on hers as he shook his head. "Won't change how I feel."

She swallowed back tears. "It will," she insisted.

"No," he replied. "It won't." He sighed and looked at Rosie, still holding her hand. "I love my sister. I don't want her to die. In fact, I am terrified at the prospect. I want you to do everything you can to save her. I would sell my soul to save her, to trade places with her, anything. But I know there are limits to what we can do. What she can endure." He swallowed and looked back at Susannah. "And what we can endure. And my limit is going one more day without you. I cannot do that."

Susannah's breath caught and she gripped the nearby counterpane for balance.

Colin stared at her as if in agony, shaking his head. "I have been horrible to you, I didn't know what you had been through, what you had suffered… I never meant that you weren't good enough for me. Quite the opposite, in fact. I am nowhere near good enough for you. That was what I meant when you came to me. But I need you anyway. No matter what happens, you are mine, Susannah. And I am yours."

Her tears fell softly down her cheeks, her heart soaring with love and hope, with fear for Rosie, and with regret for what they had lost. But mostly, she was full of a desperate need to tell him something she had never said to him. Something she should have said ages ago, years ago, and had never done.

She reached out and laid her hand alongside his cheek. "I love you," she told him, her voice breaking a little, but full of feeling.

"Say yes," he begged softly.

A smile crossed her trembling lips. "Yes."

He exhaled softly, his relief evident, and turned his head to kiss her palm, then smiled at her with so much emotion her knees shook.

The door to the room opened quietly, and Mary and Mrs. Creighton both entered with the things Susannah had requested. "Both of you?" she asked in surprise.

Mary smiled and came to her with a tight hug. "Many hands, and all that. Put us to work."

They worked steadily for hours, wiping down Rosie's burning flesh with cold rags, setting a poultice on her chest for her breathing, and trying to get her to take a sleeping draught or laudanum when she became restless. It was arduous, but eventually, they reached a point where all three felt the only thing they could do would be to wait and see what the rest of the night brought. She was not quite out of danger, but neither were they as fearful as they had been.

Mary and Mrs. Creighton left to sleep in nearby rooms, while Susannah curled up on Colin's lap. He had dozed as they worked, but was never quite asleep. When the others left, he murmured for her to come to him, insisting she sleep as well, but only in his hold. They both reached hands out to touch Rosie, and fell asleep as such. Though she was fairly insensible, neither could bear that she would ever feel that she was alone.

Sleep was limited and fitful, but it did come.

The earliest glimpse of morning light broke into the room from the open window and Susannah shivered as a cold breeze entered. Colin's arm around her tightened. "I don't mind waking up like this," he murmured in a sleep-roughened voice.

"In a chair?" she asked with an innocent air, craning her neck and sitting up.

"Of course," he said simply. "That's exactly what I meant."

She smiled with a roll of her eyes. She looked towards the bed at Rosie, whose chest rose and fell softly, steadily. Without any hint of a hitch.

"Colin," Susannah cried, her eyes going wide.

He had seen it as well and in one motion they were both on their feet, their hands on Rosie, checking her pulse and skin temperature.

She was still warm, but so markedly cooler than what she had been all night and the days before it was astonishing. Her pulse was strong and throbbing in her small wrist. Her color was rosier and her eyes fluttered when Susannah laid a hand on her cheek.

"Rosie?" she whispered, pushing back a damp curl. "Rosie, darling, can you hear me?"

Rosie licked her dry and cracked lips, her eyes opening a little. "Susannah?" she sluggishly replied, the words garbled.

Susannah hiccupped a laugh and Colin gripped her shoulder tightly. "Yes, love. It's me."

"I think I've been hit by a boulder," Rosie drawled with a wince. "My head pounds something fierce."

"You just sleep a while, pet," Colin told her, his voice clogged. "We'll sort it out later."

"Colin," she said with a smile as she nodded, her eyes closing again. "I dreamed of a pony. Can I have one?"

He laughed and kissed her hand. "You can have twelve, Rose, so long as you never get sick again."

She snored softly in response, asleep again.

Colin laughed loudly and seized Susannah in a fierce hug, his tears flowing freely as hers did. She clung to him, laughing and crying all at once.

The door to the room was suddenly flung open, breaking them apart.

Kit was in the doorway, looking haggard and rough, Ginny in his arm, fully awake, and Bitty clutching his hand tightly. Mary, Geoff, and Mrs. Creighton suddenly appeared behind them, staring into the room.

Colin smiled and waved them all in. "It's all right," he said, still laughing even as tears leaked from his eyes. "She's all right. Her fever has broken and she just told me she wants a pony."

"God save us," Kit said with a look to the ceiling, his cheeks wet.

He set Ginny down on the bed and the little girl crawled to her sister and snuggled up against her, popping her thumb in her mouth. Bitty clambered onto the bed and did the same on her sister's other side.

Kit bent to kiss Susannah's cheek and then pulled Colin into his arms for a tight hug that did not break for a long time.

Mrs. Creighton and Mary were crying and hugged Susannah in turn, then sat and watched the girls with their sister. Geoff grinned with his relief, clapped Colin and Kit on their backs, and took up position behind his wife, his hand firmly on her shoulder.

Kit thanked Susannah profusely, then went and took Colin's seat by Rosie's bed, stroking her hand with a smile.

Colin linked his fingers with Susannah's and pulled her from the room without a word. She wordlessly followed, her heart picking up speed the further away from the room they went. He led her down the stairs, moving faster with each step.

When they reached the sitting room, he turned and cupped Susannah's cheek, his eyes free of tears, but full of heat and love. "I love you," he said in an uneven voice.

She slid her hands up his chest and around his neck. "I love you, too," she whispered.

He barely let her finish before his lips were on hers, hungry and insistent, and reminiscent of that day in the gazebo. He pouring longing and need and the anguish of separation into his kiss, melting and searing every part of her so completely that she groaned against him. He moaned softly as she pulled him closer, going up on her toes. A fever threatened to rise within her, within them both, and something began to uncurl in the pit of her stomach.

A faint clearing of the throat gave them pause, their lips barely touching as they panted together.

"So…" Kit drawled in a surprisingly Colin-esque voice. "I take it a wedding is in our immediate future?"

Colin chuckled and kissed Susannah quickly. "Yes," he answered, turning Susannah a little so they could see his twin leaning casually against the doorframe.

Kit grinned mischievously. "Finally get to use that special license, eh, Colin?"

Susannah jerked and looked up at Colin. "What?" she cried.

He looked sheepish, rubbing the back of his neck with one hand. "I, erm, got a special license."

She leaned back, startled. "When, exactly?"

"Before I asked you to marry me the first time."

Her jaw dropped and her eyes widened. "That was almost six weeks ago!"

He shrugged, grinning now. "You took some convincing."

Susannah stared at the man she adored in awe, wonder filling every part of her. "You really do want to marry me, don't you?"

He took her hand and pressed a hot, fervent kiss to it. "From the very beginning."

Well. There was only one thing to do about that.

She cleared her throat and turned to face Kit fully. "In *that* case… Kit, would you fetch our friends? I must rush home."

Colin jerked and stepped back into her view. "What? Why?"

"I need my son and my things. Do you think Tibby would take us in until then? It won't be for long, obviously," she told him as she moved to the door. "I am to be married, after all. As soon as Rosie is well enough."

Kit coughed a surprised laugh, while Colin merely looked thunderstruck. "What? Susannah…"

She turned and gave him a serious look. "Colin, earlier you spoke of limits and what yours are. Mine is this: I have spent too many years and months and weeks away from you, and one more minute of loving you and not having you is more than I can bear. So your brother will get our friends, I will fetch Freddie, and you will fetch the doctor. The moment your sister is recovered, we will be wed. Prepare yourself, my love. Your boring bachelorhood is at an end. But I promise you, the rest of your life will be quite exciting."

"Exciting?" he repeated, still bewildered.

She quirked her brows. "Quite." Then, using her best Tibby impersonation, she swept boldly from the room.

As she fetched her things, she did not immediately hear a reply from within the room. But she could imagine Colin gaping openly.

She suddenly heard Kit's voice. "You'd better do as she says, brother. She is determined to have you."

"And it's about time!" Colin exclaimed cheekily.

"Where are you going?" Kit laughed.

"To find Duncan and Derek," Colin called, his voice fading a bit. "I haven't a thing to wear for a wedding!"

Two weeks later, a ball was held at the Gerrard home to close out the autumn festivities of London, the last event before winter arrived. And all of London Society was invited.

Very few people knew the truth of Colin Gerrard's rumored marriage, but word had gotten out that he had been seen at St. George's at Hanover Square in very fine attire, and that was enough to get the gossip started.

Susannah stood near one of the extraordinarily tall windows of the ballroom, looking up at it, shaking her head at such an expense. She would never get used to being mistress of such places, let alone having such funds at her disposal. Though Colin had confessed to paying off her exorbitant debts, somehow there was plenty of fortune left. It was an astonishing thought.

She smiled as Kit entered and he gave her a warm nod in response, keeping his public reserve in place. Since the wedding, Kit had removed himself to his bachelor's residence, claiming he had no desire to be about with a newly married couple. She suspected it was awkward for him, though he loved them both, and wondered faintly if he might, in some small way, miss his brother.

The girls missed him fiercely, but he came over at regular intervals and was frequently present for dinners.

Freddie delighted in having sisters, though they were technically his aunts, and they would undoubtedly get into their fair share of scrapes soon. All of the children were blessedly well and whole, no one else succumbing to the fever that had raged Colin and Rosie. They were also quite jealous that Colin and Susannah were to go on a long trip, but they were easily consoled by the fact that Kit would be staying with them while they were gone, and he had promised to make a spectacular time of it.

Whatever that meant coming from Kit Gerrard.

She might have to warn Colin about that one. She looked around the room for her husband, who was no doubt getting into mischief himself. They had avoided the awkwardness of a formal introduction of Susannah as his wife by keeping with the Gerrard tradition of informality, and no one in this room knew who she was except for their friends.

No one would even suspect.

She saw Derek nearby and smiled, moving towards him.

She was suddenly tripped by something, but caught her balance before she could do more than stumble. She heard a familiar jangling of a beaded bodice and turned with a stiffened spine to face Lady Greversham.

"Lady Greversham," she said just as stiffly, narrowing her eyes a little. Though the woman did not know it, she would not be permitted to insult or abuse the lady of this house. Susannah would not stand for it, and nor did she have to anymore.

"I don't recall being introduced to you formally," the old woman hissed. "How did you gain entrance to this event?"

Susannah opened her mouth to reply when a much taller, much more imposing person was suddenly at her side. She looked up to see Colin wearing a polite smile, though his eyes were a furious shade of their usual blue. "I know you did not just trip my wife, Lady Greversham, that is highly unlike you. So do tell me, what did you do?"

Lady Greversham's mouth worked like a caught fish. "Wife?" she croaked weakly.

"Wife," Colin said firmly with a nod. "We were married last week before family and friends, so obviously you were not invited, and we are leaving tomorrow for an extended trip, during which I shall do my very best to ignore every hurt you have done to my beloved wife so that upon my return, when I have adapted properly to the wedded bliss in which I currently reside, I will not strangle you with your own ghastly lace collars. I believe you can show yourself out? My servants have far better tasks than to assist you."

He took Susannah's arm and led her away from the gaping and gasping woman.

Susannah beamed up at him, laughing. "You've destroyed your reputation," she told him as they reached their circle of friends, who had witnessed the whole thing. "Sending Lady Greversham from your house? It is too shocking!"

"What care I for reputation?" he scoffed, which made everyone laugh. "I have been made husband of the only woman I have ever loved, and left behind my dark and dreary wasteland of bachelorhood for the brilliant paradise of being well and truly bound for eternity. What greater fortune could be had?"

Soft sniffles echoed in rapid succession as every woman in the group, Susannah included, wiped away tears. Susannah took her husband's chin in her hand and gave him a very improper sort of kiss for a ballroom, but it was natural for them by now.

"All right," Derek said with a suddenly accusing air, "who toyed with Colin's beverage?"

Susannah laughed and broke away from Colin, who settled his hand a little too close to her hip.

"Too right," Geoff agreed with a snort. "That was so poetic I forgot it was Colin."

"It was terrifying," Duncan offered with a shudder.

"It was beautiful," Annie corrected, smiling at him.

"Pity it was Colin," Moira sighed. "I enjoyed it."

"Is he feverish?" Kate asked with a wink.

Nathan slowly shook his head. "Susannah, you've married a madman."

"Aye, I have," she murmured, brushing a lock of his hair away. "And I find I am just as mad."

Someone sighed, and Colin winked at her, stroking her hip surreptitiously.

Geoff heaved a dramatic sigh and shook his head. "Well, that is the end, I suppose."

"The end of what?" Mary asked, looking confused.

"An era."

"How so?" Annie asked, her brow furrowed.

He pointed at Colin. "Colin, it seems, has reformed."

No one said anything for a moment as they considered that. "Do we have a moment of silence?" Nathan asked, looking around.

"I think I may cry," Derek said, dabbing his little finger to his eye.

"Please don't," Duncan begged. "It will set the women off."

Mary laughed. "Colin reformed? Nonsense."

Geoff shook his head. "No, he is, utterly reformed, it's all over."

"Colin…" Derek said, looking at his friend. "Come now, tell us the truth: are you reformed?"

Colin looked a bit bewildered himself. "I suppose I must be. Good heavens, I'm reformed?" He looked at Susannah in confusion.

"Please," Susannah snorted.

Colin grinned. "Well, almost, then."

"Not quite," Susannah added.

He held up a finger. "And certainly not entirely."

Susannah wrapped an arm around Colin's waist, looking up at him with adoration in her heart. "And that is just the way we like it."

Epilogue

Susannah shivered and adjusted the warm furs and blanket around her, leaning against Colin more heavily, smiling when his arm around her tightened at once.

They'd spent almost a month in Scotland, touring the countryside a little, seeing the wealth and splendor and beauty of that majestic place, and they'd even been so fortunate as to spend some time with Duncan Bray's cousin Graeme, laird of the MacLaine clan, in their historic and splendid keep, with the warm and very bustling clan. Such hospitality had been unexpected, but very pleasant, and they had received invitations to return at any time.

Thankfully, however, most of the time they had spent in Scotland had been just the two of them. It had been years since Susannah had been so much herself, without her child to think of or her life to fear. Colin was rather quickly, and efficiently, eviscerating all such fears and horrid memories. They had laughed a great deal, and talked even more.

It was the best sort of fun she could ever have imagined they would have together.

She had never known a marriage could be this way. Granted, her experience with marriage was rather skewed and unpleasant, but even the marriages she had seen up close had never been anything of this nature. Her years of friendship with Colin underscored everything, and the love and desire so addictive and ever-present had been built upon that foundation of trust and understanding. The emotions they felt were so deep, so consuming, and was acutely overwhelming for them both, but it was beginning to feel more natural and easy.

Now they were riding back to England, and would be back in London with their family in a matter of a few days. It was bittersweet, to be sure, as the time alone had been rejuvenating and beautiful, and more of that would surely be appreciated. But they missed the children, and Kit would likely go mad if they stayed away any longer. According to Colin, Kit had grown immensely since the girls had arrived, and was a wonderful guardian, but he was used to Colin being there to take some of the workload. He was not entirely sure his brother had been equipped with the proper endurance for tending all four of them, no matter how Mrs. Creighton or their friends stepped in to help.

They had brought several presents for all of them, and more grand furs for Tibby, which would delight her. She had been a godsend from the day Susannah had met her, and for Colin, even more. There would never be a proper way to thank her for that.

Christmas was soon approaching, and there would be much to see to from almost the moment they arrived. It would be best to get what rest she could on the journey in.

To her surprise, the carriage rolled to a stop. They could not have been very far into England at this point, and had only changed horses an hour ago. They should not have stopped for some time yet.

She sat up in confusion and looked around. Her heart slammed against her ribs as the imposing edifice of Pavel House met her gaze. It looked much worse than how she had left it, now appearing from the outside as horrific as the inside had ever been. Her stomach clenched in apprehension and she wondered faintly if she might be sick.

Colin brushed past her to exit the carriage, jostling it a bit with the movement. He turned and held out his hand. "Come on," he urged softly.

She looked at his hand, swallowing hard, then met his gaze, pleading wordlessly.

He pressed his hand out further, his eyes full of understanding. "Come," he murmured again.

This was not the same thing, she reminded herself. Colin was not her former husband, and this house would never again hold the same horrors. She would always be safe with her hand in his.

She exhaled softly and put her hand in his, which he instantly rubbed soothingly.

When she was down at settled at his side he cupped her cheek and kissed her brow. "It's all right," he whispered against her skin.

She remained still beneath his lips, breathing in the comforting scent of him, her hands holding herself steady against his chest.

Eventually, Colin eased away and she looked up at him, finding strength in his eyes. She nodded once, then turned and scowled at the house. "Why would you bring me back here?" she muttered, letting him take her arm and lead her away from the carriage. "I hate this place."

"No, you hate this house," Colin corrected. "Which is perfect, because I think it is an eyesore and there is no way my son is inheriting this grotesque thing."

Susannah frowned in confusion and looked up at him. "Wait, what?"

He returned her look with one of his own, and snorted. "Freddie can't possibly live here, and no wife of his would want to."

Susannah stopped and put a hand on his chest, her mind whirling under his words and the implications of them. "Hold on. Your son?"

Colin shrugged once, his eyes the barest bit uncertain. "I've arranged to make him a Gerrard."

Her heart soared to the heavens. "You did *what?*"

He beamed at her then, his blue eyes dancing against the grey of the skies. "The meeting with my solicitor before we left? Mr. Goulding was present and we set everything up. He is mine now."

Susannah swallowed, tilting her head up at him. "Can you even do that?"

"Not really," he said with a wince. "But I'm not a peer and Freddie's been irreversibly declared illegitimate, so not very many people will care." He sighed and took her hands. "The best I can do is become his guardian, and now, legally, I am his guardian, save for you. I can't actually make him mine, but that's a formality. I will treat him as if he is mine. This is as binding a thing as I can make it. He can keep the last name if you want, but…"

Susannah surged on her toes to grab his face and kiss him, pouring every bit of love, passion, and gratitude she had searing her bones at this moment into her lips. His response was enthusiastic, as always, and his arms clamped tightly around her.

"No," Susannah murmured, slowly lowering herself back down to earth with a hint of a groan. "No, Freddie is a Gerrard now."

Colin smiled and his throat worked for a moment. "Good," he finally said, roughly.

Susannah was near to tears herself. She wet her lips and cocked a brow at him. "Now what's this about the house?"

The wild grin that was so her husband was back in place. "It's his. I took care of the cousin, he's enjoying the prospect of the Shropshire estate Loughton left behind."

She gaped for a moment. "You hate Shropshire," she said in awe.

Colin chuckled and lifted his brows knowingly. "I know. It was a most excellent trade. So," he said, turning to look at Pavel House with an appraising eye, "the house is to be demolished within a fortnight, and an architect is meeting with us in London when we get back, and I will leave the new name of the house to your creative genius." He gave her a bold wink and squeezed the hand he had somehow taken hold of.

Unable to believe what was happening, Susannah could only listen and smile.

"Freddie talks about a tree all the time, I am assuming that one?" Colin asked, pointing to the old oak on the green nearby. "So we will keep that, obviously. He won't need this place for a while, so there is plenty of time to make things perfect, and when he's old enough to understand and have a voice, we can work out what sort of an entail to put on the place so it need never fall out of his hands again."

Susannah stared at him, open mouthed, her eyes welling up. He had thought of everything, for her and for her son. Their son. They really were a family, and nothing would ever convince anyone otherwise.

Colin caught her expression and turned to face her, capturing her other hand as well and holding them close to his chest. "I know your memories of this place are horrible, the stuff of nightmares. But you spoke of the land and the gardens with longing. I couldn't help myself, and Freddie deserves his rightful inheritance. But if you wish it, I'll put a stop to everything. You are his mother, and…"

Swallowing back tears, she pulled one hand free and covered his mouth, fighting for control. "And you are his father," she told him in a slightly choked voice. "I see the way he looks at you, Colin. You *are* his father, in every way that matters. And that you would do something like this for our son…"

She shook her head and cupped his face. "I didn't think I could love you any more than I did, but somehow I do. Thank you, my love."

He kissed her then, slowly, lingering, savoring every delicious caress, cradling her body against his. Then he slid his hands down her arms and interlaced their fingers. "Come on, sweetheart," he whispered, his nose touching hers. "Let's go plot the destruction of this hellhole and plant our dreams for the future."

Susannah sighed as he tugged her towards the house. "I don't care what the future is anymore, so long as you're with me."

He looked down at her with a tender smile. "I'll never be anywhere else, darling. I am always and forever yours, yours to command and direct and obey as you will."

She quirked a brow and a half smile. "Obey? Really?"

He hesitated, wincing a little. "Well, within reason."

"Oh, so now your fealty has exceptions?" she asked with a roll of her eyes. "That is a promising condition for you."

"Marriage is not exactly convenient," he protested. "Compromises must be made."

"Not convenient?" she screeched playfully. "What, you are inconvenienced by a loving and devoted wife in your bed every night? I will gladly remove such an impediment if that is the case, for the sake of your blessed compromise."

"Don't you dare."

Susannah laughed merrily as her husband pulled her flush against him and tried to walk and seduce her at the same time, which led to nothing more than their mutual laughter and a few scattered kisses as they proceeded forward.

Their future may have been uncertain, as the future always is, but their joy was anything but.

And who could resist a prospect such as that?

Coming Soon

A Bride Worth Taking

"The heart wants what it wants."

by

Rebecca Connolly

Lightning Source UK Ltd.
Milton Keynes UK
UKHW030714111022
410294UK00015B/696